Blac

Sh

This book is dedicated to my mother and father, who put my first book in my hands and many more since. Dad, thanks for giving me my first Stephen King novel. Mom, thanks for letting me read by the light of the stove when I was five.

And to my wife, Amy, without whom this would not be possible. Thank you for your love and your attention to detail.

0

Terra wasn't supposed to be here, ever. Especially not at night. She knew that, somewhere inside. And she knew that if her mother caught her here, even just on the edge of the woods, she wouldn't be able to leave the house for a week.

But she had seen...

"Dad! Daddy!"

The black trees of the Dromm woods swallowed up her words without so much as an echo. In the inky darkness of night, the thick trunks of the forest looked like an unbroken castle wall.

If Monty were here, he'd tell her that she couldn't have seen their father. That people don't die and then suddenly decide to re-emerge from the woods. That he was gone for good. A harsh truth, and one only an older brother could deliver the right way.

But Terra was alone. Monty was asleep, and deeply. Same with her mother, and anyone else who might have stopped her.

Before she took that first step into the woods, she did hesitate. She looked back over her shoulder, towards the village in the distance. She thought about her mother. The family's little farm. How tired Monty was, doing all the work their father used to do.

How happy they'd both be to see him again, if only she could catch him and bring him back.

"...Terra?"

His voice, still familiar, still in her heart. It was in the trees. She snapped her head forward, straining her eyes. If she could hear him, then he was close. She could find him.

Terra went into the forest and she didn't come out.

1

Monty awoke slowly that morning, which was unusual for him. Most of the time Terra would be knocking on his door and then pushing it open, urging him awake so he could make her breakfast. She could cook something in a pan, probably, but she wasn't able to start the cookfire on her own.

He opened his eyes to bright morning light forcing its way through the bare curtain over his window, which told him he was late in rising.

Still lying down, he turned his head toward his door, expecting to see Terra standing there waiting for him, perhaps holding an egg in her hand, faking hunger pangs. She'd done it before, and as silly as it was, it worked like a charm.

But his door was shut.

Monty sat up, his black hair falling into his eyes. It was getting too long. Same with Terra's; her blonde locks practically touched her waist, but she would never let their mother cut them. Not without a fight.

He listened for Terra's voice—her chatter was incessant, especially in the morning—but heard nothing. Perhaps it was earlier than he thought. Still, he hurried to get dressed in his working clothes. The air brimmed with cold and threatened the first frost any day.

He went to his mother's room first. She'd been sleeping a lot lately, and he worried that she was ill. Someone in the village always came down with some sickness at the cusp of winter, and as much as they tried to keep it away, it was usually Terra who caught it first, playing with some friend, brought it home, and quickly passed it to their mother. If Monty was lucky and resourceful, he'd manage to avoid it half the time.

His mother's door was ajar, which most likely meant she was still asleep. A quick peek inside confirmed her shape under the covers. Her room was even brighter than Monty's. He saw that her curtain had fallen to the floor.

He thought about waking her, but if she was sick, rest was better. It was only in his effort to be silent that he realized how quiet it was without Terra and his mother awake.

Great, so she's probably sick, too. Terra's room was down the hall, opposite his mother's. Her door was open. If they were both sick, or even starting to get sick, he was better off just letting them be. Maybe he'd get to avoid a few miserable weeks of coughing and emptying his nose into a dirty rag.

Rarely hungry in the morning, Monty walked past the pantry and to the front door, putting on his boots before descending the three steps that led out of the house.

Their farm, small enough to be managed mostly by himself, sat about three miles from the village of Irisa, named for the seventh saint.

He surveyed the land, a habit he'd picked up from his father years ago, even though nothing had changed with the farm. The small barn stood as it always did, at the left end of the farmland that stretched toward Irisa. Their two cows were inside, along with a pair of goats and their aging mare. Hidden behind it was their chicken coop and a small, fenced-in grazing pasture. The crops, doing well in advance of their final harvest, stood proud; corn and barley, mostly, with winter wheat to be planted soon.

A good crop also meant a lot of work, but Monty didn't mind that as much as he did when he was—as he would say—a kid.

At nineteen, he was still a kid to a lot of people in Irisa, but he knew that a kid couldn't handle this farm almost on their own, like he was doing. At first, when his father died, spending every morning in the field doing twice the work he used to left his body aching. But after over a year of that, he didn't feel like a child anymore.

Maybe it was the bigger muscles, or the new responsibility. Looming larger was his father's absence and his desire to fill that space, a spot that couldn't be taken by just some kid. He loved the farm and his family, and the work kept him busy. He didn't want to tend the land for the rest of his days, but now, especially, the farm needed his focus. His father had had aspirations like his, but he didn't let them get in the way of the harvest.

Monty shook his head, pushing the thoughts away. It was too easy to get lost there. He walked to the barn first to check on the animals, snapping his fingers once in the brisk air of the morning as he set on his way.

The sun had gotten higher by the time he was done, but it was before noon when he made it back to the house, dirty and ready to eat whatever would take the least time to prepare. Cradling a few eggs from the coop, he wedged the front door open with his foot and stepped inside.

His mother was awake, already working on some food. "Oh, good," she said, eyeing first Monty and then his eggs. "Let me have two of those." She plucked two eggs from him, giving him a tired smile, and cracked them both into the iron pan in about half a second.

His mother, Delila, had adjusted to life without their father fairly well after the first few months. Although he had been the one to handle the bulk of the physical farm, Delila had a way with words. Shrewd when selling their crop, when buying in town, and when overtaking her children's stubbornness.

Monty was named for his father, Montille, but he was told he looked like his mother. Certainly he got his dark hair and eyes from her, though her frame was much narrower. Terra had been named for Delila's mother, who had died before Terra was born.

"Did Terra come out to help you?" she asked.

Monty snorted. Terra had tried before to be part of Monty's farm chores, at the insistence of their mother, but was not quite capable. "Maybe she went to town."

"Don't try to find a reason to go to town." She sprinkled something on the eggs as they sizzled in the pan, then wrapped the seasoning pouch back up with deft fingers. "She probably ran off to the neighbor's to play with Kensey and his brother."

"Jeremy." Monty knew where this was going.

"Yes, I know. Go and get her, please."

"Mom…" The neighboring farm of the Gartens was a mile away. Monty had been looking forward to sitting down just for a moment.

"I'm cooking your lunch, just be happy about that." She glanced at him, looking like she already expected him to be gone. "It'll be ready for you by the time you're back with her."

The kitchen smelled good. Monty didn't bother to argue, even though the Garten family had probably fed Terra already. Monty suspected their mother loved having Terra over because they didn't have daughters of their own; they had two rowdy sons Terra's age who drove Monty crazy.

"All right, I'll be back soon," Monty said, eyeing the pork his mother had been working on. She always did pork the best.

Back out into the sunshine, Monty hustled a little bit toward the Garten farm, his hunger urging him along. The Gartens were to the east, in the direction of the rising sun. Monty squinted into the fierce light, turning his head away. To the north, across an expanse of increasingly infertile land, rose the black, leafless trees of the Dromm forest.

His gaze hung there for a moment. The black forest was not terribly large, but it dominated the northern landscape of the village with its hundred-foot trees. You could make it from one side to the other in about a day if you walked nonstop.

But people didn't do that.

The Dromm forest was said to be haunted. Or filled with monsters. Wild beasts. Some crazed tribe that survived off the dark magic in the obsidian bark, maybe.

It was hard to keep all the stories straight; Monty had heard so many over the years. He'd had such an interest in the woods as a child—a magical place less than a mile from his house where he wasn't supposed to ever go? He'd snuck away from his parents' watchful eye at least a dozen times to go in, and sometimes with a few friends.

The excitement had been real, but the results had been disappointing. No monsters; no ghosts; no loose spearheads from the *Drommenmen*, which was the name he and his friends had given the supposed tribe in the trees. Just black stains on their hands from touching the bark, something which they quickly learned to avoid so that they wouldn't get a smack from their parents when they came back home.

Terra never went in, though. She didn't share the same curiosity—far from it, she believed all the stories, even the ones that contradicted each other—and at eleven, she was eight years younger than Monty. He had lost interest in the forest by the time he might have brought her on one of his jaunts.

Still, the Dromm really was something to look at.

The Garten farm grew on the horizon until he could make out the shapes of their two boys chasing each other with sticks around the edge of their crop. As he approached, Monty braced himself for the assault.

"Monty! Get him!" Jeremy cried. He was the elder brother by eleven months, and he reminded everyone of that often and loudly. His messy blond hair was dirty with remnants of an earlier dirt clod fight, as was his brother's.

"Hey, hey!" Monty held up his hands. "I come in peace, all right?"

They brandished their sticks, but they didn't approach him. They knew Monty wasn't above clocking them one if they swung at his ankles too much.

When he was sure he wasn't going to be attacked, Monty lowered his hands. "Is Terra here?"

"Nuh-uh," Kensey said. He was a hair shorter than Jeremy, and he wore the same excited and mistrustful look, hoping that Monty would decide to brawl with them.

Kensey had been known to lie. Monty turned to Jeremy. "Is she?"

"Nope, not here," Jeremy said.

Jeremy had also been known to lie.

"I'm gonna talk to your mom and dad. You two...drop the sticks." Monty stared them down. They didn't listen, but they went back to chasing each other around.

He snuck by them and hurried up to the house, wrapping around the front to get to the door. It was open, and he could see their father inside, working the stovetop.

"Hi, Mr. Garten," he called.

The man either didn't hear him or was just ignoring him; the Garten's father was particularly distant while he was busy with something.

Monty cleared his throat. "Mr. Garten?" Monty hated when that questioning tone rose into his voice. His own mother had been specific in trying to quash that habit of his.

"Speak like you have something to say, Monty," she would tell him. *"Or no one's going to listen."*

"I'm just coming by to see if Terra is here," Monty said.

Mr. Garten looked up from his cookfire at last. "She ain't. Haven't been since three days."

"Thanks," Monty said. He was happy to turn away. Mr. Garten wasn't a pleasure to talk to, and sometimes gave him the creeps. It was hard to tell what was going on behind his eyes, or if there was anything there at all. His father had once told him that Mr. Garten had been knocked down hard by a mule as a kid and been a bit absent ever since. From the smell of the burnt fat in their kitchen, this morning wasn't one of his best.

Monty considered trying to find Mrs. Garten just to be sure about Terra, but he knew if his sister was here, he'd have seen her outside. She especially hated the smell of burning things, so she wouldn't be hanging about in the house while Mr. Garten destroyed breakfast.

"Waste of a trip," Monty muttered to himself, and it wasn't until he was past the boys' stick war and jogging back home that he realized he didn't know where to look for Terra now.

2

His mother had finished cooking by the time he got back and was putting their food into three wooden bowls. She looked up to Monty as he stepped inside.

"Did she wash up there? She gets so dirty playing with those boys."

Monty shook his head. "She wasn't there."

She hesitated as she filled the third bowl on the table. "Are you sure?"

"Yes," Monty said. He sat down at the table. "Kensey and Jeremy weren't playing with her. And Mr. Garten said he hadn't seen her in three days." He started to eat.

"She wouldn't have gone all the way to the Cherrywood's. Not without saying something." His mother leaned against the table, her food resting in front of her chair.

The Cherrywoods were the neighbors on the other side, and they were over five miles away. Monty knew Terra wouldn't be making that trip unless it was on a cart, and only then if their berry bushes were in season.

"She's not out in the barn?" she continued.

Monty shook his head. "I was out there all morning. I just figured she was sleeping in, that she got sick."

"She has been acting a little odd the past few days..." Delila walked to the front door and opened it up, looking out across the farm.

Monty knew what she meant. Terra had been a little distracted lately, and reclusive. It was peaceful, but it wasn't like her.

"Did she catch a frog or something?" Monty took a bite of his bacon, crispy and hot. "Some cat had kittens in the barn and she took one? Or maybe she's got an imaginary friend."

"She doesn't miss breakfast for silly things like that," his mother snapped. She was short when she was worried.

"Okay," Monty said. He knew she was right. He finished his food and said, "I have to swamp the barn. I'll get a look around on the trip, see where she got off to."

"Get back here fast," she said, still looking out through the door. Her food would sit there until it was cold.

Swamping the barn was mucking out the stalls, finding the rotten hay, and cleaning out any carcasses of birds and rodents the barn cats left behind. It used to make him shudder, but Monty had gotten over that by the time he was eleven years old. Now it was just another chore.

For his mother's sake, he hurried. He knew she'd just sit there staring out the window until he got back.

When the wheelbarrow was as full of refuse as it could get, he began the long trek to the compost pile. It was all the way past the crop and down a long path framed with tall weeds, towards the woods. The route wrapped around most of their property before reaching the dumping ground, beyond which lay the black expanse of the Dromm forest.

Monty gripped the well-worn handles of the wheelbarrow and hefted the bulk. The air had less of a chill now; he wore a thin sheen of sweat that glistened in the sun. He pushed the load away from the barn and around the field, where the tall stalks of corn blocked the house from his view. The sun was at his back for most of the trip, and he was grateful for it.

He was feeling mostly fine until he saw Terra's small rope bracelet lying broken on the path.

Monty stopped and dropped the wheelbarrow. He knelt down and picked up the little trinket, something she had proudly made for herself a few months ago. He wasn't surprised it broke—it was made of cheap twine and she rubbed at it constantly—but why was it here?

"Are you out here?" he said to himself, and then he stood up straight, looking around. The weeds on either side rose up to shoulder-height and there was nothing else to see.

"Terra!" he called. His voice carried away from him, absorbed in the tall grass. "Terra! Are you here?"

Silence, save the wind in the grass and its lonely melody. Terra had this bracelet yesterday, Monty was certain of it. Which meant that sometime between last night and now, she had been out here and lost it.

A pit started to form in his stomach, gnawing at his breakfast.

Why would she be out here? She never goes out here. The compost stinks to the skies and she hates it. Hell, I only ever used to come out here to... Monty looked at the not-so-distant black trees. *To sneak into the woods.*

"No way," he said. He tucked the bracelet into his pocket. Terra was scared of the Dromm. Did she grow out of it overnight?

Maybe she did, something told him. *You did.*

He chewed his lip, then picked up the wheelbarrow again. The pit in his stomach remained.

She's lost in the woods.

No, no, no. She'd never.

She's lost in the Dromm woods.

Okay, say she was. They weren't that big. They'd find her.

Unless she hurt herself. Bad. Why else wouldn't she be back?

She's lost, is all.

Or something else got to her.

Monty snorted to himself at that, dumping the weight of the barn's mess onto the three-foot-tall pile of slop and stepping back from the stench. There was nothing in the Dromm besides squirrels and birds.

"Stop talking to yourself," he said to himself, and he snapped his fingers together, the sound cracking through the air.

Stop doing that, Monty. The voices of his father and mother both rang in his head. But the snapping was a habit he'd never been able to break.

Monty pulled the wheelbarrow away from the compost and rested his hand on a clean edge, thinking. If Terra was in the woods, he had to go and find her. But his mother would have a fit if she thought Terra was lost in the Dromm. And he wasn't even sure Terra was.

Monty glanced back toward the house. He could barely see the roof past the tall grass. His mother was expecting him back, probably wringing a rag in her hands—ever since his father had died, she spent a lot of time worrying when she wasn't otherwise occupied. If she thought Terra was in the Dromm woods, she might just die right there.

His father had always had a muted, indifferent attitude toward the black forest; his mother, on the other hand, was clear: she hated those woods and she didn't want either of her kids going anywhere near them. Since father's death, that hatred had grown into fear.

If he brought all that up and Terra wasn't even in there...

Monty pushed away from the wheelbarrow and got moving, each step bringing the dark trees closer. Their leafless branches arched across the blue sky like black lightning. He would just get a closer look. Maybe Terra was here somewhere; maybe she didn't get too far from her bracelet.

The closer he got to the forest, the more the grass started to recede, like the roots of the Dromm were sucking all the life out of the surrounding land, until at last he was stepping on bare black dirt.

Monty's heart sped up a bit, feeling familiar tingles of the old excitement he used to have when approaching the forest as it stretched up and over his vision. It had been years; since taking over the farm, he hadn't even had time to spare the place a thought.

The tree trunks were thick and intimidating, but during the daytime, light penetrated into the forest; the canopy was simply crisscrossing, bare branches. He could see far in, though it was hard to tell anything apart when it was all the same color.

Monty stopped just before the tree line, rubbing his thumb and middle finger together. What did he expect to find, really? A lost slipper; a strand of blonde hair? The woods were silent and empty, as they always were. Even the wind didn't make a sound in the Dromm, as though the breeze were sucked into the bark and trapped.

He stepped along the border, looking past each trunk as it went by. Blackness, blackness, blackness. If she was in there, he wouldn't find her by skirting around the outside, hoping to catch a glimpse. He'd have to go inside, and he would do it; he wasn't afraid. But mother was waiting, and he couldn't wander in the Dromm for a couple hours without going back to her.

Monty sighed. He'd have to tell her that he was at least going to check the forest.

"It'll be fine," he told himself. "Just tell her not to worry, you'll be in and out..."

But he knew that was a dream. Her daughter, lost in the cursed woods, and she decides to send her only other child after her? No.

She'd go straight to town and call on the Judge. And then the people in town, the people who felt the same way his mother did about the forest—which was most of them—would have more reason to be wary of their family and those other families unlucky enough to be settled near the Dromm.

Monty licked his lips. He yelled her name into the woods and they didn't answer.

When he went to turn away, he saw it. A dash of white, just barely peeking out from behind a vast tree, so stark in contrast to the forest around it that he had to blink twice to make sure his eyes weren't playing tricks. How had he not seen it before?

It was inside the forest, just a bit. Monty stepped cautiously toward the shape. His throat felt suddenly tight, like he'd just seen something nauseating. The dirt under his feet took on a wretched, decaying odor; a fresh grave with a fresh body. The light in the forest seemed to dim as he approached.

Monty stopped; blinked. Turned to look at the sky, where the sun still hung, blinding. His vision wasn't going dark, and there were no corpses under his feet. When he looked back at the forest, it looked normal. Smelled normal. And he could see clearly that the patch of white on the ground, emerging from behind the tree, was part of Terra's nightgown, and her pale foot stuck out from it.

Monty's breath turned solid in his throat and he immediately bolted into the forest, stumbling over bent-up roots and fallen branches.

"Terra!" Monty dropped to his knees in the dirt. It was her. She lied facedown, head turned away from him. Her nightgown had seemed white, but up close it was marked with smears and streaks of black. How long had she been wandering around in here? He barely noticed that her hands, her feet, everything else was clean except for her clothes.

Everything slowed as he reached for her shoulder, placing his hand on her. She was warm, thank the heavens and above. But was she...

"Terra." He said it quieter, feeling the fear his mother must feel when one of her children isn't where they're supposed to be. "Terra." Monty grabbed her a little harder, then pulled, rolling her over.

Oh, saints, her eyes, they're gone, what in the blazing—

Gorge rose in his throat, hot and acidic. He squeezed his eyes shut and swallowed it down, and when he opened them again, she was normal. Her eyes were there, just closed. But he had seen empty, bloody sockets, he was *sure* of it...

Her eyes opened suddenly, her startling blue irises peering out at him. Her face was perfectly clean.

"Monty. Where are we?"

Monty let his breath out in a great big rush, and Terra closed her eyes against the flow.

"We're in the Dromm, Terra. Lords of hell, what are you doing in here?"

"Mom doesn't want you saying that." She sat up. "I'm gonna tell her."

"Well, then I'll tell her you were in the forest." Amazing, really, how quickly the situation went from life-and-death to a sibling spat.

"Oh, don't, please," Terra said, immediately forgetting her threat. She jumped up. "I don't know how I got here Monty, I swear I don't remember, I went to sleep and that's all I remember you can't tell mom—"

"Hush up," Monty said, not unkindly. Terra was scared; she was looking around at the trees, surrounded by the very thing whose horror stories had made her cry when she was younger. "Let's get out of here."

Terra just nodded. There were tears in her eyes now. Monty stood and took her hand, walking them the short distance out of the woods.

"It stinks in there," Terra said once they were out.

Monty didn't smell anything anymore, but he didn't feel like arguing. "We have to get you cleaned up. Mom's wondering where you were, and if she knows you were in the Dromm, she'll have a faint."

"Okay." Terra knew how their mother was about the forest. "But I'm all dirty. She's gonna know." She plucked at her gown with her small fingers like she was trying to peel the stains off.

Monty nibbled on the tip of his tongue for a moment, and then snapped his fingers, making Terra wince. "I've got an idea."

In one hand, Monty held Terra's balled-up nightgown, splattered with all matter of contents from the compost pile. It smelled like death itself had visited and forgotten to take his dirty clothes back with him.

In the other, he held Terra's hand, gripped tight as he marched her nakedness up to the house. Their mother was already hurrying down the steps, looking more than slightly frantic.

"Terra! Where were you?" The anger in her voice barely masked her relief.

"I...I..." Terra screwed up her face, frowning.

Monty let out a theatric sigh. "She was out hiding by the compost, mother. She wanted to scare me, probably make me tip the wheelbarrow. But when she tried to jump out at me, she just fell right in." He let a grin sweep across his face.

Terra just nodded, still holding his hand.

"Then she cried about how her nightgown stank—"

"I didn't cry!"

"—and she took it off. It's bad. I'm going to put it in the wash." He let go of Terra's hand so that she could run inside.

"I can smell it from here." Delila's stern visage softened. "Thank you, Monty. I was worried...I don't know what I was thinking."

Guilt flashed through him, but he knew the lie was for the best. "She won't be doing it again, probably. One taste of the pile was enough for her."

She gave a little shake of her head. "I'm going to make sure she gets clean. Don't bother washing that thing, it's ruined. And she's too big for it."

Monty just nodded, and once his mother had turned away to go inside, he tossed the nightgown into the waste bucket and went over to the well to wash the stuff off his hands.

The less his mother knew about what had happened, the better.

3

Two of their chickens were dead.

Monty stood by the coop. He nudged one of the dead chickens with his boot, turning it over, its legs flopping with it. Somehow a pair of them had died and rolled out of the wooden coop and into the grass.

"Did you kill each other?" Monty sighed. They only had eight chickens; to lose two of them at the same time was bad. Especially when they weren't old or unwell, at least not that he had noticed. He would have to tell mother, and she had enough to worry about already.

It had been three days since he had found Terra in the forest, and the time before the winter was the busiest for the farm. The final fall harvest had to be done. Terra, who normally helped with that, had been practically useless lately. She was distracted and not interested in the work at all; every chance she got to slip away, she took it.

The first time she disappeared, Monty was worried she was running off to the Dromm again for some reason, but that hadn't been the case. She was just in her room, lying about. The next time, she was in the barn; then, hiding by the coop. Like she wanted to do anything except help.

Monty grabbed the pair of fowls by their feet and carried them back to the house in one hand, holding them far away from his body. They smelled terrible, like

(corpses?)

they'd been dead far longer than just overnight. He whispered a silent prayer to the saints that this wasn't some sickness that would spread through the whole coop. They could, perhaps, afford two chickens. If all eight died, they'd be without eggs all winter. Monty walked silently, doing the math in his head.

His mother and father both had taught him a good deal of the business side of the farm, and he felt he had a good grasp on it. His father would talk about getting big enough to sell it to a wealthy landowner in town and move into the seat of a politician—a constable, perhaps, or chairman of the merchant or farming commerce collection. It was always a joke with his father, but the more Monty learned about it, the more he was intrigued by the idea. Selling the farm was a lot to think about, but in a position where you could actually make decisions, try to make things better—

Ugh. The chickens really reeked. Monty doubted that they would even be able to eat them; no way would he put this meat anywhere near his bowl. When he reached the front steps, he set them on the ground outside to avoid bringing the stench in.

"Mom," he called, stepping inside. She wasn't in the kitchen; he walked around the rough-hewn wooden table. "We lost a couple—"

He tripped over something, stumbled, and smacked into the wall, just narrowly missing breaking through the thin door of the pantry.

"Ouch!" It was Terra. She had been lying under the table, staring up at the underside, and Monty had tripped over her leg.

His shoulder throbbed. He crouched down, gritting his teeth. "What are you doing under there?" he hissed. "I could've broken my arm!"

"Leave me alone," Terra said. She yanked her legs back in, curling up under the table. "I'm busy."

"Busy with what?" Monty stood back up, not really expecting an answer. He needed to find their mother.

"Shhh," Terra insisted.

Monty bit back a retort, rubbing his shoulder and moving back into the hallway. If she wanted to be weird, she could at least do it out of the way.

His mother was in her bedroom, which doubled as an office for the farm, in that there was a desk about two feet from the bed. She sat there now, the curtain drawn, going over a few sheets of cheap, yellowed paper.

"Mom." Monty stopped in the doorway, and she turned in the chair to look at him. "Some chickens died. Can you take a look?"

She stood up without a word; she handled crises, large and small, in mostly stoic fashion.

"I left them by the steps," Monty said, turning. Terra wasn't in the kitchen to trip him up this time. He went outside ahead of his mother, and the two of them circled around the chickens.

"Hm." His mother knelt down and grabbed one of the dead birds' wings.

"Careful, they really smell," Monty said, as though his mother couldn't tell.

She dropped the wing and touched the breast, and when she did, the whole chicken collapsed in on itself like it was an empty eggshell. Startled, his mother jumped to her feet, taking a step back. The smell of death and decay rose up stronger, and a black fluid leaked from the flattened carcass.

"Oh my...goodness..." Delila covered her mouth and nose with her sleeve. The two of them stepped away from the mess.

"What—what happened?" Monty asked her. He couldn't look away from the empty chicken, deflated like a canvas sack.

His mother shook her head. "I don't know. The other chickens, they're all right? You checked?"

Monty's mind drifted to finding Terra in the woods, the vision he'd had. Terra with no eyes.

"Monty. Did you check the other ones?"

"Oh." He snapped his fingers, absently. "Yes. They're all fine. It's just these two."

"Well, that's good." She slowly lowered her arm from her mouth, then placed her hands on her hips. "Get these far away from the house. And wash up after so you don't catch something."

He grimaced at the thought of carrying these things anymore, but he knew better than to argue.

"We'll have to replace them," she continued. "As soon as possible. People are going to be buying up chickens left and right before winter. There might not be any left. We'll go into town today."

"I still have to harvest today," Monty said. The field was half-stripped, but that left a lot more to go.

"We have time." His mother took one last glance at the chickens. "Go on, get those out of here. I was going to make chicken tonight, but I'll cook up some beans instead." She looked away from the mess and headed inside, adding, "We'll have to go to town now to get back before sunset. I'll get the wagon ready."

Monty took the chickens back behind the farm as quickly and gently as he could, but it didn't stop the second one from caving in and assailing him with a blast of rotting stench. It caught him mid-breath, and he couldn't stop himself; he dropped the chickens to the ground—*squelch*—and heaved into the tall grass, emptying his lunch.

"Saints and gods," he croaked, spittle dripping from his lips while he wobbled on his hands and knees. "Pray I never see this again."

Getting off the farm and being a town official of some kind had never sounded better. Once he caught his breath, he ripped a clutch of the grass from the ground and wiped his mouth with it, dropping it back into the thicket. He made it the rest of the way to the compost pile without succumbing again, tossing the birds in the grass near it and backing away. The haze of the pile was almost pleasant in comparison, but the fresh air of the farm beat them both.

Monty usually hated to wash up—he was just going to get dirty again, and probably soon—but this time he did it with fervor, soaping up to his elbows to make sure it was all off of him.

His mother came from the barn with the wagon. Terra was lying down in the thin bed of straw there, staring up at the sky with her hands behind her head.

"I'm not going to pull you all the way to town," Monty told her as their mother brought the small wooden wagon to a stop by the house.

"Mom is," Terra said, and she stuck her tongue out at him.

Delila smiled. "It's been too long since I gave you a good wagon ride, dear. And I don't want you overdoing it if you're feeling sick."

Of course his mother had noticed Terra's strange behavior, too. Monty felt a little bad; maybe Terra *was* sick, and she just didn't want to admit it so she wouldn't get holed up in her room until she got better. It would explain why she kept dodging harvest work, when usually she loved to pull the corn from the parts of the stalks she could reach.

"All right. I'll pull her," Monty said to his mother. "But not all the way. You're too old to ride in the wagon like a little kid."

Delila was tying her small purse to the waist of her dress. "As I recall, Monty, you liked wagon rides just fine when you were her age. We'll go to Kettle's first. Audrey should have something to offer. And Terra, you can say hello to Ma Kettle."

Monty held back a groan. Ma Kettle was, probably, the oldest person in the whole village of Irisa, and she talked nonstop to anyone who approached her. Terra liked her because she usually gave her gifts, just small stuff from around the Kettle's general store.

He grabbed the handle of the wagon and tugged. Terra, who had sat up, fell backward with a little laugh, and he couldn't help but smile.

"Let's get moving," Delila said, setting off at a brisk pace. "It'll be dark soon."

4

Irisa had three buildings with more than one story, and two of them were the churches, each on the opposite side of the town, to accommodate the size of the gatherings. The third two-story building was Kettle's general store, which the Kettle family lived above.

The walk to the village had gone fast; his mother's urgent gait and his own barely-concealed enjoyment in pulling Terra along had hurried them along, though he did make her get out when they were a half-mile from town. They approached Irisa from the wide northern opening of the main road.

Irisa swelled with just over a thousand people. The town was not big nor wealthy, but it housed many tradesmen, and was well-built. The streets were dirt but lined with smooth stone denoting walkways through the village. The homes themselves were wood and stone, with more of the latter on the wealthier side of town. There were tall lanterns at most corners, lit every night. The fires would dance on the clean glass windows of the houses around them, and smudge to a glow in the dirty ones.

At the far end of the main road was the office of the constable and the Judge, as well as several other town officials. It was a modest building that housed not-so-modest people. Judge Mullen wouldn't spare Monty the time of day; he had tried to involve himself in the conversation when the Judge had talked to his mother about the farm, but it didn't go well. He could learn a lot from the man, but Judge Mullen was not a willing teacher. Once Monty handled more of the farm, maybe he would be more respected. He'd have liked to go into the building and look around some.

But for now, they were going to the shop.

Kettle's was toward the southern side of Irisa, opposite where they had come in, so they still had a bit of walking to do. Delila led the way, and Monty rolled his eyes as she ran into person after person that she knew; family after family she had to catch up with. People didn't like the Dromm, but they liked his mother.

"Delila! When did we come to the farm last?"

"Is this Terra? So pretty. And Monty, strong like his dad."

"So sorry about Montille, he was a good man."

"Please come by our house, Delila, we have some nice shirts the children grew out of."

Monty had been hearing the likes of these ever since his father had died. It had been saddening at first, then it had become infuriating; now, it had settled to annoying.

The last of these comments came from Meera Sand, the mother of a fairly well-off family who lived in the village. She was short, dark-haired, a bit plump, and often used more words than was strictly necessary.

She was a good friend of most town officials, but Monty didn't think he had anything to learn from Meera Sand; just the sound of her voice got his hackles up, even if she was well-meaning.

Hers wasn't the first charity offer they'd gotten, and it certainly wasn't the first time Monty had heard his mother's response.

"That's very kind, Meera, but all is well," Delila told her, which was mostly true, but she would say it when things weren't so well, too. Like when, just after father had died, the butcher had given them a second package of beef hock with a small, concerned smile. Standing next to her then, Monty could practically feel his mother's skin ice over.

"Just one, Horace. Thank you. Kindly." And she slid the wrapped meat back to the man without looking away from his eyes. Her expression was polite, but her aura bound him to meek silence.

She didn't give the same freeze to Meera, but she was just as dismissive. Meera, who had been described by Delila as 'kind, but bird-skulled,' returned Delila's thin smile with a wide one of her own.

"I know you've some shopping to do," Meera said, flipping her hand at the wagon. "With the winter coming. Farming must be such hard work.

No wonder you're so big and strong." This compliment landed on Monty, who nodded along.

Terra, bless her, started to walk ahead of them, so their mother said a quick goodbye to Meera and they continued south to Kettle's.

"I wish people would just let us be," Monty said to his mother.

"Don't say that," Delila admonished. "The people in Irisa are very thoughtful. You should be so lucky."

"But..." Monty looked toward the retreating figure of Meera as she trundled to the east side of the village. "Meera annoys you to the grave. That's what you said."

"Hmph." Delila shot a look at Monty. "Don't repeat things like that. That stays within our home."

"So you don't like her."

"Monty," Delila said. "It's not about that. Everyone deals with grief in their own way, and everyone else thinks they know what other people need. You thank them for thinking of you, and then you let it be. Do you understand?"

In all honesty, Monty replied, "Not really. Terra would like a new shirt."

"If Terra wants a new shirt, then I will get her one." His mother's words were short; clipped. "I will decide what my family needs."

Aware he was treading on dangerous territory, Monty didn't pursue the issue. He pulled the wagon along while his mother called ahead to Terra and told her to get back with them before she got lost, which made Monty think of the Dromm.

"Stay by me," Monty said to Terra when she came back.

"I hope Ma Kettle has somethin for me," Terra said, energy in her feet. A trip to the village seemed to be just what she needed to come out of her lethargic spell.

"She'll have something," Monty assured her, glancing at the sprawling building of the Irisa officials as they strolled by it.

Kettle's rose above the surrounding little shops unimpressively. The Kettle family seemed to focus all maintenance and upkeep on the lower half of the building, which served as the store. Well-stained wood; clear-

lettered signs; shining, clean glass in the windows; all united by a habit of
keeping the door wide open all day unless it was too cold outside. It was
friendly and welcoming. The top half, where the family lived, well; you
might forget it was even there.

Irisa was not densely populated. The few people going in and out of
Kettle's meant it was a busy day, busy enough that even Ma Kettle might
be doing some form of work, at the protest of her daughter.

Monty noticed worry flit across his mother's face, quickly replaced by
exasperation as Terra ran ahead again and bounded up the steps to the
entrance landing.

"Guess she really wants those chickens," Monty joked, and Delila
responded with a distracted smile. He pulled the wagon to the side of the
store, the empty wire cages they had brought for the new chickens giving a
hearty rattle as the wheels came to a stop. He dropped the handle to the
ground, where it rested alongside three others.

"Terra, wait for us!" Monty called, and she stopped just in front of the
open door, in the way of a man exiting. The man walked around her,
Terra oblivious as she watched her family come up the steps. Delila held
out her hand for her daughter's, and Terra begrudgingly took it as the
three of them went inside Kettle's.

For a small village, Kettle's was a large store, as travelers off the main
road made up a good portion of its business. Monty watched his mother's
eyes scan over the shelves and hanging baskets of goods, mostly looked
over by the bustle of customers inside. Her fingers rested on the leather
hide of her purse.

"Keep an eye on Terra," she told Monty, letting the young girl's hand
free as she spoke. Terra immediately headed to the back of the store
where Ma Kettle usually sat. "I'll look into the matter of the chickens."

"Let me talk to Mrs. Kettle. I mean, Audrey," Monty said. "I can
handle it."

"I need you to stay with your sister." She gestured to Terra, who was
now out of their view.

Another day, Monty might have argued with his mother that he should
be the one to get the chickens and talk to the Kettles—wife and husband

Audrey and Henry. He would have said it would be good for him to have this experience, to learn the family business, to learn how to dicker like his mother could, and to gain some respect from the people in Irisa who still thought of him as a kid from one of the Dromm farms.

But today, his mother was on edge from the death of the chickens and Terra's good-natured rambunctiousness and Meera's well-intended, insufferable outreach, so Monty just said, "Okay," and pardoned himself past a few patrons in the search for Terra.

He saw her slip around a family of three on her way to the opposite side of the store. Brushing past the same three, he spotted Ma Kettle, who was in fact not working today. Her daughter and son-in-law must have managed to convince her to just stay and rest in her chair, or maybe they had paid some kid from town a light coin or two to help during the end of the season. Either way, Terra was right there, and Ma Kettle was already talking to her.

As much as Terra focused on getting some trinket or other from Ma, she really did love listening to whatever she had to say. Ma Kettle had good Dromm stories; surely more than anyone else had. And she would ask Terra what she had done since she had last seen her. Monty surmised that she missed having younger children of her own, even though she had several grandchildren.

"...help Monty with the corn because I didn't feel like it this time," Terra was saying, perhaps sounding a little too proud of the fact that she had shirked most of the harvest.

"You do have to help your family, sweetheart," Ma Kettle chided, giving a little shake of her head.

"I know," Terra said. "I think I'm sick."

"Oh, and here's Montille!" Ma Kettle raised her eyes to Monty as he walked toward them.

"It's Monty, Ma Kettle," he corrected her, but warmly. Ma Kettle was old and garrulous, but that didn't mean she wasn't sharp, almost surprisingly so. She appeared slight and misty-eyed, with her long gray hair done up in a sizable bun atop her head, but she didn't forget things, and he'd seen her lift a bushel of potatoes bigger than Terra. She was raised a working woman, and she never let those roots escape her.

"You can be Monty to the young ones," Ma Kettle said. "I like a proper, full name. I let you all get away with calling me Ma this and Ma that, but that don't mean I can't have my privileges!"

Monty grinned inwardly at the thought of Ma Kettle lumping in his mother (and Audrey and Henry) among those young ones. "That's okay, Ma. You can call me Montille."

"You do remind me of your father, you know. You both do." Ma Kettle surveyed the siblings, sitting back a bit in her stiff wooden chair to get a full look at Monty. "Got his eyes, the pair of you. And you, Montille, you're a well-read boy, just like him. Not a lot of farmers are."

Terra, who had heard this from Ma Kettle about a hundred times, didn't respond, but Monty gave the old woman a smile.

"Anyway. Terra, you were telling me about the other day." She put her attention back on the girl.

Terra immediately started up again. "I wasn't sleeping very good..."

Monty resigned himself to listening to the two of them go back and forth for the next five minutes, or ten minutes, or hour, or day. He glanced around. His mother was off to the side of the counter, talking to Audrey Kettle. He wished he could hear what they were saying, but they were too far away.

"...that's when Monty found me. I didn't even know where I was!"

Monty froze. *No, Terra, you didn't.*

"In the Dromm forest?" Ma Kettle said, drawing back a bit.

Terra nodded. "Yeah. It was really scary. I just went to sleep in my bed and then I woke up in there. And I thought I saw—"

"Terra." Monty spoke her name with weight. "Come on. We have to go. Sorry, Ma."

"Aw," Terra started, but Monty grabbed her hand.

Ma Kettle looked closely at Terra, not blinking her eyes. She softened when Terra smiled. "It's a busy day, lovely girl. Here, take this, and make sure you help your brother with the harvest."

Terra brightened with about three shades of delight when Ma Kettle produced a little carved wooden doll; a girl's figure about two inches tall. It was a rough piece of work, but for the wonder in her eyes, Terra might have been handed the key to the whole store.

"Thank you, thank you, Ma!" she said. "It's so pretty, I love her!" And she broke free of Monty's hand to give the old woman a hug. Terra's hair rustled like it was blowing in the wind, then settled down over her back.

"Oh! Saints, it's not all that. Go on, now." Ma Kettle didn't return her hug, but Terra hardly noticed. She bounced away with Monty, eyes glued to the small toy in her hands.

Delila was still talking with Audrey. Monty steered Terra away, back out of the store and into the corner of the raised landing, out of the way of people coming and going.

"Are we leaving?" Terra asked, finally lifting her head from the doll.

"No." Monty got down on one knee. "Terra, why did you go and tell Ma Kettle about the Dromm? I told you not to tell anyone."

"You said not to tell mom." Terra crouched, making the stiff wooden figure walk along the ground. The arms moved back and forth, but the legs didn't.

Monty bristled. She wasn't wrong, but still. "You know better than to tell somebody from town you were in the Dromm woods. And telling her that you just woke up there! She's gonna think you're some kind of a...a changeling."

Terra gripped her toy in her first, looking up at Monty. "Am I a changeling?"

"No. You're not a changeling," Monty growled, aware that she was teasing him and taking the bait anyway, "but you know what some people think about the Dromm. Especially older folks like Ma Kettle. And if you tell people you're waking up in the Dromm, they're gonna think...it's just, it's not a good thing to go blabbing about, you get it?"

"Yeah," Terra said, playing with her toy again.

Monty didn't want to tell her that Ma Kettle talked to *everyone*, and that keeping things private wasn't counted among her skills. Not to mention that there were other townspeople around who might have heard what she said. Terra wouldn't get it. Or worse, it would make her scared enough to tell their mother what had happened.

"Just don't tell anyone else about that, okay?" Monty said, putting a finger under her chin and pulling her head up to look at her. "That is a secret for me and you only, you got it?"

Terra nodded, her eyes going wide as some of the situation's gravity settled on her.

"Tell me."

"I got it," Terra repeated. "You're being scary, Monty."

Monty let his breath out. "I'm sorry, Terra. It's just important. Come on." He stood. "Let's get back inside."

They found their mother just as she was saying goodbye to Audrey. "She doesn't have any chickens," she said to both of them, but mostly to Monty.

"Should we...see if the neighbors want to sell?" Monty suggested. It seemed no whispers of Terra's story had reached her ears.

Delila shook her head. "Audrey said she will be getting some day after next and she'll set two aside for us."

"Where's she gonna put 'em?" Terra asked.

"She'll just keep them safe, dear," Delila responded. "And we'll come back and get them."

"I'll pick them up," Monty immediately offered. He didn't want Terra coming back so soon and risk her talking about the Dromm again. And it would be nice to do some farm business on his own. "Save you the trip."

His mother nodded. "That'll be fine. Thank you. Let's get back home, now. We don't need anything else."

"In the wagon, Terra," Monty said, hopping down the steps and pulling it away from the wall. The wheels creaked. "We're still gonna have some daylight to pick corn."

5

The harvest continued that evening, and this time Terra did help. Ma Kettle's influence on her stretched all the way back to their farm, it seemed; even in the blinding wake of her new toy. Amused, Monty wondered if he'd ever be able to get that kind of respect from Terra. Thinking about how she had almost immediately broken their tacit promise of secrecy about the Dromm, he figured it wouldn't be for a long time.

The sun dipped lower and lower as he, Terra, and Delila paced through the rows of corn, plucking ears from the stalks and stuffing them in the harvesting sacks. The burlap was old and worse for wear, but resilient, and Monty relished the familiar weight of the bag as it filled with the crop. The leafy stalks cast spiky shadows on him, and corn silk clung to his hair and clothes.

Monty pulled corn silently. Every time his gaze drifted to the black forest, he pulled it away. Yet he still found himself looking again and again, wondering what exactly had happened to Terra. Even when the sun disappeared, and the forest itself was lost in the dark horizon, he looked.

His bag was full in seemingly no time; he had been able to fill two to the brim before the light was lost. He hauled it to the large shed by the barn where they stored the harvest, walking with the large bag slung over his back, his shirt wet with sweat. It had been a good evening's work, even though he had to pull himself out of reverie several times. Luckily, his mother hadn't noticed.

He returned and took his mother's bag—mostly full—and Terra's smaller one back to the shed as well, closing the door as he left it. His muscles ached, but it was a good ache.

With the work for the night finished, they all headed to the house. Terra already had her little wooden doll in her hands, keeping it in her pocket while she harvested, even though her mother had warned her she might lose it in the cornfield.

Terra went in first; Delila headed up the steps after her. Monty stopped before the door, resting his boots in the churned mud at the bottom of the stairs.

I should go into the woods.

The thought popped into his head like a fly buzzing past his ear, stealing all his focus. He turned around, looking back to the trees.

I should go into the Dromm and...and...

And what? Monty blinked, and he heard his mother's voice.

"Are you coming inside?" She was waiting, holding open the door.

"Um," Monty started. His mouth was dry. "I'm going to get a drink of water. I'll be right in."

His mother let the door close. Monty walked to the well with perfunctory steps. The small stone well sat between the barn and the field. Halfway there, Monty stopped again, and he was overwhelmed by the urge to look at the forest, though it was too dark to make out the separate trees.

I should...

Monty snapped his fingers, the idle habit bringing him back to focus. He couldn't remember why he was here. With effort, he tore his eyes away from the northern horizon and saw the well.

"Right," he said. "Drink of water."

He pulled a bucket up and ladled out a mouthful, not feeling very thirsty. More than anything, he was tired. *Must not be getting enough sleep,* he thought, swallowing the cold water, feeling it chill his belly.

He managed to finish his drink without the desire to stop and stare at the woods, which shouldn't have struck him as a victory. It was like

Terra's sudden compulsion with the Dromm had fled her body and come to him, trying to pull him that way.

That was what Ma Kettle would say, or some other storyteller. He hadn't heard a Dromm story in a long time, but that didn't make matter. They stuck to you.

He'd asked his mother and father, when he was old enough to be curious about such things (so, very young), why the trees in the Dromm were black. He imagined that their gaze to each other then had been scholarly, like they were rifling through a sheaf of stories they knew and had been told for years, deciding which one was best to share with their young son. It was his father who sat down with him in the dirt outside their house and told him the story.

Of Nal'Gee, the spirit who lived in the heart of the black forest.

Montille looked down at his son. He himself was sitting cross-legged in the dirt, but he still towered over young Monty, who was just about to turn six years old. His son waited, sitting with patience and looking up at him expectantly.

"So, you wanna know why the trees in the Dromm are black," Montille said slowly, drawing it out. "I asked my daddy the same question, right 'bout when I was your age. I told ya about granddad Montille, didn't I? 'Twas a bean farmer..."

"Dad!" Monty cried. "I wanna know about the trees!"

Montille laughed. Behind him, Delila rolled her eyes. Montille was prone to teasing, and Monty always gave in to it. She had to hide her own smile in order to set a better example.

"Right, right," Montille grinned. "The black trees of the Dromm forest. First thing, Monty, they didn't always used to be black."

"Oh," Monty said. "So, when you were a kid?"

Montille leaned back in faux offense. "No! No, no. 'Fore Ma Kettle was a kid. Before she was born, and before her parents were born, and even before her parents' parents were born. Hundreds of years ago, y'reckon?"

"Wow," Monty breathed.

"That's it." Montille nodded. "And way way back then, when magic grew like the grass and there were as many strange beasts and monsters in the forest as there were squirrels and rabbits, there was a witch who lived here."

"Really?" Monty asked. He had a habit of interrupting his father's stories. His curious nature bubbled out of him like a tide.

"Her name was Nal'Gee. And she wasn't a bad witch, y'reckon? Not like that Cromella or those Halcy sisters that Ma Kettle talks about. She did good stuff. She helped the forest grow; she loved the trees and the little animals, and even the beasties in there what were scaring most folks away."

"So what happened to her?" Monty had his little hands wrapped around his ankles, rocking slightly back and forth as he listened to his father.

"Well..." Montille glanced back at his wife, who had drifted away from them to sit on the steps of the house, working on some sewing. He lowered his voice. "She fell in love."

"Witches can fall in love?"

Montille continued, "She fell in love with a boy from the village. Nal'Gee was old—witches live forever, I've told ya that, right?—but she was a beauty. Her magic kept her youthful an' such. Long black hair, so long it could touch the ground, but it never did. Bright, smart green eyes. Probably would..." Montille dropped his voice to a whisper. "Probably drive any fellow mad with love, just the sight of her." He tipped a wink to his son.

"But there was a boy—a man, I reckon, 'bout eighteen years—that did the same to her. Walter. Had a farm by the Dromm. Matter of fact..." Montille made a show of looking around and scanning the land. "Yep, yep. Used to be right there, by the big rock. Towards the Cherrywood's, you see?"

Monty looked to where his father was pointing, visibly excited. "That's really close to us!"

"I suppose it is. 'Course, there's nothing there now. Was a long time ago. But this man, Walter, he was a darn good farmer. One of the best, even at his age; he could make things grow here that had no business growing. He grew pumpkins and watermelons and tiny little lemon trees."

Monty's eyes grew wide at the thought.

"Nal'Gee was smitten. It was like Walter was magic, himself—but he was just talented. And he spent a lot of time in the woods near his farm, the woods right behind you now. And she approached him in there one day, and she said to him, she says, 'What's your name?'

"Walter knew of Nal'Gee. Most people, all of 'em, really, were scared of any witch, so she lived way out away from town in a cottage she made herself. Walter wasn't scared, though. Musta been the farmer in him," Montille said with pride. "He appreciated her magic, and sure she was lovely as any lady he'd ever seen. So he told her his name and they talked about all manner of nature. He was in love the next moment.

"He thought they'd talked for just a couple hours, but it turned out he'd spent three days in that forest lookin' into her eyes. And when he came back to his farm, it was all wrecked up. His crop was shredded and trampled; his little barn had been burned to ashes. Animals all dead and bled out, lyin' there. Windows of his house had been smeared with their blood. Everything he had ever had was ruined."

Monty stopped rocking, his mouth falling open.

"Walter wept a while, but not long. The anger took him, swept him up onto his feet and sent him storming back into the Dromm. He knew, ya see, he knew it had to be the witch. Nal'Gee. She'd put some kinda spell on him, some enchantment, and holed him up in the woods so she could destroy his farm."

"But...but..." Monty protested, distressed. "Why? Why would she do that to him?"

"Jealousy." Montille's eyes glinted as the sun caught them. "Walter thought, for someone with magic power, someone this beautiful, to be all enamored with him, he had somethin she didn't. Somethin she wanted. And when she couldn't have it herself, she burned it. Walter didn't know any good witch, he'd never met one or never heard no story about one.

So he thought, she's got the evil in her like they all do, and it came outta her."

"What did he do?" Monty said, suddenly quiet.

"He went back into those woods and called after her. 'Nal'Gee! Nal'Gee!' Screamin his heart out, scarin' all the birds and squirrels and even the scary big-clawed tree lizards and skin-jays. And she came running; he'd only been gone an hour, but she's happy to see him again. She says, 'Walter, I'm here,' and she came up to him and put her hands on his shoulders.

"And Walter pulled his dagger from his boot and he stabbed her right in the heart."

Monty gasped, his mouth wide open now. "He killed her?"

"He killed her," Montille repeated, crossing his arms. "He put the dagger in her chest all to the hilt and dropped her to the ground. She died so fast that she didn' even get to ask why he did it."

"But..." Monty frowned, dropping his eyes to the ground. He looked back up at his father. "You said witches live forever."

"Witches live forever," he told Monty, "unless you kill them."

"So she died?"

"She died there on the forest floor, right in the Dromm. Walter left his dagger in her heart and walked away. But that wasn't the end of Nal'Gee."

Montille inched a little closer to his son. "It turns out, y'see, that Nal'Gee didn't do nothin' to Walter's farm. Someone from the village saw him cavortin' in the woods with the forest witch, and they didn't take kindly. Told ever'one else, and they got it sorted that he was bad now, too. Evil. In the village, anytime someone got sick, or a cow died, or a roof got a hole—it was always Nal'Gee's fault, so they said. 'Course, they were too scared to do anything to the witch herself. But if Walter was a consort, well, he wouldn't be welcomed in the village no more. And as far as they was all concerned, he was cursed—from his boots to his horse to his crops. So they came and they did it all in."

"That's so mean!" Monty said.

"Downright cowardly. Folks act crazy when they're scared, and saints above, they were scared of Nal'Gee. Wasn't long before Walter learned the truth, though. He went to the village for support and found nothin but hate. People spitting at him, callin' him a familiar."

"What's a...a family-year?"

"Familiar," Montille repeated. "Witch's pet, sent to do their bidding. The Judge there told him if he ever came back to the village again they'd kill him in cold blood, and he knew they meant it. And his heart turned pure to ice when he realized what he'd done to Nal'Gee." Montille grew somber and stiff; he was a good storyteller.

"So he went back to the woods—he ain't got nowhere else, now. Falls to his knees a'fore Nal'Gee's body. Her eyes are open and just as bright and green as they were when he talked to her minutes ago, but she's dead. He takes her hand in his, and it's cold and limp. He drops it and pulls the dagger from her chest, and all this blood comes out, makes him sick to his stomach. He's all despair and misery; he knows he's a murderer.

"Walter holds the dagger over the bloodstain on her dress, over the wound. He turns it so's it's pointin' at him, presses the hilt down onto her bosom, and he drops down onto the dagger. Hits his heart—man musta had a talent for that, too. And he died right there on top of Nal'Gee.

"But," Montille whispered, catching his son's wary eye, "it takes a lot more than death to escape the wrath of a witch. Nal'Gee was dead, but her spirit clung to her body, hanging on, like she knew she'd have her chance to get revenge on Walter. And when his spirit left his body, she *grabbed it.*" Montille smacked his fist into his palm, making Monty jump. "When someone dies, their spirit goes to the beyond. Becomes a saint, if they're real nice, good people. Or down to hell—to the depths—if they're bad. But if you don't get to beyond..."

"What?" Monty said. "What happens?"

"No one knows," Montille said. "Not for true. But for Nal'Gee, she snatched up Walter like he was a fleeing chicken and she gobbled up his spirit. Nal'Gee wasn't ready to die, wasn't ready to let go of this life here. She ate Walter and took his spirit into hers, but there wasn't no life in it. He was dead. So she latched onto the tree by her body, and that tree was alive, and she sucked out its life till it was all black and empty. Then the next tree, and the next.

"She wanted to come back to life, take back what had been stolen from her. She just had to gather up enough strength to do it. But she could only get enough to go from tree to tree, desperate, huntin' for something she'd never get enough of.

"Nal'Gee ate the tree spirits until every single tree in the forest was black. Then she ate the spirits of all the beasts and the monsters, creatures that knew her and trusted her—until she drained them all, and that's why you don't see those no more. And when there was nothin' left—no green trees, no beasts, nothing—she fell away into her long rest, waiting for the trees to grow again, for the beasts to come back, so she could get their lives again and again until she's strong enough to come back to life."

Montille had been leaning in toward Monty; now, he sat back, his story almost to a close. "That's why the Dromm trees are black. And why they don't grow taller, or get any leaves like the other trees—soon as they might, Nal'Gee pulls it back out of them, and leaves them just barely alive, just to make more."

"So she's, she's—she's still in there?" Monty turned toward the forest and then back to his father, fast, like he was afraid it would see him.

"She is," Montille told him, standing up. "But she's just some will-o-the-wisp, buried deep in the ground. Couldn't hurt ya. She can't even catch the squirrels." He laughed, putting his hand on Monty's shoulder. "Don't be too scared, now, Monty. You just stay away from the Dromm and you'll be fine. All right?"

Monty nodded fiercely. "Okay, dad."

Standing by the well, Monty smiled to himself, remembering how mad his mother had been that father had told him that story. That she insisted he would have nightmares for weeks. He did, for a day or two, but that had passed. His father could scare him and reassure him with remarkable juxtaposition, and anytime he got scared after that, Montille would ask him, *"Can you beat a squirrel in a fight? Uh-huh? Then you can beat Nal'Gee."*

He missed his father, suddenly, powerfully. Montille had fallen ill without warning and wasted away in a matter of days. No one understood it; not his family, and not the doctor in the village. One week he was with them, harvesting barley and carrying Terra on his shoulders, and the next week he was gone.

It wasn't fair, and the time that passed didn't change that. He wished he could change it; wished harder than he had in many, many months. That things could go back to the way they used to be. That he could hear the rest of his father's stories, about the Dromm and the saints and the ancient kingdoms.

He swallowed and emptied the rest of the bucket back into the well, the water splashing deep in the ground with a hollow echo. The well stones were cold. Monty took his hands off them and walked back to the house. It was dark, and the harvest would be waiting when dawn broke.

6

The next morning was the same as any other had been around harvest time, if perhaps more efficient, as the air was getting noticeably colder and Monty knew that the first frost could be coming any day. He moved quickly through the rows and filled bag after bag. The harvest was always the hardest work, and it lasted the longest; a combination that led to a sore back and, typically, a very good night's sleep.

But not that night.

Monty awoke alone and cold. His feet, in particular, were freezing. It was only while he stumbled backwards that he realized it was before sunrise, he was outside, and his feet were planted in the cold dirt outside of the Dromm.

He fell down, landing hard on his elbows. He groaned. Over him, the Dromm loomed, towering and silent.

What in the—how did I get out here? Monty blinked, like it was all a mirage he could make disappear.

"No. I'm dreaming. This is a dream," he assured himself. It was the only thing that made any sense. But had he ever been this cold in a dream before, with such vivid detail? His feet felt like ice blocks, stupid and heavy. He brought his fingers to the ground and curled them into the dirt, and that felt real enough. The air was snappy cold and smelled...*horrible.* It assailed him with predatory quickness, and then he was coughing, hacking, backing away from the trees on instinct. This was that smell he'd run into when he found Terra in the Dromm, the one that disappeared from his senses shortly after. He prayed that would happen now.

Holding his breath, he scrambled to his feet, and then he retreated from the Dromm until he could breathe in clean air. His eyes watered and his throat burned.

He wasn't dreaming.

Something is not right.

Monty hadn't feared the Dromm forest in a long, long time. But now that icy tendril wound its way through his belly and chest. He looked at the forest not like thousands of trees, but as one big entity, staring down at him with an eye he couldn't see. He felt watched; almost smothered. The air was clean, but it was heavy. It was cold and it stuck to the insides of his lungs.

Should've just gone to the woods, Monty, a thought ran through his head. *Should have just gone in before, like you wanted to. Now the woods are coming for you.*

Monty sucked in cold air and let it out in a wheeze. He snapped his fingers. Shook his head. Stupid, this was all stupid. He'd sleepwalked as a kid—his parents told him so, although he didn't remember it. That's what had happened now, on the tail end of Terra having her own episode, and him being thrust into the past yesterday, thinking of his father.

"Get over it," Monty said, saying the words aloud but not really hearing them. He wrenched his eyes from the Dromm and turned back toward the house. It was almost dawn, and he wouldn't be getting back to sleep. Might as well start the day.

It wasn't long after he'd gotten his boots and started his chores that his mother rose, coming down the steps from the front door and calling after him while he had an armful of hay clutched to his chest. He dropped it at the barn doors and came back to her.

"I'll take care of the rest," she told him as he approached. She was standing on the final step, so she was just about as tall as him. "Can you go into town and get those chickens? I already paid. Audrey said she'd put them aside, but I'd rather you were there first thing..." Delila halted, looking at Monty. She stepped down from the stairs to get closer to him.

"Monty, you look exhausted. What's the matter? Didn't you sleep?"

"I slept," Monty said, because it was true, and also because he didn't know what else to say.

"Can you make it to town all right?" Immediately, she put her hand on his forehead. "Well, you're certainly not warm."

"I'm fine, mother," Monty said, shying away from her hand. "I'll make it to town and back. Maybe I'll turn in early tonight if I get enough done. Are *you* sure you can take care of the chores?"

Delila huffed. "Don't get short with me, Montille. I'm not saying you look like death. But I don't want you risking your health before the winter."

"It's fine." Monty brushed some hay off his shirt. "I'll get the chickens, I'll come back—"

"I'll make some soup," his mother said. "Something to warm you up."

"I—" He wasn't going to say no to soup. "That sounds good."

"Mm." She looked him over once more, but she must not have found anything heart-stopping, because she just plucked a piece of hay off his shoulder and told him to hurry back.

Monty got the wagon and chicken cages and got onto the road before Terra could get up to pester him to bring her into town as well. For some reason, he had a strange feeling that his little sister would take one look at him and know exactly what had happened last night. Or, rather this morning. She was young, but she knew her brother. She'd see something on his face.

He had no plans to tell anyone where he had woken up today. It was just a little sleepwalk.

The cages rattled in the wagon as he pulled it along the familiar path to town. Even that grating sound wasn't enough to pull him out of his thoughts. He nibbled at his lip and kept his eyes on the ground while he walked toward Irisa. He didn't notice Mrs. Garten on the road ahead of him until he was practically running into her.

"Oh, hello, Mrs. Garten," he said, coming up beside her.

"Monty." She turned her head to him. Mrs. Garten was a very slight and short woman; Monty suspected that she didn't weigh much more than Terra. She had reddish-blonde hair that was always in a tight and thick braid. As frail as her body was, her hair was robust, as though all of her strength went into it.

"Sorry for the noise," Monty said, shrugging back toward the cages.

"That's quite all right," Mrs. Garten said.

Silence crept up on them like rising water, save for the chicken cages. Mrs. Garten was not much to hold a conversation with; she often seemed lost in her own thoughts. She would mention something, and then forget what she'd been speaking about just a moment before. Monty didn't talk to her much, but he still tried to be nice.

"We lost a couple of chickens," Monty told her.

The woman looked ahead, not saying anything.

Monty continued, "The other day. Just two of them, thank the saints. I'm going into town to replace them."

Mrs. Garten turned to him and smiled, her mousy features distant. "That's terrible." For a few moments, she didn't say anything else, and Monty was about to speak when she went on, the odd smile slipping from her face. "Our cow is sick. Fairy. She's old. Older than the boys. Almost as old as me."

"That's too bad." That cow had been around ever since Monty was born.

"It's too late in the season to find another cow," Mrs. Garten said. "Just hope she...makes it."

"Are you...getting some medicine from town?" Monty asked. Before them, Irisa grew larger, quiet this early in the morning. The sun was slowly spilling yellow light across the houses.

"Maybe," Mrs. Garten breathed. "If they have it."

That was the last she said before they parted ways as they came into town, and Monty let out a small sigh of relief as Mrs. Garten headed to the east side of the village. He always felt off while talking to her, like she was looking at something that he couldn't see.

The early day in Irisa was sleepy and slow, very far from the crack-of-dawn harvest mornings on the farm. The Kettles had been raised a farm family, though, and they would be awake. So would anyone else listening to the noise of Monty's wagon and chicken cages.

Monty looked forward to talking to Audrey, hoping that the townspeople noticed him dickering with her on his own. Maybe he'd even talk her into getting a couple coins back, if he was smart about it, or throwing in some feed with the deal.

But when he got to Kettle's, the door was closed. He didn't see anyone moving around inside.

"I guess I'm a little early," he said, his negotiation fantasies slipping to the back of his mind. He pulled the wagon to the side of the store and up against the wall, where it rested alone. Now what? If he stayed here, it was possible Mrs. Garten would wander back in her search and bump into him, which wouldn't be the worst thing in the world, but if he could avoid it—

"Monty."

He snapped from his thoughts, looking to the left and right. He didn't see a soul.

"Monty! Up here!"

It came from the second floor of the store—the Kettle's house. One of the children was poking her head through the window. Monty knew her face, but her name escaped him. The Kettles had five children, and the three girls especially looked alike.

"Oh. Hi, um..."

"Marie," the girl said, not appearing bothered by his forgetfulness. "You're...you're here for the chickens, right?"

Marie, that's right. She was the eldest of the girls, thirteen years old, if he remembered right.

"Yes," he said. "Am I too early? I can...are you all right, Marie?"

The girl was slumped in the window, and looking closer, Monty could see that she had been crying. She shook her head, but she said, "I'll be right down for the—the—the chickens."

"All right." Monty watched her close up the window, and after a moment's hesitation, he went over to the entrance of the store and climbed the steps to the landing. He heard the bolt pull from the other side of the door, and Marie stepped out.

"You got cages, right?" she asked him. It looked like she had hurriedly tried to clean the tears from her face before coming outside.

"I do..."

"Okay. Get 'em around back, I'll open up the coop." Marie hopped down the steps and ran to the other side of the building before Monty could say anything more.

A little uneasy, Monty pulled the cages from the wagon and followed Marie's path behind Kettle's, where she was pulling the key from the lock on their chicken coop.

"Marie, hold on a minute," he said, setting the cages down and coming up to her. "Is everything all right? I don't mean to pry, it's just..."

Marie looked down at the ground, and when she brought her face back up to Monty's, she burst into tears and collapsed against his chest.

7

Stunned, Monty slowly brought one hand to the crying girl's narrow shoulder. "Hey, it's, um...it's okay, Marie."

Marie sobbed against him for a few more moments before she got control of herself, pulling away and looking embarrassed. "I'm so sorry," she gasped. "I shouldn't be—you're a customer, my mother would—"

"Tell me what's going on," he insisted, knowing that when Terra was bawling about something, she had to be set straight in order to talk to anyone about it. "I'm listening."

Marie pulled in a long breath, settling the hitching of her chest. "It's grandma Kettle," she moaned, her voice quivering. "She—she died this morning. Mother found her on the f-floor by t-the bed. She was all..."

"Oh, no." Ma Kettle was plucky, but there was no arguing against time. Monty knew she was almost eighty, and though it was sad, the oldest person in the village couldn't stay that way forever. "I'm real sorry, Marie. That's terrible."

Marie just sniffed and gave a little nod. "It's awful. I saw mama pick her up, and she just lifted her right off the ground like, like...like she was a bag of f-f-feathers." Marie shook her head, fast, and reached blindly for the door to the chicken coop.

"Marie." Monty took her shoulder. "Hey, stop. You don't have to do this right now, I can come back..."

"No, no." Marie shrugged off his hand. "You're a customer, and mama—mother says the s-store comes first."

"Marie—"

The young girl took the chicken cages from his hands and set them on the short table next to the coop, then pulled open the door and went inside. Monty looked up at the second-floor windows of the store like he might see the family gathered around Ma Kettle, waiting for Marie to come back.

When Marie came out with a chicken under each arm, Monty opened the cage doors and helped her get them inside, then latched them back up.

"I'm sorry, Marie," he said to her while they walked back around toward the front of the store. "And...well, thanks for helping me this morning, with all that."

It felt insignificant, but it was the best that he could muster.

"I have to go back inside," Marie told him, ascending the steps and leaving him with the chickens.

Monty departed Irisa with two plump, sleeping chickens and a grainy cloud over his head. They'd only been talking to Ma Kettle two days ago, and just like that, she was gone. It reminded him too much of his own father's sudden illness, squeezing at his heart when he thought about all the Kettles upstairs, crowded around their eldest, a sheet covering her body.

A morbid image, and one he couldn't get out of his head. It perhaps didn't help that the cages rattled considerably less on his lonely walk home with the fat chickens weighing them down.

By the time he arrived at the farm, the chickens had awoken, but they were docile. He left the wagon over by the coop and went to tell his mother the news.

Delila was in the field working at the harvest, the last few rows of corn slowly plucked apart by her strong hands. He called out to her before slipping through the stalks to talk. He'd been snuck up on enough times in the cornfield to know that a warning was much preferred.

"That was fast, Monty," she said to him, stopping her harvest to talk. A clean rag tied back her hair, keeping it out of her face while she worked, but it still let the sweat through. She must have been going at it since the moment he left, judging by the size of her bag. She looked far from exhausted, though. Monty's mother was the only person he knew who seemed to gain more energy from hours of physical labor.

"There was no one else at the store," he said, suddenly unsure of exactly how to say what had happened.

"Oh. Did it go all right?" Delila wiped her forehead, the long sleeves of her worn shirt rolled back. "You still look awful peckish, Monty. You might want to skip the harvest today. Terra and I should be able to finish the rest of it, once I can pry her away from that little doll."

The doll. Monty sighed. "Mom, Ma Kettle died this morning. I heard from little Marie. She was...ah, she wasn't quite..."

Delila brought one hand to her mouth. Whatever pep she had gotten from harvesting left her body all at once, bringing down her shoulders. "Oh, saints, that's awful. Just this morning?"

Monty nodded. "That's what Marie said. That her mom—that Audrey found her."

Delila grabbed her son and pulled her close to him. Monty didn't know if he looked in need of cheering up, but he didn't fight it. He put his head over her shoulder, letting her wrap her arms around him. "I'm sorry, mom," he said.

"That's all right," she said. "She was old. I'd known her ever since I was a little girl. She's been around a long time. It's the way things go."

Monty thought about his father's death, and how there hadn't been a simple, comforting explanation for it like old age or frailty. How it was nice to be able to point the finger at something, even if it wasn't a thing that could accept the blame. How it made it easier to deal with—knowing, on some level, that it was something you were prepared for, something that you expected, even if you never would have said it out loud. Ma Kettle wasn't a family member, but she was part of their lives the same way their neighbors were, and the west-side church was on Gathering days.

You noticed when that something like that was gone, and you'd go on noticing for a while yet.

Delila let her son out of her embrace, still holding him by the shoulders. "Are you okay, Monty?"

"I'm fine." Monty let the somber thoughts slide away. That was something he'd gotten good at. "Like you said, she was old. It's not really...I mean, it's not a surprise."

"I suppose." Delila took back her hands. "Terra's going to be very upset. She was just telling me about how she can't wait to see Ma Kettle again and thank her for that doll."

"Yeah..." Monty glanced toward the house, though he couldn't see it through the corn.

"We won't tell her yet," Delila said, with the firm confidence of a woman used to making many decisions. "Go inside and eat some soup. I'll let her know when the time is right."

When? Monty wondered, but he didn't ask, because he felt his mother didn't quite know, either. That there wasn't a right time, really. Just a better time, and she would be the judge of that.

The harvest was finished just as morning spilled over to afternoon. It was Monty who plucked the last ear from the last stalk—not his first time doing it, but it didn't feel any less special. The sun was at its highest point in the sky, bright and blinding, but the air was still brisk. He stepped out of the stripped cornfield with his final bag and hauled it to sit with the rest.

"It's a good harvest," his mother told him when he came back to the house. "You did well this year."

"Thanks," he said, flopping back in a chair and putting a rag to his forehead to wipe away the sweat. "I had to pick up for Terra's slack, most of it."

"I helped lots." Terra was sitting at the table as well, eyes on her doll.

"She did plenty," Delila said, giving Terra a little smile.

"Must've been when I wasn't looking," Monty teased, making Terra roll her eyes and glare.

"All right, that's enough. I'm sure you're hungry." Delila was frying eggs. "Those new chickens are laying double-time. I'm almost glad we had to pick them up." She clucked her tongue. "Monty, keep an eye on these while I bring a bucket in."

"You should have asked me to get it before I came in," Monty said to his mother, but she waved him off. The kitchen was warm, filled with the smell of sizzling butter. It was always a good feeling to finish the harvest, and with a good bounty. The glow settled through the house.

Monty stood over the pan; when the eggs were done, he slid them out onto the big serving plate they kept by the stove. His mother still wasn't back with the water.

"I'll be right back," Monty said, dousing the small cookfire, thinking that the bucket pulley had gotten stuck. Terra just bobbed her head, her doll's tiny wooden feet dancing noisily across the table. He pushed open the front door.

"...brings you here?"

Monty heard his mother's voice as he left the house, and he went around the corner to see her standing, arms crossed, talking to someone else.

He didn't need to hear the man's voice to know it was Judge Mullen. He could tell just by seeing that the silver top of his head barely came up to his mother's shoulders. Though he had become quite familiar with Judge Mullen's voice lately, as the man had been coming out to their farm more and more often since father had died.

His mother didn't like to see the Judge, and Monty wasn't sure why. He suspected his mother didn't like town authority, another mild clash of her marriage with his father, who respected both the cloth and the scroll. But persistent as Monty was, she never shared her concerns with him.

Right now, he could go involve himself and learn something. She had to trust him with these sorts of things eventually. Maybe he could speak to the Judge himself, and learn a little more about his interest in their family.

But whatever brought the Judge all the way out here, Monty reminded himself, *it won't be good.*

He rounded the corner as Judge Mullen said, "I am simply here to pay a visit to the farms, Delila. How did your harvest go?" He had his hands clasped in front of him, respectful. His eyes, dark, reflected Delila's features: her crossed arms; her flat smile. They flicked over to Monty as he approached.

"It was a good harvest, yes," Delila said, glancing back toward her son and giving him a short shake of her head, which Monty chose to ignore.

"Montille." Judge Mullen nodded to him as he stood beside his mother. "But you go by Monty, right?"

"Yes, sir—your Honor." So Judge Mullen did remember him, at least a little bit.

"It's good to see you well," the Judge told him. The wind caught his cape, ruffling it around the backs of his legs.

The rites cape. Monty said, "Judge Mullen, you're wearing..."

The short Judge nodded, a solemn, slow dip of the head that was smooth as butter. "Yes, I'm afraid so. A terrible thing today."

The door of their house opened, and two small feet padded down the steps.

8

It was earlier that morning, right around the time when Monty was heading back home with his two fat chickens, that Judge Mullen was sitting down in his office.

He always preferred to be here in the early stages of dawn. At home, there were distractions; things to tend to. Unimportant things that took up too much of his time. Here, in the township, before the villagers awoke and got about their grubby business and those knocks started at his door—it was his time, alone.

He spent it as he often did, thumbing through a ledger, reading it some of the time, but mostly ignoring it while the wheels churned in his head, which rose about a foot-and-a-half over the desk. He had a full head of hair. It used to be a deep black, but was all silver now, even though he wasn't old enough to be graying. Another mishap of his body.

Elrich Mullen was not a tall man—he was short and he was stocky. Were he prone to self-examination, he might surmise that his craving for authority stemmed ultimately from the fact that the girls and the boys he grew up with made fun of him when he couldn't climb the fence of Hollins' farm like everyone else. This was back in Wilda, the large, coastal town he lived in until he was thirteen and was conscripted to the kingdom.

His mother and father had been distraught at the summons. Elrich had been thrilled at the prospect of escaping to a new place where no one would call him 'dwarfie.' He fantasized about making a new name for himself, one that garnered respect and fear. He'd be a mighty warrior and

rise through the ranks of the king's military until he was on par with
royalty himself.

But his fantasies never came to fruition; when he was younger, they
never did. Elrich was disbarred from the military due to his height,
something which the king's recruiter (an ill-fitting title, as recruitment was
not a choice, but a mandate) did not care to take into account when telling
the young man what his future would hold.

Elrich had been devastated. The one thing he wanted to leave behind
the most—the stigma of his stature—was something he'd bear for the rest
of his life. And with that burden built the fury, fury that started with the
neighbor children's teasing, fury that boiled with the sergeant's laughter at
the thought of the short, stiff-legged Elrich climbing up onto a war horse,
before dismissing him back to Wilda.

He might have left the barracks and gone back to his town to live out
the rest of his days as a tanner—his family's business—were it not for a
certain overworked advisor who had been looking for assistance.

The man had been waiting for some young conscript to be turned away
so that he could leap on the opportunity to have them for himself, and he
happened upon Elrich, who was emerging from the barracks with
clenched fists and no lapel pin to mark him as a new recruit. He pounced
on the emotional young fellow and offered him a position as his scribe.

Elrich, who was fortunate enough to have learned how to read and
write from his time spent as a social outcast in Wilda, was perfect for the
job. The advisor worked him near to death, having him write hundreds
and hundreds of scripts and scrolls out, and running them town-to-town
with barely time to sleep and barely enough pay to eat.

But Elrich hardly cared. That was how he broke into the life of
kingdom politics, learning the secrets of communication the upper classes
held—and the secrets of those upper class men and women, themselves.
How to use that to his advantage came soon after, and it was only a few
years before he was a military advisor himself. Three years there, then he
was a traveling constable. It was during that longest period of his career
that he learned what it was like to truly be in control, not to be serving or

advising or reporting. The power was his, on the road to town after town, answering only to the Judges.

Of course, his next pursuit was the position of Judge, which he attained when Irisa had grown enough to need a sitting Judge. And he'd been in Irisa the last five years, the town comfortably in his hands.

Next would come a larger town. Perhaps a port town, or maybe the big city Wilda, if that crying pansy Judge Tullard went and finally got himself killed by being too lenient on the wrong person. It was bound to happen. And wouldn't that be a glorious day?

Knock-knock-knock.

Elrich's thick fingers tore the page he was flipping, ripping it almost out of the book. He bit back a curse and set down the ledger, closing it. The torn page stuck out.

It was early—far, far too early—for someone to be knocking at his door. He pushed his chair back, its legs wearing further into the groove in the floor, and stood to his full height of five feet and three inches. His hair gave him perhaps another three-quarters of an inch, depending on the day. He crossed the twenty-five feet of his office and he opened his door.

Standing there was a nervous-looking young town courier whose name he had forgotten the day he was brought on. He knew the boy begun his duties two weeks and three days prior, and that was all he needed to know. Judge Mullen saved his attention for people who could further his career or people who might get in his way. This boy was neither.

Elrich knew, as well, that you caught more flies with honey than vinegar, and reserved his vast capacity of the latter for times when it was best suited.

"What can I do for you?" Elrich said to the boy, who couldn't have been more than thirteen. Though the boy quailed at the Judge's presence, Elrich was painfully aware (as he always was of such things) that the boy was only a few inches shorter than he.

"I've come to say—that is, they thought you should know—"

The Judge waited with what appeared to be understanding patience while his rage at being interrupted steamed behind the thin mask of his face.

The boy managed to get past his stammering and get out his thought. "Ma Kettle—Dorella Kettle. She's dead."

"Ma Kettle is dead," Elrich repeated. "Well, this is a shock."

Old sack had to die this early in the morning, unbelievable waste of my—

"Yes," the courier said, his panicked tone growing more somber. "The Kettles, they ask that you, um—that you—"

"The rites, yes. Of course." Elrich finished his sentence for him so that he might be rid of the boy sooner. "Run back, tell them I will be to the home shortly. I assume she died at home, is that right?"

The boy nodded, and Elrich closed the door in his face. He stood there, gripping the handle hard enough to turn his fingers white. One more second of talking to that inarticulate roach, and he might have done something unbecoming. He released the doorknob, the ghosts of his fingers fading from the brass, and sat back at his desk. He picked up the ledger again.

Elrich Mullen was currently in the process of obtaining personal ownership of the majority of the land in and around Irisa. He was wealthy, extremely so—no one understood quite how much, except for him. He kept it hidden. He hid a great many things, including this ledger, which normally resided in a locked compartment of his desk. The page he was currently on had detailed notes about the Cherrywood farm and land.

Once he owned more than half the land here, he would have the authority to appoint a new Judge for the town, rather than having the crown do so for him, which would take twice as long. And from there, he could move on to his next town—a real city, this time. With four times the population, ten times the gold, and a thrilling amount of *important people* who would be of use to him.

He smiled to himself, a small and humorless grin, as he surveyed the information on Cherrywood. The farms to the north of the village were easy pickings. The stupid people here were scared or tired enough of those black trees to take simple, meager offers for their land. There were only four farms left near the Dromm Forest: Cherrywood, Garten, Holcomb, and of course, Bellamy.

Elrich turned to the latter's page absentmindedly while his mind filled with the image of Delila Bellamy. She was the only woman in the whole of this unimportant, uneducated village who was worth her salt, and at first, he had seen the value in that. Now, as she continually stonewalled his offers to buy their land, he saw it as a nuisance. A nuisance that grew each passing day into a headache, then into a rage that turned his skin red if he dwelled on it.

Delila also very much resembled Elrich Mullen's mother—tall, pretty, dark of hair and stern of mouth. He would never acknowledge that connection, but it was that which had kept his eyes on her at first, an almost instant attraction.

Now, with her husband dead...well, there was opportunity there. Opportunity to get close to her, now that she'd had the time to grieve. If money wouldn't be the thing to move her, then he could do it once he was courting her. Would he take her to the city—perhaps the port city Yerta, where he'd eventually own the harbor and all the boats there, and their captains and merchant hires, too?

Maybe. If she was well-behaved. But to first break that exterior. Perhaps through the children.

His daydream was cut short as he remembered the messenger boy and his bothersome news, the death of Ma Kettle. He would have to perform the Judge's rites and talk to the family, which would devour the rest of his morning.

He closed the ledger and locked it away, leaning back in his chair to collect himself and assume the facade of the people's Judge.

Elrich arrived at the Kettle's twenty minutes later, wearing his long, black cape. It was the cape worn for the rites of the dead, and it caught the looks of villagers who were up and about. Everyone knew what the cape was for; no one knew who it was for. But when they saw Judge Mullen walk into the Kettle's, they had a fair guess.

The store was unmanned. Elrich moved through the shelves and baskets to the staircase at the back that led up to the house. A thick book hung under his arm, one of regulations, rites, readings, and other abiding minutiae. He had it memorized, but he looked more official reading off the written page.

He was greeted at open door by the Kettle parents.

"I am so very sorry," Judge Mullen said to Audrey and Henry Kettle. "Your mother was so loved here in Irisa. It will be a solemn honor to perform her rites." Delivered perfectly and crisp, as always. He'd said something similar dozens of times, to dozens of grieving families. He hardly heard the words leave his lips.

"Thank you, Judge Mullen," Henry said. His wife—Ma Kettle's only daughter—was in tears, while Henry was more composed. "If you'd like to come in, we're still waiting for Priest Erick to arrive..."

Elrich froze, but only for a second. He reanimated his smile and walked in past Henry, all the while cursing in his head, *The godsforsaken priest isn't even here yet? Why hasn't one of the little brats gotten him in?* The Judge's rites shouldn't be performed until the soul was sent by a priest, and now he was stuck even longer in this hellish, overcrowded home with seven Kettles and an old woman's dead body. They shouldn't even have sent for him until the priest was gone!

Easy. Easy.

The calming voice in Elrich's head whispered at his rage. It had to do that more and more, lately, as bogged-up land deals and an influx of papers and requests to his door piled up on him. When things weren't going to plan, his insides began to burn.

"We found her—we found her this morning," Audrey spoke from behind him, as Elrich surveyed the home with silent, invisible contempt. "I...found her. She's just...she's not right at all."

"Not right, you say?" Elrich repeated, staring a hole into the far wall. It was bare and unwashed, void of art or window or paint.

"Not right," Henry repeated. "Maybe you ought ta...Judge, sir, I mean, if you would like ta, ta see the...see her body..."

"While Priest Erick is yet to?" Elrich inquired, turning around to face the couple. Henry had his arm around Audrey's shoulders; she stood a foot underneath her husband's enviable height, and half a foot above his own. "You know that the priest should be quick to see the body, of course. Lest the soul escape."

"She's got no soul!" Audrey shrieked in a violent, throat-tearing cry, before dropping to her knees on the floor and burying her face in her hands.

Elrich seethed, but Henry was too distracted by his wife to notice, and when he looked up from her, Henry saw a patient, understanding man.

"Saints, I'm sorry, Judge Mullen, your Honor," Henry said, crouching beside Audrey and holding her. "She's a right mess, has been all day. Under the circumstances..."

"Mm." Elrich nodded. "It's...quite...all right."

Henry swallowed, his long neck stretching. "She means, though...Dorella, Ma, she's...*empty.*"

"No soul?" Elrich mused. "It is not a kind thing to say. Though I suppose, in her grief..."

Henry shook his head, standing up from his wife. "I'll show ya, sir. You'll—you'll hafta see it anyway, I guess."

"Lead the way, then," Elrich said, turning so that Henry could move past him. He followed him through the rooms and halls of the upper floor, which was larger than it seemed. They walked past several of the Kettle children, who were all in various states of mostly quiet distress. The home was rather silent for being so occupied.

"She's in here," Henry said, his voice cracking a bit. The door they approached was shut tight. "Told the kids not to go in. They're good, they...they listened."

Henry grasped the knob and pushed, the door sticking in its frame before swinging inward.

A foul, acrid smell wafted out, forcing Elrich to take a step back. Henry was used to it, though he winced. The room was dark, with no window or flame.

"It's—it's bad, I know," Henry managed, his voice wavering. "I ain't never, your Honor, never seen anything like it. Not in my life."

Neither have I. And that was a very rare thing for Elrich Mullen, who'd traveled the entire kingdom a dozen times over and attended hundreds of rites.

He buried his surprise and said to Henry Kettle, "A lantern, please."

The man returned with a lit one. Elrich took it in his hand and raised it high, but not above his head. He breathed in a lungful of fresh air and went into the room.

Had he not been holding his breath, he might have sworn aloud. The scene before him was ghastly. Ma Kettle was lying facedown on the floor, naked. A blanket was wrapped around her ankle, pulled from the bed and hanging off.

"Audrey tried ta cover her," Henry said, his words short and clipped to avoid breathing in. "She couldn't—couldn't stay in the room."

Dorella Kettle's corpse was shrunken and shriveled like an ancient hide. It was unnatural. Wretched. Her arms were two narrow sticks, tucked in close to her wasted body, and her legs were just as thin. Her hair had fallen out and lay scattered around her head, spread across the floor, wispy and grey. She was as small as the smallest of the Kettle children.

Elrich was forced to take a breath, and as he did, he noticed what the flickering lantern had hidden at first. What he had thought was the shadow of the corpse was actually a black puddle spreading from the abdomen.

Elrich stepped out of the room and closed the door.

"What do you think, Judge Mullen?" Henry asked him, hushed.

"It's not for me to say," Elrich answered. He was learned in many things, but he was not a physician, and this wasn't something he had ever encountered. He handed the lantern back to Henry.

Henry took it, snuffing the flame. "But do ya...I mean, what Audrey said...her soul, is it still there?"

"That is also not for me to say," Elrich advised, starting to lose his patience with the man. Hoping it would cease the questioning, he added, "But I am sure a woman as strong as Dorella kept her spirit."

That was enough to relieve Henry, who grasped the lantern handle with both hands and nodded. A knock sounded, soft and muffled from the faraway front door.

"That will be Priest Erick," Elrich said, looking toward the front. "Come. Let's bring him in."

And get this damned thing over with.

9

Delila's sharp ears picked up the sound of the door closing before Monty's, but Terra was already running along the grass.

"It's Ma Kettle, right?" Monty said, eager to be on the forefront of the news the Judge was bringing. "I heard earlier today from Marie that she had—"

"Monty!" Delila chided. Terra had come up between the two of them, peering at the Judge through their legs.

"Hi, Judge," Terra said.

"Hello, dear," Judge Mullen said, looking down upon the blonde child. "Your name is...?"

"Terra."

"Ah, yes. Terra. It's a shame we must see each other under these circumstances, all of you," Judge Mullen said, looking to the whole of the Bellamy family. "I'm afraid I bear the news that Dorella Kettle passed on this morning."

Delila closed her eyes. Maybe she was hoping that Terra didn't know Ma Kettle's real name, but that wasn't to be.

"Ma Kettle is dead?" Terra pushed through her mother's and brother's legs, bringing her toy up to her chest and pressing it against her shirt. "Are you telling the truth, Judge?"

"I am, Terra," Mullen said, looking into her shining eyes for a moment. "I performed the rites this morning, and Priest Erick rested her soul as it left. She is ready to go to the beyond. I volunteered to bring the news to the surrounding farms, to give our new messenger boy some...rest."

"No! I just saw her, she can't be dead!" Terra cried.

Delila threw a glare at Mullen, then knelt down. "It's okay, Terra. Ma Kettle lived a very long and happy life. It's good that you got to see her again before she passed." Delila took her hand, opening the fingers and revealing the wooden doll. "And you always have this to remember her by."

Terra nodded, calming down some, though tears were spilling down her cheeks. Delila stood again.

"Monty was at Kettle's this morning," she told Judge Mullen. "He heard from Marie. It's a shame. We were *waiting* to tell Terra."

"I see," Mullen said, looking over at Monty. "So you may have been the very first to know outside of the family."

"Oh," Monty said. "Well, I guess so. I didn't—didn't see anything. Marie came downstairs and told me."

"She was comfortable with you," Mullen said. "That's good. You probably eased her grief a great deal."

Monty thought back to how he had stammered through their interaction. "Maybe."

Judge Mullen smiled, narrow and grim. "We will be performing the final sending of Ma Kettle this evening after sundown. I am inviting all families to come, as Ma Kettle was a friend to everyone in the village."

"The final sending, so soon?" Delila said, rising up and holding Terra's hand in hers.

"This is a...special circumstance," Judge Mullen said. "Dorella's remains are in a precarious state. I felt it was best to ensure we send them as soon as possible."

What does that mean? Monty thought of Marie's tear-streaked face, and what she'd said about Audrey lifting her mother's body right off the ground. The final sending usually wasn't done for several days.

"It's short notice," Delila said. "I'm sorry to say that we may not be able to attend. And the children don't need to see something like that right now."

"Of course, I am just here to provide the word," the Judge said, unlinking his hands. "It would be good to see you there, if you can. I am sure the Kettle family would appreciate seeing you as well, Monty."

Monty's heart swelled a bit. Judge Mullen was personally asking him to be there?

"We'll see," Delila said, cutting in before Monty could say anything. "Thank you, Judge. We have to get back to the house, now. We were just about to eat."

"Please, don't let me keep you longer." Judge Mullen dipped his head again, as smoothly as he had done before. "I must inform the Gartens next."

Monty watched him move back the road and follow the path to the Gartens farm, rather than cut across their land to get there sooner. He turned to his mother once the Judge was out of earshot. "Mother, why can't we go? We should be there."

"As I said, it's not something that either of you should be seeing right now," she said.

Monty figured she was thinking of their own father's sending, which had been very difficult to get through.

Still holding Terra's hand, she started to walk back to the house.

Monty followed after her. "But Judge Mullen asked me to be there himself!"

"Judge Mullen asks many things of many people," his mother responded, not turning. "That does not mean they have to be done."

Monty let out a frustrated groan. "It's not like it's a favor to him. Why are you so cold with him all the time?"

"I am perfectly pleasant," Delila said. "Terra, go on inside. We can talk more about Ma Kettle later, if you want."

"Yeah." Terra nodded, still hushed, before going up the steps.

He waited patiently for his mother to round on him, which she did with deliberate ease. He crossed his arms. It hadn't taken much to feel like he *needed* to go this sending, but now that he was stuck on it, he didn't feel like letting it go.

"I saw you give him the evil eye when he told Terra about Ma Kettle," he said to her. "No one else would do that to Judge Mullen."

"Don't concern yourself with that," Delila said, hands on her hips, her dark eyes sharp. "Judge Mullen's business with us should not cost you any sleep, Monty. Nor should you be worried what a man like that thinks of you."

She had hit the matter right on the head, as she was good at doing, so Monty went around it. "'A man like that?' See, you do have a problem with him."

"We are not going to discuss that," Delila told him. Her tone was heavy; final. "You and I both know that bare cornstalks do not mean that our work is done. Tonight is just as important as the rest of the harvest. We have to go to town almost every day from here until the crop is sold."

"I know that," Monty said, defensive. "I know how the farm works, I've been doing this ever since I was half Terra's age, you know."

"If I didn't know better," Delila responded, "I'd say you're half Terra's age right now."

Monty flushed. "I'm not a kid anymore. I should be able to know—"

"You should know when to stop." She crossed her arms now, too. "No one is going to that sending, and that's all I have to say about it."

"Fine," Monty said. "I'll load the cart for tomorrow, then."

"You have to eat."

"Not hungry anymore," Monty said, and he turned and paced toward the shed before his mother could stop him.

Whatever she called after him, he didn't hear. All he wanted to do was be recognized and given some responsibility. He was his father's son, and his mother's son, and Terra's older brother, but he was more than that, too. What was it going to take for people to see that?

Mom's never going to let me grow up.

He flung open the wide doors to the shed where all the harvest was stored and began hauling bag after heavy bag to the cart by the barn.

I'm going to be her kid forever. She hasn't let me even look at the farm papers once, and dad's been gone over a year.

He grunted, tossing a bag into the cart. Some corn spilled out, rolling over the beaten wood. He ignored it.

Everyone in Kettle's just saw me babysitting Terra while mom handled the business, like usual.

Sweat beaded on his brow as he hefted the eighth heavy sack of corn into his arms.

I'm normally invisible to Judge Mullen, too, and when he finally asks something of me, she tells him that I can't. Like I can't even speak for myself!

Monty heaved the last sack into the cart, filling it up about as full as it could be. He was still antsy.

"I'm going," he said. He snapped his fingers and leaned against the cart, looking toward Irisa. The decision, sudden and clear, made him feel better instantly. He nodded, reaffirming to himself. "I'm going to the sending no matter what."

10

The days were shorter in winter, and the sun was finding the horizon by the time Monty returned from the cart. He shoveled down a dinner of cold eggs and bread and told his mother that he was going to sleep early, tired from his before-dawn journey into town.

"Cart's ready for tomorrow," he said shortly to her. She was sitting at the desk in her room, and she turned in her chair.

"I know you want to be more involved, Monty," she said to him. She sounded a little pained and stressed, papers spread all over the desk. "After the harvest time—we're just so busy now."

"Yeah," Monty said, and he almost left to go back down the hall to his room. But he knew his mother well, and that she might suspect his evening's plans if he stayed stubborn. So he told her, "I get it. I'm sorry about...you know, getting on you about Mullen and the sending and all. You're right, it's...not something I want to see."

He held his breath until she replied, "I appreciate that, Monty. Go on, get to bed."

She gave him a smile that danced in the flickering candlelight before he returned it and went back to his room.

We're just so busy now.

It was something he'd heard before. Getting put off. He could see all the papers on the desk, and how she'd burned through candles every night working on things there. If she really was going to teach him, she'd do it now when she needed his help.

Tonight, he'd be helping himself. He'd be the sole representative of his family at this sending. He'd talk to the Kettles, offer his condolences. Maybe be asked to say something, or stand with the Judge.

These thoughts, chaining together one after the other, kept him awake in bed until the sun was long gone and he knew his mother was asleep.

The sending would be happening soon.

Carefully, he slid his blanket off until it was rumpled at the foot of his bed. The house was silent; no scratching of quill or fidgeting, which just meant that Monty had to be as quiet as possible. He set his bare feet down on the floor and stood out of bed.

He'd snuck out of the house plenty of times, and the floor hadn't gotten any less squeaky since he was a child. He just knew the spots better now, and stepped easily around them.

Monty eased the door open and slipped through the narrow space before. He had left his boots outside by the steps earlier, so he wouldn't have to fumble with them inside. He slipped them on his feet, muffled by the grass, and crept carefully around the house to the road.

The night was dark, and the horizon of Irisa was clear of light. He knew he would be on time for the sending, but it was still a relief to see it hadn't proceeded without him.

He made much quicker time to Irisa without the wagon in tow. The sending was to take place outside of town, in a northern plain just astride the village proper, and it was there he saw the people gathered—a great number of them, though it was too dark to truly tell how many.

He approached with uncertainty. Monty had been to final sendings, of course, his own father's fresh in his memory, but this was different. Should he seek out Marie, or one of the other Kettles? Judge Mullen?

His indecision was snuffed by the approach of the Judge himself, moving with grace along the grass. Most of the villagers were gathered around the platform; the Judge broke away from that crowd, coming over to Monty on the outskirts.

"Monty," he said, quiet yet very easy to hear. "So you were able to make it, after all. Your mother as well?"

"No, your Honor. It's just me," Monty said, and quickly decided that it was best the Judge didn't know about his indiscretion. "Mother...couldn't get away from the farm. But she—I understood that it was important for someone from our family to be here. For me to be here."

"It is too bad she couldn't come," Judge Mullen said, looking none too displeased at that fact, "but I am glad you are here, Monty. It will be nice to speak with another of the Bellamys about your farm."

"The farm?" Monty repeated. Whatever he was expecting Judge Mullen to say amid the sending, it wasn't about their farm. "Sure, I mean, if you have were wondering about the harvest, we'll be coming to town tomorrow..."

Judge Mullen offered him a smile. "No, I am sure it was a good harvest, Monty. I wanted to ask about your mother. She does seem very stressed, the last few times we have crossed paths."

Monty shrugged. "I guess. The farm has been a lot of work this year, with...well, with my father passing."

"Yes." Judge Mullen bowed his head. "A terrible thing. I worry about each and every one of my constituents, you know. It does not matter to me if your house is next to mine or your farm is miles from the village. I want to make sure that everyone is doing well."

"Right," Monty said.

"With the harvest ended and your selling to culminate over this next week, it occurred to me that a virile young man like yourself might have some free time," Judge Mullen said.

Monty just nodded. The winter after harvest was a fairly idle time, excepting the one winter where the roof of the barn had needed to be fixed. But it was sturdy now.

"To put it simply, Monty, this latest messenger boy we've had among town has been...leaving something desired." Judge Mullen cracked one of his knuckles. "Not that I wish to speak ill of the boy. He is kind and puts forth an effort..."

Monty's features lit up, eagerness hidden by the dark. A messenger position was about as low on the ladder one could be on the town coin, but it was still a position within the village. Something that could lead to

more, and in the meantime, get him familiar with the operations of the
town. The merchants and commerce; the farmers' collective and their
officials. In an instant, his mind filled with images of selling the farm and
putting his family up in a nice house in Irisa, or of hiring others to run the
farm while they reaped the profits.

"...but I fear I am going to have to replace the lad, as the busiest time
of all approaches in the wake of the traveling merchants and buyers."
Judge Mullen sighed, low and long. "Well, Monty, I have been impressed
with your capability in handling the Bellamy farm work in the absence of
your father. If you do have the time this off-season, I would be quite
pleased to have you as the new recruit courier."

Recruit courier—the official name. The sound of it warmed him in the
chill night.

"Of course, if your mother allows," Judge Mullen added with a small
smile.

"I would be thrilled to, your Honor," Monty said immediately, and
when Judge Mullen held out his hand, he shook it with a sense of
independent purpose.

"Wonderful, wonderful," Judge Mullen said to him, letting go of
Monty's hand, which had swallowed up his own. "Pay me a visit next time
you are in town, then, and we can take care of the arrangements. It will be
good to have someone so capable working for the village."

Mullen gave a farewell and disappeared into the black of the night,
back to the sending. Monty let his excitement out in a big rush of breath,
knowing he couldn't walk into the sending with a big grin on his face.

So Mullen had wanted to get him alone, away from his mother, to offer
him the courier position. He appreciated the man's savvy; Judge Mullen
knew that his mother might not be as keen on the idea. But what he
didn't realize was that the decision was not his mother's—it was Monty's.
And she would have no reason to be upset about it, anyway. The winter
would bring little work and even less coin once the harvest was sold;
meanwhile, he'd be earning more keep and making a name for himself
within Irisa. It couldn't be more perfect.

The lighting of a torch nearby reminded him of where he was and why he was here. Monty quickly walked into the crowd of villagers gathered around the platform that held Ma Kettle's body, losing himself among their count. It was warmer among the people. He didn't know where the Kettles were, but that was quickly answered when he saw Judge Mullen, holder of the torch, pass it to Audrey Kettle. She and the rest of her family stood in the front, facing the Judge and the expanse. The torchlight lit them all orange, dancing in the soft breeze.

Judge Mullen's voice boomed, oddly powerful from his small frame. "I thank you all, as does the Kettle family, for being here at the final sending of Dorella Kettle. May she thrive among the saints."

Together with the swell of villagers, Monty spoke the prayer in gentle tones: "May she thrive among the saints." He saw most of the Kettles' lips move with everyone else's, but not Audrey's. She held the torch stoic and stricken. Her husband was reserved, his hands joined at his waist. Their children, all five of them, stood around him. Marie stepped toward her mother and put her hand on her arm; Audrey seemed not to notice.

"We will now send Dorella to the beyond, where she will watch over us," Judge Mullen said, his voice washing over everyone there. "Audrey, you may now commence the pyre."

Audrey Kettle moved stiffly, her daughter's fingers falling from her arm. She approached the small platform, where, piled upon a neatly-arranged mass of dry branches and logs, her mother's body rested in a simple wooden casket. The shiny iron handles adorning its sides would later be retrieved by Irisa's gravekeeper when he came to bury the bones, but he would find only ashes when this sending was done.

Her back to the crowd, Audrey dropped the torch at the foot of the pyre. The dry wood caught immediately, crackling. As the Kettles and Mullen retreated from the platform, it grew to a blaze, the licking tips of the fire reaching far above the three-foot height of the pyre itself. Light cast out over the field, followed shortly by the warmth of the sending flame.

Monty looked around to see most of the village surrounding him, close to a thousand people, gathered here to bid farewell to Ma Kettle. It was a good thing to see, and it reinforced his conviction to be here; that it was important to be a part of this.

"...from the Dromm..."

His ears tingled at the word, and he looked back to see who had whispered it, but all he saw was half-shadowed faces.

"...said she...just woke up there..."

He looked around again, and now it seemed that everyone was looking at him, or was looking away when he turned. He did see some faces he knew, now; Meera Sand, off in the distance; a builder from the guild whose name was either Brice or Brick. But who was talking? No one? Everyone?

"So sudden..."

"...just like that, an' she said..."

"...they ain't here, are they? Just him, and..."

"...cursed."

Monty felt surrounded by whispers, soft words that roared louder than the fire before him. He turned around fully, now, daring someone to say something to him, but there was no challenge. It was the same it always was; behind his back, whispered; hinted; teased. Just enough to keep him at arm's length, to make him feel like he didn't belong in the village.

Terra didn't talk to anyone in town, really; she didn't understand. He didn't know how his mother was able to just cast this stupid stigma aside the way she had. When he heard the whispers, it always made his ears hot. It was never overt; he was never refused service or shooed away like he'd heard of happening to lepers and the like. But the whispers. The whispers were there.

And here, they were louder. Turned away from the fire, he heard them from the people who were behind him now. Black trees, little girls, curses. Ma Kettle had told people what Terra had said, and those people had told people, and now he was sinking in a pile of hushed rumors he'd never hear told to his face.

Monty pushed through the crowd, retreating from the noise of the fire and the voices and the light and warmth, into the cold and black embrace of the night that lied over everything else. Were people watching him leave the sending before the fire was burned out? Certainly, they were.

"To hell with this," Monty growled, shrugging his coat around his shoulders, bracing against the cold. The attraction of working for the town, living there and thriving, grew sour in his mind. He was a Dromm farmer kid. His family grew up by the Dromm. It was nothing but a bunch of trees, but it ruined everything.

Was everyone in the village thick in the head? He, Terra, and their mother were *fine.* The Gartens were *fine.* So were the Cherrywoods and the Holcombs. The woods weren't cursed, they were just dark and scary to the people who didn't know any better. The village kids he had played with went into the woods, too. Were they now numbered among their superstitious parents? Did they remember their jaunts with Monty? He'd forgotten their names, now, so it was only fair they'd forgotten him.

"As though their little kids never sleepwalked?" Monty muttered. He snapped his fingers. "Of course they have. Of course they have! They just woke up in the road, or in a stable, or sleeping in the pantry." He cursed. "If they had trees to wake up in, they'd wake up there!"

Snap. Snap. Snap. His fingertips burned. He clenched his hands into fists. So he'd never belong to the town? He'd never get to move on from their farm? They would all be trapped there, trapped until they died and the villagers were grateful to burn their bodies.

It would be better to stay on the farm.

The wind blew around Monty. He stopped on the path back home, one foot on the path and the other on the grass.

Isn't that what they'd expect? For him to just go back to the farm and stay there, by the Dromm? Would that change anything?

No. He would have to change it himself. And he would start by taking the courier job.

It would be the first step in getting off the farm and moving on from the black forest.

11

"I thought you'd grown out of this, Monty!"

Monty and his mother stood in the kitchen, one of them on each side of the small, round table. Monty opened his mouth to speak, but Delila cut him off.

"Sneaking off in the night? Doing something just because I told you not to?" Delila huffed. "I am just—"

"I'm not a kid anymore, *mother*," Monty said, his voice edging close to a growl. It was the day after the sending, and his mother had noticed that his jacket and boots weren't where they usually were, and his boots were dirty. Monty had been too preoccupied to bother being careful about that. She had gathered the truth quickly. "In case you forgot, the town Judge himself had asked me to be there! Personally!"

"That's nonsense," Delila said with a shake of her head. "There's no reason for Judge Mullen to want to you at a final sending when you're not even a relative. He's only..."

"What? What is it you think he's up to, exactly?"

"You're really pushing me, Monty," Delila told him. "I shouldn't have to hear this from you. Terra is having a hard enough time with Ma Kettle's death, just when she was getting over your father's."

There it was; the fact of Montille's passing, uttered aloud, used as a weapon in an argument. It hung in the air.

"I'm fine," Terra said, standing in the doorway of the kitchen. "I'm not a baby, either."

Oh, so I'm a baby, now, Monty thought. He whipped his head to Terra. "And if you had just kept your mouth shut about the Dromm, the people in town wouldn't think we were all cursed!"

Terra said, "I tell Ma Kettle everything! She's nice to me! She was nice to me!"

Delila clapped her hands, spiking the argument. "What are you talking about, now? What about the Dromm?"

If she could use their father's death, then he could tell her about this. "Terra sleepwalked into the Dromm. When I went looking for her that morning? I found her there. And the first thing she did when she got to town was tell Ma Kettle about it, even though I told her not to. And now everyone in Irisa knows!"

Delila blanched. "You didn't tell me that."

"Of course I didn't!" Monty snapped. "You're just as crazy about the Dromm as the other—" Monty stopped himself from saying *grown-ups*— "the other people in town! I didn't want you having a fit." The sympathy he felt for his mother those days ago was far away and out of reach.

"So you lied to me?"

"It was going to get back to you anyway, apparently," Monty said. "It was all I heard about at the sending, people talking behind my back. I'm tired of being outcast just because we live out here! Everyone thinks the Gartens are weird, and the Cherrywoods never, ever go to town. I don't want to be like them!"

"This is your home. It is not a burden."

"I'm okay, mom," Terra spoke up, climbing onto a chair. "I don't even remember anything about the woods. I didn't get sick or get hurt."

"You are in just as much trouble, Terra," Delila told her, making her shrink back in the chair. "You lied to me, too. And Monty, you're completely overreacting about the townspeople. We are not outcasts, and no one thinks less of us for living near the Dromm. Just because you're getting teased by the other kids—"

Monty growled, waving his hand in the air. "It's not the *kids.* It's everyone."

"Who?" she asked simply.

"It's..." Monty hesitated. He didn't have a real answer. "I didn't see who it was. It was too dark. But people were talking."

"Maybe you thought they were." Delila's voice softened. "And if you really feel that way, Monty, then you should know we have to stick together as a family. We can't be undermining each other. The farm is on the line. Our livelihoods. All it would take is one bad harvest for everything to take a turn, and without your father around, we can't take chances."

"I don't know any of that, because you never tell me." He didn't feel like shouting anymore. A bitterness filled his throat, the same old struggles he'd felt since dad died. "I'm just a farm hand to you."

"That isn't fair," Delila said. "We're all busy during the harvest. We all work hard. This winter will be different."

Another thing he'd heard before. Monty bit back the words on his lips, about the courier offer. He would talk to Judge Mullen today to arrange it, and *then* he would tell his mother about it.

"Fine," he said. "I'll go and hitch the horse so we can get to town."

Delila had more to say, but time wasn't on their side. "Go on. Terra, come here and talk to me. What happened with the woods?"

Monty grabbed his boots and left the kitchen, his anger reduced to embers, but still burning. It felt good to say what he'd been thinking, even if his mother wasn't listening to it. And now she was probably working herself into a mild frenzy as Terra babbled about her little misadventure in the black trees. Let her.

He brought their old mare out of the barn and hitched her to the cart, leading her back to the house. At least she was still strong, not struggling with the heavy load at all. He kept his hand on her neck while he walked her back.

Delila and Terra came out shortly, boots on. Terra said she wanted to walk with them instead of riding in the cart, so they all set off toward town. The traveling merchants would arrive on this day, the people to whom they'd promised some harvest the year before last. They would sell to them first, and then to the people of Irisa, until the yield was gone.

The argument was left in the kitchen of their home. Delila seemed to be in better spirits after talking to Terra; perhaps she'd been put at ease knowing that her daughter could have ventured into the Dromm and come out again just fine. Terra, too, was well. Monty noticed that she didn't have her doll with her, and he thought that she'd finally grown tired of carrying it with her everywhere she went.

The travel was easy and fast, with no company on the road, since they'd left early. They arrived in Irisa well before the merchants would get there, and they set up their cart by the town's front gate, where travelers off the main road would enter. The gate itself was not a measure of security; it had no doors, nor even a complete arch over the road. It was two sturdy, square wooden pillars buried in the earth, stretching twelve feet above the ground.

"We're early," Monty said to his mother, once they had locked their wheels and he'd fed the horse a pair of carrots from the sack they'd brought. "I'll go and check with the town merchants, see if they've heard any news of the road."

"All right," Delila said, both she and Terra working on lifting a fallen harvest sack. Terra stood in the cart, pulling at the canvas. "Hurry back. I'd like to stop by and talk to the Kettles before the selling begins."

"I'll be quick," Monty promised, and he headed back toward the direction of Kettle's store. He did give it a quick look as he walked past it and toward the center of town, and it seemed to be business-as-usual with the open door and trickle of customers. Back to normal so soon? Likely not, and Audrey had looked terrible the evening past. Her family was in grief, but she was somewhere else entirely. He almost stopped, just to go in and see if she was doing all right; but there was another pressing matter. And she had her family to support her.

Monty's destination stretched across the corner of the next road: the large, one-story building of the Irisa officials. It was the village hall, but it was mostly referred to as the Commons. All were welcome there, but rarely was there reason to visit.

Monty had one, and it wasn't to speak to the town merchants. He was here for the Judge.

He hesitated at the main doors. The large glass windows—the biggest pieces of glass in the whole town—were intimidating. He had only been here once before, and that was five or six years ago, when he had come with his mother while she brought in some kind of record that needed to be delivered. The door had seemed even bigger then, reflecting him wholly. Now it showed most of him, cutting him off at the knees.

He pulled the door open, stepping inside. Immediately he was warmer. The Commons had several ongoing fires spread throughout in brick enclosures, with short, fat chimneys on the roof letting out smoke. It was a well-maintained place, and just stepping in made Monty feel like he didn't belong.

I'm going to change that, he told himself, shaking off the trepidation. *I am going to be part of this.*

12

Judge Mullen's office was farther back. He remembered from when his mother had brought him here. That had been when Judge Mullen was new to the town.

The corridors were long, but not confusing; though the Commons was big, it only stretched in three directions, and Judge Mullen was at the end of the hall that continued straight ahead. He walked down the polished wooden floor as quickly as he felt was appropriate.

The Judge's door was closed, but Monty heard that it was always closed; that the Judge was a busy man, often buried in his work. He had also heard that Judge Mullen hated to be interrupted. But he had asked him here, had he not?

Monty knocked on the sleek door, his knuckles rapping on the wood next to the engraving: *Judge Elrich Mullen.*

The door was pulled open a half-minute later, though that thirty seconds felt much longer to Monty as he waited on the other side. Judge Mullen greeted him with a smile.

"Monty! Fantastic, please come in, and close the door. Have a seat." Mullen swept back to his desk. He wore his traditional Judge's robes today.

Monty did as asked, pushing the heavy door shut and sitting down in the chair in front of Judge Mullen's desk. The office smelled of wood and ink and candle flame, though no candle burned. The desk took up most of the back wall, behind which was a shuttered window, with slats eased open to let in enough light to read by, the rest of the big space dim. Bookshelves built into the wall braced the desk on either side, neatly packed with volumes thick and thin, some labeled, some not. It was the most books Monty had ever seen in one place. He'd read a few, but they were keepsakes from his mother's parents, grandparents he'd never met.

Judge Mullen saw him looking at the shelves. "Quite a lot, yes? I brought the majority of them with me. I do hate to be without my collection."

"You've read all of these? Your Honor?" Monty was amazed.

"Several times over, if you would believe it," Judge Mullen said. "But we are here to talk about you as a recruit courier, are we not? I know you are here with your family to sell to the merchants. I imagine you are in a hurry."

Monty straightened in his chair. "Yes, sir. I'm still very interested in the job. The position."

"Certainly," Judge Mullen said, his face showing that he never doubted Monty's acceptance for a moment. "There is one thing I neglected to bring up to you at the sending. If you are the recruit courier, you will need to be in town often, and throughout the day. There is a small quarters here in the Commons that I can arrange for you."

"You'd have me live here, your Honor?"

"Yes," Judge Mullen said, his eyes distant, as though he were looking right through Monty. "Now, I realize this might interfere with your duties at the farm, so I must ask: is this something that you could make work?"

He was slow to respond, choosing his words carefully. The idea of it practically made him want to leap out of his chair in delight, but the question was there: *could* he make it work? Winter was winter, but to not be home at all?

"I sense your hesitation," Judge Mullen said, and Monty wondered if he had just spoiled the entire prospect. "This is something we could...transition into, if necessary. You are not terribly far from Irisa, and your first day in this role would be a week from today. If you are not in your quarters, then I will need you to report directly to me each morning with the sunrise to ensure we start each day on the right foot."

"I can do that, sir," Monty said quickly, gripping the arms of the chair to stop himself from snapping his fingers.

"It would be ideal for you to be here at all times, of course," Judge Mullen added, "but this is something we can work with for now. As long as you are willing to extend the extra effort."

"Yes!" Monty said. "I'll do it, Judge. I really—I appreciate you doing this for me."

Judge Mullen laughed, a short chuckle. "Trust me, Monty, you are doing far more for me and for Irisa than I am doing for you. I am pleased with your fortitude." Quick as a whip, the Judge drew a quill from the stout inkwell on his desk and scribbled something down on the paper before him. "That makes it official."

Wow. Just like that.

"All right, Monty. Our short meeting is over. You can get back to your family now." Judge Mullen dropped his gaze and looked to the papers on his desk.

The office went quiet. Monty tried not to move the chair as he stood, and took his paces to the door. Once it was open, he hesitated, his hand on the warm brass handle.

"Judge Mullen?"

"Mm?" The Judge didn't look up from his desk.

"I just wanted to ask...Audrey Kettle. Is she doing all right? At the sending last night, she seemed very..." Monty shrugged. "I don't know. She wasn't doing well."

"That is kind of you to notice." Judge Mullen did look up from his desk now, fixing Monty with his dark eyes. "She is not well, that is true. Her family says she's come down with some affliction. Grief; illness; sometimes these things look alike. She will get better as time goes on."

Monty hoped that was true. "Thank you again, Judge," he said, and he stepped out of the office and closed the door, then let out his breath in a long exhale. That had gone well. Better than expected—his own quarters in the Commons? He didn't care if it was a closet and he had to sleep standing up. It was incredible.

The town of Irisa greeted him outside, shining bright in a different sort of light now. The only obstacle left was his mother.

She wouldn't like any of this, but the simple facts couldn't be contested: he wouldn't need to start until after the bulk of their selling was done, and he wouldn't be entirely away from the farm. Some days and nights, maybe, if the agenda was long and he chose to stay over in his quarters. But it would be simple. Better than him sitting around at home, watching the light snowfall through the window. And he'd be bringing home money in the bargain.

He relieved his mother at the cart so that she could go and check up with the Kettles, telling her that he'd heard no news about the road—which wasn't exactly a lie.

"How are they?" he asked her when she returned.

"Mostly well," his mother said. "Henry is a rock, he always has been. They need that now. But Audrey..."

"She didn't look good," Monty said. "At the, uh—at the sending."

He thought his mother might get angry at the mention of it, but she was more focused on the Kettles. "Henry wouldn't let me see her. She was in bed. He said she's been in bed, mostly, since her mother passed."

"Is she ill?"

Delila shook her head, unsure. "Henry thinks so. It could be the pain of loss pinning her down. I want to talk to her soon. I would have pressed Henry more, but—well, here they come."

In the distance, the road billowed dust as the horde of horse-drawn merchants rolled to Irisa.

The buyers were eager this year. The yield the merchants usually arrived with was smaller than it had been in the years past, speaking to a difficult harvest further in the west.

As it were, their own batch of harvest was sold through over the next few hours, even before the last merchant rolled past to see what was available. The sun started to set on the villagers at the gates, the merchants moved further into town to find quarters, and the packing up of the carts and stands began in tired earnest.

The wheels of the Bellamy cart (empty, save for Terra) rolled toward home. With his mother in a fairly cheery mood at their successful outing, Monty broached the subject of the courier job. He divulged all the details: The title. The duties. The quarters. As well as his opinion that that there was no better time than now.

Delila's reserved energy had retreated by the time Monty had finished speaking. "When did you talk to Judge Mullen about this?" she asked him, after remaining silent for few moments.

"At the sending," Monty told her, holding the reins of their horse a little tighter than he needed to. "He was really serious, mother. This is a huge opportunity. A rare one."

"What's it an opportunity for, exactly?"

"To..." Monty searched for the words. "To get *in*. In the town, in the Commons. To get to a place where I can do more for the family."

Monty watched his mother look straight ahead, unspeaking. Was she considering it? Understanding his point of view? Or just thinking of a new way to say no? The silence stretched out as they moved. Terra slept in the cart, exhausted from the day's work and talking to two dozen travelers.

Finally, Delila said, "I don't know why the farm isn't enough for you, Monty. It's enough for me. It was enough for your father."

Monty said, "He wanted more, too. You know he did. He was too...he had to be there, to carry us along. I'm grateful for it," he added. "But even today, we sold our harvest quickly. From the sounds of it, the rest should go just as fast. This is a good year for us, even without him. Without dad."

His mother didn't have a response. He wanted her to be supportive, or at least all right with the idea, but he realized now that all his logic couldn't change what his mother was feeling.

"I'm going to start next week," Monty told her. "I've already talked to Judge Mullen about it. It won't be till after we've sold our harvest and the shed is cleaned out. He understands."

"I am sure that he does," Delila said, her words measured.

She was angry; maybe a little hurt. Monty resisted the urge to apologize. It wasn't her place to dictate his life anymore. He was nineteen, and he'd be twenty when the winter was over. It was time for him to be the one telling his mother what he was doing. It wasn't as though he were abandoning the family forever.

There was no more talk of the job, the harvest, or anything else before they got back home. Delila took Terra out of the cart, carrying her back to the house in her arms while the girl slept, undisturbed.

Monty loaded the cart for the next day and tried not to think about the look on his mother's face.

13

The more complex the plan, the more steps involved in its execution, and the more ways it could go wrong. That was what ultimately made it most satisfying as things clicked into place.

Elrich slid Monty's paperwork into one of the many drawers on his desk after the boy had left. That was one thing taken care of.

He was fairly certain that the Bellamy boy would have done the job for free, but the pittance of coin he'd be getting would ensure his loyalty, and his effort. All else aside, the Judge *was* in need of a competent courier.

Which brought up the next matter, and it was only a few minutes before said issue was knocking at his door. This time, when he drew himself out of his chair and around his desk, he did it with a smile.

"Remind me," he said as he opened the door and greeted the young courier with a toothy smile, "what was your name again?"

"Rod—Rodney, your Honor." The twig-skinny, brown-haired recruit courier had his head lowered, like he was afraid to look up and see the Judge's face.

"Rod Rodney," Elrich repeated, and before the boy could correct him, he said, "if you're not too busy, I'd like you to come in to my office for a spell, please. Have a seat, right there before the desk."

There was no option for refusal. Elrich simply stood aside the door until the squire shuffled his way inside, and then he closed the door and watched him approach the chair. The boy was so skinny and ungainly that

Elrich half-expected to hear the child's bones knocking together as he walked.

Elrich waited, back to the closed door, until his guest was seated. He stood silent and stared at the back of the lad's head. How long would he sit there, waiting for the Judge, before he got up the nerve in his air-filled head to turn around and wonder where his master was, why he was making him wait? It would be terribly rude, to turn around and stare as if to hurry along the Judge of Irisa. He would never have the heart. No, the boy would sit there, fidgeting, until he pissed himself in his chair.

Elrich might have waited for that if he didn't have other things to do today. As it was, he was content to watch the boy squirm for half a minute before he took measured, deliberate steps toward the desk.

Before sitting, Elrich narrowed the window slats, casting the room in a dim pallor. The dark wood soaked up the light, and Elrich was framed by the shuttered window, short but broad, his silver hair blackened.

He sat down and did his best to prevent a smile from curling up the corners of his lips. He managed it, but it was a close thing.

"Rodney," he began. "Now that I recall your name, I remember the reason you were brought on. You're the son of Rodney Talhauer, the chief builder. Which makes you Rodney, Junior—am I right about that?"

"Yes. Yes sir, Judge Mullen." Rodney's voice was tiny like his arms, but shakier. Elrich though the boy might be absorbed into the chair.

"And here I'd thought my judgment was slipping," Elrich said, and now the grin was coming out. "But that's not it at all. It's just good, old-fashioned nepotism."

The courier clearly didn't know what to say to that; his mouth just hung open slightly, his eyes darting around the Judge's, waiting for what he had to say next.

"It would have been nice for your father to let me know you were close to useless before I went ahead and signed you on," Elrich said to the boy. "Lesson learned, there. I'll have to be having a talk with him, too."

"Sir—Judge—what do you mean?"

"Quiet." Elrich learned forward, resting his arms on the desk. This wasn't as fun with someone who didn't understand. What exactly was happening in this child's head? The wonder was fleeting, for he didn't truly care to know.

"As of today, your duties as courier have been absolved. You have been replaced." He leaned further across the desk, getting as close as he could to the boy without standing from his chair. "And while this does serve to benefit me regardless, believe me when I say that you will not be missed. Every half-second I've seen you dawdle at my doorway has been hell. You've made my life much harder than it needs to be in just the few weeks I've suffered your employ, and the fleeting relief of this conversation is diminished by the need for me to do even more paperwork to make it final. The fact that this will be the last time I ever write your name brings me joy so grand that I can't properly express it to you. Not due to any pitfall of my own, but rather your inability to comprehend even the simplest subject or command that involves anything beyond putting a sheet of paper under someone's...fucking...door."

Elrich reclined. By the end of his tirade, the tear-streaked boy was so small in the chair that he might have been trying to escape through back of it.

"Get out," he said, intertwining his fingers and resting them on the small paunch that was usually hidden by his robes.

The former squire was quick to stand, jerking out of the chair and tumbling to his knees before the desk. Elrich suppressed a laugh as the gangly boy stumbled to his feet, then made quick paces across the sleek floor of the office, grabbing at the door handle like he was drowning.

As he opened the door a narrow crack to slip through, Elrich said, "Wait, boy."

Rodney stopped, halfway out of the room. He slipped back in, still looking stricken, but with a tiny glimmer of hope lighting his eyes. "Yes, sir?"

"I'd almost forgotten." Elrich rapped his knuckles on his desk. "You came here to deliver a message, didn't you?"

Fitting, of course, that the boy would forget his duty in the first place. He'd like berate him further, but he needed whatever information the boy had managed to carry here.

"Oh. Oh, right." Rodney frowned. "Doctor Tobias, he—he wants to come and see you. He said he wants to talk to you about Mrs—er, Audrey Kettle. I told him he could come to your office once I got back to him."

"Then get back to him," Elrich said, annoyed at the prospect of the future interruption. "And close the door on your way out."

Elrich watched that small glimmer leave the boy; his posture slumped again; his head went down. Then he was gone, and the door was shut good and tight.

Dr. Tobias. Elrich had at first respected the doctor, when he first arrived in Irisa as the new town Judge. Dr. Tobias was old, and he was fairly short, himself, especially because he suffered from a bad back that kept him bowed over most of the time. Still, the man tottered about town at a good pace, visiting people and carrying his worn, scuffed brown leather bag that he claimed was older than he was.

Over the years, however, the man had become a nuisance, at first shaking the boat by recommending a remedy for Elrich's gray hair, and then insisting that the Judge be along for most of his home visits. Why the hell would people want the Judge at their home when they were lying in bed, sick? They'd think they were about to be delivered their rites.

Elrich had shouted as much at the doctor when he'd pestered him for the third or fourth time about coming on a home visit, but frustratingly enough, the anger seemed to slide right off of him. That was the worst of it all. Dr. Tobias was a generally cheery fellow. Just the sight of him made Elrich's stomach give a twinge.

Knock, knock, knock-knock-knock-knock.

Even the man's knock chafed at Elrich's nerves. Luckily for the doctor, Elrich had just had a chance to release a bit of his frustration. Once again, he stood from his desk and walked over to the door. Paused to take a breath. Closed his eyes. Then opened them and grasped the handle.

"Doctor," Elrich said with a smile, pulling the door open wide. Tobias was hunched over, per usual. His hair was wispy on the top and gray on the sides, with wrinkles pitting his face and a stringy beard dangling from his chin and cheeks. His clothes, as always, were clean and tidy, if loose-fitting.

"Good afternoon, Judge Mullen," Doctor Tobias said. "May I come in and sit with you?"

"Certainly." *If you must.*

Elrich withdrew, letting the man pass and shutting the door, wishing briefly that his office were only accessible via a hatch in the floor. He moved swiftly to his desk and sat down. "Rodney, the courier—he tells me you have news about Audrey Kettle?"

Tobias nodded, his wispy beard moving in delayed fashion. His body may have been bowed, but his voice was strong and quick. "I visited her today. The woman's been in bed since her mother died, saints save her soul. The family thought it was unusual. I told Henry that it's likely just the grief of—"

"Right," Elrich cut in. "She needs time."

"Aye." Tobias cleared his throat, a wet and appalling sound. "So I thought. But Henry insisted that I come have a look. The children are in tatters about the whole affair. So I did." Tobias's mouth tightened, his eyes growing more misty than usual. "I did not have the chance to see Dorella's corpse. She died quickly and she was sent quickly. Henry told me what he saw, something you can corroborate, I'm sure, Judge. That she was shriveled and blackened, like she'd been burned over a spit. All the meat was gone from her bones. Her body was unnaturally positioned. Yes?"

The memory of that morning came to Elrich easily; it was still fresh, and it was not an image that disappeared on its own. Ma Kettle uncovered and naked. Audrey screaming that her soul was gone. Her body nothing but a husk, the hair all fallen from her scalp.

"Yes," he said. "That is accurate."

Tobias chewed on his lip, another unsightly habit the man presented regardless of his company. "I've never seen something like that, in all my years. Even when that fungus swept up on Gerrich's farm and family."

That was not a family Elrich knew of. He assumed they had died. "What of Audrey?" Elrich inquired, moving the old man along to the point.

"Mm. She's certainly unwell. Awake, but lethargic. She spoke to me, but she sounded as though she had just woken up, or was speaking in her sleep. Her eyes were open, but she wasn't looking at me or anything in particular."

Enrich waited with thinning patience for Tobias to get to the point.

"At first glance I would assume one of the winter illnesses, but she hasn't vomited or been in other distress..."

Elrich folded his hands on the desk, wondering if the doctor could see the fury behind his eyes while the man rambled about a myriad of symptoms that Audrey Kettle was not exhibiting. Tobias's insistence on departing his entire knowledge of human illness on Elrich showed no signs of stopping, so he interrupted.

"Tobias." He let his fingers relax, the blood flowing back into them. "I've got...I have some other appointments. What are you trying to tell me about the woman?"

"Yes, right...well, Judge, I fear that she may have caught the same sickness her mother came down with," Tobias said.

"Do you."

"Most of her symptoms are not uncommon, but they don't lead me to any diagnosis. This lack of energy could be caused by many things. But she also has graying of the hair, and sometimes she is short in breath."

Elrich could have pointed out that Dr. Tobias himself exhibited those things, but instead he said, "And your concern is...?"

"That it may spread!"

"There are six other family members in that house. I was there, myself. Have any of them been acting this way?"

"No, they have not," Tobias said, shifting in his chair, "but it could only be a matter of time."

"I'm no doctor," Elrich continued, "but if this were some dangerously contagious illness, I would think it would have spread to the rest of the family if it were going to spread at all. Spare your concern of that matter. Focus on treating the woman, and whomever else needs your care. And to be clear—I do not want anyone in my village thinking they're going to fall ill just because the oldest woman here has passed. Do you understand?"

"Well, I wouldn't want to incite any sort of panic among the people," Tobias agreed, needling Elrich with his upbeat tone. "I will keep an eye on how Audrey does and I'll let you be the first to know if there are further developments with any...contagion."

"Please do," Elrich said dryly. He relaxed his fingers and pulled his arms back to his lap. "Is that all, doctor?"

Tobias thanked the Judge for seeing him on such short notice (*You mean* no *notice,* Elrich thought) and started to stand from his chair, but stopped short.

"Oh, I'd almost forgotten, Judge," Tobias said, chuckling to himself. "One last thing..."

Thunder roared inside Elrich as the doctor reached inside of his jacket. If Tobias was about to tell him of another sick villager, he would force the old man through the small opening beneath the door.

"Young Rodney gave this to me when he returned from your office." Tobias pulled a wax-sealed scroll from his cloak and set it down on the desk. "He told me he was too busy to run it back, but truth be told, he looked an awful mess, scared and maybe a bit tear-wet, if I saw it right..."

The scroll on the desk was sealed with the kingdom's crest. Tobias's words fell dead on Elrich's ears as he looked at the small document. For what reason would the kingdom send a missive? Was it orders? A request to move to another town? The latter had never sounded sweeter, Dromm farms and Delila Bellamy be damned.

"...talk to him for you, you Honor?"

Elrich blinked, bringing his eyes back to Tobias, who, for some reason, was still there. "What?"

"I said, do you want me to talk to him for you? Rodney?"

"I have talked to Rodney plenty." Elrich grabbed the scroll from the glossy wood of the desk, running his thumb over the wax seal. "That is all. I really must attend to this message, now."

"Of course." A nod, a few steps; at last, the doctor was gone.

The moment his door was closed, Elrich broke the scroll's seal and unfurled it. The red wax crumbled and tumbled down the desk, where he swept it to the floor with his forearm before laying the paper down on the surface.

Elrich read it fast, his excitement running from a boil down to a simmer, and then souring inside him as he reached the end.

"Absolutely not," he muttered, reading it over once more. "Absolutely not. Absolutely not." He repeated the words to himself even as he cast the letter aside and pulled out parchment of his own. The first pen he grabbed from his desk drawer, he flung across the room. The nib had broken off, probably from the last time he had tossed it in there. He took a second pen and dipped it in the inkwell, tapping it on the side. *Clink-clink-clink.*

The words he let spill aloud didn't exactly match his writing, but they were in the spirit of the return message. "I do not...need...a gods-be-damned...*assistant..,Judge...in MY town!"* His pen blackened the page, furious in execution but courteous in result. "No...no, no, no...I refuse your...very kind...offer...of assistance...you arrogant, squirmy little ferret..."

The unwritten insult was directed toward the king's residential advisor, the writer of the scroll, and a man who outranked Elrich Mullen by about four degrees and many thousands of constituents. Elrich set his own page aside to dry, his wet signature blanketing the bottom of the sheet.

The advisor's message was not a mandate—not yet. It was an offer to allow him to appoint an assistant Judge in the town from the list of candidates the advisor had been *so kind* to include. A list of people he owed favors to for pushing him this far up the ladder, Elrich surmised, because none of the names he recognized on the list carried any merit with them.

If they were trying to push an assistant Judge on him, it wouldn't be long before he didn't have a choice in the matter. But once he owned most of the land here, once Irisa was, in fact, *his*...well, then the kingdom couldn't do anything short of starting a war to get their own men sitting in the town's official chairs.

Like the ink on his answer, his time was drying up. He needed that land.

14

The rest of the Bellamy harvest sold in similar quick fashion, though with only one cart, it still took them the full week to unload all of their wares. Monty's mother had not warmed up to the courier position at all; in fact, the only time they had spoken about it since he first told her was the previous night, when he reminded her that he'd be going to the Commons early the next morning.

She'd acknowledged it, and she'd told him to be safe and polite. Monty supposed that was better than nothing. Terra had been mostly indifferent to the idea when Monty explained to her that he'd be in town a lot after the harvest. He was just glad to see that she was back to normal after that episode in the Dromm, and that she wasn't taking Ma Kettle's death too hard. He wouldn't admit it fully to himself, but he was relieved to confirm that his family—and the farm—would, in fact, be okay while he was gone, even if it was only a day at a time.

And now, with dawn breaking over the east horizon, Monty was walking into the Commons building with a ball of nerves buzzing in his stomach, nervous energy propelling his steps down the straight hall to the Judge's office.

This early, the Commons was even quieter than normal. He knocked on the Judge's door and the sound seemed thunderously loud.

Judge Mullen answered promptly.

"Good morning, your Honor," Monty greeted him.

"And to you, Monty," Mullen responded. He didn't invite Monty inside. "These first few days as a courier are going to be a trial by fire, of sorts. I am assuming you know the town fairly well, but you need to know the offices in the Commons and other official buildings even better."

"Not a problem, Judge."

"That's what I like to hear." Mullen reached into his robes and pulled out a scroll that was tied by a string. "Your first job is to deliver this message to Rodney Talhauer."

The builder chief. His house was on the opposite side of town. He took the scroll from Judge Mullen, asking, "What's it about?"

He immediately realized his mistake as Mullen's expression shifted.

"That is not the business of a courier," Judge Mullen said. "You are to be knowledgeable, fast, and you are not to ask questions. If you come to my door and I hand you a bloody dagger and tell you to deliver it to the Dromm woods, then I want you back here empty-handed in under an hour. Is that clear?"

"Yes, your Honor," Monty answered.

"Good. When you have handed that off, come back for the next missive. I would give it to you now, but I have not finished it. It is an incredibly busy morning. We are backed up since last week." Judge Mullen readjusted his robes. "When you have no message to deliver, you may retreat to your quarters or go about town. But you will need to check your door every fifteen minutes."

Judge Mullen explained that if he was needed, either himself or another official would leave a courier badge in the slot by his door, which he would then return to the proper office and get his assignment. He also pointed out where his quarters were, off to the far-right side of the entrance down the branching hall.

"Get moving," Mullen said. "I need you back here as soon as possible."

Scroll in hand, Monty hurried back down the hall and exited the Commons. The sun was waking the village, but the streets were mostly empty. He broke left onto the streets and left again, moving at a quick pace towards the east. The sun poked at his eyes.

Monty hadn't visited Rodney Talhauer's home before, but he'd seen it many times. The chief builder had an impressive domicile, almost as big as the Commons itself, taking up a high-rising corner of Irisa. It was one story, though in its center rose a tall peak, with a triangular glass window showing the thick beams that reached up to support the roof. The whole house was painted a clean white. Many people in Irisa would come by just to admire the structure.

With a small grin, he reminded himself that he was here to work. He hustled up to the front door and knocked with purpose. He imagined the thudding of his fist echoing throughout the inside of the expansive home.

There was no answer. Monty knocked again. Judge Mullen had explained the importance of handing messages directly to their recipients, not just sliding them under doors.

When Monty was about to knock a third time, Rodney Talhauer opened the door and looked down at him.

The man was massive; it was like he was made out of tree trunks. He was the only official in Irisa who wore a beard, and it grew as thick as the muscles with which he swung sledges and laid brick. He stood over Monty by a foot.

"Sir," Monty said, holding out the scroll. "A message for you."

Rodney was silent, looking Monty over. His weather-worn face was passive and unchanging. He stepped forward, out onto the street, closing the door behind him. Monty moved back to accommodate the approach, wondering what was going on.

"What's yer name," Rodney said, a question with no inquisitive tone; he spat it like he might spit a curse at a horse who was walking too slowly.

"I'm Monty, sir. I'm the—" He suppressed a smile. "The new recruit courier. It's my first day."

"Are ya." Rodney let a long breath out of his nose. "Bellamy boy. And Mullen sent ya here. To gimme that."

"Yes—"

Rodney plucked the scroll from Monty's hand. "This a message from him?"

"I don't know, sir. I'm just bringing it from the Commons."

"It's from him," Rodney said. "Tied it with string, see? Not even bothered to use wax. Tryin' to send a message."

Monty thought, *Well, yes, exactly,* but he didn't dare say it aloud. Rodney was clearly not in the best of moods. Or was he always like this?

"How ya know the Judge?"

"I don't know him personally, sir," Monty answered. "He just brought me on as courier last week."

"Y'ever meet my son?" Rodney was gripping the scroll in a closed fist, crumpling it in the middle.

"I...haven't had the pleasure." Monty knew of Little Rodney, the skinny young child so vastly different from his father that one could hardly believe they were cut from the same cloth. He'd seem him around town before, but never spoken to him.

"Hmph." Another blow of air from his nose. Rodney kept his mouth tight-lipped, barely opening it when he spoke. "He was courier. Till last week. Mullen did a number on him. He din' come out the house fer a couple days."

Monty's stomach fell into a pit. He remembered Judge Mullen saying something at the sending about the old courier not working out. Of all people, Monty had replaced Rodney Talhauer's son?

"Still won't tell me what the man said," Rodney continued. He looked Monty in the eye, a withering gaze. "What you think of the Judge, kid?"

Normally, the 'kid' comment would have made Monty bristle, but he resisted. "Judge Mullen is—"

"Ah, save it. Save it. I dun'wanna hear it." Rodney waved his slab of a hand. "You ain't know better, I ain't gonna take it out on ya. That's one thing separates me an' that little dwarf. That an' about two'n'a'half feet." He crushed the scroll further. "Listen here, cuz I know your ma and she's a good one. Mullen ain't any good. Don't trust a word out his mouth. He breaks promises, he uses people. Uses their kids."

Monty decided that Rodney must be in a poor state because of his son being let go. It would be best to just go along with him. "I'll keep that in mind, sir."

"Aye." Rodney shoved the scroll in his pocket like it was a loose coin. "You better. Yer first day on th'job and Mullen sends you here, to me, at the crack o'dawn, knowin' full well what he did to my boy. You think

about that. And if ya tell the Judge any what I said here, I'll kill ya."
Rodney turned back and went into the house, slamming the door behind
him with a brutal thud.

Monty stood in silence before remembering that was a luxury he could
not afford. He was probably already late after this hell of a first delivery.

Rodney's words knocked around in his head on the way back, but they
were quickly shoved out by the motion of the day. Monty returned for the
next message as fast as he could, and he was whisked off to the outskirts
of town to hand off three scrolls to a western farm. It seemed the morning
messages took him all over town, and as the afternoon wore on, he spent
more time dashing around the Commons and closer parts of Irisa.

It was exhausting work. He was a farmer, and had labored for most of
his life, but there wasn't a whole lot of running back and forth involved.
He did get a few minutes to rest in his quarters and hurriedly munch
down an apple.

The quarters were about as small as could be, but it didn't make
stepping into his very own room in the Commons any less special. There
was a narrow bed that was surprisingly comfortable once he found the
right position in it, and a single oil lamp rested, unlit, on a sturdy
nightstand that looked to be professionally-made. Most of the furniture in
their small farmhouse had been put together by his father, and while it
served its purpose, it was far from elegant.

On his last visit to Judge Mullen for the day, the Judge informed him
that his tasks were at an end and told him he did well, a warm
compliment that breathed life back into Monty's winded lungs. His
encounter with Rodney that morning had left his mind entirely; the day
had gone by so fast that he could hardly remember how long he had been
in town. Only the setting sun told him it had been almost twelve hours of
running around the village.

"I will need you to stay the night, Monty," the Judge said as he was
closing his office door and locking it behind him. "I will be in very early,
and we must start the day as soon as we can. Is that a problem?"

Monty shook his head. "I can do it, sir."

"Good, good. And I'd almost forgotten." Judge Mullen pulled something from his belt and handed it to Monty.

It was a small coin sack. Small, but heavy. Monty hefted it in his palm. "Are you paying me in advance, Judge Mullen?"

"No, you will be paid at the end of the week, the same as everyone else under the town's employ." Judge Mullen nodded to the money. "That is your food stipend. It should cover the winter as long as you are not foolish with it."

Judging by the weight of the coin, that was more than true. "Wow. Thank you, Judge. I didn't expect this."

Mullen smiled, meeting Monty's eyes. "I treat my people well, Monty. Especially when they perform. I expect the same out of you tomorrow." He began walking down the hall, and Monty moved with him. "Report to me before the sun rises, and we will be off to a good start."

The Judge left the Commons to go back to his house, leaving Monty the last person in the building. He went back to his new quarters, rolling the coin pouch in his fingers, enjoying the feeling of the gold. He had held this much money before—more, and recently, from their sales to the merchants—but never had it just belonged to him. It was a good feeling, but it was a better one to think about bringing this home and presenting it to his mother. Maybe he could even buy her one of those nice nightstands, so she wouldn't be getting splinters every time she set down a lamp. He resolved to buy just the food he needed and try to have as much coin left as possible by the time winter was over.

Monty tucked the coin into the nightstand's drawer, along with the key to his quarters, and climbed into the skinny bed. It was the first night he'd spent away from his farm in years, not since the one end-harvest, on the last day of selling, when it had snowed so much that they couldn't safely get the cart back to the farm. Their family, and the other farmers, flush with coin and the content of a season done, had booked up whatever was left of Irisa's inn, spending the evening there along with many of the same merchants they had been bargaining with all week.

He remembered it being fun, warm, and loud. He remembered his mother succumbing to his father's insistence that she join the other adults with the Cherrywood's ale cask, and how she was pink in the face before the fire died down. He remembered Terra not understanding what everyone was laughing about, and their father picking her up and telling her a joke that got her giggling along with everyone else.

He couldn't bring back their father, but he could help his family make new memories like that.

Right now, they were too few and far between.

15

The door to his quarters was thin, and he heard the larger door of the Commons knock shut when someone came in. He had slept on edge, nervous that he wouldn't wake up on time, but he was fairly sure it wasn't morning yet. Though without a window, it was hard to tell.

Monty rose from bed and gently pulled open his door, peering out into the hall. Quiet darkness greeted him; it was indeed too early for morning light. Was the Judge here even earlier than he had said he would be?

He shut his own door and changed out of the simple nightclothes he had brought with him, getting into a clean white shirt and lightly-wrinkled pants. No one seemed to mind if the courier wasn't the peak of professional. Aside from Rodney and Judge Mullen, most people he visited hardly seemed to notice him at all.

He left his quarters and locked the door, slipping the key into his pocket. The Commons were just as quiet now as they had been the evening previous, and he hadn't heard any footsteps after the front door had opened. If the Judge had gotten to his office, though, it was too far away from his quarters to hear the door. He could already be waiting.

The building was much chillier at night without the fires lit. Someone came in to do it after sunrise, which would be at least an hour from now. Monty rubbed at his arms, turning right once he reached the end of his hall, where the front doors opened up into the three branching directions.

When he reached the Judge's office at the end, he gave a few small knocks at the door and waited. It really was cold here without the fires blazing throughout the building. It hadn't been this cold last night.

There was no answer from the Judge. Monty went to knock again, and that was when he noticed that the Judge's lock was still turned. Unless

Mullen had come in, unlocked the door, went inside, then closed it and locked it again, it shouldn't be turned still. And why would he do that if he was expecting Monty?

"Maybe..." Monty half-turned, looking back towards the front doors, where he could see out clear into the dark village. "Maybe I didn't actually hear anything."

He had been anxious, sleeping thin. It wasn't crazy to think he might have heard a door open only because he was ready to hear such a thing.

Well, he didn't want to try to go back to sleep. Morning would come soon.

Take a look around. Maybe it was the firelighter, or some other official getting an early start. It would be good to start learning the habits of the office-holders here. There was definitely no one else in the Judge's wing, and he was certain no one had come walking down the wing where his quarters were.

"How certain are you?" Monty whispered. "You may have just imagined the sound of a door."

He really had to stop talking to himself. What if someone else was here, and they heard him? If he was going to spread a reputation for himself around Irisa, it wasn't going to be as some loon.

He turned right again at the end of the hall, to the third and final wing of the Commons. There were no fires lit here—

"—of course there aren't, there weren't any when you came down the hall ten seconds ago—"

—nor were there any open doors, self-indulgent humming, or shuffling of papers. Still, he strolled all the way down, reciting the names of the officials to himself as he passed each of their offices.

"Hanlon...Firn...Barley—no, Bartell...Decalt..."

The end of this hall opened into a larger common area housing the largest fireplace in the building, filled with last night's ashes. All the chairs were empty; all the curtains were drawn.

"All right. All right. I made it up," Monty chided himself, turning back around. His room was warmer than the rest of this place. If he couldn't sleep, then he would at least be able to heat up a little.

It was only when he got back to the front door that he realized it was open. Just a bit. The wooden frame, nestled snugly around the plate of glass, hung slightly ajar.

It hadn't been open when he had just come by. He was sure of it. Well, he was almost sure of it.

He pressed his hand against the door, pushing it shut. It clicked into place. The front door of the Commons was always unlocked, per the name. The offices were locked, not that anyone would come in to steal the inkwells. Irisa was safe.

Monty was suddenly very aware that standing here, where all three halls met, made him visible from every direction. He eased his way back to his hall, leaning on one shoulder against the wall. Surely Judge Mullen had closed the door last night. Monty had watched him do it.

"Hello?" Monty called. He checked the door again, and it was still closed. It hadn't come open on its own. And no one answered his call. Why would anyone come here and disappear inside before the sun even rose?

Thud. Thudthud.

Monty snapped upright, his ears perking painfully. He had definitely heard that; there was no mistaking it. It had come from the direction of the large common room.

Someone was here.

All right. All right. Easy. Could just be the firelighter.

But he would have seen someone head toward the common room, even in the dark. He hesitated only a moment longer before moving, feeling stiff as he forced his muscles into action. Whatever was going on, whoever it was, he wasn't going to go and hide in his quarters, and he wasn't about to let someone just come into the Commons and try to cram something into their pockets.

He'd deal with them. Unless is was Rodney Talhauer. In that case, he would have to run.

Monty didn't hear anything else as he approached the common room; as he got closer, the room slowly clarified in the minimal light. He didn't see anyone. But the common room was big, and it stretched wide enough to where someone could be hiding around the corner. If they wanted to.

Monty held his breath as he approached. The floor was silent as he stepped carefully into the common room; in fact, it had been silent all throughout the Commons, without a squeak or a groan. If someone had wanted to sneak around the place, they could have.

He let his breath out slowly when he confirmed that the room was empty. He wasn't exactly sure what he would have done if there had been someone here, but he didn't have to worry about that now. But what—

Something tugged at his hair, and Monty spun, lashing out his arm. It swung through the air, hitting nothing and throwing him off-balance. He stumbled to the right, pinpricks of pain flashing on his scalp as some of his hair was yanked free.

"What the—"

Fwapfwapfwap!

Monty brought his hand to his head, rubbing at the spot where the crow had snagged its claws. The bird, big and black and almost invisible in the dark, was now standing on the back of a chair.

Monty broke into laughter, leaning against the wall. He had pictured Rodney ready to close one hand around his throat. He had pictured a vagrant from the merchants' troupe slinking around town. He had pictured—and he hated to admit it—some monster, narrow enough to slip through a crack in the door, but strong enough to tear him in two.

"All that for a crow," he said, staring at the bird, which stared right back at him. "Let's get you out of here."

Monty went to a window on the far wall of the common room, pulling back the curtains and pushing it open. Chill night air eased in.

"Come on," Monty said, trying to draw the bird's attention to the window. When it just stayed put, he came around to its opposite side and advanced, shooing it forward. "Go! Go!"

The crow took off in a few mighty flaps, and saints be good, it flew towards and out the window, ruffling the curtains in its wake. Monty shut the window and drew the curtains behind it.

And someone called his name.

16

The voice filled Monty's veins with ice. He turned, forgetting to let go of the curtain he was holding. The rod pulled off the wall, clattering to the floor. He didn't hear it.

He was staring into the face of his father.

Montille was his height to the inch, with a short, unkempt beard and sparkling green eyes beneath dirty blond hair. He looked just as Monty remembered him, and why wouldn't he? It had only been a little over a year.

Because he's dead, that's why, because he is dead—

"Monty," Montille said again, and he was watching his dead father's lips move, he was hearing his dead father's voice in his ears, he was watching his dead father step toward him one slow shuffle at a time. He could see him just fine, like he was lit by daylight coming from somewhere else.

Monty's own voice died in his throat. Still clutching the curtain in one hand, he swallowed, finding something.

"Fa...dad?"

The word made Montille's face break into a smile. He had his arms out; big, strong arms from a lifetime of farming and carrying his kids above his head until they got too big for it. Terra never got too big.

"Come with me, Monty," his father said. "I want us all together again."

Monty dropped the curtain. "You—you're dead."

"Not dead," he answered. *Step.* "Just gone. Come on and be gone with me."

Step. Step.

"We'll go an' get your mother, and your sister..."

Step.

Monty screamed, a terror that sounded loud in his head but came out as only a gasping whisper of guttural air. He backed up one pace before bumping to the wall, and Montille kept coming.

"An' we'll go into the woods."

This is wrong, this is wrong, this is wrong this is wrong this is wrong

Monty grabbed the curtain rod from the floor, the curtain sliding off of it. It was brass, and heavy. It was real.

this is wrong this is wrong this

"Don't make me go back alone, Monty."

is wrong this is wrong this is not him

Monty swung the curtain rod at his father and connected solidly with the side of his head, a meaty hit that jarred the muscles in his arms. Montille fell to the side, hitting the floor like a pile of bricks.

"Oh saints, oh no, oh gods..." Monty was mumbling to himself without even realizing it, trying not to look at what he had just done, gripping the rod tight. It was bent, and bloody at the curve. "Oh lords of all what is going on..."

Montille sat up, and Monty did scream this time, a real scream that ripped up his throat and rang his skull in his head and shook the insides of his ears. His father's head was smashed in, blood pouring out of the hole where his left ear had been. His head was caved, half his teeth scattered across the floor. The skin of his face was hanging loose, ripped off in strips, showing shiny flesh underneath.

I didn't do that, how did I do that, what's happening—

That was when the smell hit Monty, a gagging, putrid cloud of wet death and rot that made him drop the curtain rod and cover his face with both hands, his eyes filling with water. He choked on it. He remembered the dead chickens, and spilling his guts into the tall grass.

"Monty..." Montille spoke, spoke as though his head weren't sunken like a rotten pumpkin, like his teeth weren't spread across the floor, like his lips hadn't peeled off to show his bleeding gums. "Don't be afraid, kiddo. I got a place for us."

He stood up, more of his flesh falling to the floor. It hit with wet slaps. "Nice an' big. We can stay there forever."

Monty forgot about the curtain rod and just ran. The smell of fresh death wrapped its arms around him and held him back, like he was fighting his way through the cloud. He closed his burning eyes and barreled forward, hitting one of the stuffed chairs and falling to his hands and knees, and then he crawled, eyeing the long hall through blurred vision.

"Don't touch me," Monty said, still crawling, only struggling to his feet once he reached the common room entrance and could pull himself up. "Don't touch me. Don't touch me!"

He didn't dare look back. What would happen if this thing got its hands on him? It wasn't his father. It was a monster wearing his skin, and that skin was falling off.

Up on his feet, he ran, thundering down the hall, knowing that no one would hear him because he was alone, all alone here with that thing. Every breath was fiery pain down his throat; the wretched smell wasn't getting any weaker. What if it was right behind him? What if—

He looked back as he crossed past the front doors, just in time to see his father close in. His breath locked up—Montille reached one hand out and grabbed his shoulder, lancing him with exquisite, searing pain as his fingers dug into the meat of his collar up to the knuckle, and he screamed—

It was gone.

Monty tumbled to the floor, clutching at his shoulder. He skittered backward and looked wildly down the hall. Nothing. No noise; no monster.

And no smell. That was what really convinced Monty that it was over.

He looked at his hand, expecting it to be covered in blood, not realizing that his shoulder didn't hurt anymore until he saw that it was clean. He felt for the wound and encountered unbroken, clammy skin.

"What...the blazing...fuck..." Monty squeezed at his shoulder again, expecting it to suddenly spout forth a bucket of blood. He leaned against the wall, catching his breath, which was jumping around inside his chest like it was sizzling on a hot pan. But his shoulder was fine. He was fine. He was alone.

He had to be sure.

Slowly, he stood, pressing his weight against the wall while he pushed up from the floor. Nothing to his left or right. He stepped to the divergent entrance, peering down the Judge's hallway. Nothing there either; no unnaturally-lit figure waiting for him at the end.

Have to check the common room. Have to.

With leaden feet, Monty walked down the long hall, where he'd fled in terror just moments ago. His steps were ungainly and heavy. He wasn't concerned about being quiet. If it was there, let it come, but don't let it hide away and wait to ambush him. Let this be done.

The common room was empty. Monty let his stale breath escape and wash into the room. It smelled clean; perfectly normal. In fact...

"That's...impossible."

The curtain rod was hung up on the window, the curtain drawn. Heart pounding, Monty approached it, looking down at the floor. This was where the father-creature had fallen, struck hard enough by the rod to start breaking into pieces.

The floor was clean. Spotless. No flesh; no blood; no tiny white specks of teeth and bone fragments.

Monty looked up to the curtain. The rod wasn't bent or broken. It was like it had never been taken down from the wall.

Fuzziness crept in on his vision and he felt like he might just float up to the ceiling. He fell backwards into one of the chairs, arms hanging loosely over the sides. Gradually, the blurriness in his vision faded, and he could breathe deeper.

Did it happen? Monty mouthed, trying to speak out loud but not summoning the breath. *Did any of this*

"Actually happen?" he said. *The monster? The* "Crow?"

He touched his head, but he couldn't tell if he'd really lost those few strands of hair to the crow's claws. It had all felt real. Smelled real. Just the memory of it made nausea churn in his stomach.

"Dreams can feel real," he spoke, his eyes drooping. "Dreams" *can feel too real. It's a dream. It was a dream. It still is* "a dream. You're asleep in your quarters. You fell asleep thinking" *about your dad and that night at the inn and* "then you dreamed about him."

I've never dreamed like this.

Fine, you're "sleepwalking." Like Terra. Like the other night, when he awoke facing the Dromm. But this was so much worse.

"It's not real," he told himself, and gathered up the assurance to rise from the chair. A nightmare was a nightmare, and if you could have them while sleeping, surely you could have them while sleep*walking*. He would go back to bed and try to sleep, just for a little, and shake this off.

The Commons were so dark and quiet. It would be good to see the sun.

17

Monty's sleep was bare, but it got him through the next hour or so. There were no more haunting visits or noises outside his room. The Commons was quiet, and he breathed easier, though quietly, in his bed.

When it was time to rise, he did so with gratitude.

Dressed and sitting on the bed, he rolled his room key around in his fingers and listened for the Judge's footsteps. He had no concerns about missing them in the night; if he wasn't a light sleeper at home, he certainly was here, and seeing the crack of dawn thousands of times had instilled his early-rising habit just fine.

At last, the sound of the front door and the quick, purposeful steps of the Judge brought the day to a start and the night to a close. Monty gave the Judge enough time to get to his office and settle in before heading over.

Judge Mullen's door was closed when he arrived, and he gave it three small knocks. The Judge was quick to answer.

"A pleasure to see you so punctual, Monty," Judge Mullen said. He always seemed energized in the morning, his eyes kind and aware. "How was your first night here in the Commons?"

Monty's throat tightened. He fought through it and answered, "It was great, Judge. The bed in the quarters is very comfortable."

"If only it were bigger." Mullen had a scroll in his hand, which he brought up to Monty. "This has to get to Bolton when he makes his delivery rounds. It must go to Ponsia today."

The capital city, and home of the king. Monty took the scroll, holding it as though it weighed more than the others before it. "I'll make sure of it."

"Very good. In the meantime..."

Mullen beckoned Monty into his office to pepper him with the morning's assignments, which were few in number but large in distance. Just like the day before, he'd be crossing town several times over before the sun was all the way in the sky.

"Make sure you get something to eat," Mullen told him as he walked Monty out of his office. "I cannot have you fainting in the middle of the street to get run over by a horsecart."

With that stipulation, Monty left the Commons with a light bag slung over his shoulder, full of scrolls. The inside was sewn full of leather straps to hold down messages and keep them separate, with an indent to slide the wax seal into and protect it.

He made his rounds as the sun crept upward, making sure to get the Judge's scroll to Bolton, the inter-town courier, as soon as he saw him. The silent, skinny man gave Monty a thin grunt from atop his horse before continuing on his own route.

It would be nice to do this on a horse, Monty thought, shrugging his bag up on his shoulder.

When he returned from a quick lunch at the small cafe near the Commons, his bag empty, Judge Mullen was waiting at his quarters. He had a thick book under one arm.

"Is there more, sir?" Monty asked, flipping open his bag as he approached.

"Yes, but there's a more pressing matter to attend to." Judge Mullen's face was tight; solemn. "Doctor Tobias has just left. It seems that Audrey Kettle has passed away."

The news froze Monty in place, one hand pinching the leather flap of his bag. "She's...she's dead?"

Judge Mullen nodded. "She has not been well."

"My mother said something about that." On the first day of merchant sales, his mother had tried to visit Audrey. That was only a week ago; it felt like years. "I just thought…"

"We all hoped she would improve as time went on and her mother's death was not so fresh," Judge Mullen said. "Alas…I have been called upon to read her rites."

"Oh." He hadn't considered that. The thought cast him back to his own father's death, and the Judge's attendance there, something that had entirely left his mind until now. He shook off the heavy image, saying, "Please let me take any messages I can before you leave, then."

"Actually, Monty, I would like you to join me at the reading." Judge Mullen shifted the heavy book, which Monty could now see was officially-bound, into two hands. "If that sits well with you. You are a representative of the town, now, and I know you were there when Dorella was found. I think it would be good for the Kettles."

"I…" Monty didn't think his presence had done much for Marie, let alone the rest of the family. But if the Judge was asking… "Of course, Judge, I can go with you."

Mullen nodded. "Drop your bag and lock up. This may take some time, and there are no terribly pressing deliveries that need be made in the immediate hours."

From the desk, the Judge pulled out a neatly-folded black square of fabric. The rites cape.

With his quarters locked, Monty fell into Judge Mullen's wake, breezing out of the Commons. He was always surprised at how quickly the short man walked. Their steps kicked up small clouds of dust as they made haste to the Kettles.

Audrey is dead. He couldn't believe it. There was no reason for Audrey to have perished. Though, he supposed, everyone took losing a parent in a different way. His own father was hard…but Ma Kettle had been around three times as long.

The Judge didn't speak on the walk, nor did he don his black cape. He must have been trying to keep the news in the family, though Monty

remembered hearing that he had worn the cape directly to the Kettles'
when he crossed town for Ma Kettle's rites. Why not now?

The door to the store was locked, and Judge Mullen rapped on the
door in three quick strikes. Henry Kettle answered.

The man looked like the grave. At a glance, one would assume he
hadn't slept for three days. His eyes were saddled with deep purple bags,
his hair unkempt and dirty. His arms hung at his sides like dead animals,
and when he blinked, it seemed the shiny lids of his eyes weighed on him
like stones. When Henry's glossy gaze drifted over him like an aimless
weathervane, Monty felt all his words dry up inside of him.

Judge Mullen had no such issue. "Henry, I am so very sorry."

Henry's normally talkative demeanor was dust; shattered. He said
nothing, but moved aside so that the Judge could walk in. Monty followed
on tender feet, uneasy. He'd never been inside of Kettle's when it was
closed. Seeing the store quiet and dark, when it was normally filled with
sun and boisterous voices, was a haunting thing. Like the shelves and
counters, too, knew that Audrey was dead.

Judge Mullen fastened his cape to his cowl once they were inside and
the door was shut behind them. He gave a nod to Henry, who responded
by turning to lead them up the stairs. His steps were heavy and awkward,
the thumps of his boots the only sound in the stale air.

They ascended the stairs and went through the Kettles' front door,
wide open. The house was quiet like midnight, and it stank like

dad

death.

Henry had not said a word since they'd come. His silence was broken
with a small, lifeless "This way."

Tacitly, Judge Mullen and Monty followed Henry through the house,
its surprisingly-confusing halls eventually leading back to a room with a
door only slightly ajar.

The Judge didn't need to ask if Audrey was in here. Monty could smell
it. He regretted his lunch.

I will not vomit here, I will not vomit in their house, I will not...

His gorge was ever-present, a new part of him amid the stench, but he held it at bay. He was here for a reason, and he mustn't forget that, and in the company of the Judge. Perform well, even if the performance is simply silence and holding back your bile.

Judge Mullen did not hesitate to move past Henry; the short official did not seem perturbed by the smell. Monty hoped he looked half as composed, yet he doubted that Henry would notice anyway. The man's eyes were empty and faraway.

"With me, Monty," Mullen said, his tone hushed but firm as he pushed open the door and stepped into the room.

Henry didn't follow.

Monty braced himself against the burning, rotting smell while he walked inside. If he breathed through his mouth, it was better, but then he imagined it going down into his stomach and nesting there, filling him with the rot from the inside. Lungs or stomach? Which was better?

It was dark. There was a window, but it was shut and curtained. Monty resisted the urge to dart over to it and let the sun in. He approached the bed alongside Judge Mullen, who had the Rites book in the crook of his elbow, resting against his side.

The corpse of Audrey Kettle waited for them.

18

O nce his eyes adjusted, Monty could see the form of Audrey
Kettle lying in the bed. Only her head was visible, the rest
underneath three or four thick, heavy blankets. Had she been freezing,
begging her husband for more and more blankets, until she finally expired
in the night?

The vision of that suffering spiked Monty's mind so sharply that it
made his eyes water and his heart wrench. This smell of death; this
wrecked widower outside the door; this quiet house, with the children all
shut up in their own rooms; this was a home. A home with first a dead
grandmother, and now a dead mother, a corpse that was still here, like it
wasn't ready to give up its time in its house.

Audrey. Audrey's house.

The Kettle mother's head was shrunken. It was so odd, so dissimilar to
her, that Monty at first wasn't sure what he was looking at. He thought that
it was another balled-up, dirty shawl at the head of the bed. But the
blanket of hair around her skull made it clear that this was Audrey; her
long, brown locks had fallen from her scalp like a scythe had been taken
to her, leaving her bare.

She looked like a skull that had been set in the sun for months and
months.

Her skin was dark and stretched, almost like leather, yet it gave the
sense that it would crumble with the faintest touch. The rest of her body
was completely hidden beneath her excess of blankets. Monty had no
desire to see any more.

"Judge...she's..." Monty had to say something. "I've never seen..."

Mullen nodded. He spoke quietly, keeping his voice to himself and Monty. "It is a shame. It appears she suffered a great deal."

Monty tried not to imagine it.

"I sent for the priest earlier," Judge Mullen continued. "He should be here shortly. Once he has rested and sent her, I will perform the rites."

A priest, right. The ritual of death had escaped Monty's mind, cast away ever since going through it for his father.

Had a priest ever seen anything like this before? Marie had implied that Ma Kettle was skin and bones on her last day. Did this same thing happen to her?

Why did you bring me here, Judge?

The question clawed at his lips, but he didn't put it forth. It wasn't as though he could leave. He would be seeing this through until the Judge was finished. No matter how long it—

Audrey moved.

Monty's jaw slid open as he watched her small head turn ever so slightly, the loose hair rustling as it did. The blankets moved; barely, but they did, as her body shifted beneath them.

He looked to Judge Mullen, who registered this impassively, though his eyes were wide. He turned to Monty, moving his head only slightly.

"Close the door." The words came out fast and firm, a strict order. "Henry should not see this."

Monty tried to move and felt frozen. His eyes drifted back to Audrey, turning her head toward them. Her eyes shifted beneath black lids.

"Go!"

The harsh whisper snapped Monty out, and he managed to shuffle his feet to the side and shut the door. No one outside tried to open it again. It was just them...and her.

Audrey breathed—she must have been breathing the entire time, but it was so small and insignificant that they hadn't noticed. It had gone unnoticed by her family, as well, and who could blame them? Who would lift up those shrouds and press their ears against what remained of the woman's chest? Who could lower themselves within an inch of that tortured skull and search for life? Not even the woman's husband.

Audrey was beyond hope and beyond approach, and yet here she was, lying alive in this bed in the back of her house.

She must be in terrible pain, Monty thought. *Her skin...her bones...everything is all...*

Judge Mullen grabbed Monty by the shoulder and gave him a single, strong shake, and he realized that he had been on the verge of passing out on the bedroom floor.

"Stay with me," Mullen said, his strong fingers pressing divots into Monty's flesh. "She is...she cannot last for long." He paused. "Not like this. Whatever is keeping her here...it will pass."

Monty's vision steadied. Even in the dark, he could see that Audrey was looking at him. Right at him.

But no—her eyes were...

Gone?

Lidded. The skin there was taut, like it had been sewn shut. Eyes or no, the sight made shivers crawl up and down his back like squirming bugs. He fought off the urge to shake, with the Judge's hand still holding his shoulder.

"I'm okay," he breathed, and the hard fingers eased. "You...she's close." He chewed on his lips. "To dying."

The Judge nodded, a gesture which Monty barely caught in the darkness. All the light was coming from the crack under the door and a tiny gap in the curtains.

The blanket shifted. An arm slipped out from underneath, falling off the edge of the bed and hanging there. It was narrow and black, like a burned stick. The hand was clenched in a tiny, shrunken fist. As it hung there, it slowly uncurled, the fingers so thin that Monty half-expected them to break off and fall to the floor.

Then there was silence. Even their own breathing was hushed. The room was heavy and the air was thick. Monty was almost used to the smell, but he could still feel it pressing in around him.

Judge Mullen broke the silence.

"It's over. Open the door, Monty," he said, his fingers running across the edges of his book. "I believe I just heard the priest arrive."

Monty emerged from the back room like he was breaking free of a tomb, leaving and finding Henry and the priest at the front door. The latter moved past him, Henry in his wake, and Monty followed.

He stood quietly by while Priest Erick performed his duties and Judge Mullen finished with the rites. Henry was the only one who was in attendance. The children were nowhere to be seen, even on their walk out of the house.

Halfway through Mullen's speech, Monty thought he saw Audrey move again. A subtle shift, barely rustling the blankets. He stared, expecting more, fearing that she would breathe again, that she wasn't gone, that she was still suffering.

But she remained still till it was over, and hadn't moved again by the time they'd left.

It felt strange to see sunshine once they were outside. Monty blinked in it, looking down toward the ground.

"That poor family," Judge Mullen said. "It is very..."

Monty could hardly hear him. Some faraway part of him knew that he should be listening to the Judge, but that part was buried beneath images of horror and death. Audrey's emaciated form would fade away only to be replaced by his father's crushed head, dripping blood and grinning its inviting grin.

He breathed, tasting dust on his tongue. His feet carried him along with the Judge, back toward the Commons.

"...Tobias, well, he may be a fearmonger..."

His shoulders slumped; it occurred to him that he felt nothing good had happened in quite some time. He and Terra had those sleepwalking episodes...Ma Kettle's death, and then Audrey's...the chickens, too, though that hardly compared...

But this job was a good thing. Their harvest, that had been good, and the sale had been quick and bountiful.

"...once this is behind us..."

Bad things come in threes. An old saying, and one he'd heard from his father, and his mother, and Ma Kettle herself; others too numerous to draw forth. The chickens, Ma Kettle, and Audrey. Three untimely deaths, unexplained, but in the past.

The thought was a little childish, but it made him feel better. Enough to look up and let the sun hit his face without feeling like he should be back in that room, waiting for Audrey to move again.

Judge Mullen stopped them down the road from the Commons. "The Kettles won't be ready to send Audrey tonight, regardless of what doctor Tobias thinks should be done. I told them that the sending can wait till tomorrow evening. The priests will handle Audrey's remains until then."

Monty nodded. *Stop thinking. You have to listen.*

"There will be more work today, but I want to you to hurry it along." Judge Mullen glanced toward the north. "It would be good for you to inform Delila...your family about Audrey's passing. Let them know the sending will be tomorrow evening. With the harvest over, you all should be able to attend."

"We'll be there," Monty affirmed.

The Judge gave him a nod, and the pair of them went into the Commons to catch the time that had been lost.

There was still light in the sky by the time Monty left Irisa and headed home. The key to his quarters in his pocket, he was amazed at how long it felt since he had taken the northern path back to the farm. It had only been one night.

But a lot had happened in that time.

He barely beat the sunlight home, and he smiled as he saw the familiar curves of the land roll up to him, their house sitting comfortably in the grass with a narrow stream of smoke coming through their chimney. Mother had the cookfire on. His stomach rumbled.

It was nice to be away from home, but it was better to be back.

19

Monty didn't know what to expect from his mother, but the hug she encased him in hadn't been on the top of his list.

"You really had to stay away your first day on the job?" she said into his ear, holding him with a strength that reminded him of his father.

"The Judge...needed me," he said, after catching his breath. "There was a lot to do."

"Hmm." Delila released him, pulling back just a bit so that she could look into his eyes. "Well, I expect you to tell me everything, then. I want to know what he has you doing all day and all night." She turned back to the cookfire so their dinner wouldn't burn. "Go on, sit down and fill me in."

Monty was actually excited to tell his mother about the courier job, rather than irritated to give her a report. He drew a cup of water from the bucket on the counter and drank some down before sitting.

He started by telling his mother about his quarters, and how they were small but the bed was soft. He then told her what exactly was expected of him as the recruit courier; the beck and call of the officials, his messenger bag—which he regretted not bringing home—and getting to talk to various town officials, however briefly.

"Rodney Talhauer is kind of, um," Monty said, "gruff, I guess." Apparently his son was the courier before me, and he doesn't seem all that happy that I have his son's job."

"Rodney." His mother shook her head. "He's a good man, but he's got a bit of a temper. Especially when it comes to Judge Mullen." She smiled. "He and your father always got along well."

Monty didn't know that. Thinking about it now, he never knew much about his father's friends from town, or what those relationships were like. It had never occurred to him to wonder.

"Selman—Mr. Selman, from the Buyers' Committee—he's nice, though. I went to his office three times and ran into him a couple times outside of that, and he always asked how I was doing. But I didn't have any time to talk."

Delila was serving their food by about the time Monty was reaching the end of his day, today, and Terra came in through the front door around the same time.

"Monty!" she exclaimed upon seeing him sitting at the table. "Where'd you go?"

"I was working," he said, a smile coming across his face at her excitement. "Didn't mom tell you?"

"I'm sure I did," Delila said, sitting down at the table once the food was laid out, hot and steaming, slices of fresh beef and sweetened carrots that were purchased in town.

"I don't remember," Terra said, hopping up into a chair. "I was playing with Jeremy and Kensey. It's more fun when the corn's all grown."

"It'll be back soon," Delila assured her. "Then all you kids can get lost in it, like usual."

All you kids. Somehow, the scene at the Kettle house had been completely driven from his mind, but it came back over him like a stinking tide at the thought of the Kettle children driven into the furthest corners of their home by the specter of their mother.

He paused, his fork halfway to his mouth.

"Something wrong with the food?" his mother asked, raising an eyebrow.

"Huh...? No...no." Monty ate his bite, taking time to chew so that he could think of a response. He didn't want to bring up Audrey during dinner, and not in front of Terra, who was happily chewing a carrot. He swallowed and said, "I was just thinking that I should have brought my messenger bag home, but it's fine if it's locked in my quarters there."

"I'm sure." Delila's eyes drifted to her daughter as she ate her dinner with sloppy eagerness. "Don't make too much a mess, Terra. Or you'll be cleaning it up."

Once dinner was over and Delila had handed Terra a clean cloth to wipe the table with, Monty brought up the subject of Audrey.

"Can we go outside while she wipes up, mom?" he asked. "There's something I gotta tell you about. In private."

"Aw, you gotta help me," Terra insisted. The cloth, still clean, was balled up in her hands.

Delila said, "You can certainly manage, Terra. When I'm back, I want that table clean enough to eat off of. All right?"

"Fine," Terra said, shaking out the rag.

Monty stepped outside, Delila following after him. They walked away from the house for a few paces until Monty was sure Terra wouldn't hear.

"So..." Monty wasn't sure how to say it, even though he'd done the same thing only days before. It might not be something that someone ever got used to. "Today, the Judge and I went to the Kettles'. Audrey, you know, she wasn't, um...doing too good."

"Monty..."

"She died, mom." Monty just forced the words out, before the images could overtake him again. "I was there, with Judge Mullen, and with—with Priest Erick. For the resting and the rites."

"Oh, no..." Delila was hushed, looking downward for a moment before wrapping Monty up in another hug. "This is terrible. The poor Kettles..."

This time when she released Monty, her look was harsher. Her hands found her hips. "You were at the rites? Why in heaven's name would Judge Mullen bring you along to a rites reading?"

"It wasn't so bad," Monty said, which was a lie big enough to be almost completely untrue. He supposed it would have been worse if he had vomited, or passed out on the floor. "The Judge said the family would appreciate me there."

"Like they appreciated you at the sending," Delila fumed. "That is absolutely ridiculous, bringing you to something like that. That is *not* part of your responsibility."

Monty had been about to tell her what had happened, that Audrey had been still alive, but now he held it back. "It was for the family, mom. For the Kettles."

"Did you talk to them? Henry? The children?"

She was always able to get right to the heart of the matter. Monty flushed, trying to think of the right words. "It wasn't...it wasn't a good time for talking. They just needed...support."

"I am going to tell Mullen that if he—"

"Mom!" Monty held up his hands. "Please, please don't. Don't *yell* at Judge Mullen. Please. For me? It would ruin everything."

Delila relaxed a little bit. "Well, you're right about that. Mullen doesn't take too kindly to being questioned." Her hands came up from her hips, now crossing in front of her chest. "I know this is important to you, Monty. I just don't want you getting in over your head, or getting hurt."

"I won't," Monty said, regretting telling her about Rodney Talhauer, though she didn't seem worried about that. "It's just delivering messages and being by the Judge's side as he asks. Nothing dangerous."

Judge Mullen's comment about the bloody dagger floated to the front of his mind. He quickly knocked it away.

"There's dangerous," Delila said, "and there's reckless, and uncaring. You're going to have nightmares."

"I'm not some little kid," Monty huffed, and then of course that made him think of the vision of his father, and he wondered what might be going on in his head, after all. "Can't you trust me?"

"I trust you," she said. "I don't trust the Judge."

He knew better than to argue with his mother about that, no matter how different his opinion of the Judge was. Maybe later, in his career as a town official, she would understand.

"I'll be careful," he stated as a form of compromise.

"I hope so." Delila let out a little sigh, still meeting Monty's eyes. "I know you're not a kid anymore, Monty. That's clearer every day. But you're still my son, and I am always going to protect you." A little smile eased onto her face. "Whether you like it or not."

She went up to her son and patted his shoulder before he could respond. "Do you know when the sending will be?"

"Tomorrow evening," Monty said. "We can all go?"

"We will," Delila said. "I regret not being able to attend Ma Kettle's. I will make sure we're there for the rest of the family."

"Okay." Monty took in a breath. It appeared the hard part of this conversation was over. "I'll be reporting back to the Judge in the morning, but with the sending, there won't be many evening messages to deliver. I'll be able to meet you and Terra there."

"That's fine. Let's go back inside, now. It's chilly."

The next morning, Monty beat the sun to Irisa and reported to the Judge right on time, prompting a smile from the man as he opened the door to his office.

"Your punctuality is appreciated, Monty," Judge Mullen said, handing him no fewer than five scrolls to sort in his messenger bag. "You are doing much better than our previous courier, already."

"Thank you, sir," Monty responded, the compliment slightly soured in memory of Rodney Talhauer's visage. He wondered, briefly, just how poor a job the man's son had done, and what it would take to be released from the position even though your father was a town official.

"Get on with it, now," Judge Mullen said, starting to close his door as he spoke. "With the sending tonight, we both have a lot to take care of before we must depart."

Click. The door shut, and Monty stared at the blurry outline of his reflection in the glossy wood.

The Judge wasn't wrong. Five messages to start the day was heavy, and Monty knew there'd probably be twice as many once he returned. It would be busy, and he would have to be fast.

The town pulsed in slow contrast to Monty's pace through the streets. He noticed it as he moved through Irisa, saying hello to the more gregarious early risers, and watching the more tacit, sleepy folk open their shutters or pull in their wash. There was a pallor here. A sadness. Over the tops of all the other homes and buildings, the Kettle's two-story loomed.

So the word had spread. As it needed to, with the sending this evening. The turnout for Ma Kettle had been large, and Monty imagined the same would hold true for Audrey. But while people were somewhat prepared for Dorella's passing, Audrey's seemed to have left many villagers numb.

People were muted and prickled by fear. In his goings, Monty heard plenty of conversations; talk of Audrey's death and what caused it. Speculation that the rest of the Kettles might be falling off, one by one.

"Whatcha think, boy?" a stable worker asked him of the last. The stocky man was chatting with two other workers on an east-side estate, leaning against a dirty shovel planted in the ground. "You seen any of it? Are we all dead men?"

The workers laughed, and Monty joined in with a little chuckle of his own, though it lacked any mirth. The memory of Audrey rustling under the covers pulled any humor from the situation. The workers' own laughter seemed a little strained, though, and they waited on Monty for an answer.

"I didn't see much," Monty said, unsure if word of his presence at the rites was common knowledge. "The rest of the family seems fine. It's just the grief."

"Aye." The stable worker pulled the shovel from the ground. "Wish I had time to grieve."

Monty moved on until his bag was almost empty. He stopped for something quick to eat, a hot bun with gravy from the west corner baker, Bradley. Monty had known him for a while, and now he was seeing him more; perhaps that was why Bradley, too, brought up Audrey's death.

"Can't believe it," he said to Monty. "First the grandma, Ma Kettle herself, and now the daughter? Ya know..." Bradley lowered his voice down from his standard shout to simply indoor-speaking volume. "I think that Henry might've had something to do with it. Been talking to Joelle, she thought up the idea."

Monty managed to swallow his mouthful of hot food without choking. He didn't want to talk about this, much less engage in rumors so ridiculous. Joelle was the baker's assistant, fourteen years old, and all Monty knew about her was that she liked to whisper in anyone's ear about anything.

"That's ridiculous," he said, sounding just like his mother and not realizing it. "You can't really believe that."

Bradley just shrugged, not at all deterred by Monty's dismissal. "Marries into the Kettle family, then takes out the heirs? That happens all the time, don't it?"

"In stories, and the heirs are usually children, not the other way around." Monty was quick to finish the last of his food and heft his bag over his shoulder again. "They got sick. That's all."

"Maybe sick. Maybe...*poisoned.*"

"I have to go, Bradley," Monty said.

He left, suddenly angry. He'd known the Kettles his whole life, and he'd been around two of their deaths, now. To hear Bradley talk that way, and knowing that both he and Joelle were probably saying the same thing to everyone who came to buy their bread...

He clenched his fist. The Kettles didn't deserve that. They'd been through enough as it was.

Next time I hear someone say something like that, I'm putting a stop to it, Monty promised himself, letting his fingers relax before he reached into his bag for the final scroll. He had saved it for last because it was the delivery closest to the Commons, a trick he had picked up after the first day walking back across town with an empty bag.

When it was done, he went and got some more.

20

The work took him till just before twilight, where Judge Mullen walked them both out of the Commons toward the sending grounds. The evening was chill, the diffused light of the setting sun clinging to the streets along with the shoes and boots of most of the village. Despite the crowd, the air was silent save for the scuffling of feet and an errant cough or child's unintelligible voice lost among the legs. Judge Mullen steered the pair of them away from the crowd.

Monty looked back over the swell of people walking north out of Irisa. "This might be everyone in the entire village," he said, unaware he was saying it loud enough for the Judge to hear.

"It might well be," Mullen said, not bothering to follow Monty's gaze. "The rumor mill has begun to grind, Monty. I am sure you witnessed it while you were out and about today."

"Rumors? I guess."

"Mm." Judge Mullen had a book under his arm, as he always did when attending anything as a representative of the village. "Rumors and hearsay. Speculation. The dirty things that weave their way in and around a town and its people. Impossible to scrub out. They always linger, no matter how much effort you give."

Monty looked at the Judge to find Mullen's eyes forward, locked and impassioned.

"Rumors unsettle the populace, Monty. You'll find that. The more time you spend above them, the easier it is to see the things that wind through their minds and mouths like poisonous snakes."

"I...see."

"You don't." Mullen looked to him, and his eyes seemed to glow in the faint light. "You don't yet. Perhaps you never will, and you might count yourself lucky. Finding things out of your control...it is irritating."

Monty remained silent.

"I have been hearing rumors all through the day. It does not matter if people are trying to keep them secret from me." They stepped from the packed dirt of the village proper onto grass, moving into the field. "They say that the Kettles are diseased. That their sickness will spread through the town and kill each and every one of us. You have heard that rumor today, I'm sure."

"I guess I have, sir," Monty said, wondering where in the crowd those stable workers were.

"People want a look at the body," Judge Mullen said, resuming his speech the moment Monty's lips were closed. "Sickening, it truly is. They want to see what's happened, see if it's something they know. This crowd here, it's even more than what Dorella had. You think all these people knew Audrey well?"

"I—"

"Vultures at best, that's what we're witness to." Judge Mullen was looking away and forward, unblinking. He clenched his book with short, strong fingers. "That damned Tobias, he went and opened his mouth, I know it. After I told him..."

"Did the doctor say something about Audrey?" Monty asked.

Judge Mullen dismissed his inquiry with a wave of his free hand, sweeping the voluminous sleeve of his black robe. "I forbade him to see the body after what he spilled in my ears about Ma Kettle."

Mullen sighed, and then blinked once; twice; three times, rapidly. He gave a little shake of his head, and when he spoke again, his voice was calmer. Measured.

"Monty," he said, and now he did look at him. "I need your help to quell these rumors as best we can. For the people. I am certain that this is not a worry for the village, and everyone must understand that. The last thing we want is unrest and discontent. People often fall ill in winter, and if on every corner there is someone whispering about some kind of nonsense plague, the town will be in chaos."

He understood what the Judge was saying, and he imagined that rumors about murder and poisonings wouldn't be any better. "I can help," he told Mullen. "Anything I hear about that, I'll put a stop to it."

"I appreciate your vigor," Judge Mullen said, "but you are only one man, and the best thing is to spread the word by scroll. These next few days will be hectic. I will be writing many messages for you to carry."

They were at the site now. The pyre was in place, set up earlier in the day. Audrey's body rested atop it, hidden in a simple casket reminiscent of her mother's. The neatly-stacked pile of wood and branches was braced by a priest and three laborers whom Monty didn't recognize.

"I'll need you overnight the next three days, I surmise," Mullen said. "Starting tonight. Can you do that?"

His mother wouldn't be happy about it, but it had to be done. "I'll be there."

"Good, good," he said. "Go and find your family. I must begin the preparations."

Mullen broke off from their gait and to the pyre, approaching the priest and saying something Monty couldn't hear.

Moving past the pyre and continuing north, Monty set his sights on the dark horizon toward home, where his mother and sister would come from. He could have waited back at the gathering for them to arrive, but something made him restless. He couldn't quite put his finger on it, but wanted to move.

In the gloom, he couldn't make out his family until they were a hundred feet from him. Seeing his mother guide Terra along by the hand helped to dispel the unease that was clinging to him, and he hurried up to them with a suppressed smile. It was a solemn occasion, after all.

"Hi, Monty," Terra said, breaking free of Delila's hand to run up to him.

"Hi, Terra," he responded in kind. He glanced up to his mother.

"She knows about Audrey," she said to him, reading his mind.

Terra nodded. "It's sad."

"It is," Monty agreed.

"But everyone's here to see her to the beyond," Delila said, holding out her hand again once Terra looked back.

"I won't get lost," Terra said, putting her hands into the small pockets of her pants.

Delila didn't argue the claim, but gave Monty a look that read clearly as 'keep an eye on her.' The three of them began walking to the pyre, where the two torches that straddled the gathering blazed into existence.

Monty decided to get it over with. "Judge Mullen needs me overnight the next few days."

Delila flinched, but she kept walking. Monty heard her exhale through her nose, a huff of hers that he always referred to as 'dragon's breath,' because it generally preceded a roar.

But she didn't yell or raise her voice. She slowed her pace just a little and said, "Is that really necessary?"

"There's a lot going on," Monty said. "He said he's going to have a lot of work. He's counting on me."

Delila looked back to Monty, then toward the crowd and the Judge. Her posture slumped, ever so slightly. "I won't argue with you, Monty. But if I need to, I will make sure the Judge understands that it cannot be this way during the season."

"I'll take care of that," Monty said quickly. "And if you need me for anything, you can send for me."

She didn't respond, and Monty accepted it. If she wanted to be mad, let her be mad.

As they neared the site, the Judge's voice carried back to them, growing clearer with each step forward as he addressed the gathering.

Delila broke her silence. "We're going to be close to the sending. We owe Audrey that, at least, after not being able to be there for her when Ma Kettle was sent."

Given the haunted visage Audrey had adorned that night, Monty thought it might have been best for neither Terra nor his mother to have seen her that way. But if she *had* been there to comfort her, would things have turned out differently? Would she have been stronger, able to fend off whatever combination of sickness and grief had sucked the life out of her body?

If so, maybe Henry Kettle needed that now. Or the children.

"We can be close," Monty said, and it wasn't long before they were near the crowd. It was easy to come to rest close to the sending site; as they approached from the north, they simply settled at the front of the swell. Monty noticed that Terra hadn't taken his mother's hand again, but she was just a bare inch or two from her legs.

"...is a sacred rite bestowed to all..."

Judge Mullen's voice cast out over the crowd, repeating words they'd heard far too recently. Henry Kettle stood on small platform by the pyre, where he'd been at Ma Kettle's sending, but with no wife before him now. Just him and their five children. The family shared the same haunted look their mother had worn, and Monty's heart wrenched with pity. There had to be something that could be done for this family.

"...sent by her husband, Henry. He will start the flame that will carry her beyond..."

This was the part where Henry was to take the torch. As it was handed first to Judge Mullen, Monty felt a small hand slip into his. Terra. He looked down to her, but she wasn't looking at him. Her eyes were straight ahead. A little river of warmth, of brotherly love, wound through him as he held her cold fingers.

Judge Mullen held the torch out to Henry, saying something else that drifted past Monty's ears. He watched Henry, close enough to see the emptiness in his features, just the same as yesterday when he'd been in their house.

Henry lifted his arm for the torch—Mullen pushed it into his hand—and he dropped it on the stage. The crowd flinched as a whole, Monty included. It wasn't dropped near enough to light the pyre; it simply rested on the platform, burning.

Henry stared down at it like he was trying to read words in the fire. He made no motion to pick it up.

Judge Mullen swiftly pulled the torch from the short wooden platform before it could catch light.

Monty turned to his mother only to see her gone; she was walking up to the stage, not to Judge Mullen, but to Henry. She went up to the much taller man and rested a hand on his shoulder, saying something too quiet to be heard by anyone but the two of them and perhaps the more attentive of the Kettle children. Henry's head swung to look at her in awkward, broad motion, and Delila's eyes were sympathetic when they met his. The Kettle father nodded, and Delila turned to the Judge, holding out her hand.

"If I may, Judge," Delila said.

Judge Mullen nodded. He handed the torch to her and stepped back off the stage, the Kettle family following shortly after.

Once they were all clear, Delila set the torch down at the foot of Audrey's pyre. She moved back gracefully as the kindling caught, crackling and popping, before the fire swept upward, engulfing the pile and Audrey's casket and billowing out a cloud of heat to the villagers.

The black air above the flames swirled in invisible torment.

Delila raised her arm, shielding herself from the brightness of the blaze and the swelling heat. She stepped backwards, faltering. Monty moved forward, stepping quickly to catch her, but she regained her balance and made it safely off of the platform. Terra's hand was still enclosed in his own.

Their mother rejoined them at the crest of the gathering, and the town of Irisa watched Audrey Kettle burn.

<u>21</u>

The day after the burning was the first time Monty felt afraid of Judge Mullen.

Once the sending was over, he and his family had parted ways; Delila and Terra headed home, and Monty went back to Irisa with the rest of the villagers to spend the night in his quarters. His mother had wished him well, but she had seemed distracted and far away. He knew she'd need some time to feel all right about the courier job, and two days wasn't enough, especially with him being gone this much.

He had slept through the night without incident; no ghosts or visions.

The next day had started off well, with Monty grabbing his usual morning quarry from Judge Mullen and greeting the sun as it swept over Irisa. The town was lethargic. People were sleepy, and everyone seemed drained after the sending. Even the sunlight was weak through the clouds.

Henry Kettle's stony silence—during and after the sending, while his children wept—settled like a weight on the villagers, and no one was in the mood for talking.

As a result, Monty's deliveries went quicker than usual, though they left him with a somber reminder of the past evening's events. The pallor of Audrey's passing was uniform among the people of Irisa, save for the Judge.

Mullen was not morose today. The man was furious.

He had seemed fine in the morning when Monty was filling his bag with scrolls, but when it came time to replenish his load, what answered the door was an entirely different man.

Monty knocked on the Judge's office door, his first round of deliveries done. He was sure the Judge would be pleased with how the morning had gone.

The door ripped away from his knuckles shortly after his last knock. It was such a sudden and violent motion that Monty fell back a half-step. The Judge stood in the opening. His face was not the visage of kindness and patience it normally was; veins throbbed underneath the sweep of his gray hair. The color in his face was harsh and loud, enough that Monty thought he would feel the heat from it, were he a few inches closer.

"What in the blazes took you so long?" Judge Mullen snarled.

Monty's jaw dropped, and he struggled to find a response. He held his bag with one hand, raising it slightly, as though it would answer the Judge's question.

"I told you today would be busy." Mullen tore the bag from his hand, catching his shirt with one of the clasps and popping loose three threads. "Fucking non-stop, did I not say that? Did I not?"

He hadn't, but Monty dared not to share that with him. His cheeks flushed, burning. He found his jaw again, and with it, some semblance of response: "I know it—"

"You're here for one reason, and that's to make my life easier. Look at me, Monty. Do I look like a man whose life is easy?"

Another impossible question that sewed his lips shut. What had happened between this morning and now?

Rather than wait for a response, the Judge yanked open the flap of his bag and stretched it open, thrusting the empty insides at Monty's face.

"You see this, courier? Do you know how many scrolls this bag can hold?"

Wise to the fact that an answer was not what the Judge was looking for, Monty let the Judge continue.

"Seventeen," Mullen said, snapping the bag back down to his chest. "Seventeen slots to keep them nice and orderly. Yet you left this morning with only nine. You left before I could give you the rest of your work, and now an entire half-day has been wasted!"

The accusation was so unexpected that Monty couldn't restrain his surprise. "Judge, I took everything you gave me—"

"And then you ran right off. Unconscionable." Mullen was reaching into his robes now, pulling out scroll after scroll and sliding them into the inner straps of the messenger bag. "I won't have you pulling a mockery of your duties again, is that clear?"

Monty bit back a retort, feeling the heat in his face. He knew he hadn't messed up, that he'd taken the full morning's load and gotten it done quick. He'd made mistakes before—late delivery, wrong house, wrong recipient—and Mullen had never resembled anything close to what was burning before Monty right now. Monty knew he'd taken his armload of scrolls and then Mullen had shut the door, just this morning.

But losing this job was small stakes compared to being an enemy of the Judge's, and what that would mean to his family. So he let it go.

"I understand, Judge," he said.

"Good." Mullen shoved the bag at him, filled with scrolls. "Get back to work."

Slam.

Monty stared at the door, holding his bag in one hand. It was a side of the Judge he'd never seen, and it made him wonder what the man was capable of. He thought again of the Judge's comment about the bloody dagger. He thought about what it would be like to have Judge Mullen rallied against you in his rage, vindictive and powerful. Why Rodney Talhauer, thrice the man's size and bespoken of his ire toward the Judge, didn't move against him.

Maybe, Monty thought, *this man is more than what he likes to show to everyone else.*

The next two days in town proceeded as normal. Judge Mullen had eschewed his frothing anger by the time Monty saw him again that first night, but Mullen did not acknowledge their previous meeting, nor did he apologize for it. Monty thought he might have detected a hint of aloof disdain in the man's dark eyes, but chalked that up to being paranoid. Mullen had lost his temper and taken it out on Monty, and it was over.

But he wouldn't forget the way the Judge had looked then. How he called him 'courier,' and seemed to not care who he was; only that Monty had wronged him. Just because that part of Judge Mullen wasn't bubbling to the surface right now...that didn't mean it was gone. It only meant that it was waiting.

Had his mother seen it before? Was that why she had such distrust of the man? For the first time since accepting the job, Monty was prodded by doubt about his future. Did he truly want to align himself with the Judge?

And did he have a choice now, not knowing what might befall him or his family if he were to decide to part ways?

The answer wasn't written, but he felt it, heavy as stone. He had no choice. And to that end, he found himself relieved when locking his quarters that third evening and heading home, missing the faces of his mother and sister.

<u>22</u>

"Why didn't you send for me?"

Monty knelt beside his mother, who didn't have the strength to get out of her bed.

"Don't be silly," she said. Her words were strong as ever, but her voice sounded weak. "It's just the winter illness. I was bound to catch something among all those people at the sending. We're just lucky...we're not all sick."

Sick. Monty had heard enough of that word lately. Far too much.

"Stop your worrying," Delila said, brushing a hand across his shoulder. There was a fine sheen of sweat on her forehead, plastering a few strands of black hair to her skin. "I can see it all over your face, Monty. Just let me rest. It will get worse before it gets better. I'll be up and about in a...a couple of days."

"You need some water," Monty said.

"Yes...I could use some."

"I'll be right back." Monty stood, his mind clouded as he left the house. Terra was rummaging through the pantry, collecting root vegetables for dinner per their mother's instructions. She wasn't worried. His mother wasn't worried. Why should he be worried?

Because I was there. I saw Audrey.

But he didn't know anything. He was no doctor. Whatever disease had killed the two Kettles had no reason to spread all the way out to their farm from Irisa. He'd heard not a peep of more illness or sudden, unexplained deaths within town over the last three days, and he'd been all over, talking to everyone. Winter sickness, sure; plenty of townspeople were bedridden with that, and nothing more.

That made him feel better, and he rested his palms on the well stones, closing his eyes. Everyone in town felt a little more relieved, it seemed. With days passing since Audrey's death, the fear that the strange sickness would spread through Irisa had dissipated.

Monty let out his breath and opened his eyes. He'd bring in the bucket of water, he'd help Terra cook, and he could relax for a bit. He felt ragged after three full, taxing days as courier, and he looked forward to sitting down with his family for dinner.

Well, with his sister. His mother would take her bowl in bed.

He dipped the bucket and began pulling it up, winding the crank with the absent motions he'd been doing all his life. His gaze drifted to the Dromm woods, and the wooden handle creaked to a stop.

"What...?"

Monty almost let the full bucket drop. He pulled it up and set it on the stones, keeping his eyes on the trees. He thought he was seeing something he'd never seen before, but he had to get closer to be sure.

Monty moved to the path through the tall grass, past the compost pile and back to where the plants started to thin and the ground became dark, dry earth as it approached the black forest. What he had seen rested upon a branch some twenty-five feet above his head.

The budding green of a new leaf.

It was so jarring that Monty blinked and expected it to disappear. Never, not once in all his life, in his dozens of youthful jaunts through the forest or the thousands of times he looked at it from across the field, had he ever seen anything growing on a Dromm tree. Ever.

If it were closer, he might have reached up to pluck it off and make sure it was real. But he could see it plainly. A sprout—small enough to fit between two fingertips, but alive all the same.

Water. He remembered why he had come outside, and it wasn't to go investigate the Dromm. His sick mother was thirsty, and waiting on him. He looked away from the speck of green and went back home, picking up the bucket and bringing it inside.

His mother thanked him for the water, her voice heavy and tired. She sat up and drank the cup down in three big gulps, and Monty got her another.

"Stay there," he told her as she drained half of the second cup. "I'll help Terra cook."

Delila didn't protest.

Terra had done a fine job assembling the ingredients for vegetable stew, and Monty let her chop the carrots while he worked on the rest, letting a pot of water boil and collecting the scraps to toss outside.

When he went to go see if Delila wanted more water, he found she was asleep. Her cup rested, empty, on the small table beside her bed. He refilled it and set it down again in case she wanted more, remembering how she'd done the same for him and Terra when they were sick, and how it was nice to wake up with water there for you.

When the stew was done, he left his mother's serving in the pot and sat down with Terra to eat.

"When did mom get sick?" he asked her.

Terra shrugged, shoveling a spoon of stew into her mouth. "I dunno. After the, um, the sending."

"Right after?"

"No..." Terra set her spoon down into her bowl, screwing up her eyes. "Tomorrow. The day after, I mean. While you were gone."

While you were gone. Terra hadn't meant the words to hurt, but they did, needling at Monty and raising a small flush in his cheeks.

Terra's face darkened, her eyes going down. "She's not gonna die like Ma Kettle, is she?"

"Terra!" Monty said, harsh but quiet. "Don't say that. Of course she's not. It's just winter sickness."

"That's what she said it was." She brightened and picked up her spoon again, eating. "I hope I don't get it. Last time my nose was runny for weeks."

"I remember," Monty said. "You ruined three good shirts because you kept blowing your boogers into them instead of a kerchief like Mom told you."

"You can't say *boogers* at the table," Terra told him, but she giggled at the word, and so did Monty. He wished their mother were sitting with them.

"Take good care of her while I'm working," he told Terra. "Okay? Let her sleep, don't let her try to do any work. Get her lots of water. Can you carry the bucket?"

"Yes, I can carry the bucket! I'm strong, you know."

"Good. I guess you have to let her cook, but...make sure she eats, too." Monty realized he sounded just like his mother when she was instructing him on how to care for his little sister when she was sick, and found he was grateful to have that to cling to. "She'll get better in a few days."

"I hope I don't get sick," Terra repeated, and she was well ahead of Monty on her dinner because he had been talking so much. He hurried to catch up.

When he was done, he decided it was best to wake his mother up with a bowl of stew while it was still hot. He brought it back to her while Terra cleaned out her bowl (not grumbling about it like she usually did), setting it on the table by her cup, which was still full.

"Hey, mom," he said softly, kneeling down again. "Got some food for you."

She was silent and still, but when he repeated himself, she stirred. He smiled at her, but it was laced with sadness, the way you smile at someone you care about when they're in pain.

"Huh? Oh...dinner..." Delila was sleep-ridden and weary, blinking her eyes. "How long did I sleep?"

"Not long," he said. "It's still hot."

"I don't really have any...appetite," she said, letting her head sink back down into the pillow.

"Eat it anyway," Monty told her, pushing the table closer to the edge of the bed. "You'd make me do the same thing, you know."

She smiled, and it lifted Monty's spirit a bit. "You bet I would."

"I have to work in town tomorrow, but I'll be back as soon as I can."

Delila sat up, a slow task. "You're a hard worker. I've always been proud of you for that. I'm sorry I've been so...so crotchety about all of this."

"Crotchety..." Monty almost laughed, settling on a grin. "I don't think I've ever seen you be crotchety."

"No?" she asked, matching his grin with a weak smile of her own. "Your father did, when he let my dinner burn."

"Lucky for me, it's hard to burn stew."

"It looks good." She cupped the bowl with both hands, lifting it off the table. "Go on...don't want you getting sick, too."

He left her room and helped Terra clean up the kitchen. It was late now, fully dark, and his sister was sleepy. He checked on his mother once more afterward.

She had eaten only a little of the stew before lying back down. Monty looked down at the remaining food, twisting his lips. At least she had taken the water.

"Good night, mom," Monty said, and she stirred a little at his words, which was enough. He filled her water again before he went to lie down in his own bed.

As comfortable as the Commons quarters were, this was better. He found sleep.

<h2 style="text-align:center">23</h2>

When he woke the next morning, beating the sun as usual, Terra was already up, sitting at the table in the kitchen. He stepped in slowly, rubbing the sleep from his eyes with the back of his hand. There was a candle lit on the table, and her hands were busy.

"Are you hungry?" he asked her.

Terra shook her head. "I had some stew. It's still good."

She had something on the table before her. Blinking, Monty recognized it as a shirt, and the thing shining between her fingers was a sewing needle.

"Are you...sewing?"

"Yeah. Mom's been teaching me." Her tongue poked out between her lips as she plunged the needle into the fabric, her rough movements making Monty wince. Still, she seemed to be doing a fair job fixing up the tear in the shirt. It was strange, seeing Terra sew up a shirt instead of playing with a neighbor kid, or a doll.

She has to grow up sometime. I just didn't think I'd miss it.

Monty went to check on his mother. Her water was gone—good. She was asleep, and she looked buried in it. He let her lie.

"You have to go?" Terra asked him when he came back out into the kitchen.

"Yeah." He had Delila's cup, and he filled it again, setting it on the table by Terra. "Bring this to her when you can. And don't poke a bunch of holes in your fingers."

"I already did." Terra frowned, flexing her small hands. "But Mom says that's part of it."

A tired grin came over him. "You'll have to show me how, once you're better at it."

"I'm already better than you," she said, sticking her tongue out.

"I'll be back tonight," Monty said. Even if the Judge asked him to stay over, he'd just sacrifice some sleep to be to town on time.

Terra said, "Okay," and she hopped down from the chair to bring the cup of water to their mother's room. Monty was out the door before she returned.

The day's work was heavy, but not unusual. Monty heard far fewer whispers of death and doom as he hustled through the streets.

Mullen, meanwhile, seemed distracted. He spoke few words to Monty, and was always halfway turned away and hurrying back toward his desk as his office door closed. Whatever set off his rage those days ago must have carried a tide of work with it, as evidenced by the bulging contents of his messenger bag.

The time went fast, and Mullen didn't ask him to stay the night. Perhaps he was too preoccupied to bother. Monty dropped his bag in his quarters and locked it tight, and he was back home again with a sliver of sun slipping behind the horizon.

Terra was outside, waiting for him.

"Hey..." he said, uneasy as she ran up to him. Was it mom?

"Monty!" Terra stopped right before him. "Hi. Mom wants you to get another water bucket, before you come inside."

"Oh. Okay." Monty looked toward the house. "Is she...doing all right?"

Terra nodded. "She's awake. She got up and put more salt and something else in the stew. She said it needed more...um, I don't know what she put in it."

Monty broke into a smile. A weight he wasn't even aware he'd been carrying lifted off him, and he clapped Terra lightly on the shoulder. "She's just too nice to tell us our dinner wasn't very good."

"Aw. I liked it."

"Me, too. I'll get that water."

He brought in a fresh bucket and saw his mother hovering over the pot of stew, stirring. She turned to him when he came through the door.

Delila didn't look quite back to normal, but it was better than yesterday. Her face was shiny with sweat, but the color in her cheeks looked healthier, as opposed to flushed and hot. Her eyes were brighter, but lethargy still hung on her frame.

"Mom, shouldn't you be in bed?" he said to her.

"Probably," she admitted. "Terra pricked her finger, and I had to wrap her up, and then since I was up anyway...well..."

"You didn't like the stew." Monty accused her with a twitch of his lips.

"I liked it fine. Don't be...silly. Ooh." Delila wavered, dropping the spoon into the pot and steadying herself against the counter.

Monty got to her side. "Are you all right?"

"I'm fine. I..." Delila closed her eyes. "Got a bit...lightheaded..."

"You shouldn't be up," he said, putting a hand on the back of her shoulder. Her skin was hot even through her shirt. "Go and lay down. I'll bring you some stew, if you want."

"Ah...well, all right." Delila patted Monty's arm, and he lowered his hand. "Just give it a good stir. Mix the spices in."

"Okay," he said, and he did so, bringing her a hot bowl once she was in bed.

Delila fell asleep soon after she ate. She did seem to be doing better than yesterday.

While the last vestiges of light were slipping away, Monty brought the bucket back to the well. The Dromm stared at him. He had forgotten about the little sprout from the other day, and now there were more. Whole leaves, it looked like. In the fading light, they stood out in stark contrast to the black wall of trees they sprouted from.

Monty counted six or seven little patches of green before it grew too dark to be sure. It bothered him, and he wasn't sure why. But it wasn't enough to keep him awake, and he slept well again in his own bed.

The next morning, Delila was awake before Monty was. The noise of the front door opening roused him from sleep, and he left his room to see his mother coming back with the bucket. She was alert, but she still looked pallid. She read the concern on his face.

"Good morning. Yes, I should be in bed. But you have to go to town, and Terra can't fetch water without spilling half of it."

"I could have gotten it," he said, the sincerity in his words dampened by a stifled yawn.

"And now you don't have to." She set the half-full bucket on the table with a thud.

Usually she was much quieter in the morning. Monty suspected she'd be able to cook a full meal in this kitchen with a blindfold on, but today she was leaning against the counter and table more than usual. He held back a comment about it, instead opting to drink a scoop of water from the bucket himself and clear his throat.

"Well...I'm glad you're feeling better," he said, and the sincerity there wasn't muted; he felt it burn his cheeks.

Delila smiled. "Thanks for picking up my slack, Monty. You won't have to do it much longer."

She crossed over the kitchen and plucked at the front of his shirt. "Is that what you're wearing? It hasn't been washed."

"It's fine," Monty said. "I rinsed it."

"Let me—"

"No, no—" He slid around her arms, rounding the table towards the front door. "I have to go."

"Mm." His mother didn't give chase. She rested her palms flat on the table. "All right. But I'll wash that shirt next time I see you."

"If you must," Monty said, and he left wearing an abashed grin that he carried almost all the way to Irisa.

Judge Mullen was a little more present that day, if not exactly cheery. Monty was bestowed with a "Good morning," from the Judge, and was further surprised when Mullen asked him how things were going.

"Fine," Monty hastened to answer. "Mother's a little sick—winter illness, it looks like."

"Delila? That is a shame," Mullen replied. "Are you under the weather, yourself? Your sister?"

Monty shook his head. "No."

Mullen was silent for a moment, his eyes tipping away from Monty's own. The pause stretched long enough for Monty to want to say something, but finally Mullen spoke again.

"Well, let me know if she takes a turn," Judge Mullen said. He placed his hand on the edge of the door, signaling the end of the conversation. "I will have Dr. Tobias over there to give her something to nip at the sickness."

"Thank you, Judge," Monty said. The tension he'd lately felt when talking to Mullen eased a little bit. "But she's on the upswing of it. She'll be all right."

The door closed, and the rest of the day was lost in work and footprints in the packed dirt.

24

Monty returned home from courier work the next day a little earlier than normal. Things had slowed down in town, and Judge Mullen had dismissed him while the sun was still fat in the evening sky.

Approaching the farm, Monty was surprised to see the shapes of two people standing outside. Adults. Not friends that Terra had brought over.

Once he was close enough, he recognized their neighbors, Mr. and Mrs. Garten. Their own children were nowhere to be seen, but Terra was sitting on the front step, mostly hidden by the Gartens, who were facing toward her and away from Monty.

His footsteps alerted them before he could say anything, and when the Gartens turned to look, Terra burst through the gap between them and ran to him. She grabbed him around the waist and pressed her face into his stomach.

"Terra—" He put a hand on her shoulder. "What's going on?"

Whatever she said, it was lost in the combination of gasping tears and muffling of Monty's midriff.

The Gartens came over. Mrs. Garten's face was colored in sympathy, and Mr. Garten's wore the same drifting gaze he always did.

"Monty, I'm sorry. It's Delila..." Mrs. Garten trailed off, wrapping her thin fingers around her wrist. "She's..."

Monty picked up Terra, holding her against his side with one arm. His vision blurred. He moved past Mrs. Garten, her words fading into nothing. His heartbeat filled his ears.

She was okay. She was okay.

The words thumped steadily in his head as he climbed the front steps and opened the door. As soon as he did, the smell hit him. It pulled tears from his eyes, making the kitchen wobble, and he leaned against the door frame with Terra in his arms.

She was okay. She was okay, Terra can't be in here, she can't—

Monty set her down. She was still crying. He didn't want to leave her alone, but he couldn't bring her in there. The smell, that godawful smell, that horrid stench that he knew—

"Go back outside," he choked. "I'll be—I'll..."

He didn't know what he was going to say, but Terra either understood or just didn't want to be in there anymore. She pushed out the door, one hand on her face.

Monty was alone here now.

Wiping his eyes, he pressed forward. He bumped the kitchen table, the sharp pain in his hip focusing his vision. He tried not to breathe, but of course he had to. Had to inhale that stench. Had to feel it burn his insides like hot smoke.

Mother's room. Dark; the curtain drawn. Had she drawn it herself? Had she asked Terra to?

Her bed, covers high. Concealing her. What about that—had she pulled up her blankets? Or had it been the Gartens?

"Mom..." Monty's call was weak; almost silent. He crept forward, the floor creaking underneath him like it always did. "Mom..."

No answer. Standing at her bed now, he grabbed a fistful of blankets. The smell was so strong, but he wouldn't retch, not here in the house.

He pulled the blankets back. Slowly. They weighed hundreds of pounds. Yet still, fine wisps of black hair went flying as they were freed.

Audrey—

Not Audrey. Delila. His mother. Terra's mother.

Dead.

The smell disappeared; his vision cleared. He gripped the blanket hard enough to bend his nails back. The wasted, blackened corpse of his mother laid below him, unmoving and empty. There was no semblance of clinging life, like Audrey at the end. Delila's body looked like it would crumble into black, ashy flakes at the slightest touch.

Monty felt a scream bubbling up in his throat. He jerked involuntarily, pulling the blankets off further, revealing bedclothes smeared with black, ashy remnants of her skin. Her inhuman remains stained the bed.

"I'll wash that shirt next time I see you."

He knew he should look away. And he knew it didn't matter, that one bare second of this image was enough to burn it into him for the rest of his life. That it would follow him into the beyond itself.

"Mix the spices in."

The only thing that helped him bury his scream was Terra, knowing his little sister was outside, that she would hear it. That it would haunt her nightmares, bringing them more crystal-clear detail to reflect on in the dead of nights to come.

Monty didn't scream. He let go of the blankets and he closed his eyes, falling to the doorframe, tripping backward and landing hard. The dark room was sprouting eerie gray. His mother's body, eye level now, was a black line in his vision.

Don't pass out, don't pass "out, don't pass out..."

The words slid through Monty's lips like sludge as he crawled backwards, eyes closed, hands scraping against the wooden floor. Inch by inch, through the hall, to the kitchen. The smell was back, assailing him in the wake of his shock. He held his breath and found he had none to hold.

Gasping in burning air, Monty made it to the front door. He pushed it open and tried to crawl out, putting his hands down on the steps, but he slipped. A thick splinter dug into his palm, the pain sudden and sharp. He felt blood dribble down his hand as he fell and turned, landing on his shoulder.

Strong hands grabbed him and hauled him up, pulling him to his feet without hesitation or strain. It was Mr. Garten. He didn't speak; instead, he grabbed the long splinter of wood by its end and yanked it out of Monty's palm. More pain; spots of red in his vision. More blood, covering his palm. He winced.

"You're okay."

Monty looked up to Mr. Garten. The tall man was eyeing the bloody splinter. He flicked it away and looked over to his wife, who was holding Terra against her. Monty couldn't see Terra's face.

"Wrap that," Mr. Garten said, nodding towards his hand.

Monty said, "I need to take Terra...she needs to..."

His blood dripped onto the grass, bright red against dull green. Take her where? Back in the house?

"Wrap that," the man repeated, and he motioned for his wife to come over. "We'll take Terra. And you. Until this is..." He made a motion in the air, waving his hand to the horizon.

He's talking about my mother. Her soul going to the beyond. Monty was numb, watching things unfold. Watching Mrs. Garten pet Terra's head and make sympathetic noises, words he didn't understand.

She'd been fixing their dinner two days ago. Just two days ago.

"Come on, Monty. You don't...we shouldn't be here." It was Mrs. Garten, approaching him, holding Terra's hand. He could see his sister now, strands of hair caught in her tears. She looked up to Monty, meeting his eyes. She needed him.

Mrs. Garten was right. They couldn't be here. But...

"I can't...I don't..." Monty swallowed. "Mom. She...I can't just leave her here. She has to...I have to tell the, the priest. The doctor. So they can..."

Mrs. Garten's hand was on his shoulder. "We will take care of that. Right now, come home with us."

Home? This was home. Were they going to abandon it? They'd leave their mother all alone in that house, roasting in the smell...

"Monty."

He was staring at the ground, not realizing it. Mrs. Garten was in front of him. He tilted his head up just a bit to look at the shorter woman.

"Nathan will go to town and make sure your mother is taken care of," she told him.

"Nathan..." The name meant nothing to Monty.

"Mr. Garten," she said, softly, the way she said everything. "Mr. Garten will go to town right now, and someone will be back with him very fast. Nathan?"

Mrs. Garten looked to her husband, and the man nodded.

"Aye. I'll go." And without hesitation, he did, heading towards Irisa without so much as a nod in their direction.

Monty watched him walk away, Mr. Garten's long strides carrying him quickly towards the town.

He'll get there faster than I would, he thought, and then, *No, I would run, I'd be to town in minutes, I—*

A hand tugged on his. Terra. She wasn't talking; just pulling. Urging him along.

He went with her, and the three of them walked back to the Garten's home. Mrs. Garten held Terra's hand, and Terra held her brother's.

No sense in rushing to town, Monty thought, his head turned toward town. *It's too late to save her. It's too late.*

The thought didn't sting like he expected. Everything was numb. All he felt was the weight of his feet as they pressed into the ground with each step.

At the Garten farm, it was quiet, almost as quiet as his own house. The young Garten boys must have been inside; Monty managed to string together the realization that Terra must have run to the Garten's house for their help, that the neighbors didn't just come over with no provocation. So the boys probably knew something was wrong, too.

The numbness swept over him again, burying the image of Terra running across the field; panicking; crying.

When they went inside, Mrs. Garten said something. Monty thought she might have asked if they wanted something to eat.

He saw Terra shake her head, and he did the same. She looked exhausted.

"Lay down," he said, and then cleared his throat. "I think Terra is—somewhere we can lay down?"

Mrs. Garten showed them to one of the rooms, but whether it was hers and Nathan's or one of the children's, Monty didn't know. The memories of being in this house were fuzzy, just close enough to make it passingly familiar. He let Terra climb into the bed first, but once he got in, she laid across his chest, her slight weight warm and trembling.

He stared at an unfamiliar ceiling and put his arm around his sister, holding her close to him.

I never should have gone back, he thought. *Never should have left her when she was sick. It's my fault.*

"Not your fault."

Terra. He must have said his thoughts aloud, or part of them. She spoke, but she didn't move or try to look at him. Her head was on his chest, facing toward his toes.

"I should have been home," Monty said, whisper-quiet. "I should have been there."

"Not your fault," Terra said again, and her words were sleepy and drifting. "It's the forest. The forest took her."

Monty shifted, looking down at the back of her head. "What do you mean?"

"I tried to get Daddy back," Terra murmured, fading away into sleep. "But...I couldn't. Now it's...got them both..."

"Terra?" Monty whispered, but she was gone, her trembles disappearing into her doze, her breath evening out. He let out his own long breath, slowly, so as not to disturb her. He heard Mrs. Garten say something unintelligible, presumably to her boys. He wanted to lie awake until Mr. Garten got back, but he was burdened with sudden, immense tiredness.

He regretted going to town and trusting his mother's health. Some part of him knew there was nothing he would have been able to do, but it wasn't the part that was lying in an unfamiliar bed and holding his sister close to him.

Monty closed his eyes. His mother's corpse didn't float there, as he feared it would; he instead found blessed blackness. Terra, hopefully, wouldn't give herself nightmares about the forest taking their parents, whatever that meant.

Maybe he'd show her the leaves that were growing there.

See, Terra—it's just a regular forest.

The room was warm, and he was cold. He wished the forest really had taken their mother. Then they might be able to get her back.

25

Monty opened his eyes to see weak morning light. Terra hadn't moved and was still sleeping like a stone. There was an instant where, upon waking, his mind was empty, before the weight of the world came back on him with crushing force.

He closed his eyes, chewing the insides of his lips. If nothing else, he had to stay strong for Terra.

"Hey," he said, nudging her. "Wake up, Terra."

She did, slowly, raising her head and blinking. She looked around. "Where..."

"The Gartens."

It was all Monty had to say. He could practically see reality returning to her, and it tugged at his heart. He put a hand on her head, losing the tips of his fingers in her hair.

"We're gonna go home," he told her. "We're gonna...get through this."

He hoped she believed him. He didn't know if he believed himself.

The smell of cooking was in the air, scents he knew but couldn't place. They were just different enough, and they didn't stir his appetite. His stomach didn't feel full; it felt like it wasn't there at all.

"Stay here for a minute," he told Terra, getting up. But she clutched at him, grabbing two tiny fistfuls of his shirt.

"Where are you going?"

"It's okay." He didn't push her away, just waited for her to relax enough to let him go. "I'm just going to talk to Mrs. Garten. I'll be right back. You can come if you want."

She considered it, then shook her head.

Monty left the room, taking a moment to remember which way to turn, trying to follow the sounds of cooking. When he came into the kitchen and saw Mrs. Garten there, working on breakfast, pain swept over him so suddenly and with such power that he couldn't speak.

"I'm cooking," Mrs. Garten said with some uncertainty when she saw him. "Usually Nathan does, he's better..."

"Um," Monty said, trying to find himself. "Did he...did Mr. Garten get to town?"

"Oh." Mrs. Garten nodded. "Yes. And back. He's fixing the shed now, with the boys. They should be doing most of the work."

"And..." Monty hesitated, but Mrs. Garten didn't seem to have any inclination to finish his thought. "Did he, you know...bring someone? For—for my mother?"

"He did, yes. They took her to town. To prepare for, ah—" Now Mrs. Garten hesitated, perhaps realizing the pain Monty was in. "Her sending. Tomorrow. The Judge said...well, to Nathan, he said that you don't have to work, until after the sending. You're welcome to stay here until then."

"I..." Monty thought, *I need to go home and open the windows.* "That's very kind. I'd like to take Terra home, though."

"I understand." Mrs. Garten shook the pan over the stove, a burning smell emerging in the kitchen. "Will you eat? It's just a little burnt. Nathan usually does the cooking. He's better."

After letting her know that neither he nor Terra were hungry, Monty got his sister from the bedroom and the pair of them left the house. Talking with Mrs. Garten always made him feel odd.

The walk back home was long and quiet. They stopped outside the house, standing some yards back and staring. Monty wanted to think it looked different; eerie or foreboding—but the truth was, it looked the same. Short but well-built; small but welcoming. Strong wood stained dark and pretty. Everything inside would be the same, except for the most important thing.

"Mom's not in there anymore, is she?" Terra was holding him now, her hand on his wrist.

"No," he said. "It's okay to go inside."

He noticed that the windows were open; whoever had come to retrieve his mother's body must have done that. Would the smell be all gone?

Terra let go of him and approached the house, but she didn't go inside. Instead, she turned and sat down on the steps, looking towards Monty and the Dromm behind him. He sat next to her, looking at those dark trees.

"Can you see the leaves?" Monty said, pointing at the swatches of green peppering the black trees. "It's growing, can you believe it?"

Terra followed his finger, blinking. "Those are leaves?"

"Yeah."

"That's weird." Terra didn't seem all that interested, dropping her gaze down between her feet. "I don't like the forest, Monty. I don't want to live here anymore."

Monty looked over at Terra, who kept her eyes on the ground. She was bringing up the forest again. Since he had found her in the Dromm, she hardly ever talked about it.

"Why don't you like the forest?"

Terra shrugged. A breeze blew, cold enough to draw a shiver out of Monty, but it made no sound. Monty would have let it go, but something was prodding him, something he couldn't quite identify. Like a key hunting for a lock in the dark.

"You said it took dad. Last night, remember?"

She nodded, still looking down. Her legs were closed, hands on her thighs.

"What did you mean?"

The cold wind came by again, chilling them down to their bones. But neither of them made a move to go inside the house. He wanted to ask her again. Instead, he waited.

"I didn't remember before," Terra said, so quietly that Monty leaned in to hear her better.

"Remember what?" he asked.

"Seeing Daddy," she responded, and she looked up at him. "I saw dad in the forest."

"Come with me, Monty. I want us all together again."

His breath caught like there was a lock in his throat.

"I forgot when I woke up," she continued, "like how you forget a dream, you know? But I know it wasn't a dream. I went in after him, but...I wasn't fast enough. He got away. The forest got him."

The horrifying image of his father in the Commons reared up in his mind. "When you saw him, was he...was he normal? Or like he was...like he'd been dead?"

"Um...normal, I guess. I didn't get close. I wasn't fast enough."

Monty breathed in cold air and let it out in a puff of white. "Do you think it was really him?"

"I..." Terra curled her fingers, picking at her thumbs with her nails. "I think so. I did think it was him, or I wouldn't go in the woods. I'd never go in there."

"But do you still think it was him? That it was really dad?"

She paused, then shook her head. "No," she whispered. "It was the forest."

Monty looked at the leaves, sprouting after what was said to be hundreds of years of blackness.

"Did you see him, too?" Terra put her hand on his leg, and when he looked into her eyes, he saw the weight of her question there. Felt her fingers dig into his skin.

If he told her, would that be worse? Would she be more scared, or feel less alone? He wasn't used to having a conversation like this with Terra. It was uncharted territory.

"I saw him," Monty breathed, and Terra's fingers pressed in harder.

"Where?" she asked him.

"It was a dream," Monty said. "Or I was sleepwalking, or something. He was in the Commons, in town. I woke up in the middle of the night and heard something and...I saw him. But he was..." Monty shook his head. "It wasn't him. It was just some trick. It sounded like him, but it looked...like a corpse." Monty left out the fact that he had bashed its head in with a curtain rod, because he never actually did, because none of it had happened. It was just a dream.

Terra frowned, and she looked like she was going to cry, but she didn't. "Did it try to make you go into the woods, like me?"

"I was in town," Monty said, but the last word came out choked, because he remembered what Montille's dream specter had said.

"We'll go an' get your mother, and your sister...

"An' we'll go into the woods."

Monty didn't answer the question, but Terra didn't ask again. Instead she said, "If it wasn't him, who was it?"

And that was when the prodding key clicked into place.

That story that he'd heard so long ago from his father, and one he hadn't remembered until his own strange brush with the forest, when it seemed like it was calling to him, beckoning him in. He remembered that the urge had come over him with no warning or explanation, but that he had shaken it off.

Perhaps the same thing had come over Terra, and she hadn't been able to shake it off so easy.

It had been a long time since he'd been scared of the Dromm. Since he'd been scared of the stories he heard about it. It was an old feeling with haunting familiarity, and it crept over him now.

The tall black trees of the Dromm loomed in the distance.

It was crazy. Just considering it made his head feel like it was cracking inside and something was leaking out. But...

What if Nal'Gee was real?

A spirit lying dormant in the forest, surviving off the trees. The black trees of the Dromm, black forever because the life was being sucked out of them over and over.

Those leaves were the tipping point—what really drove into Monty the idea that something, something beyond his understanding of the world, was happening.

There was life in the dead forest.

26

If Nal'Gee was real, and everything in the story his father told him was true, then why would the leaves suddenly be growing after all this time? Because she was gone to the beyond? Maybe.

Or maybe because she didn't need the trees anymore.

Maybe she was sucking the life out of the town. Out of the people. They turned black, didn't they? Just like the trees.

No, no, that's crazy, Monty thought to himself, and he made sure not to say it out loud this time, because he didn't want to scare Terra. No way he could tell her what he was beginning to suspect. Even if she knew something strange was happening, herself.

That's not enough to justify what you're thinking, he told himself. *It's a coincidence.*

His dad had told him she was a will-o-the-wisp, too weak to even catch a squirrel. How could she drain the life from a person?

He could be wrong, the voice in his head said, and it was a scary thought. *It's just a tale. It can't all be right. And she's stronger, now. Stronger than anyone thinks.*

If she's real, he countered, but it felt a lot weaker than he wanted it to. Whatever sickness had killed Ma Kettle, Audrey Kettle, and now his own mother—it wasn't a normal sickness. It didn't spread to people like normal sickness. None of the other Kettles were sick. No one in town was, now, and he would know.

So maybe it wasn't a sickness at all...it was a spirit. It was Nal'Gee.

"Monty, are you okay?"

Terra's voice snapped him from his thoughts. He'd been staring silently at the black forest while his mind ran like a river.

"Huh? Oh." He shook his head. "I'm fine. I just—" *Don't let it slip.* "— I was thinking about the nightmare I had. About dad. That's all it was, you know, and yours too. It was just a nightmare. The forest—it's not trying to get us."

Just the spirit inside of it. Maybe.

But those damned leaves, growing after all this time. Growing because they were allowed to for the first time in centuries. Growing because they weren't food for Nal'Gee's spirit anymore. After hundreds of years, was she strong enough now to leave the forest?

Monty resisted the urge to put his head in his hands. There was too much happening, and none of it was simple. If he wanted to give in to the idea of Nal'Gee—and insane as it was, he couldn't shake it off—how would he even explore it? Leave Terra in the house and go poking around in the Dromm, knocking on newly-sprouting trees to see if Nal'Gee lived in one of them? Put himself up for offer to be taken next by wandering around her territory, investigating?

There was no proof. There was only the leaves on the trees.

"Let's go inside," he said to Terra, standing up from the steps and finally looking away from the trees. She followed after him.

The smell of death in the house was gone, and Monty was grateful for that, but he still wasn't going to go back into mom's room. He didn't know what they were going to do here. Mother's sending was tomorrow night, and there was a lot of empty time between now and then. He didn't want to spend it sitting in the house where she had just died.

"Are you hungry?" he asked Terra, and she shook her head. She was just standing there in the kitchen, making no move to sit down or go back to her room. She didn't want to be here, either.

It was rare when two siblings agreed so perfectly on something; even rarer was the fact that it happened in complete silence. Monty caught Terra's eye, and they both stepped out of the house, down the steps, and out into the grass. The air was cold, but it was fresh, and the grayness of the day was better than the darkness of the house. The empty spaces out here were less confining. Lighter. Easier to ignore.

The Dromm was there, too. Itching at Monty, making him second-guess himself and everything he knew about how the world worked. Under that pressure, he realized there was only one other person in the whole world who was on his side and knew exactly what he was going through. Even the crazy parts.

That was Terra. And she deserved to know what he was thinking.

Besides that, he thought, *she might even know more than I do.* He didn't really believe in the legends once he grew out of it, and he hadn't for a long time—not until now, when this inkling had come through.

But Terra...she always had, and she still did.

"Let's go for a walk," Monty said. He started to suggest going into town, but bit his tongue on that. He wasn't quite up to talking to people, hearing their sympathies, and struggling to come up with a response. He wasn't sure how he was going to do it at the sending, either, but that worry at least had the luxury of being for tomorrow.

"Okay." Terra looked towards Irisa. "Where, to town?"

"No..." Monty darted his eyes toward the black trees. If Nal'Gee was able to get to Ma Kettle, it wasn't like it mattered if there were in town or brushing against the bark, right? "I wanna get a closer look at those leaves in the Dromm."

"You wanna go in there?" Terra asked, hesitant.

Monty shook his head. "Not inside. I just want to get a closer look. It's not scary, and it's not going to get us." Which, even if he was right, wasn't a lie. The danger wasn't the forest—it was what was now free of it. "But I do want to ask you about it."

As they approached the tall grass that marked the transition of their land towards the Dromm, Monty said, "Did dad ever tell you the story about Nal'Gee?"

Terra was walking on his right side, looking straight ahead. "I don't know...what was he?"

"She," Monty corrected. "She was a witch who got killed in the forest by, um…" It didn't feel right to say *lover*, so he chose, "by her boyfriend. She used to live on our land, or near it, hundreds of years ago."

"Oh!" Terra perked up. "Dad told me about that when I asked him why the trees were black. She was the witch who helped the forest grow."

"That's her."

Past the compost pile, small and useless in this part of winter. Now the grass was getting shorter, and there was nothing between them and the tall trees.

"Do you remember the rest of the story?" Monty asked.

Terra nodded. "Dad said she died, but she never let go. That she ate the boyfriend's soul, and then she ate the whole forest. His name was Walter."

Walter. That was right; he recalled it, too, now that she said it. Was there more? "What else do you remember? He told me a long time ago. I forget how it all went."

"Ummm." Terra grabbed at her hair, twisting it between her fingers while she thought. "He said…oh. It's kind of scary." She looked up at the trees. They were close enough now to block most of the sky. She had to crane her neck back to see where they ended.

"It's okay," Monty said. "You can tell me. I won't be scared."

When she looked at him, he tipped her a little wink, and she smiled and everything felt a little bit warmer. Just a little bit.

"Well…he said that Nal'Gee didn't eat up that life and then need more, like we do. She just kept it. Every day she gets a little more…and eventually she'd be strong enough to be alive again."

Wind whistled in Monty's ears and died in the trees. He was sure that their father had never told him that. And truth be told, it *did* scare him.

"Dad said that?"

Terra nodded, and Monty thought, *Maybe he really wanted to make sure she stayed out of the forest.*

They turned, strolling along the edge of the forest in the direction of the Cherrywood farm, leaving a berth between their shoulders and the trees. Terra had moved over to his left side, away from the Dromm.

"I was thinking about the people who got sick," Monty said. "The Kettles, and...and mom. How it doesn't make sense for people to get sick and die this fast, and how it doesn't spread like a normal sickness...you know?"

"I guess," Terra responded. Of course, she hadn't been there to see the bodies. But no—she had seen their mother's. Was she all black and drained when Terra found her?

He didn't ask. He said, "I'm thinking that Nal'Gee might be real."

Monty stopped walking, but only because Terra did. She was looking into the woods, but she looked to him when he turned.

"Monty, you really think that?"

There was no sense in lying to her. "I do. Or, I'm starting to. I don't know. Me seeing dad, after never ever having a nightmare like that—and you seeing him, too. It's just so many weird things happening, too close together. And so awful, with no reason or—or sense."

Monty's next breath was great and shuddering, as the toll of what he'd been through the last couple of weeks started to ring in his ears.

"These people died so horribly, Terra, and I wish you hadn't had to see any of it, but I did. They were just..."

"Empty," Terra finished for him, and she grabbed his hand with both of hers. "Is that what you were gonna say?"

Monty nodded. His eyes were wet and it was hard to see. He rubbed them, trying to hold it together.

"When I saw—when I saw mom yesterday, when I—" Now it was Terra's turn to quaver, and she shook her head, her hair flying. But she kept on going. "When I saw her in bed, she was all small and skinny. And her skin was black, and—and her hair was falling out. She looked...empty."

"Yeah," Monty croaked, and he pulled Terra a little closer to him. "You're right. I saw Audrey Kettle, and she looked the same way. Like the life is being pulled out of them."

"And they're turning black like the trees," Terra said slowly, her words painted with halting awe as she looked up the vast trunk of the closest Dromm tree.

"If Nal'Gee is real, and she's stronger now, maybe she's strong enough to start taking people instead of plants," Monty said, "and she'll get a lot stronger a lot quicker. Enough to come back."

"What'll happen if she comes back?"

"I don't know," Monty said. Who could know? But he had an idea. An idea of someone lying dormant for hundreds of years, clinging to life using pure hate. An idea of what that person would be like if she returned to find a thousand new people on her land, and other people farming where she used to live.

"I think she'd be mad," Terra said. "In the story, she hated Walter in the end. She probably hates everybody now."

"She probably does," Monty said. "And she'll keep killing people until she gets what she wants. Maybe even all of us."

Terra grabbed her hair again, worrying at it. "What are we gonna do?"

His little sister seemed to have grown up a lot in the last few weeks, and it had happened without Monty even noticing. He thought she'd be scared, and surely she was, the same way he was—but she was curious and asking questions. She wanted to fix it.

He wished he had an answer for her.

27

Monty and Terra spent the night at the Gartens' once again. To Monty's surprise, Mr. Garten had come to check on them, and insisted that they come over. Well, insisted in his tacit way, with few words and distant stares. That was just before dinner time, and they both had grown hungry in spite of the clouds filling their minds, so they enjoyed the food that Mr. Garten cooked and took Mrs. Garten's invitation to stay over once more.

They went back home after sleeping in late, something neither of them had done in a long time.

There was no more talk of Nal'Gee. In the new day's light, it felt farther away and a bit silly. There was nothing else to say—they didn't know how they would even begin to challenge a witch's sprit. But like the Dromm, the idea was still there behind them, looming. Their house was less foreboding, and they spent some time cleaning out the pantry of any rotten vegetables, and bringing in fresh water.

Soon the afternoon light faded, and the evening of Delila's sending was upon them.

Part of Monty didn't want to go, and the rest of him knew that he must. He wasn't ready, and he imagined that he never would be, but his mother deserved for them to be there.

"Is it time?" Terra asked, almost as soon as the sun was halfway down. The sending had been on their minds all day.

"Just about," Monty said. "Do you—"

"I'm not hungry," Terra interrupted. "I can feed myself, you know."

On another day that might have come with a little grin, but not today.

When the sun was almost gone, they left the farm behind them, setting on the narrow road to Irisa. They walked close together.

There weren't many people, which was expected. Delila Bellamy wasn't a Kettle; she was a border farmer, people saw her now and then, and some knew her face, but that was about it.

Evening came fast, and it wasn't until they got very close that Monty could make out the pyre, already built. And his mother's casket, already placed. The iron handles caught what tiny bit of light remained, and Monty thought, *how many fires have they been through?*

Terra made a small noise in her throat at the sight, and she drew closer to Monty, but only slightly. Monty rested a hand on her upper back, his touch light and comforting. If she wanted to be strong in front of the people here, she could, but no one would judge her if she let some tears out. He wanted to say that to her, but he wasn't sure he could speak.

They went to the front of the gathering. It was like when they had come to Audrey's sending, only so very, very different. Monty recognized some of the faces there, but in a blurry and distant sense. It felt like he was floating above his body, looking down on the scene from a foot over his head. It was only his hand on his sister that kept him tethered to reality.

He was being touched; some older man putting a hand on his shoulder, someone he didn't recognize. Words were murmured, fuzzy and quiet. They dripped away.

Terra tugged on his arm, and he crouched down to hear her better.

"Can we get away from the people? I wanna see mom."

"We can't see her," Monty said, but he knew what she meant.

He led them to the pyre, where the torches were not yet lit. Together, they stared at the small wooden box that held what remained of Delila's body. Was there any left at all, or had it all crumbled into dust? Was Nal'Gee still feasting on her?

That last intrusive thought made his stomach clench, and he stared hard at the coffin. The dragging hours of the last couple days had taken

him back and forth between his beliefs and his skepticism; his outlook
and the unexplained.

Those leaves.

Would Nal'Gee still be in his mother's body, waiting to strike the next
victim?

"Monty—you're hurting me."

"Mm?" He looked down—he was holding Terra's hand tightly, and
growing tighter by the second. His teeth were clenched. Breathing out, he
loosened his grip and his jaw and apologized. "Don't know what's wrong
with me," he muttered.

To his surprise, Terra grabbed his own hand tighter now, though she
wasn't quite strong enough to hurt him.

"Nothing's wrong with you," she said, in a way that made it sound like
he was stupid to think otherwise.

Was she right? Maybe about him. But something was just...wrong.

The box sat there, plain; unmarked and unremarkable, atop a pile of
wood that would burn easy and hot, the sending fire and reading of the
rites carrying his mother's soul to the beyond forever.

Unless Nal'Gee eats that, too.

"Stop it," he whispered, and hoped it was too quiet for Terra to hear.
You're going to drive yourself crazy, and Terra needs you.

He kept telling himself that, but who needed whom right now? Who
was the one holding onto him, bringing him back to the here and now
when all he wanted to do was float away, scream, maybe go to the beyond
himself so he could somehow see if a witch's vengeful spirit was
destroying his town and his family one person at a time?

Monty held Terra's hand and he breathed in deep, smelling the dry
wood and the cool night air.

"Monty. Terra."

The two of them turned inward and around, their hands coming apart.
Judge Mullen was there, hands behind his back, face dripping with
solemnity.

"Hello, Judge," Monty said, more out of reflex than anything, his
words hollow.

"I am so very sorry," Judge Mullen said. "I know the words don't help much, but I will make sure that Delila—your mother—is sent peacefully and swiftly into the beyond."

Can you do that, Judge? Can you guarantee that to us? I'd give you our whole house and everything inside if you could make sure it was true. I'd—

Terra was pulling on him again, tearing him out of his thoughts—again. Time and the world around him was disappearing in great gouges.

"Come on, Monty." She was pulling him to the side, where they could step off the platform. "We have to get down." A note of pleading came through. She was starting to break.

He followed his sister, barely noticing the Judge as he walked past him. It was darker now. Someone had lit the torches further back, and Monty saw that the crowd had grown significantly in size. More people had flocked to the sending while he had his back to them, eyes boring into the unlit pyre. Were all these people really here for his mother? It seemed there were over two hundred, with more emerging from the darkness and into the torchlight as he watched.

Fwump. A nearby torch flared into existence, one of the two that braced the stage. The lighter doused his own torch and slipped into the crowd.

"Monty." A hand on his shoulder.

He turned, holding Terra's hand, and it was the Judge, looking at him with some kind of pity and patience, stopping him from leaving the platform.

"You two can stay," Mullen said. "The pyre is for the family and the Judge."

"Oh...right." Terra blushed, embarrassed. "I saw other people leaving..."

"That's quite all right. Here, come to my other side. I will read your mother the words of the sending now." Mullen slipped his hand off Monty's shoulder and hefted his thick book up to chest level, nodding slightly to his right to direct the two Bellamy children.

"I'm sorry," Terra whispered, and Monty told her it was okay, and then the Judge was reading those damned familiar words, and all he could do was stare out at the crowd, holding his sister's hand.

"We have gathered for the final sending of Delila Bellamy, a life lost too soon..."

Did Judge Mullen say that about Ma Kettle? It was a crass and unfunny thought, and it brought no smile.

He found himself looking for the Kettles, though he wasn't sure why. Last time, and the time before that, this platform had been crowded with Kettles. It was just the two of them now, Monty and Terra, their combined size perhaps matching that of Henry Kettle's stature. Though the man had lost some meat off his bones lately.

Judge Mullen continued to read. "The beyond awaits, the soul ready to be burned free of the worldly remains. Delila Bellamy will watch her family from the other side."

Terra was crying now, and Monty pulled her closer, her head resting above his hip. He felt her narrow frame shuddering, but her sobs were silent. She was always a quiet crier. Mom had worried that if she ever got hurt in the field or the barn and no one was looking, they wouldn't be able to find her.

He had no tears to give. Mullen's reading crowded around his ears like a swarm of bugs, a muffled and unintelligible buzzing that he couldn't swat away.

Someone was approaching the stage, and Monty recognized him as the torch lighter, holding a freshly-wrapped-and-soaked torch in one hand. Carrying it to the stage for him, because surely he would be the one asked to light their mother's pyre.

The lighter walked slowly. Everything moved slowly; even Terra's sobs against him felt rigid and measured. When he took a breath, he heard it rattle around his mouth and brush across his teeth on the way to his lungs. And a moment of piercing, crystal clarity followed.

This is how she gets to another body.

This is how she gets to another body.

Out came the breath, slow and harsh. Nal'Gee, latching onto people, draining their life force into her own—it was one at a time. Ma Kettle was burnt, and then it got her daughter. Audrey was burnt, and then mom got sick. And who was right there, closest to the pyre, dropping the torch? Delila, when Henry couldn't.

Breathe. Blink.

Once his mother was sent, once her pyre was lit and her body was burnt away, Nal'Gee would be free. Released, once again, to swirl into someone else. Inhaled, perhaps, or something more otherworldly.

The lighter stopped before the stage, right before Monty. He raised the torch to him. The Judge was done reading, looking at Monty easily, but expectantly. Terra was still at his side, but her crying was done. She stared at the torch.

"Go on, Monty," Judge Mullen said, and Terra tightened her grip on him, letting out a small, pained sound.

What if he lit this pyre and Nal'Gee flew into Terra? Or into him? The Judge; the torch handler; one of the townspeople who were kind enough to be here when his mother was sent into the beyond? He couldn't let that happen.

His breath came faster now, and his heart started to hammer in his chest. The world grew sharp in his vision. He could see each tongue of the torch flames in the crowd, and he realized that a panic was upon him, one far too powerful and fast to stop.

When the lighter pushed the torch closer to him, he shrieked. He batted it away like it was a snake and it went tumbling to the ground.

"Monty!" The Judge closed his book with a heavy thud. "It's time to—"

"No! Don't light it!" Monty had found his voice, and he was using it to scream. It all made sense, so suddenly, and it filled him with terror. "Don't light it, she'll get free!"

The lighter bent down to pick up the torch, and Monty pulled free of Terra's hand and jumped down into the grass. He shoved the handler away, grabbing the torch from the ground and heaving it over the pyre. He was strong, and it was a good throw. It disappeared completely in the darkness before it even hit the ground.

The crowd was murmuring, but no one approached him, not even the torch handler. Monty panted, unable to catch his breath.

"Monty, what's going on?" Terra said, making him turn around. She was on her hands and knees on the stage, looking down at him.

"She's in mom!" he said to her. "Nal'Gee's in mom, and if we burn her body, she's going to get into someone else!"

He didn't know if anyone else heard him, but he didn't care. Terra's eyes were wide with shock, but Monty saw the understanding there. The agreement, with only a little hesitance. Terra knew. He knew. No one else knew, and he couldn't let this sending happen.

Judge Mullen was frozen on the platform at first, but only briefly. In fluid strides, he descended the platform stairs and came down to Monty, while the villagers backed away. The crowd curved around the two of them.

"It's all right, son," Mullen said, putting a hand on Monty's forearm. "I know this is hard. But it's what needs to be done for her soul."

"No, you don't—" *Understand,* was what Monty planned to say, but of course Mullen didn't understand, and of course he wouldn't. There was no explanation of this that would make the Judge change his mind.

Monty said, "Her soul needs more time here," and he brushed off the Judge's arm and hauled himself up onto the platform, swinging his leg up onto the wood.

He had to get her off the pyre.

"Monty!" The Judge cried, and he heard several other shouts from the crowd. It didn't matter. Mullen's short frame wouldn't allow him to climb the platform—he'd have to go all the way around to the stairs. And Monty would have his mother in his arms by then. He'd pull her body out of the casket and run it to the next town if that was what it took.

Up and onto the stage and past Terra, he ran. The pyre stretched over him, vast and wide. The casket rested just above eye level. He grabbed onto the thick branches and started climbing.

28

The shouts were louder now, and Monty could hear the crowd start to move around. Were they all coming to get him?

It didn't matter. He wrapped his fingers around a heavy branch and pulled himself up, his feet lifting off the ground. He was going to get there.

The branch slid out of the pile, jostled free, and he dropped back down. Loosing a frustrated grunt, he grabbed another one and pulled, but the same thing happened. They were thick and dry, ready to burn, but it was just a pile of wood.

"No!" Monty said, and he bunched up the big muscles of his legs and leapt up, thrusting his chest over the top of the pyre. Sharp sticks and bark dug into him, drawing blood from a half-dozen places, but he barely felt the pain. He scrabbled for purchase, his feet finding gaps to slide in, his fingers finding stiff knobs to grab hold of. He pulled, and he knew he'd get there. The casket was inches from him now.

Someone had his feet. They pulled, and a broken stick scraped along his belly and drew pain like thin fire. He cried out and he reached for a more stable grip, but then there was another pair of hands on him, and he couldn't fight it.

"Don't hurt him! Monty!" Terra's voice cut through the din, and as he was yanked off the pyre, he looked down to see her reaching for him, held back by the group of people who had come up onto the stage. One of them, he noticed, was the elder Rodney Talhauer, and it was he who pushed the rest of the men away and threw Monty over his shoulder like he was a sack of potatoes.

"Don't wiggle, kid," Rodney said, his gruff voice deadly serious. "You're bein' all kinds of nuts, and I get it, but don't you fight me. Let yer mom get sent."

He walked Monty away from the pyre, back toward the stairs. Terra turned after them, but someone else had her, too, holding her around the waist while she screamed.

Monty tried to yell something at the man holding his sister, but his breath was gone. His chest and stomach flared with pain, and he was sure he was bleeding all over Rodney's shoulder. By the time he could talk, they were down the steps.

"It's not good," he gasped. "Rodney—Mr. Talhauer—I'm not nuts. Nal'Gee is in her, and if she burns, she'll be free again to kill someone else!"

Rodney bent and set him down, but stood in front of him. His wide frame completely blocked any view of the stage.

"Don't," he told Monty, and he didn't need to finish the thought. The behemoth of a man was like a brick wall with arms; Monty knew he'd never get past him.

He peered around Rodney to see the stage mostly empty, with just the lighter and the Judge preset. The lighter held a new torch.

"You have to believe me," he said, and that was when someone approached and set Terra down right next to him. She looked frightened to death, staring up at Rodney's bulk.

"I got 'em," Rodney told the man. "Go on."

"The sickness that killed the Kettles and my mom isn't a sickness," Monty continued. "It's a spirit from the Dromm forest sucking the life out of people!"

Rodney didn't offer a response to that. He stood stoic, arms at his sides. When Monty tried to speak again, he cut him off.

"It's almost over," he said. "Then ya move on, however you do it. Don't make a bunch of enemies here, now, kid. Wilhelm is already sick of ya."

Monty didn't know who that was, but he imagined it was the torch carrier who was now handing the lit torch to Judge Mullen, and the Judge was delivering the final set of rites now, naming the burner as himself.

It was Terra who broke free from her spot, but even her small, quick frame wasn't fast enough to escape Rodney. While he stopped her dead with just one hand, Judge Mullen lowered the torch to the pyre, and the pile of dried wood, the casket, and Delila's body all went up in the blaze.

The heat washed over them, and Monty sunk to the ground.

"Come here, Terra," he said, sitting in the cold grass. Rodney let her go, and Monty pulled her to him, closing his eyes and holding his head against hers. The crowd disappeared; the torchlight; Rodney Talhauer. All that remained was the pulsing heat and his shivering sister at his side. Monty prayed, and Terra joined him.

"Take her, gods, and bless her journey." The words, murmured softly at all sendings, overwhelmed him now, reminding him of his father's death. Terra spoke with him.

"Grant her passage and hold her in esteem, so that she may do the same for us when we arrive."

The fire roared. By now, her body would be consumed, cast bit by bit into the night sky, and releasing two souls instead of one.

Monty prayed that he was wrong, but he knew he was not.

29

Two weeks after the burning of Delila Bellamy, Elrich Mullen was once more planted in his office, looking over the plans and documents of her farm. He had been holed up there, almost completely without contact, for the last eighteen hours, because words on official documents were all that made sense to him right now. Words were all that kept him from losing his mind.

His villagers were dying.

Whatever strange illness had swept away the matriarchs of those two families was now laying waste to more and more people throughout the town. How many had gone over the past fortnight? A dozen? Was it more? Elrich couldn't remember, and he gave great effort not to, but he thought that it was.

"Allotted an acreage of two-hundred and twenty, to be expanded..." He started reading aloud, fighting the whirling questions in his mind.

It had gotten so bad that, upon conference with the priests and with Dr. Tobias, he had begun reading the rites and performing the final sending at the site of the bodies, burning them in small fires on the grass behind their homes with only the family in attendance, if there was any.

It was easy to burn the bodies. There was almost nothing left. Wrap it in a blanket, soak it in kerosene, and light it. It burned hot, and most importantly, it burned fast. It almost took longer to read the sending words than it did to burn the damned corpse.

Of course, hardly a day would go by before he'd be called again.

"...granted to Montille Bellamy and Delila Bellamy, the latter with child to be named for the father or the deceased aunt, Terramia Bellamy, for the total sum..."

And when he was called, he was forced to leave his office, to go out into the streets. Among the villagers, who had questions. Questions that grew increasingly anxious, loud, and incessant as the days wore on and the deaths piled up.

Judge Elrich Mullen had no answers for them. Neither did Dr. Tobias, no matter how many of the blackened bodies he examined. He called it an autopsy, but how does one autopsy an empty bag full of viscous swill that used to be organs? The bones were like jelly, barely holding shape, and they collapsed into mush when they were touched. Elrich knew this because Tobias had shared, and not because he had asked.

"...taxes assessed yearly as follows...paid...paid...paid..."

He licked his lips. His eyes moved frantically across the page. He read the words aloud, but he didn't listen to himself.

The last rushed sending he had attended was for the brother-by-marriage of Rodney Talhauer, the father of the boy he'd had a chance to berate in the short weeks before his uncle's body was shriveled into nothing and burned like the same.

His father—

"Dim-witted, bellowing *behemoth!*" Elrich screeched without realizing it.

—had gone so far as to take Elrich by the shoulders, shouting in his face, blaming him for the death of his family and his neighbors. Elrich had put that to bed quickly, pinching his strong fingers into the fleshy web of fat and tendon beneath each of Rodney's thumbs, digging hard enough to make the beast hiss and withdraw (of course, Tobias and Priest Yorick, or Yanelle, or whoever-the-fuck-it-was, had sat there and watched with stupid, hanging jaws), reminding the overgrown fellow in short words that laying hands on a Judge was a capital offense

And then they had burned the body and left, Mullen striding ahead and ignoring any person who tried to get his attention.

Since then, he'd been locked in here, reading and muttering. Exhaustion dragged his eyes down and colored the skin below them, but he read and pulled more scrolls and read those, all the while knowing one simple thing: he was losing control of his town. People were dying, and there was no end in sight. It would only be a matter of time before the unease and worry became a full panic—even in his bare brushes with the public, he'd heard the word *plague* uttered more than once—and from there would come an exodus.

Bellamy. He needed the Bellamy farm. And he wouldn't get it if the children decided to flee town, or if Monty caught sick next and died before he could strike a deal with him. He might be able to buy it from the kingdom in that case, but that could take months. A direct deal with the family could be done the next day.

Monty was being peppered with questions and inquiries just the same as he was, as the courier told him all the same, no doubt curious for the answers himself.

People are wondering what's going on...

Is there anything I can say to Meera Sand? She's relentless.

Has Dr. Tobias said anything?

Elrich shook his head hard enough to make it throb, though gods knew that was happening enough on its own lately. He thought he could wait until things settled down, but things weren't moving in that direction. It was getting worse, it was getting *bad,* and it was happening faster with every passing day.

He had to act fast if he was going to secure the land he needed. And the way to do it had just slithered into him, a plan drawn from his frantic plotting inch-by-inch until it was fully formulated.

Mullen would sleep later. It was time to talk to Monty.

30

For Monty, the last two weeks had been a mix of dragging, painful hours and a horrifying blur of death constantly visiting him each day. If it wasn't memories of his mother's sending, it was wondering who at the sending had seen his outburst, and who had just been told secondhand. The time with his mother on his mind was slow, and the times when he was told there had been another death—and he was the first to hear about half of them—made everything feel like it was flying by, and *he* was the lethargic one.

But what could he do?

The tears had come within that time, two days after the sending. He knew they would have to, and he was just glad he was alone when they did.

It was an evening when he was heading back to his quarters in the Commons. With no warning, the sadness had overwhelmed him like a tall wave, and he ducked off the street and into an alley. There, he collapsed against a wall, his messenger bag slapping into the wood. He slid down to the ground, his knees bent, legs askew, his vision blurred until he closed his eyes and let the Tears come out. There was no sound. Just a deep, deep pool of loss escaping him a drop at a time.

He felt better, in some small way, when it was over, but he still thought that his mother deserved more. He wondered if Terra had had a breakdown of her own, and imagined that she must have. He just didn't think that she'd want to hide it in the same way that he did.

But it was a trait they had learned from their mother: a strong face for others, but not to be afraid of yourself.

Terra was staying in his quarters now, ever since the sending. It was snug, but Monty didn't mind. He much preferred it to her being alone at home, and he knew that she did, too, even though he was the one to suggest that she come and live in town, after ensuring the Gartens could house their few farm animals.

She had gotten into reading lately, ever since he'd secured a book on fairy tales and legends for her. Terra had asked for it the day after the sending. And since then, she'd pulled at least three more books from the small library in the Commons, sitting and reading by the light of the sun and the candles.

Two weeks after the sending, the two of them were sitting on the bed in his quarters. Terra was reading, and Monty, preoccupied, was pretending to look along when a knock sounded. They both jerked their heads up.

Monty got up from the bed, taking the few short steps across the room to the door. It was late in the evening, so when he opened the door to find Judge Mullen there, surprise flickered across his face. He assumed that the man had gone home by now. In fact, Monty had seen him leave his office and lock the door behind him.

Mullen didn't miss the surprise. He spoke with his usual formality, sounding tired. "I do hate to disturb you after hours, Monty," he said, and looking past him, added, "And you, Terra. But I need to borrow you for a minute, Monty, if you don't mind."

Monty did mind, a bit—he always felt reluctant to leave Terra alone, as though he might somehow be able to stop a Dromm spirit from entering her body and pulling out her life as long as he was within a few feet of her.

But like most requests from the Judge, it wasn't really a request.

The man didn't look well—his eyes held heavy circles beneath, his hair was a little unkempt, and his robe was shifted off to the side and dirty on the bottom from road dust. He looked like he hadn't slept in over a day, and as far as Monty knew, that was true. So it was best not to try any temper he might be treading on.

He told Terra he'd be back soon, hoping it wasn't a lie, and he closed the door behind him.

Instead of walking the two of them back to his office, Mullen took them outside through the front doors of the Commons and to the street. It was winter-dark and cold, but Monty liked the brisk snip of the air and how quiet and empty the streets were.

"This must be a difficult time for you and Terra," the Judge said, as they started down the main road of Irisa.

"It has been," Monty agreed, wondering why the Judge was walking him through town, especially since lately he'd seemed so eager to be shut up in his office. Maybe he needed fresh air.

"It has been difficult for me as well," Mullen commented. "The deaths...the endless sendings. And of course now I am worried about you, my confidant and courier, and his family. I noticed that you have been having Terra stay in your quarters."

It hadn't occurred to Monty that such a thing might be against the rules. "I hope that's all right, Judge Mullen. I just don't want her to be alone."

The Judge waved away his concerns with a lazy hand. "It's fine. I mean to say—I understand, you know. I think of Terra alone in that house, and it makes even me worry. It's good of you to be with her. You're strong for your family, Monty. And now you're the one who has to make the tough decisions. The ones that will affect your future, and your sister's."

They turned onto another road, Mullen falling silent while Monty took in those words. *Don't suppose you can help me decide how to deal with Nal'Gee, sir?* he thought, and the darkness hid his humorless grin.

"Your farm," Mullen said after a pause. "I'll be frank, Monty, because I'm too tired for much else. I don't think you and Terra will be able to maintain it with your mother gone."

Mild indignation thrummed in Monty, and he said, "That isn't true, I've been running—"

"You've done a lot," Mullen said, and his tone was firm, "but for every part of that business you've touched, there's five more you've never seen. Trust me. I've done it myself. And I ask, have you given the farm any thought since the sending?"

With burning in his cheeks, Monty realized that he hadn't. In fact, he'd barely been back to the house at all after that night, not even to sort through his mother's papers. The sheaves and stacks which had once been so important to him had completely disappeared from his mind. Thinking of them now, he felt a little sick.

He hadn't given the Judge an answer, and Mullen didn't need one; silence was enough. "I'm concerned for you and Terra, Monty. You have enough to handle right now, and your living situation shouldn't have to be a burden."

"We're fine, Judge."

"Let me say what I have to say." Judge Mullen stopped, and he looked up at Monty. "I will buy your farm from you, Monty. I will pay you a hefty sum, fifty percent more than the worth of the land. Enough money for you to build a house here in town and pay the taxes on it for the next five years, at least. You and Terra can move on from this tragedy."

The unexpected proposal sat down heavily on Monty. He struggled with it.

"Sell the farm?" he asked.

"Move on," Judge Mullen repeated. "I know you don't want to live in that house anymore, Monty, and I know the pain you feel when you walk through the front door. I've been thinking about it at length the past few days, and I knew I had to find a solution for you. I think this is a good idea for you and for your sister."

The words sounded sincere, and Monty actually felt a little touched that the Judge would think of his family in such a way. His cheeks burned again. Since Mullen's furious outburst, Monty had been staying at arm's length from him. But thinking on it now, he'd been judging Mullen at the tail end of an extremely stressful time—and now the man was willing to offer him a wheelbarrow full of gold for his farm so that he and his sister could have another place to live.

He was glad the Judge couldn't see him in the darkness. He was sure his face was pasted with shame.

"Judge Mullen...that's very generous of you." And it was. Kind, even. "What do you think?"

The night was quiet, and Monty's mind was blank. Accepting was the right thing to do...right?

"It's what your mother would have wanted," Judge Mullen said, and that snapped Monty's thoughts into focus.

No, it's not.

But this wasn't just about his mother and her distrust of Judge Mullen. She was gone. Whatever the Judge's motivations were, his points were true, and it probably would be better for Monty and Terra to be away from home.

Away from home...forever?

"I'll need to think about it some," Monty said at last. There was no way he could sort through his thoughts in the next few minutes.

Judge Mullen didn't respond. Monty thought he saw his brow furrow, but in the dark, he couldn't be sure. Before he could look any closer, Judge Mullen gave him a nod.

"Yes, of course. It's not an easy decision. But you know what the right thing is to do. In the meantime..." Mullen began walking again, turning them around to head back towards the Commons. "The quarters in the Commons are far too small for both you and Terra."

Monty could have refuted that, but it would have been a lie.

"I am going to arrange a better living space for the two of you here in town," Judge Mullen said. "No argument. It will be paid for, so don't worry about that."

"I—Judge, are you serious?"

"Always, Monty," Mullen replied. "Consider it collateral—a gesture of my goodwill and intent toward the deal for the farm. It will be an experiment, of sorts, to see how the two of you feel about living in town. I think you'll find it pleasant."

Another flush of warmth. "Thank you, sir. We both appreciate that very much."

Careful, his mother's voice whispered, making the hairs on his neck stand. *Careful with this man.*

Mullen smiled, his visage visible as they approached the Commons and the single torch that illuminated the doors. "I try to achieve some good, even if it's for only a pair of my townspeople." He snuffed the torch with the tin cap that hung from the sconce. The smoke dispelled, tickling Monty's nose. "I pray that this difficult time passes soon, so that I might do more. This is where I'll leave you, Monty. Tomorrow, I'll have someone get you and Terra moved into your new quarters."

Mullen bade him farewell and set off in the opposite direction, toward his own home. Monty lingered outside the doors of the Commons for only a moment before pulling them open and stepping inside.

It was a short walk from the front door to his quarters where Terra was waiting, but he didn't take it just yet. He leaned back against the wall, closing his eyes. He wanted to hear the voice of his mother again and listen to her advice. But he couldn't make it come.

The last two weeks had been a strange, blurring hell, and the only thing that kept him focused was Terra. He did his work and made few mistakes, which was surprising, considering how muddled his head felt. Whenever he could latch onto a thought, it was a sad string of memories, or the threatening rope of Nal'Gee—the threat he still had no proof of, but could not shake from his mind.

And all the while, people had continued to die.

He went back to his quarters, seeing that Terra had made it through an impressive amount of pages in the time that he had been gone. She read faster than he did, and faster than their mother had. It made him smile.

"How's the book?" Monty asked her, sitting down on the bed.

"It's good," Terra said. "I still haven't found anything about Nal'Gee, though."

"I'm not sure it's in there," Monty said. He'd never read the legend, and neither had Terra; they'd only heard it from dad. It might not be written anywhere, but it didn't hurt to look and try to learn more.

"What did the Judge want?" Terra looked up from her book.

"He..." Monty tilted his head, stalling, but only for a moment. If he was going to be honest with Terra about Nal'Gee, there was no sense in keeping secrets about anything else. "He wants to buy the farm."

"The whole farm? Our house and everything?"

"Yeah," Monty said. "He said he'd give us a lot for it. So that we could build a house in town."

Terra twisted her hair around one finger. "Why's he want our house?"

"He just wants to do a nice thing for us," Monty said. "We talked about how...hard it is to be there. And that it might be better for us to, um—" What had Mullen said? "—*move on.*"

It seemed obvious now that the Judge just wanted the land. He had his own mansion on the east side of town, and Monty was sure he wouldn't be doing any farming. People didn't buy land over its value out of the goodness of their hearts, even if it that was part of it.

But was that worth worrying about when it had nothing to do with them?

"I don't like living there right now," Terra said. She curled her hair around her fingers, uncurled it, and then did it again. "But mom would hate it if we sold the farm. I mean, she would—she would have hated it."

"I know."

Monty sat up a little straighter. Terra was thinking the same way he was, and that was something that he noticed more and more. It was probably time to stop being surprised by it, and maybe even time to stop thinking of her as a little kid.

"He's gonna move us into a bigger quarters tomorrow," he told her. "Let's give it some time. See how you like living in town after a little while. Then we can decide."

"Really? I'll have my own bed? And a place to put books?" Terra let her fingers slide out of her hair.

"Probably," Monty said, and added, "but I get the biggest bedroom."

They read the book together for a while before Monty slept. The legends about other monsters and spirits helped, oddly enough, to push Nal'Gee from his mind, and he dozed off before his sister did.

Terra stayed up to read.

31

The unlikely thing to set Monty's actions in motion was a visit from Meera Sand, the woman who irked his mother with her polite but unwelcome offers of help. In his work in town, he'd seen her husband quite a bit, but not her.

Mullen did indeed come by the next day to move them into their new quarters, which he'd managed to arrange during the early morning. He waited till Monty's lunchtime lull in work to bring him and Terra to the new place, which was five minutes from the Commons.

"Patricia Stetter will be your landlord, of sorts. She owns the house," Mullen had told them, but mostly Monty, as they walked along. Terra had her ears perked and listening. "You know her."

He did know Patricia, barely—you can only get to know someone so well by delivering scrolls to them, unless they were the kind to stop you and talk to you as you were trying to leave, and Patricia wasn't.

The house was big—big enough to take Monty's breath away at the thought of living in it, but Judge Mullen explained that Patricia had split the space inside into five separate living quarters that she rented out. That was fine with Monty; there was such a thing as too much space. He had only to think of his house on the farm, sitting empty, to know that.

They had carried everything they wanted to bring with them, so moving in was done the moment they stepped through the door. Their space was on the ground floor, and it had two bedrooms, and a kitchen that was big enough to house a little sitting area beside its narrow table. The windows were wide, and let in a lot of light.

This is really nice, Monty thought, and almost protested to the Judge—he was really willing to pay for this? He knew the Judge would just smile and nod and Monty would feel stupid for asking, so he instead thanked the Judge again, and Terra did, too, commenting on how much she liked it.

"I am glad to hear that," he'd told them. "If you need anything else or have trouble, Patricia would be the one to speak to. But I am sure that will not be needed."

Mullen was right about that. The quarters were spacious and clean, but still cozy enough for the siblings to not feel too far apart from one another, even in their separate rooms. Monty did have the chance to briefly meet Patricia, an older blonde woman who walked stooped over but looked strong enough to throw him ten feet through the air. She was businesslike and pleasant, thanking him for being a tenant, and Monty didn't probe into whether or not she knew the money was coming from Judge Mullen. Probably she did.

It was just before Meera Sand's visit that Monty was thinking that living in town—really living there, not just having an eight-by-eight space tucked into the Commons—was actually quite nice. They'd spent two nights there so far, and he wasn't pining for home the way he thought he might, nor did Terra seem to be homesick. Not for the house, nor for their tiny former quarters.

"Imagine having a whole house here," Monty was saying to Terra, before their conversation was cut short by a knock at the door.

It was the first visitor they'd had. They knocked again, three taps that weren't heavy or particularly loud. Monty knew how the Judge knocked, and it wasn't like that. Perhaps the landlord?

Monty opened the door to see the plump, solemn face of Meera Sand. She quickly lowered her raised fist, folding her hands in front of her.

"Hello, Monty," she said, adding, "and Terra," when she joined Monty at the door.

"Oh—hi, Meera." Monty wanted to ask why she was here, but wasn't sure how to do it without sounding rude. His mom would have known how.

"I heard you two were living in town," Meera said, moving her gaze down to Terra and putting on a small, sad smile. "I wanted to come by and offer my condolences for the loss of your mother. I hadn't had a chance to say so."

Monty tried not to think about the burning, and how Meera had almost certainly there been there to see what happened.

"Um, thanks, Meera," he said, the words coming out awkwardly, while Terra nodded along.

Meera moved right along, not perturbed. "I wish I'd known the two of you were here sooner. I'm sure your space could use some warming up. You don't decorate, do you, Monty? Terra?" Before either of them had finished shaking their heads, she continued, "I have some lovely hanging shawls that would really brighten the walls in here, especially with all the light coming in."

Monty thought that the walls were plenty bright. "Thanks, Meera, but that's okay. We're still getting used to the place."

"Aren't shawls for wearing?" Terra asked, but Meera either didn't hear her or thought she was joking, because she just smiled and kept talking.

"Everything could use a little brightening." The smile slipped off her face, and she leaned forward a bit, her hands still held together before her. "It's been so terrible lately, but you know that, don't you, Monty? Town courier and all. So many people are getting sick, and from what I hear, Dr. Tobias doesn't know the first thing about it. Even after looking at all the bodies!"

Monty glanced down to Terra, but she didn't seem bothered. "I know, it's—"

"Yesterday they sent three people at once! Just stacked up the bodies on a tiny little pyre and lit them all! I've never heard of anything like that." Meera sounded truly horrified. One of her hands came up to her chest, pressing against her heart. "Neither of you are feeling sick, are you?"

"No." Terra had to answer for Monty, because he was stunned. Three people being burned at once? Dying, right after the other?

She's getting stronger. Strong enough to live in multiple people, or to kill them so fast she can go to another one before the day is over.

"That's good, that's good." Meera's voice quavered. "It's all happening so fast. If my Ed got sick, I don't know what I'd do."

And this is all happening while I bury my head in the sand inside this house.

He was ashamed. He'd been running without even realizing it.

"Don't worry, Meera," Monty said, and it felt right to put his hand on her shoulder, so he did. He looked down at her shorter frame. "This will—this will run its course."

"I hope so," Meera said, and her voice was a whisper, but she did meet Monty's eye. "I've lived here my whole life, you know. Ed moved here some twenty years ago, but I've been an Irisa woman since I was a babe, and I've never felt this scared of my own town. Both of you stay safe. Stay inside, maybe, just in case."

After she left, Monty closed the door but didn't move. He said to Terra, "This is getting bad."

"It's already pretty bad," she responded. "Do you really think they're sending a bunch of people at a time?"

"I don't think she lied about it." He looked back toward Terra's bedroom, where he knew the book she was reading—a new one, now—rested on her bed, the corner of her blanket tucked between the pages to mark her place. "Is there anything about Nal'Gee in that book?"

"Nothing," Terra said with disappointment. "I wish there was someone we could ask. It might take me forever to find the right book."

Monty had never heard about Nal'Gee from anyone but his parents. Could he pull any information from the Gartens? Not Mr. Garten, that was for sure, and his hopes weren't much higher for his wife.

"I want to take a look around town," Monty said. "You wanna come?" It felt like he hadn't really paid attention to Irisa since his mother's sending, just drifting through his work and not listening to what people were saying.

It shouldn't take Meera Sand arriving at his door to show him how bad things were getting.

32

It only took a quick jaunt through town and a few conversations to show him that things were even worse.

Before the unsettling news started coming in, they went to Kettle's, surprised to see it open and doing business, with the usual amount of people—maybe a little less—walking in and out. The sight made Monty smile, and he imagined Henry working behind the counter.

"Let's go in and say hi," Terra said, heading towards the store, but Monty stopped her.

"I don't know if Henry would want to see us. I mean, I'm sure he would," Monty corrected, "but it might bring up some bad memories. I was in his house when Audrey died, and mom's sending was the last big one with the whole town..." Monty wasn't sure if Henry had been there.

Terra said, "I didn't think about that. Maybe you're right."

"Come on. I want to keep going."

Their stroll through town took them to sharing a meat pie at the west corner bakery, Bradley's shop. The same man who burned his ear with talk of poisoning and conspiracies turned out to be the one who let him in on the next piece of information.

Monty had expected Bradley, garrulous at best and a blabbermouth at worst, to have something to say, but he didn't expect it to be useful. When he asked Bradley how things were going lately, Bradley was quick to spill.

Very quick.

"Business would probably be worse with all the people dyin', except that no one is able to leave town," Bradley said. "So I have lots of folks coming here for lunch and dinner and talking up a storm. I'm thinking of starting to open up early for breakfast now, if people—"

"What did you say?"

"No one's able to leave?"

Monty spoke first, then Terra a split second later. Bradley stopped his jawing and looked back and forth between the two siblings sitting at the small table outside his bakery.

"Well, yeah, you ain't heard? I was about to ask *you* about it, courier," Bradley said, a smug smile settling onto his face.

"I hadn't," Monty said, annoyed with the man but needing to hear what he had to say.

"I think Henry was the first," Bradley said, talking again the moment Monty's lips closed. "Henry Kettle. Heard he tried to pack up his store and take his family elsewhere. Can't blame him, I guess, even though I know he makes more gold than he needs without even tryin'."

"All the Kettles are gonna leave?" Terra asked.

Bradley shook his head. " *Were.* Henry went to talk to the Judge—selling the building back to the town, or somethin'—and I dunno what all was said, but the bottom line was that Henry couldn't leave. Violation of contract or somethin'. Henry didn't put up much of a fight. Just went ahead and reopened the store instead."

"So he—"

"But he ain't the only one I heard of." Bradley put the heels of his hands on the table and leaned in closer, but he didn't lower his voice. "Townspeople, too. I mean, folks here who ain't got businesses or land. They talk to the landlords and the officials about movin'—cuz they're scared, lot of 'em. And they're either talked out of it by Mullen himself, gods know how, or they're strong-armed into staying."

Monty looked at Bradley until he moved back a bit, giving him some space. "How can they do that?"

Bradley shrugged, standing up straight again. "Relocation fees. Unpaid taxes, plenty of that in Irisa. And if that don't work, threatening 'em, straight up. Heard the Judge got himself a well-paid crew of...I guess you can call 'em 'residency enforcers.' They'll dangle tax levies, and they'll break your wagon wheels if that ain't enough. Even some travelers got trapped, someone was saying."

Terra scoffed, a sound Monty had never heard from her before. But he felt just as skeptical.

"I've never heard of anything like that," Monty told him.

"Ain't nothing official." He gave another shrug. "Just what I heard. People try to leave, they find reasons to make 'em stay. Not that I'm going anywhere."

Monty nodded, although he hadn't asked. "All right. We're gonna eat now, Bradley."

Once he was gone, Terra asked, "You think that's true?"

"Not all of it," Monty said. "Probably not even most of it. Bradley's known to exaggerate. But..."

"But you think some of it might be true."

Monty grinned before taking a bite of the pie while it was still hot. "He's not an outright liar. He's just a little stupid."

That made Terra laugh. They finished their lunch with lighter talk, but Bradley's rumor drilled its own little space into the back of Monty's head, nesting. Even if it was only partly true, it was something unheard of. Just like burning multiple bodies at once.

The final piece dropped into place after lunch. They were moving steadily towards the east side of town when Monty was stopped in the street by the frantic housekeeper of Tobias Pelkin, or as he was more well-known around town: Dr. Tobias.

The housekeeper grabbed his arm with both hands and pleaded for him to come with her.

"He was fine earlier, I think he was," the young woman said to him, after pulling him off the street to Dr. Tobias's front door with Terra in tow. Monty knew her name was Bella—she was the one who took messages for Dr. Tobias when he wasn't around. "But he hasn't been himself all day, I think he's sick, I was making him some soup and cutting bread and—"

"Stop, stop," Monty said, holding steady while Bella tugged on him. "What's going on?"

"I think he's dead," Bella whispered, and then the tears came. "I think he got what's getting everyone else. I can't bear to look, but I saw his head poking out of the covers, and it was—his hair's all..."

Dr. Tobias was dead?

"He was talking to me, and then I think he fell asleep for a little while, that's when I went to cook, but I went to go check on him cuz he was so awful quiet and he just...he looks small. Under the blankets. Like...like what happens to the people who die of the black."

The black. So it had a name now.

"Monty." Terra was tugging on him now, pulling hard on his shirt. "We should go and see."

"Terra, you shouldn't—"

"Please come inside," Bella sobbed. "I don't want to have to do it myself. I can't bear it!"

"I found something about Nal'Gee," she said to him, and the look in her eyes was urgent. Insistent. "I didn't tell you yet because it wasn't anything big like we wanted. But if she's really in him right now, I think we can see her."

33

M onty let Bella take them into the house, and he made sure to shut the front door behind them. He needed to talk to Terra, but it would be better if Bella didn't hear anything. She was worked up enough.

"Bella, go and sit down. Let me check on him. If he's—then I'll take the news to Judge Mullen. You don't need to do anything."

"Okay, okay," Bella said, wiping her face with the backs of her hands. "I'll just...the soup..."

She wandered back towards the kitchen. She didn't seem to notice that Terra was there, the small girl looking curiously around the house from where they stood.

Monty ushered them a little farther away, into a branching hall. The house was big, and Bella hadn't told them where Dr. Tobias had been lying down. But if he was dead, they'd find him. The smell would take them there.

"Okay," Monty said, hushed. "I really don't like taking you in here, but..."

"I saw mom, you know," Terra said, her lip quivering only a little bit. "I've seen stuff like this."

That doesn't mean you should make a habit of it, Monty wanted to say, but now wasn't the time to argue. They were in this together, till the end of it. Instead he asked her, "What do you know?"

Terra's eyes flashed with a moment of guilt. "It wasn't exactly about Nal'Gee, the story. But it sounded like her. It wasn't a story about one spirit, but just...how they work. Um, usually."

They jerked at a noise from the kitchen, shattering glass or porcelain. Bella had dropped something. As she muttered to herself, their broken tension eased back into cohesion.

"So?"

"So, yeah," Terra said. "The spirits—the evil ones who try to steal bodies—they don't like to leave the body until it's empty. They can, but it's harder, I guess. So when someone dies and their soul goes to the beyond, that's when they like to leave."

"When someone is sent," Monty said.

Terra nodded. "Or when the rites get read, you know? They'll leave then. They don't have to. They can leave before, but it's harder 'cuz they're attached, it said. But..." Terra looked down the hall, where Dr. Tobias's body was surely waiting. "There's signs. If you're watching when they start to leave, you can see it."

"Signs like what?"

"The book said..." Terra closed her eyes, thinking back. "Their hair moves. *Rustles*, it said. Like there's a breeze, even when there's no breeze. The eyes open if they're closed. If they're open, they'll, um, they'll *gleam*. The body might move, or roll over for no reason. And the book said sometimes the body will talk, but that sounded kinda silly. I think it was just trying to make the story good."

"I don't know, Terra," Monty said. "I've been to a lot of these readings. I haven't seen any of that."

She shrugged, catching his eyes. "Were you really looking?"

"I..." He didn't want to admit it, but that was a good question. Of course he hadn't been paying attention to those specific things, and he'd been a little out of it, especially with Audrey's...

"Audrey moved," he said slowly, the memory flooding him. "When Mullen was reading the rites, she moved, at least I think she did. Just a little. I thought she was still alive..."

He remembered staring at her body, praying to the gods and saints that she wouldn't move again, fearing that she would come back to life and open her eyes and see them all.

"It was her," Terra said, nodding, like a sage.

Monty almost wanted to snap at her, tell her that she hadn't been there and she didn't know what she was talking about, and he bit it back.

I just don't want her to have to deal with stuff like this, he told himself.

Yet he was also more and more sure that he couldn't do it without her, no matter how much he wanted to. She knew things, and she would learn more. She paid attention to things that he missed.

"I smell him," Terra said, still quiet. "It's what...it's what mom smelled like when I found her."

Yes, the smell was there now, brushing at him. The smell of death. The smell of the black. And Terra had noticed first, while he was busy reeling about something that had happened weeks ago.

"Let's go," he said. "Before she leaves again."

Bella cried loudly in the kitchen.

34

It was easy to find the room and the body, and not just because of the smell. Pieces of a broken bowl were scattered where the hall turned. There was no spill. Bella must have been carrying an empty bowl, walking back to talk to Dr. Tobias, and lost it when she stumbled back from the room.

More shattered porcelain, Monty thought. *Expensive. He'd probably be mad if he weren't dead.*

He was glad Terra was here.

The bedroom awaited them, the door hanging open like a gaping mouth. Darkness lay beyond.

"Are you ready?" Monty asked her, but she was already going in. He followed after her.

Terra hesitated once she reached the bed. The smell was strong and sickening, as it had been before. But it was the sight of the body that stopped her in her tracks.

The blanket was down past Dr. Tobias's chest, which was just as narrow as his shrunken skull. His body, like the others, was blackened; not wholly black, but tanner than the tannest leather Monty had ever seen sold.

Terra wavered, standing a foot from the bed. "It really stinks."

"Yeah," Monty said, aware that they were both breathing in the wretched air. "So let's do this. What am I supposed to look for?"

"She has to..." Terra coughed, hard, and Monty was worried she might vomit. But the coughing stopped. "She has to leave. I don't think we'll see anything unless she leaves."

"What if she already did?"

Terra shook her head. "I dunno. But if she's here, you can make her leave."

"How can I—" Monty stopped. "Are you talking about the rites? I don't know the rites, Terra."

"Come on," she said, looking up at him instead of at the body. "You went to a lot of these, didn't you?"

"Yeah, but..."

"You remembered dad's whole story about Nal'Gee," she said. "If you can remember that from so long ago, you can remember something you heard the Judge say a bunch of times." Her voice slid into a teasing note. He wondered if she was aware of it.

"I don't," he said. "Even Judge Mullen reads it from his book when he does it."

Although Mullen didn't always look at the book when he read, and Monty suspected he brought it just for show.

"Just try," Terra urged him. "I dunno what else to do. This is the only idea I got from all that reading."

It wasn't much, but Monty didn't need to tell her that. "All right, I'll try."

He thought back to the readings he'd been present at; Ma Kettle's and Audrey's, of course, and others since.

"Did the book say the rites or a prayer?" he asked. "Priest Erick prayed over the body before the Judge would read. It was all quiet, and even what I heard was in old tongue. I don't know anything about the prayer."

"Um..." Terra stuck her fingers in the ends of her hair. "It didn't say. It's an old book, it didn't even really talk about sendings. Not like we do them. But I don't think it's the prayer." She nodded to herself, affirming, and took her fingers from her blonde strands. "Because the prayer..."

"The prayer blesses the dead." Monty picked up where she left off. "And comforts the soul. The rites prepare the soul for sending."

"Yeah!" Terra said. "So if anything is gonna make Nal'Gee leave—"

"It would be the rites." Monty's trepidation was forming into excitement now. If they could really see something, something that proved they were right, it would be...well, it would be terrible, but it would mean they knew what they were dealing with, and the 'how' of it all could come later.

"But," Terra said, "you said that she gets into another body when the soul is sent. At the burning."

"I said, I *think* that she does," Monty responded, flexing his fingers. "But I could be wrong. We could be wrong about this whole thing."

Wouldn't that be nice? He wasn't sure if he'd rather have an evil spirit among them, or an unknown sickness with no cure. Was there a difference?

"It's worth a try," he continued.

"Yeah," Terra said. "Go on, do it."

Dr. Tobias's body waited beside them. Monty looked down at the small remains and summoned what memory he had of the rites.

Once he started talking, he realized how strange it felt to be saying the sacred words. Blasphemous, even, if only a little. Was it possible to be only a little blasphemous? He was doing it for a good reason, and he hoped that was enough.

"I...I speak to the soul of our friend, Tobias..." Monty paused, trying to draw up the doctor's last name. "Tobias Pelkin. I brace thee in the comfort that the beyond awaits, and that..." He stopped again, reaching for the words.

Terra remained quiet at his side, glancing up to Monty only briefly. Mostly, she kept her eyes locked on Dr. Tobias's body.

Monty remembered, and he pressed on. His heart pumped faster. "And that the souls of those before you await your passage. Your journey will be eased by the mortal efforts to set you onward."

He was surprised by how much he remembered. He talked for a little over a minute, his confidence growing as more and more came back to him.

Monty might have made it halfway through the rites and beyond if Dr. Tobias's head hadn't turned toward the two them, cutting Monty's words off as clean as a cleaver.

The corpse's eyes opened. They gleamed.

And it began to speak.

35

It wasn't Dr. Tobias's voice that emerged from the rattling jaw of the wasted body. Because it wasn't Dr. Tobias that was speaking to them.

It was Nal'Gee.

"I...hearrrrd...you..."

The sound was like wind, if wind could be dried up like dead skin and crumbled into pieces. It was guttural and deep and yet still airy and barely feminine. The lips of the body did not move; the jaw simply rocked up and down as it spoke, like it was a puppet.

It is *a puppet*, Monty thought. And then, *she's real, gods above, saints, she is* real *and she is* here.

Terra was clutching him with one hand, her ragged fingernails drawing blood from Monty's forearm. He didn't feel a thing.

The corpse laughed, the jaw flapping so hard that Monty expected to it to break. It stopped abruptly.

He was afraid. He was more afraid than he'd been in his whole life, even when he was staring at his mother's dead body-box atop the pyre, but there was anger, too. Anger at what this monster had done, and was still doing, and it broke him out of his paralysis.

Monty felt the pain of Terra's nails now, but he didn't care. "You're— Nal'Gee. Of the Dromm."

The jaw flapped again, and the body grew blacker before their eyes, like they were watching the life drain out of it. It spoke, and it was stronger this time. Monty understood that its first breathy words had been a semblance of teasing singsong.

"You know me. I know you, Bellamys. And I'll have you all."

The eyes closed; the jaw went slack. Dr. Tobias's body rolled, his head drooping off the edge of the bed. The hair around him rustled in an invisible breeze.

Monty grabbed Terra, suddenly acutely aware of the danger they were in. They hadn't thought about this at all.

"Don't let her in you!" Monty said, holding Terra tightly by the shoulders. *"Don't let her in!"*

He had no idea if they could hope to resist; it might already be too late. He didn't feel any different, but would he? Did his mother; did Audrey? The disease of the spirit could be inside him already, attaching to his bones and leaching out the marrow.

No. He would know. Bella had said that Dr. Tobias was acting strange, right?

"Monty..."

"What is it? Do you feel all right?" He felt the crazed heat from his mother's sending again. There was a powerful urge to jump through the window, or perhaps to run out into the street.

"I'm fine," Terra said, and she sounded mostly calm but looked scared, about as scared and wild-eyed as he felt. "Let go of me!"

Monty did so, his fingers stiff and hooked into claws. He forced them to relax, and all was quiet. He could hear Bella crying, still, in the other room.

"I think we're okay," Terra said slowly, looking back at the body. "I think she's gone."

Monty followed her gaze. Dr. Tobias's eyes were closed, and his hair—both what was still attached and what had fallen out, which was most of it—wasn't moving. He let out a long, shaky breath.

"She *talked* to us," Monty said to Terra.

"I didn't think..." Terra's brave face began to tremble, her eyes growing wet. A tear spilled out, rolling down her cheek. "I didn't think this would happen. I knew—I knew she was real, but I—I didn't think she'd *talk,* she's really here, Monty, and she said she's gonna—that she's gonna have us!"

Terra was crying now, her breath hitching in her chest. Monty got hold of himself and pulled her out of the room, into the hall. He was careful to avoid the shattered bowl that still laid in pieces on the floor. He knelt down.

"It's okay," he told her. "We're safe, right? She said...she said 'soon.' She wants us, but she can't get us. We're stronger than her."

Can you beat a squirrel in a fight? His father's words came back to him. *Then you can beat Nal'Gee.*

The echo of Montille's voice in his head hurt, but it made him feel warm at the same time. If he hadn't shared that story with them, where would they be?

I think she's stronger than a squirrel now, Monty thought gravely. *Not strong enough to take us, somehow. But I think she's a lot stronger.*

Yet she was strong enough to take their mother, and Audrey, and a dozen others. Why not them?

"Nal'Gee has only gotten to adults so far," Monty told Terra, toying with the idea as he said it aloud. She was settling down a bit, pushing her hair out of her face. "Older people, you know? I've heard about every death, and none of them have been, um...kids. Even all the Kettle kids are still fine. So maybe she can't get into kids, for some reason."

Terra sniffed. "But why? Grown-ups are stronger."

What Monty was thinking—and didn't want to say—was that maybe kids didn't have enough life force for her, or whatever it was that she fed on. Maybe Nal'Gee would kill every adult in town before she'd start feasting on the kids, too.

"I don't know," he said, and hated how much he didn't know, hated how powerless he felt, and hated that the best he could do was to stop his sister from crying for a little while until the next horrible thing happened.

"And she *knows* us, how can she know us?" Terra wailed, and the tears brimmed again.

Monty stood up and took hold of her hand, cutting off the flow. "She knows us because she knows we're onto her, and she doesn't know how to stop us," he said. "Come on, we have to get out of here. I have to tell the Judge about Dr. Tobias. Watch the shards."

"Then what?" Terra asked as he pulled her along.

"We've seen it with our own eyes," Monty said. "It's time to tell Judge Mullen what's really going on."

36

Monty stopped to let Bella know that Dr. Tobias was gone, leaving out the rest of what had happened and hoping she hadn't heard over her own sobs, which were now finally coming to a close.

"I'm so tired," she told him. "Poor Dr. Tobias, he didn't deserve this, he was just trying to help everyone..."

"It's terrible," Monty agreed, both to placate her and because it *was* terrible. Dr. Tobias succumbing to Nal'Gee was a shock, one that would spread throughout the town—that their only doctor had been taken by the black. Whatever muttered unrest stirred through Irisa now might well turn to an actual panic. All the more reason to talk to Judge Mullen.

"Go home and rest," Monty told Bella, putting a hand on her back and walking her out of the kitchen. Terra, meanwhile, slipped away to douse the cookfire that was currently boiling the soup over. "I'm going to let Judge Mullen know about Dr. Tobias, and he and the priest will be here soon to take care of everything."

Bella took to that without much of a fight, most of her energy spent on tears and worry. Monty walked her out of the house and Terra closed the door behind them.

"It smells better out here," Bella said, and her face started to quiver again. "Oh, the poor man..."

Monty said some reassuring words and made sure that she started walking toward wherever she lived. Once she was on her way, he and Terra hurried toward the Commons.

"Is the Judge gonna listen?" she asked Monty, jogging to keep up with his long strides. "No one listened at mom's sending."

Monty grimaced. "That was different. I'm going to be much...clearer, now. And we know for sure what's going on, too. Before it was just a guess."

It was more than a guess before, and Terra knew it.

"No one listened at mom's sending," Terra repeated, anger creeping into her words. "No one cares what kids think."

"The adults around here are the ones who believe in the Dromm legends," Monty said. The Commons was just around the corner. "I didn't once I grew out of it, but the older people were raised on it. Mom and dad both believed it, you know that. Or...even if they didn't *believe* it, they were scared of the forest. They stayed away and they tried to keep us away." Monty stopped in front of the glass doors of the Commons. "We're not the only ones. We can't be."

Through the doors, Monty could see straight down the main hall. The Judge's office was closed, as usual, and the man himself would be inside, sitting at his desk, like he had been almost every hour of the past few days. Someone inside walked past the doors and cast a quick, curious glance at the two of them, but he didn't slow down.

"Let's go." Monty pulled open the doors.

"You want me to come?" Terra asked.

"Yes," Monty said, a little surprised at her hesitance. "Do you want to?"

"I...guess." Terra stepped inside with him. "I never talked to the Judge before, not really."

It was almost funny. Moments ago, Terra had practically led the way into a room with a dead body and an evil spirit.

"It'll be all right. He'll understand," Monty said, with no idea how wrong he was.

They walked down the long hall to Judge Mullen's door, their footsteps loud between the walls. Some of the office doors lining the halls were open, with people working inside. Monty barely noticed them. His eyes were set ahead.

With adrenaline still surging through him, he was sure he'd be able to make Judge Mullen understand. Terra at his side, he knocked on the Judge's door.

The answer came shortly, the door pulled open and left ajar, the Judge looking mildly surprised to see Terra standing next to Monty.

"What is it?" he asked. The Judge was clearly annoyed and not in the best of moods, which wasn't much of a change from how things had been.

"It's urgent, sir. And...delicate." Monty shifted, remembering all the open doors behind him. He lowered his voice. "Can we come inside?"

"We? Both of you have business with me, now?" Mullen inquired, almost sneering, planting a seed of doubt in Monty's mind.

Terra nodded, but Mullen moved back before Monty could say more. "In, then. I have little time to waste, so let's get on with it. I hope this is about the farm."

They walked inside the office, Mullen closing the door behind them. It was dark and quiet. Monty suspected that the walls of this room were thicker than the others in the Commons. Mullen did not go back to his desk to sit, but simply stood there in front of the door, waiting for them to speak.

"Dr. Tobias is dead," Monty said, starting with the normal, albeit troubling news. "I just heard from his housekeeper. It was the black."

"The black," Judge Mullen repeated. "So they've got you calling it that now, too, have they?"

Mullen didn't seem at all perturbed by the doctor's death, and Monty didn't know who 'they' were supposed to be.

"I—we saw his body just a while ago," he continued, moving past the Judge's question. "It's certain."

"Mm." Mullen swept across them, walking away from the door and back to his desk. The slats of light let in through his blinds painted bright stripes across him. "Is that all?"

"No," Monty said. "There's more, Judge. Something me and Terra both saw. We know where the black comes from, and why people are getting sick."

Judge Mullen sat down in his chair, placing his hands flat on his desk. The papers there rustled. His mouth was a thin line, and even in the gloom of his office, Monty could see the muscles in his face twitching. It was a look he recognized—the one that came before the storm of the Judge's temper.

But it didn't matter. He had to know. Monty approached the desk, and Terra stuck with him. "This is going to sound crazy, sir, and I know that. I know how it looks. But I swear I am telling you the truth."

Mullen said nothing, but he gave a short nod. His face stayed the same.

Monty licked his lips. "It's not a sickness that's killing people. It's something from the Dromm forest. Have you heard the legend of Nal'Gee, sir? The witch spirit of the Dromm?"

At that, Mullen's features did shift. The muscle atop his eye still twitched, making his eyelid dance, but his narrow lips relaxed some. His eyes flicked down to Terra, then back to Monty, and he said, "I've heard it."

"Then you know how she drained the forest and turned all the trees black," Monty said, barreling ahead. "I saw the other day—you can see for yourself—the forest is growing again, there's leaves. New green ones. I noticed it after Audrey Kettle died, and it's been growing ever since, even faster."

Mullen let out a small breath, like a sigh, but he didn't stop Monty.

Monty got to the point. "It's never grown, ever. I've lived here my whole life. I thought that it might be growing because Nal'Gee wasn't there to drain it anymore. That she came out into the town, and now she's draining *people.*

"Judge, Terra and I both just saw Dr. Tobias's body. It was luck, pure luck, but Bella found us and brought us in just as he died. We went in looking for a sign, and—"

I'll have you all.

"—he talked. *She* talked to us. Nal'Gee. She was in him, Judge, and she said she was going to kill us all."

<u>37</u>

Monty didn't know when he had grabbed the Judge's desk, but his hands were there, fingers digging into the edge. He forced them to relax and pull away, having said his piece.

Mullen leaned back slightly in his chair, panning his gaze over them and landing on Terra. "And you saw this as well, Terra? Is that so?"

Terra nodded, but then she said, "Yes. I saw it, Judge Mullen."

Mullen clasped his hands. "I'll ask you this once, Monty. Will you be selling the farm to me?"

"I—what?" Monty was sure he hadn't heard correctly. "The farm? Judge, there is a monster out there—"

"Enough." Mullen slammed his hands on the desk. His face was crawling with fury and twitching muscles. Sweat beaded on his forehead. He stood.

"Do you think," Mullen said, "that you are the first idiot villagers to come into my office and tell me that my town is being terrorized by something supernatural?"

He came around the desk. Monty pulled Terra close, but Mullen simply walked around them, pacing on his short legs.

"Every time I hear a knock at my door, I am *flooded with stupidity!*" Mullen roared, the words booming in the space of his office. "Monsters, curses, and spirits. Are all you backwards people having secret meetings where you come up with this nonsense?"

"Judge," Monty said, "I'm not lying to you. The Dromm is—"

"That damned forest, too, I've heard enough about that to last me ten lifetimes!" Mullen laughed, a frantic and harried cackle. "Even Tobias brought up those fucking black trees to me. When I thought the man couldn't get any more annoying. Even in death, he's managed to dent the brain of my courier."

Mullen was circling around them, pounding his feet into the wood. Now he came back around to his desk, moving to the front and forcing Monty and Terra to back up. The short man seemed to stand seven feet tall. The contempt on his face made him ugly and twisted, and when he barked another laugh at them, it rang like a snarl.

"I am done with the both of you, and with this town. People trying to leave, blaming me for getting sick. Getting in my way. *I've had enough!"*

Mullen stepped forward, darting his hands out lightning-quick and grabbing two fistfuls of Monty's shirt.

The small man was strong, almost eerily strong. Monty stumbled forward, and Mullen held him up, pushing on him with arms like iron bars. Terra grabbed on Mullen's arm and he shoved her away, hard. She fell and rolled back on the floor, smacking into a bookshelf.

"Hey!" Monty flared, putting his hands on Judge Mullen's upper arms. It was like grabbing onto a pair of bricks, and he wasn't budging. "Let go of me, or I swear—"

"You're in no position to make threats, child," Mullen said, and he pulled Monty closer. He had no fear of retaliation from Monty, or from Terra, or from anyone. Whatever was in his eyes was writhing and wild. Untamed.

Still, Monty could claw at the Judge's eyes. Grab his head and wrench it. Close his bigger hands around the man's neck. But he let him speak.

"You listen to me," Mullen said, staring into Monty's eyes and holding him firm. "You are going to sell me your land. You are going to vacate the house. You are going to take the money and leave this town. And if you don't, I will *kill you both."*

Mullen released him, and Monty pushed off him and went to Terra. She was sitting up, looking dazed, but she seemed okay. He didn't see any blood.

Mullen's hands were balled into fists, and they slowly unclenched.
"You are not going to spread any more rumors around this town, either. I
should've taken action on this long ago. If I see you talking to someone
about spirits or curses, if I hear about it, the both of you are dead, and so
is whoever you open your mouth to."

"You're crazy," Monty said. "Your town is dying around you, and all
you care about is buying our land?"

"No one will know what happened to you," Mullen said, ignoring
Monty's words. "Trust me when I say that I have done this before, and
with people much more important than you. No one will care that you're
gone, and the farm will be mine regardless." He sat down at his desk
again, looking them over with sudden, remarkable calm. "The only
reason I won't just kill you now is because it will complicate the
acquisition process."

Terra was up now, brushing Monty off when he tried to help her. "I
knew you wouldn't listen," she said to the Judge. "You remind me of the
monsters I read about. It's no wonder my mom hated you."

Mullen's eyes glinted. "If she were around, maybe she could talk some
sense into her spawn. It's a shame; she had such potential, and it was
wasted on that little plot of land."

"I'm not your courier anymore," Monty said, suddenly so angry at
himself that he hadn't seen behind this man's mask. "You're going to let
this town die, is that it?"

"I don't care," Mullen said, either about Monty quitting, or Irisa, or
perhaps both. "I will give you one week to make arrangements for the
land. If it's not signed over by then, I will be taking it."

Monty took Terra by the arm, pulling her away from her still-standing
glare. Mullen's fury was down to a simmer. He sat in his chair and
watched them go.

"Children," he added, before Monty opened the door. "You are free
to flee, as well. Abandonment calls for the same paperwork as death, and
I have the forms ready."

38

Elrich watched the Bellamy children exit his office, the older boy slamming the door behind him. Monty's rage filled Elrich with a thin glee, something he hadn't felt in a while. It was good. Good to take action! Good to *do* something, instead of sitting here and letting the townspeople come to him over and over!

And they had been. Each face he saw made it clearer that the town was slipping out of his control. If it wasn't someone crying over their dead mother or father, it was someone asking him to do something about it. As if he was a doctor. As if he had time for that.

The Bellamy papers had been stuck to the top of his desk for weeks, and he stared down at them now. It was all he had been focused on, and he'd been lathering the eldest living Bellamy with honey when he knew that vinegar was the most effective. Well, so did the child, now. Both of them. Elrich Mullen was not one for idle threats.

He resisted the urge to crumple the papers on his desk, closing his fingers into empty fists. If they were his only problem, he might be grateful. And to think, weeks ago, he had been planning on approaching Delila Bellamy with an offer for the farm. A generous offer, more even than what he had offered her distasteful progeny.

But like the one settled on Monty's shoulders, it would have had its own undertones. Problems with the farm that could be created, causing much trouble for the woman and her family...and problems that he would be all-too-happy to undo, once the farm was in his hands.

She would have been overwhelmed with gratitude. She would have seen him as a hero and savior. Now she was ashes and blackened bones.

But he still had the town, or at least he would soon.

"Spirits," he spat, sprinkling the paper. He pulled his hands away. It didn't matter what came over the town—sickness, rumors, or morbid nicknames like 'the black'—it inevitably spread from person to person and made it to his desk. He'd heard a fresh dozen tales of monsters and spirits. Entities brought by traveling merchants; wraiths emerging from the Dromm forest; monsters sucking the souls out of people like they were mugs of beer. And that name that Monty had given it, what was it? Nal'Gee.

It was the fault of the bards and storytellers traveling with the merchants. So much outside trade only lead to poison in the town.

Nal'Gee. The name rang a bell. Some man—no, it had been a woman, from a troupe that had come through the town recently.

Some evening past, Elrich had made the mistake of stopping by the Moon tavern for a bottle to take home, and he had seen this crone sitting on a table, feet on a chair, blue shawl wrapped around her head and a bowl for coin resting between her knees. She'd been surrounded by a crowd, telling some tale, and he'd heard that name from her lips. Nal'Gee.

Her bowl had filled up just fine. The villagers had eaten up whatever she fed them, then probably asked for more when it was done. And it had gone so far as to make its way into his own head, and now too the heads of the Bellamys, the only gods-damned family in the town he needed. Any sane person would take the money for the land and be happy with it.

But the people, Monty included, were clearly going crazy.

They were trying to leave his town, to go where they felt it would be safer. He had to put a stop to that, of course. Owning a town with half its population gone was practically worthless, and would do nothing to further his goals.

No. No one was going to escape him. The doctor had confirmed that this *black* was not an illness. Whatever it was, it would run its course and leave the town a few citizens lighter, and that was all.

And if it does kill everyone?

The thought crept into his head as it had before, and he ignored it. He'd seen plagues. He'd seen infections wipe out whole square miles of cities. This wasn't anything like that. He didn't know what it was, but he'd seen people die a lot faster and a lot more horribly, and more widespread to boot. This was nothing. If someone died every day, it would be years before it would matter to him.

But villagers fleeing the town would cripple his office much quicker.

Elrich stood from his desk and moved briskly out of his room, locking the door as he always did. The light was bright out here, and he narrowed his eyes against the biting cold of the breeze. He swept forward through the hall, ignoring the sycophantic greetings called from the offices on either side of him, and pushed through the glass front doors.

He hated the idea of being forced to talk to another idiot, but he needed to make himself known as the Judge of Irisa, not just some desk-rider who sat behind a door. He had to get his hands wrapped back around the town, tight enough so that nothing and no one would be slipping through his fingers.

He'd first go to the Moon. It was time to start keeping a bottle of the good stuff in his office, not just his house. He'd prefer not to be seen buying it, but he didn't have a courier to run such things right now, did he? Like all things, it was better handled by himself.

He was undisturbed through the streets, and that was because they were empty. Unusual at daytime after lunch, but not as of late. Mullen hardly noticed; his quick gait took him to the Moon tavern, and he pushed in through the door as though he owned the place.

Technically speaking, he did.

The bar was empty, too, and he walked up to it and smacked his palm on the wood, summoning the barkeep from the next room.

"Judge, sir," the man said, and his name was Barton. Mullen knew it, and ignored it.

"Bottle of Welshire, barkeep," Mullen said, and when the man set it on the counter, Mullen laid down coin and said, "I have some questions for you, friend. That vagabond storyteller woman who was in here some nights ago, do you remember her? With the blue wrap on her head?"

"Aye." Barton slid the coin beneath the counter. "Kept a lotta drinkers in here. I wish she could stay all the time."

"Mm." Mullen wrapped his fingers around the neck of the liquor bottle. The sight of that wench had been what made him arrange the Keepers, his small crew of enforcers that stopped travel out of the town. Which meant that she should still be here. "I heard she is still in town, and I want to talk with her some. Did she tell you where she was staying?"

Barton hesitated. He might have seen the dangerous glint in Mullen's eyes. But when those same eyes bore into him further, he spoke. "She did, sir. The inn down east lane, the nice one. Montgomery."

"Wonderful." Elrich pulled the bottle off the bar and tipped Barton a nod. "Stay well, then. I am sure that I will be back."

He left the Moon, tucking the whiskey into his robes, connecting lines in his head. He didn't want anyone leaving Irisa, but there was always an exception to the rule. That exception was nestled around this raconteur and whatever band of vagrants he had managed to pin down within Irisa's borders.

If you wanted to stop a rumor, you killed it at the source.

39

Shaking with rage, Monty slammed Mullen's office door behind him and left the Commons with Terra.

A few short weeks ago, an altercation like that with the Judge might have left him in fear. But now, with Nal'Gee threatening their lives, Mullen seemed like nothing more than a petulant bully. A dangerous one, but nothing compared to what was really at stake.

"We're not selling anything to that pile of horse shit," Monty swore, moving with long strides toward nothing in particular.

Terra gasped at the curse—silly, considering all they'd been through—and then she let out a giggle before turning more serious. "He said he'd kill us."

"He'll have to get in line, won't he?" Monty stopped them where the street turned, nestling them in a shady corner between two buildings. It was cold, but he didn't notice. He felt so heated that he thought steam might be rising from his hair. "I don't care what Mullen says or threatens us with. We're done with him, and we have bigger stuff to worry about."

"Yeah." Terra looked out at the street. "Where is everybody?"

Monty looked up, too, seeing the streets completely empty in the middle of the day. "Maybe everyone's too scared to come outside," he surmised.

"So he won't pay for our house anymore," Terra said, quickly changing tack.

Monty blinked. "Yeah, I suppose that's true. That's okay. I've got some money from the courier work." What he didn't add was that it wouldn't matter for anything if Nal'Gee was free to tear through the village.

"Let's go home," he said, stepping back into the sun. "I'll talk to Patricia, see how much we'd owe her to stay there."

The one-week clock Judge Mullen had given them began to tick.

Monty knew there was a lot to do in that time, but he didn't know what any of it was. The first thing was to talk to the landlord, Patricia, about the cost of the quarters in town.

The number she gave to Monty made him balk. One month would clean him out completely, with barely enough left over to buy a sack to carry their things back to the farm. Which it looked like they'd be doing, once the money Judge Mullen had paid had run out. In a useless bit of luck, that wouldn't be for ten more days. Good news, but not quite enough to make Monty jump for joy.

One week wasn't enough time to pore through all the books necessary to find the answers they needed, if they were there at all. Still, they both read everything they could get their hands on. Monty hated to go back to the Commons library, but it had to be done. Certainly he wouldn't let Terra go alone. To his surprise, Mullen was rarely in the building. Busy with other things, apparently, and ones that brought him out of the office.

He felt disconnected from town and goings-on since he wasn't running messages anymore. He decided it was better to be out and about rather than behind closed doors. Maybe someone else could tell them more. Two days of reading until their eyes dragged had yielded nothing.

That was how they found out that Bella, Dr. Tobias's housekeeper, had been the next to die. She had succumbed the day after Dr. Tobias, and apparently she'd never left the house again. Judge Mullen and a pair of priests had read both of their rites together. Efficient.

Monty wondered if they'd be burned together, too, and if anyone else would be lumped in.

Going out into town and asking around about old legends was difficult to plan out, and even harder to execute. Monty knew plenty of townspeople, but had no idea who to talk to.

He spoke to Bradley, and he was hopeful there would be something there, but there wasn't. The baker was far more interested in actual gossip than some legend, especially if it wasn't something he'd heard about. Though his young assistant, Joelle, did have something to say.

"I heard about Nal'Gee," the girl said to them, bouncing up to the counter once Bradley had moved away to serve someone else.

Terra perked up, standing on tiptoe to see better over the counter. "From who? Your mom and dad?"

Joelle shook her head. "Nah, they don't tell ghost stories like that. There was a storyteller from one of the caravans in the Moon the other night. My parents would never let me go there, but I snuck in to get a nip of the beer."

She looked rather proud of herself for that.

"The storyteller talked about Nal'Gee?" Monty said in disbelief. "Why would someone from out of town know about a local legend?"

"If they're a storyteller, they know lots of stories," Terra said, answering before Joelle could. Her eyes were lighting up. "Didn't you read about bards and gypsies? The really good ones remember hundreds of stories, even more than a book could fit!"

Joelle nodded along. "Yeah, she was talking there for hours, I heard. All night! I hung around for a while, and she was still going after I left."

Monty turned the idea over in his head. "If that's true, then it makes sense that she would tell stories from around here..."

They would have to visit the Moon, talk to someone there, and try to find the storyteller. If she was still here at all. Joelle had seen her three or four nights ago, and caravans didn't tend to hang around the town very long.

Unless they got trapped.

It was a hope, but a slim one. Would the Judge care if outsiders tried to leave, or were his men only stopping villagers?

Monty thought, for a moment, about running away—if it was even possible. Taking Terra and getting the hell out of here was probably the safest option...but then again, was it? Mullen had a long arm, and

Nal'Gee—if she could leave the forest, what was to stop her from leaving the town? From finding them wherever they went?

Besides all that, he didn't want to abandon his home. His farm; his friends and villagers. Dromm family or not, there was love there. There were bonds, and they were strained by death and discontent, but they held. Monty couldn't leave that behind, and he couldn't ask Terra to do it, either. They would fight this. They would protect their home.

Their mother would have done the same.

They would look for this woman from the tavern, and if there was any luck, she would still be in town.

40

The Moon tavern was not a big place, but it did enough business to keep uncorking barrels and pouring them into mugs. They made their own beer, and most people would say it was fine, because most people in Irisa had never tasted good beer. The bottles of whiskey and good liquor were shipped in and sold at thrice their value. It was usually only east-side people who walked out with glass.

The tavern itself barely poked into the east side, sticking out from the other line of buildings like it didn't quite belong. There was a small, hanging sign over the door that simply read 'MOON'.

Monty had never been inside. He'd heard of the place, but only since he had been running messages. Had he arrived just twenty minutes earlier, he would have seen Judge Mullen coming out of the front door, tucking his bottle into his robes.

As it were, he and Terra walked in to the empty tavern, but the barkeep was there behind the polished length of bar, working on something beneath the counter. He was thin and balding, but his eyes were lively. He looked up and saw the young man and little girl approach him.

"Don't get people your age in here much," he said as they walked up to the bar. "Yer parents know you're wandrin' around a drinkin' spot?"

"I just have a question," Monty said, regretting bringing Terra inside. She was mature for her age and size, but you couldn't tell that by looking at her. And the barkeep was definitely looking at her.

"No, you can't have any beer," the man said. "Go on, kids in here ain't any good for my business."

"We don't want any beer!" Terra got annoyed quickly when people treated her like a little kid (*Something she might have picked up from me*, Monty thought). She put her feet on the bottom of the bar and climbed up so her head and shoulders were standing over the edge. "There was a storyteller in here, right?"

"My name's Monty," he told the barkeep. "This is Terra." His little sister glanced back at him and gave him a little nod, and he understood what she was doing. He grinned abashedly. "Sorry, she just gets real excited about stories. We're both hoping that the lady storyteller is still around."

The barkeep didn't offer his own name, he just shrugged and went back to whatever he was fiddling with beneath the counter. "She ain't here. We don't have rooms here, if ya didn't know."

Terra peeked over the bar, pulling herself up further. "What are you doing?"

"Counting money," he muttered, staring at Terra until she backed up.

"Looks like a lot," she said.

The barkeep huffed. "Unless you got some yerself, hop down off my counter and get the hell outta here."

"Do you know where she's staying, sir?" Monty asked, coming up behind Terra and putting his hands under her arms, but not lifting her off right away. "We can go find her and get out of your hair."

The man behind the bar stopped counting his money, pulling his hands up and leaning on the wood. The annoyance slipped off his face, and he eyed them both closely. "What you wanna go findin' her for, now?"

"We wanna hear some stories," Terra said, layering on eagerness. "I have a coin for her."

One hand still tucked around Terra, Monty reached into his own pocket for a coin, laying it on the counter. It wasn't a heavy one, but it was more than a pence. "Here's a coin for you, if you can help us out."

"You're the courier, ain'tcha?" He slid his eyes down the coin, then back up to Monty. "You got some message for the woman?"

It didn't bear explaining that he was no longer the courier. "Nothing official, sir. Just trying to get my little sister a story so she'll stop pestering me to read to her every night."

The barkeep did grin now, relaxing. "If you say so, kid. She's staying at the Montgomery. I'd hurry, though. You might not get to her first."

"What do you mean?" Monty said.

The barkeep plucked the coin with long, strong fingers, adding it to the pile below. The friendliness came off his face as quick as it had settled in. "It'll cost ya a lot more for that information, boy. Take your sister off my bar and get out, or I'll get my hittin' rod."

Monty knew he was done talking. He took Terra off the bar before she could say anything else. "Thanks," Monty said.

Silence was the response, and it followed them to the door as they left.

"Good job in there," Monty said to Terra in a low voice. "Reminded me of when you'd bother me for stuff."

She smiled, a trifle mischievous. "He probably woulda talked without paying, I think."

"I'm not so sure." The barkeep had tightened up very suddenly when they asked where the woman was staying. "Something was off. I think he's right—we'd better hurry."

Night was coming on fast, the afternoon light sliding away between the houses. Montgomery was a place he knew, and he'd been inside plenty of times. Luckier still, it was close to the Moon, just a few streets deeper into the east side of Irisa.

Had Monty decided to wait another day, all would have been lost. But as willing as Mullen had been to stroll into the Moon, the Judge was not foolish enough to hunt after the storyteller himself. He left that to his men, and his men had to be informed, instructed, and paid in advance. This took time.

Monty and Terra entered the Montgomery to find the small band of caravaners eating in the downstairs room of the inn, taking up a table by the fire. There were four of them; loud, cheery, and—judging by the smell of beer in the air—mostly on their way to being drunk.

Among the four bodies seated and eating was a woman with a blue scarf wrapped around her head. She was the only one who didn't have a mug in front of her, but that didn't seem to have dampened her spirits.

"Let me do the talking here," he said to Terra. A tingling crept across the back of his neck. He approached the table, ignoring the other few patrons who were scattered around the dining area. They paid him the same courtesy.

The woman in blue looked around as he got near, and unbelievably, her eyes flashed with recognition. She was older than Monty by a decade or so, and she fleetingly reminded him of his mother. She had the same dark hair, but with white woven into it, visible even in the little bit that stuck out from under the scarf.

She stood and walked over to them, the rest of her party talking loudly and not paying her any attention.

Monty put a protective hand on Terra's shoulder.

The woman pointed a finger at him. The nail was painted a deep, dark red.

"You," she said.

<u>41</u>

The storyteller's face broke into a smile. It made her look even more like his mother, but that might have been his aching heart speaking. Her eyes were the wrong color; not brown, but a crisp blue, a few shades lighter than the scarf that sat above them.

"It is you, isn't it? You're the Monty boy?"

What? His mind ran in circles, first trying to determine if he did, in fact, know this woman, but he knew that he didn't. A friend of the Judge? That would be a bad thing, almost for sure. Had the barkeep known something else?

I should have asked him more, shouldn't have just walked away so easily—

"You know us?" Terra asked, breaking the short silence.

"No. I've heard of you," the woman said. "You're here to ask me about Nal'Gee."

Terra nodded, while Monty gaped. The storyteller moved closer, and she noticed Monty tense up, ready to run with Terra in his arms if he had to.

"I'm a friend," she said. "I can be, if you like. My name is Iselle. And if you're Monty, then you must be his sister, Terra."

"Yep," Terra said. "Do you know about Nal'Gee?"

"Hold on." Monty held up a hand. "How do you know who we are?"

Iselle turned her palms up. "I have big ears," she told him with a grin. "Every town I go to, I hear everything. And I heard a few tales about you and the show you put on at your mother's funeral."

His ears grew hot, and he shook it off.

"Okay," Monty said. "Well, you're right. We do want to talk to you. But..." He looked around the place, counting heads. "It's a little crowded here."

And I'd rather not spread any more rumors about myself if I want people to take this seriously.

"Can you come to our house? Now?"

"Lead the way," Iselle said, leaning into the idea with surprising ease. She must have seen Monty looking at her fellows still sitting at the table, because she waved her hand in front of his eyes. "Don't worry about the family. They know I come and go, just like they all do."

"They're your family?" Terra asked, as Monty turned and gestured for Iselle to follow them out.

"Not blood," Iselle answered. The three of them walked out of the Montgomery inn, cloaked now in the darkness of night. "But they might as well be. We're a caravan, you know that. But you don't know that we've been together riding the roads for over ten years! You spend ten years with anyone, you're family." Stopping only for a beat, she continued, "Nal'Gee, she's one of my favorite legends, you know. I'm interested in what you've—"

"Stop," Monty said, glancing back. "I just—we shouldn't talk about it out here. Our house is close."

"All right," Iselle said, her voice brimming with intrigue. Curiosity practically radiated around her in an aura.

As they went around the corner and moved down the street, three men entered through the front door of the Montgomery inn. The villagers who recognized them were quick to leave their tables and go outside or back up to their rooms.

Monty, Terra and Iselle got to the house undisturbed. Monty opened the door and let them inside, then locked it once they were in. That tingling, uneasy feeling had yet to leave him, the hairs on his neck brushing against his shirt.

"Okay, we're safe and secure," Iselle said, giving the place a quick once-over before plopping down in a chair that sat by the desk in the main room. "Not likely to draw a crowd in here, are we?"

She crossed her legs, her long skirt shifting over her calves.

Monty pulled another pair of chairs out of the bedrooms and set them close to Iselle, but not too close. He sat on the edge of his, toes on the floor. Terra climbed into hers and crossed her legs ankles-to-ankles.

Terra seemed very excited, so Monty spoke before she could, wanting to stay focused. "Tell me what you know about Nal'Gee, Iselle. The story you know."

"I usually charge for that," she replied, stretching her foot in the air where it dangled over her knee. "But you do have something to offer me besides coin, I'm hoping."

The tale she told was the one she knew, albeit far more detailed than Monty recalled. It had been years, and his memory wasn't perfect, but he was fairly certain his father had never mentioned the names of Walter's family or the village, or the kinds of magic Nal'Gee used before she settled near the woods.

A bubble of hope began to grow in his chest. It seemed Iselle knew quite well what she was talking about.

"Wow," Terra breathed as Iselle finished. "You tell it a lot better than my dad did."

Iselle said, "It's my calling, little Terra. Now, I'll ask the both of you— no, just Monty, here. What happened at the sending?"

Monty's bubble wavered. "What did you hear, exactly?"

The storyteller gave a little shrug of her shoulders. "A few things. Most of it rubbish, I'm sure. But the common thread was that *you* seem to think Nal'Gee was present at the sending. That she was there to claim the souls of everyone there."

"I don't remember saying anything like that," Monty said, which was true. Could he say with certainty that he hadn't, though? That evening had been hell brought to life.

Iselle merely looked at him, blinking once. Waiting. Monty gave Terra a glance before he started to speak.

"There's truth to that," he admitted. "Something has been happening here. You probably heard about all of the...deaths."

"It's been quite interesting gossip around the place," Iselle acknowledged, her glee in it just barely hidden. "Small towns are usually so boring."

"So you know how people have been dying."

"*The black*," Iselle said, slipping into her storytelling voice for the phrase. "People are shriveling up like old vegetables. First an old lady, and then more of her family. Then it would have been..."

Iselle trailed off there, like she just realized she was talking to people whose mother who had, in fact, *shriveled up* just a few weeks past.

"Hells and saints, I'm sorry," she said. "My mouth gets going and it takes me a while to catch up. I never knew my mom, but I imagine it would be very tough to lose her."

"Yeah," Terra whispered.

Iselle blinked slowly, drawing in a breath. "Go on, tell me. What's your piece?"

Monty told Iselle the same story he'd told Judge Mullen, leaving nothing out and adding more. The legend he knew; the growth in the forest; finally, the appearance of Nal'Gee in the body of Dr. Tobias.

Through the tale, Iselle sat quietly. Her hands found their way to the scarf on her head, fiddling with it unconsciously, until she eventually unwound it and held it in her lap. Her long, dark hair fell around her shoulders, streaks of white shocking among the black. Her nails stroked the scarf gently, not picking at or tearing it, but turning it over and touching every inch while she looked in Monty's eyes, and Terra's when she spoke.

"The Judge threatened us," Terra said at the end of it. "He laughed when we told him. He thinks we're up to something. We just want to stop Nal'Gee."

Monty winced. He hadn't wanted to share that.

Iselle said, "Sounds like a lot of Judges I've run into. Like to have things wrapped around their little fingers. *Especially* little, in the case of this Mullen." Her eyes sparkled with the joke. "You don't need to ask if I believe you. I might, I might not. I wouldn't know all these stories if I didn't believe in them a little bit. But so far, I like what I'm hearing." She hesitated again, catching herself. "I am *interested*. This is something I can take with me. I want to know more."

Terra's whole face brightened at that, but Monty was slower to cheer. A maybe wasn't a yes, and even a yes wouldn't get them anywhere. They needed her help, not to be added to her catalogue.

"Okay. But we need more from you." Monty met her eyes, determined. "What else do you know?"

The storyteller pulled her scarf taut in her hands. The sparkle in her eyes disappeared, going solemn. "You may not like what I have to say."

42

"I'm not a demon hunter," Iselle said, looking back and forth between Monty and Terra, weight on her words. "I'm not a monster slayer or a spirit catcher. I'm a storyteller."

"I know," Monty responded, the bubble in his chest getting smaller.

"But," she continued, and she raised a hand, one long finger pointing straight up, "knowledge *is* power. That is something I have, and it's something I can share." That captivating energy she had began to spiral in again, lifting her shoulders and pulling her forward.

"Nal'Gee is not a monster or a demon. She's not a witch, either. Not anymore. She is a corrupted spirit trapped in our realm. Most corrupted spirits will kill off a nest of animals or poison a well with their spite, and then all their energy is gone and they...fade away." She danced her fingers in the air. "Nal'Gee is different. She's strong. She has *guile.* I respect it. Few wills are strong enough for what she's done. But she's evil. She's a life stealer. The Dromm forest was hers for centuries, and now—perhaps— she's taking to people."

"Lots of people," Terra murmured, shifting in her chair. Anger touched her brow.

Iselle dipped her head once. "If this is true, it will lead to a horror this world has never seen."

Monty's throat trickled dry. "What do you mean?"

Her face was grim. "A corrupted spirit like Nal'Gee...there *is* no other one like her. She is powerful, and she is filled with hate. Hate that's grown for many years. Spirits that don't relinquish life have one goal, and that is to get it back. I've never heard a story about a spirit managing to claw all the way back to our realm, but...it would take a lot of life. A lot of *lives.* And by your count, she's swallowed dozens now."

"Yes."

"She spoke to you." Iselle's scarf was bunched up now, tucked into one fist. "That can only mean that she is close. I don't know how much life she needs, but she's much, much closer now than when she was trapped in the black forest."

"Why did she kill our mom?" Terra asked, and there were tears in her eyes, but her face was hard and angry. "She said she'd kill us too. Why does she want *us*?"

"That," Iselle said, her head tilting back, "is something I don't understand. Why she'd threaten you, choose to speak to you... Yet, there is a particular way that a spirit like her would choose her victims." The scarf went from one hand to the other. "It's about potential."

"Potential," Monty repeated.

"A person's potential. Not the life they have, but the life they have left. Has Nal'Gee killed any children?"

Monty thought back, revisiting a familiar path. "No. Not that I've heard."

A sagely nod from Iselle. "And the first to die was the oldest woman in the village. An easy target. Someone with life to live, someone with *potential*, is much harder for Nal'Gee to wrestle with. She's been building up her strength, I would say."

"But the next person to die was Audrey," Monty protested. "The woman's daughter. She wasn't that old. There's plenty of older people in the village."

"Ah," Iselle said, "but potential doesn't simply mean age. It means what is left in a person's life. This woman, the daughter—Audrey. Did you see her after her mother died?"

"I was there," Monty said. "At the burning."

"Tell me." Iselle set the scarf in her lap, folding her hands over it.

"Well..." Monty brought himself back to that night. He remembered the Kettle family on the platform. "The whole family was sad. In tears. Audrey was quiet, though. Like she was lost."

"Distraught," Iselle commented. "Natural at a sending, for the family. She was married, correct? Children, a big family? How were they?"

"Sad," Monty recalled. "But not like Audrey."

Iselle asked, "And after the sending? Did either of you see Audrey?"

"I did," Monty said. "Kind of. She was the next person to die, and the Judge and I were there, too. Before she died, my mother had tried to visit her, but she couldn't. She was unwell, just lying in bed. And by the time I saw her, she was dead." His mouth twitched, and the words started coming faster. "Mostly. She moved. Her head turned toward me and the Judge, and I saw her eyes move under the eyelids. Then it was...it was like she took a breath. Her arm fell off the bed and just...hung there, making a fist. And then the fingers uncurled and everything just stopped, and she was dead."

Iselle's eyes widened the tiniest bit. "You may have witnessed Nal'Gee leaving the body...or trying to." She paused, and her fingers wound up in the scarf again, turning it over and over. Her eyes dropped down to it, briefly, before rising back up to meet his. "Are you speaking truly to me, Monty? This body moved in that exact way, and the doctor's body spoke to you?"

"I swear it," Monty said. He would never forget what he'd seen. "I swear it on the souls of my mother and father."

"If you were older..." She rubbed her thumb at a frayed patch on the scarf, not looking down. "I might think you were having a trick with me. Some well-read townsies will do that, and then they'll laugh when I get excited. What you're describing here matches many...*many* of the legends I've heard about vengeful spirits and possession." Her eyes narrowed, crisp and sharp. "Only people who knew what I know would be telling me things like this. Storytellers. Orators."

Iselle leaned back in the chair, and the tension in her shoulders slackened a little bit. "Since you are neither, I believe you. I admit that I don't want to. After we're done here, my people and I are leaving this town, barricaded or not. Death lives here. Audrey was taken because she had given up—you understand? Her potential was gone, and it made her an easy target."

"Bella," Terra said, tapping Monty on the leg. "Bella was crying because Dr. Tobias died. And then Nal'Gee got her, too!"

"Just like that?" Monty said. "He wasn't her father."

A small smile snuck onto Iselle's face, but it was gone as quickly as it came. "Nal'Gee is stronger now. It's harder for people fight back."

"But...my...our mother..." Monty watched the pity gather on Iselle's face, and all at once he understood.

"It was my fault." He looked down, speaking the words to the ground. It suddenly made perfect, horrible sense. "I abandoned her. I went to go and live in town even though she didn't want me to. I worked for a man she hated. I...I told her I wanted a different life!" Monty clutched at his thighs, digging his fingers into his skin. "I killed her. I let her die."

"No!" Terra cried. "Monty, you didn't. Mom wasn't sad!"

"She wouldn't show it to you," he muttered, "or to me. But she...I *weakened* her enough to let Nal'Gee take her. She must have thought I was going to abandon the family, or...I don't know. I don't know. I don't know. I thought she was getting better, but it only took days and she...she..."

A hand on his knee. It was Iselle.

"Don't presume to understand what's happened," she said. "No one truly knows how a spirit chooses their victims, or how their power works. All the same, no one knows what is inside another person's mind. Nal'Gee had consumed two human lives before taking her. She was strong, and so was your mother."

Monty's eyes were dry, but his chest felt both empty and painfully heavy. He managed to pull in some air and look back up.

"If your mother survived as long as she did with the spirit inside her, I am certain that she did not give up." Iselle squeezed his leg, then she blinked and pulled back. She brought her hands to her head and pulled her hair up, tying it back into the scarf with practiced, fluid motions. "I'm sorry, to both of you. But I can't help, and to be honest, I'm not sure that anyone could."

She stood up, her chair sliding back a few inches and hitting the desk behind it. "I'm leaving. If you want to live, you do the same."

43

"**W**ait!"

Terra followed Iselle out of the house, and Monty went after both of them, leaving behind the guilt at the role he had played in his mother's death—for now.

The woman was a fast walker, and she didn't look back. Terra ran to catch up with her.

"You have to help us!" Terra pleaded.

"There's nothing that I can do," Iselle said. She kept her eyes forward...but glanced down briefly and said, "Don't trip."

"You don't need to do anything," Monty told her, coming up on the other side. "We just want to talk some more. Learn what you know, and see if there's anything that we can use. You can still leave tonight."

Though, he wondered, *can she really?*

"I can assure you that I know nothing about fighting spirits," Iselle responded. Their place was not terribly far from the Montgomery; already, they were only one short street away. "In fact, all I know is what great harm they can do to people. Not things you want to hear right now."

"Any of that could help!" Monty said.

"We won't know unless you tell us," Terra added, her breath coming a little harsher with keeping up their pace.

"There's nothing to know," Iselle said, and Monty heard the annoyance there. But she was the only person who even had a chance of offering something that might help. He couldn't let it go.

"I'll pay you," he insisted, promising money he didn't have. "Whatever you want. I've got—"

"What in the world?" Iselle stopped dead, raising a hand, reaching out for nothing.

Monty had been so distracted trying to stall the storyteller, he hadn't been paying attention. He looked up and saw the Montgomery across the road. The outside lanterns were lit, throwing soft light onto the sign and on what appeared to be three bodies lying in the dirt outside. Smoke rose off them in fading wisps. Lying on their backs, their faces were easy to see. Even through the burns, Monty knew them. He didn't get a long look at them, but he had seen the three of them less than an hour ago.

It was Iselle's caravan. All of them. Dead.

A few other people were outside, gathered around the bodies. He thought some were inn-goers, looking shaken and scared—but he clearly recognized three of the men there, even partially clad in darkness. It was hard to mistake people that big. He'd seen them talking to Mullen in the days past.

It's true, he thought. *They're really doing this.*

And then he thought, *Mullen has gone completely crazy.*

Iselle unfroze and lunged forward toward the inn, and Monty grabbed her around the waist. It was a fast move, and he didn't get good purchase, but he had her. Thank the saints it was a dark and cloudy night—he didn't think they'd been seen. Hurriedly, he pulled her back, deeper in the darkness by a storefront.

"What are you doing? Let me go!"

"Monty!"

"Both of you, quiet!" Monty's voice was a harsh whisper. "Iselle, if you go over there, you're going to be killed."

"If you don't—"

"Those men work for the Judge!" he spat through gritted teeth. "Iselle, they're looking for you. They want you dead."

"You don't know what you're talking about!" She spun in his grasp, twisting an arm around to grab at his face. He pulled back, narrowly avoiding her long nails. "You let me go you little monster, *that's my family out there!*"

"I know," Monty said, and he stayed strong in his grip. "I know."

It was coming together in broken little pieces. Mullen's vitriol toward the rumors; Bradley's talk about the so-called residency enforcers; the Moon barkeep's cryptic comment about getting to Iselle first. How close had they come to losing her, too?

"I'm sorry," Monty said to Iselle. "Really, I am. I didn't—I had no idea the Judge would go this far."

Iselle said nothing, but her pulling and twisting felt half-hearted now, like the weight of what happened was beginning to hold her down.

"We have to go back to our house," Monty said to Iselle, and he pulled harder, bringing her close. She had stopped struggling, but he wasn't sure that she wouldn't bolt away. "Please. You have to trust me. We can't help them, but we can save you."

"Let me go. I won't run. Just let me go." Iselle was still, her arms hanging down. Her scarf had shaken loose, half her hair spilling out and down her neck.

Monty didn't hesitate; Iselle would never trust them if he couldn't show her the same courtesy. He let go of her. She didn't run, but she didn't move back, either.

When she did make a sudden jerking motion, Monty reached for her—but she wasn't running. Someone was coming from the direction of the inn, and she was hailing them. It wasn't one of the men, fortunately. It was a boy who looked young and a little shaken, perhaps thirteen. Still—

"Iselle! Don't!" Monty whispered.

"You there! Boy!" she called, not too loudly. "Please, quickly—tell us what happened at the inn. There's a heavy coin for you if you're fast."

The boy ran across the street at Iselle's beckoning. He was short and skinny, with brown hair. There was soot on his face, smeared around his shining eyes.

"How heavy a coin?" he asked.

"Out with it," Iselle prodded.

"Awright, I was in just to get a nip," he said. "I know one of the girls who works the kitchen. I was gonna eat at a table in there when these three big men come in. They look awful scary, I seen them around. They head right for the gypsies by the fire."

"Caravaners," Iselle corrected flatly.

"Whatever," the boy said, and hurried along. "One of the big guys yells out that the man's coat is on fire, the gyp sitting real close to the fireplace. And then—I saw it —another of the big guys threw a little bottle in the fire, and the whole thing went up, it exploded like magic! The whole table and all the people at it caught on."

Iselle raised a hand to her mouth.

The boy, excited, went on. "The three of 'em grabbed the gypsies like they was gonna put 'em out, like they're patting the fire down. They put their coats over their faces, and they dragged 'em outside so the whole place didn't catch. I run outside, and I heard one of 'em say it's too late, and they're all dead. Just like that. That's all I saw, I just got out of there before I got in trouble. You ain't gonna tell on me, are ya?"

Unbelievable, Monty thought. *The...the brazenness of it. To not be challenged, because everyone is scared. What is happening to our town?*

Mutely, Iselle plucked a coin from her pocket and dropped it in the boy's palm. The boy sniffed.

"Not very heavy..."

"Get out of here!" Monty snarled at the kid, and the look on his face was enough to jolt the boy. He scurried away, tucking the coin in his shirt.

"They're going to come," Monty said to Iselle and Terra. "We have to be gone."

Iselle stared in the direction of the inn, unmoving. He didn't know what she was thinking, what she was feeling, and yet...perhaps he did, a little. At the very least, he knew that she was stunned, and she wasn't going to make a decision on her own.

He took her hand, pulling her. "Let's go. We have to go."

She moved, letting him take her at first, then turning, sliding her hand out of his and running, running like he and Terra were, going faster with each stride until they had to stop.

"Wait," Monty panted, grinding his feet to a halt. They were seconds from his door. "Wait."

"What is it?" Terra asked.

"We can't...here. People at the inn saw us. Know you're...with us." Monty shook his head. "If they tell the Judge's men, they might come here looking for you."

"Do you have somewhere else?" Iselle said, the first words she'd spoken since the boy's story.

"Yes. The farm." Monty caught Terra's eye, and she gave a little shrug. "It's quiet out there. If they come for us, we'd hear them. We could run to the Dromm and hide, if we needed to." He gave a weak smile that barely lifted his mouth. "It's not like Nal'Gee is in there anymore."

"Okay," Iselle said, her voice flat. "Let's go."

They hadn't been to the farm in some time, but years could pass and the path would still feel familiar, where the roads gave way to loose dirt and then grass, where the stars filled the whole sky (when the clouds weren't in the way), and where the black forest began to creep up the horizon, taking over the distance.

They slowed down once they got out of town and no one seemed to be on their trail. The walk was silent, all three of them muted by what they had seen.

Maybe I'm paranoid, but I have good reason. Would the men be fixated enough on this goal to try to track Iselle down through the night? That would depend on the Judge's orders. The way Mullen had throbbed with anger about the rumors, Monty thought it was possible. Better to be safe than dead.

There was the farm house. Even right in front of them, it felt very far away.

"We can make up a bed for you," Monty said as they approached, turning from the main path to the worn grass that led to the door. Even in the dark, his footsteps fell into the same spots they always did. "Or you can use..."

Monty trailed off, following Iselle's gaze. She wasn't looking at the house or at him, but at the Dromm where it rose in the night. It was too dark to see the leaves. It looked as black and foreboding as it ever had.

"I'd like to see the forest," she said, her voice light with awe. "This will be my only chance. I'm either going to die here or never come back."

"Um, sure," Monty said, a touch uneasy. But with Nal'Gee gone, the Dromm had probably never been safer. "Terra, do you want to come?"

"Yeah," she said. "I'm not scared of it anymore."

It didn't sound terribly convincing, but it made Monty smile all the same.

"Follow me," he said. "There's a path."

Another familiar path. Subconsciously, Monty was quite fine not having to go into the house yet. He didn't want to lose it to Judge Mullen, but there was still a mountain to climb there, and one he would have to climb later...but not right now.

They passed by the compost pile, which had whittled down to nothing but a space carved into the tall, wilting grass. Images of brisk and sunny days flooded him, and he closed his mind to the memories. He breathed in the cold air and focused on the trees, so black that they were visible only as they blocked the starlight poking through the clouds.

"They're huge," Iselle breathed, stopping a few dozen feet before them and craning her neck upward. "The stories don't lie about that. I could see them from the town, but..."

"You can't tell until you're up close," Monty finished for her, standing at her side, and Terra at his. "It's too dark, but there's leaves there now. Ever since Nal'Gee let the trees start to live again."

"I wish I could see them," Iselle said.

As they stood quiet for a while, Iselle's wish came slowly true. The cloud cover that concealed the half-moon had been gradually moving west, and at last it was gone. Pale moonlight dripped down into the forest, and it shone brightest against the green leaves.

Monty saw her eyes widen as she watched the color appear. It wouldn't ease what had happened to her for long, but it was something. The passion in her eyes, gleaming even in the heaviness of the death around her. The incomparable thrill of living within a legend, even one that would suck the flesh from her bones if it had a chance. Monty could see how she could get wrapped up in tales, tall or otherwise. It was something she lived for; something she *craved.*

Would you really have left Irisa? he thought. *I think you might have stayed. I think you would have come to this forest without me tomorrow, looking for the hole Nal'Gee was living in.*

"Monty!" Terra screamed his name and grabbed at his wrist. She was pointing into the forest. He followed her hand, where the moonlight had fallen on something else. A shape in the trees.

Someone was in the woods.

44

Monty stepped forward, putting his arm in front of Terra and pushing her back. "Iselle, you may have to run."

"Is it them?" Iselle asked, sounding as though she hardly cared.

"I don't know," Monty said, but who else would it be? Someone at the inn must have told the men that Iselle had left with Monty—almost everyone in town knew his face. And then they'd sent someone to the house to ambush them.

I wasn't smart enough, he lamented, and what were they going to do now? Where would they go?

The person in the woods was unmoving, a dark silhouette. Perhaps he was facing the other way. If not, he must have seen them; they could see him, easily, even among the trees.

"Unlikely they would beat us here," Iselle said, making no move to flee. She either didn't believe it was one of the Judge's men, or she just didn't care.

That made Monty think—why not have someone in the house? Why would someone be waiting in the woods for them?

Someone could be in the house, too.

True, and they'd have to investigate that carefully, but out here, in the woods?

"They wouldn't," he said. "They wouldn't."

Then...who was it?

He was tired of running, and there wasn't even anywhere left to run to. He wouldn't abandon his home because of some figure in the woods.

Monty bent down and picked up a thick fallen branch. It was heavy.

"I'm going to see who it is," he said. "You two stay back here."

Iselle said, "Don't be stupid. If it's some thug, there's a better chance with two of us. And if it's some other Dromm monster, I want to see it with my own eyes." She gave a little titter at that.

"Terra—"

"I'm not staying here," she said quietly, her eyes locked ahead. "I can fight."

"You're not going to fight," Monty told her. "Stay behind me. That's that."

All the same, he heard her pick up a stick from the ground. There wasn't time to argue further. If there was a chance of getting the drop on whoever was waiting in the woods, it had to be done before they saw them.

Monty moved forward. There was enough moonlight to walk around the broken sticks that might clue into their approach, and it seemed like Iselle and Terra were following suit, stepping carefully.

They made it to the border of the Dromm and stepped inside.

A little closer now, Monty could see that whoever it was, there was something wrong with them. Their arms were narrow and oddly bent; their shoulders were uneven. They didn't seem to have any hair, and they were eerily still. They hadn't moved a single muscle the entire time they'd stood there.

His heart was climbing steadily into his throat. Black Dromm trees surrounded him on all sides, and a few dozen feet away was...what? A foe? A trick? Some plot of Nal'Gee's, luring them into her territory?

We should have run, he thought, but he moved closer, a tight grip on his flimsy weapon, and he told himself, *No. No running. We fight.*

But he'd keep Terra out of it, if he could.

Monty wished there was more light. Even this close now, all they could see was the outline of this person, and it was such an odd shape. He had no idea what he was looking at. It couldn't be a person. It had to be something else.

He held his hand up, indicating to both Terra and Iselle: *Stay back. Let me handle this.*

Monty stepped forward quickly, disregarding the noise. He raised his branch with one strong hand and demanded, "Who are you?"

But it was no one.

"Terra. Iselle." He lowered his branch. "It's safe."

They came to either side of him, and all three of them stared at the intruder in the wood.

"What is it?" Terra asked.

Monty prodded it with his stick, finding it unyielding. Which wasn't surprising, considering it was made of Dromm logs, hardened mud, and heavy rocks. It was an assembly of forest pieces that was roughly in the shape of a person. Easy to mistake from far away, but clearly lacking up close.

The head was a single large rock, unadorned. The torso was thick, but the shoulders were narrow. The legs were not legs at all, but more of a roughly circular pedestal, wider at the base, holding the whole thing up. There were two thick, knobby branches stuck into the sides, approximating arms.

Monty dropped his heavy branch on the ground. "Who would do something like this?"

Iselle, meanwhile, reached out to touch it. She placed her hands on the rock, gently running her fingers over the surface. She appeared enthralled, her energy bouncing back again as she examined the creation.

"I'll be twice-damned..." she muttered to herself, wrapping her fingers around one of the arms. "You know what this is? No, of course you don't. I was wondering if we might find something like this in town, but it makes sense she would build it out here where it's safer."

Monty glanced at her. "What are you saying? Is this thing from Nal'Gee?"

Iselle's eyes glinted in the moonlight, a fascinated smile across her face. "Exactly that, Monty. It's a golem. She's trying to build a new body."

The earthly pile of sticks and mud in front of him took on a sudden sinister aura. He stepped back from it, but Iselle had no such reservations.

Terra was skeptical. "She wants to be a big pile of rocks?"

"No." Iselle examined the torso. "She'd use her power to turn this golem alive, and then she'd live within it. It would look much more human by then...though not perfect. Can you imagine? The power it would take to make this walk. And she's close."

Monty imagined the rocky golem coming to life, jerking toward the village with heavy steps. Crushing people and taking their souls.

He grabbed the head with both hands and wrenched it off the body. The heavy rock strained his shoulders, but he threw it away, where it hit a tree trunk with a heavy thud. He tore through the rest of the body quickly, yanking out and breaking the arms, pulling out the smaller rocks and kicking over the stiff mud until it was nothing but a scattered and broken pile. By the time he finished, he was panting and his hands ached.

Iselle had moved back from his frenzy. Now she stared down at the mess, stoic. "She can build another. She will. We could come out here tomorrow and this will be standing again."

Monty flexed his fingers, flaking dirt from them. His heart was racing, refusing to settle down. "I don't care," he said, grinding his heel down on one of the rocks, burying it further in the dirt. "I'll break it again. She's not taking us. She's not having any more of this village."

Iselle was calm when she said, "It may well be out of your hands."

"We'll see about that!" Monty's voice was a snarl. He clenched his hands into fists, feeling the dirt caked there like dried blood. He was furious. Nal'Gee was so brazenly confident that she would make her golem at the edge of the forest? Right behind their house?

She was teasing them. She was laughing, wherever she was. Laughing while she drained the life out of someone else that he knew.

"She's playing with us." Monty pointed at the wrecked golem behind him. "She's playing with us, and I'm not following her rules. She wants us to be scared, and run screaming at any sign of her. Maybe we would have before." Their home rested in the darkness, empty. He could see it between Terra and Iselle, between the trees, beyond the wilting grass. "Not now."

He pointed to Iselle. "I wasn't trying to drag you into this fight, but the fact is that if you hadn't come out of that inn with us, you'd be dead."

That drew her out from stillness. Her eyes narrowed. "If I was there, I could have helped."

"The smallest person there besides you looked to outweigh you by a hundred pounds," he told her. "It was happenstance. It was a coincidence. But we saved your life. What are you going to do with it? Don't you want revenge? Because none of this would have ever happened if it weren't for Nal'Gee."

Monty lowered his hand. He thought she might run at him, but the lines on her forehead softened slightly.

"Caravan life—what is done is done. I will mourn." Iselle's face was redolent with pain, but her words came through clearly. "Then I will move on."

"Not from here, you won't," he said.

"You could learn a lesson from me, *boy*," Iselle responded, and now she was the one pointing at him. "I've told you more than once that there is nothing that can be done here. You can run, or you can die."

"We're not running anywhere," Terra said, turning to the side to look at Iselle. "Nal'Gee took our mom. She took Ma Kettle, and a lot of other people. We can't run. They didn't get to run."

Iselle held Terra's gaze, but she didn't have a response to that.

Monty blinked, slowly, letting himself settle down. He wasn't thinking clearly, but with the golem destroyed and behind him, he could let himself be rational. Iselle didn't want revenge. He knew what she wanted.

"You're in the middle of something you tell stories about," Monty said to her. "Me and Terra, we're here because it's our home. We've lost family and friends, and we're going to stop this so that we can save our village. You're here because you got stuck and your caravan came along at a bad time, but that doesn't mean you can't stay for a better reason."

Monty threw his hands up—at the forest, at the village, at everything. He'd seen her eyes when they lit upon that golem and drank in what its existence meant. He'd heard the thrilled shiver in her voice when she shared her tales with them, and asked them for theirs.

"This is a chance to witness a real legend. Even more—this is a chance to be part of that legend. On the right side of it. To be a hero." Monty dropped his arms. "You don't have to risk your life to do something important here."

"I'm already risking my life," Iselle said, but her anger was dissipating.

"Just talk with us," Terra said. "Please? We can help each other."

Iselle's hand flicked upward, just an inch, like she was going to reach up for her scarf and yank it out of her hair. She stopped herself. She looked at Terra, and then at Monty.

"If I die here," she said, a ghost of a smile finding its way to her face, "then you must tell *my* story. And you make it good."

45

The house was clear, Monty's earlier worries of intruders dispelled as they poked carefully through the rooms to find them empty. All that was foul in the house was the rotting food in the pantry he had neglected to clean out. He threw that outside a few steps beyond the door, leaving a window open to air out the smell, and lit the small lantern on the table.

"Let's talk," Monty said, wiping his hands and sitting down. He swept an open hand across the surface and the two remaining chairs. "For real, this time. For longer than twenty minutes."

"Mm." Iselle took the chair where their mother usually sat. The resemblance between them was not lost on him. "I'm happy to talk, but the truth is that I've really told you all I know about Nal'Gee."

"Okay," Monty said, "but what else do you know about spirits?"

"That's a big question." Iselle took the scarf from her head, beginning its dance through her fingers. "I know a lot, but do I really *know* it? I've never had to think about if my stories might affect real life beyond someone hanging a ward over their door."

"Then maybe we should assume everything is true," Monty suggested.

"Unless it's wrong," Terra added.

"Wrong?" Iselle drew back the tiniest bit at that, but then relaxed. "No, you're right. I don't spread lies if I can help it, but it would be dangerous to treat everything as fact. The wrong assumption in something like this could get you killed."

"True, but—" Monty said.

"*But,*" Iselle continued for him, tapping a nail on the table, "we are in a situation where assumptions *must* be made. Whole *leaps* will have to be made. Because we are dealing with something that has never been dealt with before."

She grasped her scarf with both hands before continuing, tossing her hair back with a twist of her head. "Of course, Nal'Gee isn't the only spirit I've heard tales of. I could tell you the stories of Amallion the Cursed, or the brother spirits who lived inside of their family's dog...but now's not the time."

Iselle laid her headscarf on the table and spread it out flat so that it was a big, crinkled square of blue fabric. She planted two fingers just above the center, arcing them.

"Here we have a person. It can be a regular, everyday human, or it can be a king, or it can be a witch like Nal'Gee. They can be good, they can be poor, they can be rich, they can be evil. It doesn't matter. When they die, the same thing happens. The spirit or the soul, whatever you want to call it...pulls away." She split her fingers, curling one up into her palm. "What happens then?"

Terra answered, "They go to the beyond. With the saints. Or..."

"Or the depths," Monty said.

Iselle nodded. "The lonely depths, the big empty space inside of our world, so big that you can wander around forever and never find anyone in the darkness. At least, that is what the legends say. But we can't be sure, can we? That is where we stand."

"Scriptures are different from legends," Monty said, glancing at her curled finger. "All the priests say the same about the beyond and about the depths. So do the books and scrolls."

"I'm sure a lot of people tell the same stories about monsters," Iselle said with a shrug. "I've met plenty of them. Does that make them true? Perhaps some. But we're not here to question the church." She tapped her finger on the table, the click of her nail dulled by the scarf. "There is a third possibility for a separated soul, as you both know. It can be trapped in this realm." Slowly, she lowered her curled finger back to the tabletop.

"Right," Monty said. "Nal'Gee clung to the forest."

"She ate up all the animals and the trees," Terra said.

"Yes," Iselle nodded along, "and there are other spirits who have done similar things. Not devoured like Nal'Gee has, but they live among other things. Animals and people. The forest attachment is also unique to Nal'Gee, most likely due to her own early powers as a witch of the Dromm. But there is something all of these stories have in common: Spirits cannot survive here on their own."

Monty blinked. "They have to be attached to something."

"They do, but..." The storyteller drew her fingers back together again. "They have to be attached to something *alive*. Something with worldly roots."

"I've read stories about haunted suits of armor, though," Terra offered. "They're not alive."

Iselle shook her head, a slight motion. "Haunted is different from possessed. A witch can curse armor and make it walk. But a spirit cannot live inside of it. This is one of the first assumptions we must make."

"I agree with it," Monty said. It lined up with the stories he knew— though admittedly they were few—and it *felt* right. "It's definitely what Nal'Gee is doing."

"It is," Iselle said, grim now. She drew her fingers back. "And the golem in the woods proves her intent. Not to kill everyone in the village in a form of revenge for her death, but to steal enough life force to create a body of her own. Perhaps even her old body, drawn from the decay in the woods."

"That was hundreds of years ago," Monty said, his mouth dry. "There wouldn't be anything left."

Iselle shrugged. "We speculate. Now, you tell me what you're thinking, because I can see it waiting behind your eyes. Both of yours."

"She could still kill everybody," Terra said. "Once she got a body. She'd be magic again, right? She could do even more things. She could come and get us."

"If that was her intent," Iselle replied.

Monty said, "It might be. When she spoke to us through Dr. Tobias, she threatened us directly—by name."

"Yes…" Iselle seemed put off by the idea. "But it doesn't make sense to me. If she was kept in this world by spite, her ire would not be toward your family, which was not even around when she was alive. The Bellamy name does not live in any stories I know. She should not harbor you ill will."

"Maybe it's because we're trying to stop her." Terra grabbed the edge of the table, pulling herself close.

More doubt from Iselle, plain on her face. "I just don't think she would concern herself so deeply with one mortal family."

"There's more," Monty said. "Even before this—before I even suspected she was behind this—Terra and I both had strange visions. Our father died a little while ago, but Terra was drawn into the Dromm forest by a vision of him. Not a dream. And I saw him, too, on a night when I was staying in town. He visited me in the night and told me to…to go into the woods with him. It was horrible."

"When was this?" Iselle asked.

"Terra's…" Monty glanced at her. "A month ago, maybe a little longer. It was before Ma Kettle died. Mine was after."

"Hmm." Iselle gathered up the scarf from the table again, feeding it between her hands. "If it was indeed Nal'Gee who sent these visions after you, they show her growing strength quite well. The first one to you, Terra, stayed in the woods where she was held. She didn't have the power to reach out farther. But once she did, she came to you in Irisa."

Twist, pull, furl, unfurl.

"That is…telling," Iselle continued after a moment. "I'm having my own doubts now. She lies dormant for years, then reaches out like that? When most of her energy must be spent on staying here and not getting pulled to the beyond."

"We live on her land," Monty said. "My dad told me—when he told me Nal'Gee's story, he said her cottage was on our farm, or really close to it. She could be angry about that."

"Perhaps...if that's indeed true."

"I think it is," Monty continued, determined. "Our neighbors, the Gartens, aren't very far from us. They have two young kids, but the parents—Mr. and Mrs. Garten, they're not...not really all there. It's like they're dazed, a lot, especially Mr. Garten. I mean, they're nice. They helped us." Monty shook his head. He didn't mean to speak ill of them. "What I'm saying is, it seems to me like they might have been easier targets, if she wanted to kill Dromm families. But she's going after us. It must be true."

"Why didn't she kill me?" Terra asked, bringing her hands to her shoulders. "She got me all the way into the woods. I was asleep out there all night. Couldn't she have gotten me?"

Iselle's eyes flashed, and she leaned forward on the table. "She must have wanted to. That would be why she brought you into the woods."

"Gods," Monty breathed. "After I found you, for a couple days...do you remember, Terra? You were sick, or at least we thought you were. You were always hiding alone, and sleeping, and you wouldn't help with any chores. But you got better after we went to town."

"How long?" Iselle asked. "How long was she like that?"

Monty thought back. He snapped his fingers. "Three days."

Iselle slumped back. "Three days? You're sure it was that long?"

"Yeah..." Monty wasn't sure what the problem was.

"The chickens!" Terra said. "Monty, the chickens!"

"What do you...oh." Monty nodded. "Two of our chickens died around then. They were..."

He remembered their empty shell bodies; the foul, slick blackness inside them; their awful stench. "She must have killed those chickens. Sucked their life out."

"Yes!" Iselle slammed a fist on the table, and both Monty and Terra jumped. The storyteller paid that no mind, now pointing a long nail at Terra. "She wanted you, Terra. *She wanted you.* Nal'Gee latched onto you and left the forest. Gods, she did! What an incredible risk! She didn't know her own limitations, she just thought she would be able to take you, but *she couldn't!*"

"So when I was sick that time, that was actually...Nal'Gee?" Terra's voice quivered, and she looked ill at the thought. Monty felt a bit sick, himself.

"Nal'Gee!" Iselle practically cried, ecstatic at the conclusion. "She clung to you, and she tried to take you—she tried, but she failed. You were too strong for her. She weakened you with that vision of your father, a father you'd only lost recently, and she thought it was enough, but it wasn't!

"She must have almost lost, but she had the chickens. How many chickens do you have? Did you have?"

Iselle was in a fast-talking rant now, and Monty quickly replied, "Eight. Six afterward."

"Ha!" she cawed. "Oh, to think of it. The witch was almost wasted away, but she found those damn chickens, and she only had strength enough to kill two of them."

"I was hiding by the coop," Terra said, looking down at her hands while scrounging for the memory. "It wasn't for long. I took a nap, I was so tired. And when I woke up, I just went back to the house."

Iselle nodded, her head bobbing excitedly. "Not strength, then, but *time.* She knew she could either stay and kill all the chickens and then perish, or eat what she could before jumping back to you. If this is true, this would mean that animals don't have souls! Not chickens, at least, if she's able to bounce between them and you...but she couldn't cling to your soul, no, you're too strong, she was stuck to you like a bit of tar, like dung on your shoe, she was expiring...

"Monty was too strong. Your mother, Delila, was too strong. The witch had nowhere else to go, because none of you were going back to the forest! She gambled and she almost lost, until you went to town and you ran into the old woman!"

Iselle stopped, having talked herself out of breath.

"Oh, no," Terra moaned, curling her fingers and scratching at the surface of the table. "Oh no, it was me, wasn't it? I carried Nal'Gee all the way out of the woods and into town and she—she was able to get into—e-everyone!"

She dropped down onto the table, crying. Iselle grimaced and shook her head. "Sorry. Sorry. Again."

Monty moved his chair next to Terra. She had her face buried in her arms; small, muffled sobs escaped. He put a hand on her back.

"Hey," he said, leaning in close to her. "Hey. Listen here, you didn't *carry* anything, okay? Did you pick up Nal'Gee and put her in your pocket? Did you throw her into the wagon?"

"N-no..." Terra said from within her arms.

"No," Monty repeated for her, firm. "She stuck to you. She's a parasite. And if it didn't happen now, it was bound to happen sooner or later. There was nothing you could have done to stop it, Terra. But we can do something now."

"I'm sorry," she gasped, pulling her head up. She wiped at her eyes. "I was so stupid. I followed Daddy—I followed dad into the woods even though I knew he was dead. I was just...I don't know!"

"She manipulated you," Iselle said, her words soft with contrition. "She felt your pain over the months and years, and she used it against you. And Monty's right. If it didn't work, she would have kept trying with you, or with your family. It's clear that she is...tenacious."

Monty took his hand from Terra and stood up.

"I think that's enough for tonight. We're all tired." He couldn't speak for Iselle, but it had been an extremely long day for the two of them.

"All right," Iselle said. "I..." She hesitated, perhaps shying away from making another apology. "I have some things to think about."

"I'll show you where you can sleep," Monty told her, though it was more likely the woman would lie up in bed, running things through her head. "But I want to talk more in the morning, and I think we've done enough...speculating. I want to make a plan."

Iselle smiled, but it was weak, stifled by the burden of reality returning in the aftermath of their discussion. "That's exactly what I'm thinking about."

46

The next morning came early and cold on the tail of fitful, ragged sleep. Monty, pulling himself from bed as quietly as possible so as to not wake Terra (which he did anyway), first wondered if Iselle had left in the night. But she hadn't; she slept in Terra's bed, which was only somewhat smaller than Monty's and fit her just fine.

Delila's room remained empty.

Waking up in the house for the first time since his mother had died was hard, though it had been weeks since the sending. The quiet, normal in the morning, was strange and heavy. The house was devoid of smell, which Monty supposed was not a wholly awful thing. It was cold—not terribly so, but it would do to light the kitchen fire.

He stood in the kitchen, looking at the snuffed lantern on the table; the open pane, with soot smudges on the glass. Sleep had not come easy nor lasted long, but he wasn't tired. He felt like last night was still pressing on, long hours stretching into the early morning, and that his work was not done.

By the time he moved—and he wasn't sure how long he had stood there—Terra was up with him, leaning against the doorway of the kitchen and tugging at her hair.

"Hi," she said.

"Mm." Monty knelt down and saw there was still wood by the cookfire circle. Not a lot, but enough for today. He arranged it as he'd done many hundreds of times, lighting it just as easily. The fire slowly crept across the small, chopped logs. He inhaled the woodsmoke as it came, finding a moment of peace.

Terra was in the pantry, her feet crinkling on old onion skins laying on the floor. Monty looked after her while she rooted around.

"There's some potatoes," she said, pulling out a pair of the same, one in each hand. "They don't look bad."

"Potatoes last a long time," Monty said.

"I know." She set them on the table, then grabbed three more. "I'll make some for breakfast."

Monty thought of her sitting at the table, sewing. Staying up late to read page after page. The books that would stack on the table next to the bed.

"Sure," he said. "Let me help you cut them."

They chopped the potatoes together on the table, and when that was done, Monty gabbed the skillet, which hung from the ceiling where Terra couldn't reach. She was tall enough to use the cookfire, though, and she did that just fine.

Iselle came out of Terra's room and into the kitchen once the potatoes had been sizzling for a few minutes. Monty had heard the familiar creaks of the hall as she approached.

"Wish I had a change of clothes," Iselle said. Her scarf was gone, her hair fallen in a not-unappealing tumble of black splashed with thin streaks of white. "It's all in the caravan."

The mention of her roots didn't seem to affect her. Monty got the feeling that the emotional outburst she'd had while struggling in his arms was a rare moment of transparency for Iselle. That, and her excitement when coming across new information about Nal'Gee.

Iselle sat at the table, her eyes lingering on Terra while the girl stood almost on tiptoe to watch the frying potatoes. "Smells good," she said, looking away with a smile. "I hope you have some salt."

"We do," Terra said, not turning around.

"Well." Iselle laid her palms flat on the table, eyeing the small flaws that had accumulated in the color on her nails. "I have been doing some thinking."

Monty, remembering her parting words before they slept, sat down with her. "You have a plan?"

She tilted her head, equivocating with her shoulders. "I have ideas. I would hope that you have some ideas, too."

Reluctant to admit that the night's intermittent pondering had yielded little, Monty said nothing.

"I thought of some stuff," Terra said, scraping at the pan with a long spoon.

"Let's hear it," Iselle said.

"Hold on, I'm almost done."

Monty got up to help scoop the potatoes into three bowls, lifting the heavy skillet while Terra divided the portions and sprinkled some salt on the top, pulling pinches from the half-full sack on the counter.

"Thanks," Iselle said when Terra set a bowl and spoon in front of her. "Do you cook a lot, Terra?"

"No. Just a little." Terra took her seat, and Monty took his. She dug her spoon into her bowl, burying it in the mound of potatoes and leaving it there. "There's something me and Monty didn't tell you about Dr. Tobias."

Monty chewed his food, thinking back. Had they left something out?

"When we went to go see the body, we tried—well, Monty tried to read the rites. We thought it might, um...disturb Nal'Gee, if she was still in there. Make her come out, so that we'd know for sure."

"Oh." Iselle paused, letting her spoon rest. "That's an interesting idea. And it worked."

"Yeah." Terra nodded.

"Or it didn't," Monty said, tapping his bowl with his fingers. "And Nal'Gee just came out to laugh at us. I didn't know all the rites by heart."

"I thought it was good," Terra said, "and I think it did work."

"It may have," Iselle said. "You could be right, too, Monty. So." She took a huge spoonful of food, delaying her next words. Monty suspected it was for dramatic effect. "My thoughts are also about Dr. Tobias. Rather, about his housekeeper. What was her name?"

"Bella," Terra answered.

"Yes, Bella. And how Nal'Gee went right from Tobias to Bella. From the old Kettle woman to her daughter. From her daughter to your mother—who was at her sending. And, I assume, from your mother's sending into the next victim, who most likely was at *that* sending."

"Yes..." Monty agreed, waiting for more.

"She cannot leap *far.*" Iselle punctuated the last word with a rattling of her nails on the table. "When she first lured you into the Dromm, Terra, it was to clutch onto you. I assumed that as her power grew, then so would her ability to transfer from person to person. And yet, even after all these killings, she seems to go to someone *close.* Her power is greater now, surely, but this fact remains. Both when she first emerged, and recently with Bella."

"It does make sense," Monty said, "but I don't see how that helps us."

"I told you it wasn't a plan," Iselle said, seeming cross with the fact that Monty didn't find this as enlightening as she did. "It is an idea. It is a thought on the matter. If we're going to plan, we need a basis—"

Thunk. Thunk. Thunk.

Someone knocked at the door.

47

Monty got up fast, tipping his bowl over as he pushed away from the table.

"Who is it?" Terra asked. She looked sharply at the door, tense and still.

"I didn't see a back door that we can leave through," Iselle said, calm. "Maybe I missed it?"

Who could—it has to be the Judge's men. Who else? But why would they knock? They can just barge right in if they want. They know we're here, there's smoke through the chimney pipe.

Thunkthunkthunk.

"Go in the bedroom. Mom's room has the biggest window," Monty murmured. "If there's trouble, get out through it and run. The forest is probably the safest place." *Oddly enough.*

"You're gonna answer the door?" Terra gaped.

"Go!" A fierce whisper; a wave of his hand. He moved to the door, not giving them a choice in the matter. Terra and Iselle slipped out of the kitchen.

As Monty grasped the door handle, he was suddenly very aware that he had never actually fought anyone in his life. Before this moment, that had seemed like a good thing.

He pulled open the door, balling his left hand into a fist—

And was greeted by a scroll. A scroll in the hand of a kid who, at first glance, reminded Monty a lot of Rodney Talhauer's son; slight, and dressed in clothes a little too big for him. But he lacked the mousy demeanor of the former courier. His words were crisp and rehearsed.

"Missive for Monty Bellamy from the home of Judge Elrich Mullen," the kid recited. He had clearly taken over the duties of town courier.

Was I the oldest recruit courier ever? The inane question passed through Monty's head as he took the scroll, processing the lad's words. He didn't say thank you or ask for the courier's name, just gave him a dull nod and shut the door in his face. His heart was thudding in is chest, slowing down only once he managed to breathe more than a little sip.

"A message from Mullen." Monty thumbed the wax seal. It was unbroken, indeed from the desk of the Judge. Although the courier said it came from the Judge's home. He closed his fist around it, suppressing the urge to crush the paper.

"It's safe," he called past the kitchen. "Just a courier. He's gone."

Monty was handling the scroll as they came back into the kitchen.

"Who's it from?" Terra asked.

"The Judge." Monty's face was grim as he broke the wax seal and let the pieces fall. Absentmindedly, he kicked them under the table.

"How did he know we were here?" Iselle questioned.

"He probably sent the courier to our place in town first, then instructed him to come here if he didn't find us." The farm house wasn't exactly a hiding place; it just created enough distance to make them feel safe. He glanced up at Iselle before opening the scroll. "Since we weren't visited in the night by any of Mullen's goons, I'm assuming no one at the inn told them that you ran off with us."

"Or they didn't recognize us," Terra said.

That was possible, but Monty thought it was the former, and that after seeing what had happened, no one in the inn felt particularly friendly toward the Judge's men.

"Well? Are you going to open the scroll?" Iselle rested a hand on the table. "I admit I'm very curious to see what the man has to say to you."

Monty felt the same, though it was mixed with a heavy sense of foreboding. Not fear—his fear of Mullen was gone. He did fear for Iselle's safety, and his sister's, but the Judge himself was not the threat. Just an obstacle.

He unrolled the scroll and read it aloud.

"'The week you were granted has been cut short. I await your response at my home. Come alone or with your sister, it does not matter to me. Bring me your answer or I will come to get it from you.'"

The message ended there, taking up only a small portion of the paper in the Judge's small handwriting. It was compact, yet it looked a little sloppy. Monty imagined the small man brimming with anger, scratching the quill into the paper hard enough to splinter the tip.

"What's this about a week?" Iselle asked, raising one curious eyebrow.

Monty informed her of the ultimatum the Judge had laid on them.

"He wants your land, is it? He might have to get in line behind Nal'Gee." The storyteller smirked.

Monty wasn't in a laughing mood. "We have enough going on without Mullen forcing his way in. But if he's serious about this, I can't just ignore it."

"Monty, you can't go to his house!" Terra pulled on his arm, lowering the missive so that she could take a look. "It has to be a trap. He said he would kill us."

"If he wanted to kill us, he'd just come and do it, or send his men," Monty said. The words came out with an odd casualness.

"Maybe he's just lazy," Iselle offered, then held up her hands. "Sorry. I know this is serious. It's just funny to think of that short little man as some big danger while we're discussing all of this."

"Actually," Monty said, letting Terra take the paper from his hands, "laziness could have something to do with it. He did say us being alive made it easier. Otherwise he wouldn't be asking."

"He's not really asking," Iselle pointed out.

Monty shrugged. "Whatever you want to call it. But yes, Terra—I'm going to go. We're not going to get anything done with Mullen breathing down our necks this whole time."

"What are you gonna do?" Terra threw the paper aside, where it brushed against the table and then fell to the floor. "Are you gonna give him the farm?"

The fire was burning low. It would go out soon.

"I don't know," Monty said, and he put more wood on the fire.

48

They decided that Terra would stay behind with Iselle. There was no need to bring her along into the belly of the beast, as it were, and it was still better for Iselle to be further from town. In the daylight and the clear, cold air, they could see anyone approaching from miles away. As long as either of them kept a passing eye on the horizon, they'd be able to flee any danger.

But Monty knew the danger wasn't out there, not anymore. It was where he was headed,

It was early—not too early for courier runs, evidently, but too early for most of Irisa to be up and about. The fires were lit at the Commons, and the smoke rose from the four chimneys that sprouted up from the roof.

It could be a trap. The fear in Terra's eyes glinted in his mind. *It could be a trap, and all my assumptions about what Mullen wants won't mean a thing if I'm wrong.*

The only thing he knew at this moment was that he didn't know anything about anything. Everything he thought he knew—about Mullen, about the town, about foreboding tales of spirits told to children—had been shaken with violent force. He clung only to hopes and some mutual understanding between him, his sister, and a woman he'd met less than a day ago.

Mullen's house was far into the east side, an area Monty normally had never gone until he was a courier. He'd become quite familiar with it since then. He'd never visited the Judge's house directly, but he'd seen it plenty of times, and it was impossible to mistake. Whatever semblance of humbleness Mullen tried to portray in the office or about town was discarded right about where his estate gate thrust upward from the ground.

It was tall and spiked, and the iron was flawless; Monty had seen pairs of men working on it often. The gate itself was ajar, slightly. He wondered if Mullen had opened it himself, or if he had sent someone down the long walk to do it.

Monty pushed the gate open a little further and passed through, stepping from packed dirt onto impeccable cobblestone, a long path that curved slightly left on its journey from the gated entry to the tall front door.

Mullen's mansion was not a castle, but it made Monty's modest farm house look like a chicken coop. It was two stories of stone, darker on the bottom, rising in lighter gray shades to the barely-slanting roof. Huge windows sat in the walls, darkened by drawn curtains. Mullen often complained about the setting sun blinding him through the glass, and Monty had never seen the curtains opened. It appeared Mullen did not care for the morning light, either.

He looked left and right, scanning over the expansive yard. Maybe he was looking for a man hiding behind a tree trunk with a sword—he wasn't sure. Mullen's estate did not have many trees, and the ones that were there had trunks too narrow to hide even Monty himself.

If it was a trap, all he could do was walk right into it.

His boots thudded on the stones as he followed the path up to the door. Why would the Judge choose to have such a big door on the front of his house? It would only serve to make him look smaller, not to mention how heavy it must be. Would the Judge expect him so soon, immediately after the message was delivered?

He will, Monty knew. The man was focused and arrogant. He would assume that things would go as he wanted them to.

Monty didn't know what he was going to say. But the moment the Judge opened the front door and Monty laid eyes on him, he began to form his plan.

49

"So...you came alone."

The Judge's first words were likely meant to be strong and imposing, but the highest-ranked official in Irisa was leaning on his door frame for support. His hair was disheveled and his face lacked color, making the heaviness of his brow look like a burden.

Sympathy never crossed Monty's mind. The gears began turning.

"I did," Monty said, deciding to be direct. "Do you plan to kill me?"

Mullen smiled, and the evil there was shaky and dotted with spittle, but it still laid thick. "I have many plans, boy, and you'll never know them. But no...this is not the time of your death." He paused, straightening up. "My message was...clear. It is time for you to make your decision. I pray it is wise...for you and your sister both."

I pray the same, Monty thought.

"The land," Monty told him. "The farm. You can have it."

Surprise flicked in Mullen's eyes. Perhaps he had expected more of a fight before Monty would yield.

"Wise, indeed," Mullen said, and Monty noticed a change there. Color came back to his face; his posture straightened, ever slightly.

Doubt cast tingling fingers across Monty's heart, and he ignored it.

"My office." Mullen's eyes flicked upward, narrowing, then returned to Monty's face. "We'll sign the papers there."

"No," Monty said.

"This is not—"

"I assume you'll require our deed," Monty said, "and probably other things. Other papers. It's all a mess on our desk, and I don't know what to look for. You can bring what you need to bring to our house, and we can do the deal there."

Mullen breathed deeply. "It would be unwise to try to trick me, Monty. Whatever clemency I am willing to extend could be cut very, very short."

"It's not a trick," Monty said, lying through his teeth and doing a damned good job of it. "I want this done. I don't want to have to bring Terra back into town. I don't want to have to come back into town again to sign anything that crops up, or any more than I have to. I don't want a courier involved, either, and I assume you don't, given how this all...came about."

Mullen said nothing, and Monty knew he was right.

"Let's finish this in private, and be done with it. I'll pick up the payment at the treasurer's box. You can have one of your men leave it." Monty didn't care about the coin, but he knew that Mullen would.

Most importantly, he knew—he *knew*—that he was right about Mullen wanting this to be as simple as possible. The man was a monster, but he was also a bureaucrat, and he wanted their land badly enough to murder. Further complications would be the last thing he wanted.

"Fine," Mullen said. "This is an agreement, all told. You can have your...stipulation, since it's small. I'll be there before the sun sets. Have a lantern lit if we'll need it."

The door shut in his face, a gesture he was quite familiar with by now.

Monty exhaled the hot air inside his chest, hoping the tension in his neck would slide away. It didn't. The plan was hasty and only one step had gone right so far. There were many more to go, and many ways it could go wrong. It would only take one for them to lose everything.

Though Mullen had said he wasn't planning to kill him, Monty was still relieved to get off of the Judge's property and back onto the road heading west. There was one more stop he wanted to make before he went back home.

The Commons was in full bustle, but no one paid Monty any attention. They hadn't when he was courier, either, for the most part. He breezed in through the glass doors and pulled the key to the quarters from his pocket, something he'd never returned. It didn't occur to him until he was unlocking the door that the new courier might be inside, but the quarters were empty.

He knew that Terra had left a book here—the one book that actually mentioned the Dromm woods, if not Nal'Gee. He wanted to bring it back to Iselle for her to have a look, but the book was gone. Someone must have cleaned out the room. Perhaps it was moved back to the small library shelf.

Crossing past the main hall, he glanced to the end where the Judge's office was, and he saw that the door was ajar. His mouth opened in surprise; Mullen was rarely so careless. He pictured the Judge's eyes flicking upward when he mentioned the office, like he had forgotten something. Today was not Elrich Mullen's best day.

He hoped that would hold true through the night.

The decision was quick. He walked down the main hall like he belonged, expecting someone to stop him or hold him up, but no one did. He slipped inside the office and closed the door.

The Judge would surely be back here to get what he needed for the signing, so he couldn't ransack the place or set it on fire, much as he might like to. Nor could he take anything that would be missed.

What he wanted, however, was something he figured would not be noticed absent. He found it quickly and tucked it under his arm, leaving the office just as casually as he had strolled in. He made sure to leave the door just barely ajar, as it had been.

He left Irisa behind him and went back home, piecing together his plan even as he climbed the front steps of the house and pushed open the door.

Terra and Iselle were sitting at the table. His sister lit up when she saw him walk inside.

"Monty! I was worried. Me and Iselle talked about some stuff..." She looked at what he had taken from the Judge's office. "Why do you have that?"

"Change of plans," Monty said, dropping the book from Mullen's office onto the table. It shook the surface with its weight. "She's in him. Nal'Gee is inside of Mullen."

50

There were, as Monty knew, a dozen things that could go wrong. Probably more.

"How do you know?" Iselle asked him right away, and Monty explained how Mullen had looked, and how suddenly the change had come on.

"We just saw him yesterday, and he was fine," Monty said.

"It could be anything, though," Iselle said. "Any number of sicknesses. You know that. It's winter, and this man interacts with a lot of people throughout the town."

"It could be," Monty said. "But I'm sure of it. I can feel it."

It was mostly true. Was he really sure? No.

Iselle's next question came: "When would Nal'Gee have had the chance?"

"Easy," Terra answered quickly, catching on with excitement. "The Judge goes to all the sendings, and to all the houses to read the rites. So—so he must have gone to Dr. Tobias's house! Bella died there, too."

"That's exactly what I was thinking," Monty said, flashing a grin at Terra. "Mullen is older, too."

But Iselle shook her head. "I told you, it's not about being old. It's about potential. And look at this man—a kingdom-report official. On the cusp of getting your land, and presumably hungry for more power. He's brimming with potential. It would be a very hard leap for Nal'Gee to take him."

"You're right," Monty agreed, and he sat down. "He's not bedridden, but he *is* sick. And he's strong-willed. I think he's fighting her. I don't think he can win, but his stubbornness is getting him on his feet. And hopefully out to our farm."

"It sounds to me like you have a plan," Iselle said, her dismissal slipping easily into interest as her doubts were subdued. She had her scarf in her hands, twirling it around her fingers as she listened.

"We don't have a lot of time," Monty said. "It's going to take all of us, and even that might not be enough to get it done."

"We can do it," Terra said. "But...what do we have to do?"

"For starters, we're all going to be getting our hands dirty," Monty said. "Iselle, I hope that's all right with you."

Iselle laughed and held up her palms.

"Aren't you a storyteller?" Monty asked.

There was a surprising amount of callus painting a broken ring around each of her palms, and coloring between the bends of some of her fingers.

"I'm a caravaner," Iselle told him, flexing her hands and lowering them again. "When I'm not telling stories, I'm whipping the oxen or helping with the load. Or helping to fix broken wheels. Don't worry about my hands; they've seen plenty a day's work."

"Let's go then." Monty stood up. "We're going to need some tools from the barn."

There was no need to bundle up against the cold; their blood ran hot as Monty talked them through what he was thinking. The three of them discussed, heated, while they walked to the barn; while they pulled out the tools; while they went to the clearing to dig and pull at the dirt.

"It's all got to be gone." Monty swept his arm over the area they stood, the grassy field that stretched for a mile between their house and the Gartens'. "As much as we can get, the biggest it can be, just to be safe."

"Is this really gonna work?" Terra asked, panting. She was carrying a twenty-pound bag of salt, which she insisted on taking all the way here by herself.

"I have no idea," Monty said, and then he corrected himself as Iselle laughed. "I have *some* idea. We just have to hope it's right. And we have to do as much as we can."

With shovels and hoes between them, the three of them dug out the earth in an expanding circle, ripping out and discarding every piece of grass and weed they could see. It was exhausting work. The hours stretched ahead of them, but there wasn't time for rest.

When the sun was high in the sky, they stopped briefly to eat some food Monty had brought along—old bread with salted butter. Then it was back to tilling and yanking and discarding. Their hands grew caked with dirt and their backs burned with the effort. The cold didn't stop them from sweating as they tore at the earth.

"Okay." Monty breathed heavily, pinning his weight on the shovel in his hands, his arms and forehead shining with sweat. They'd worked for hours. He swept the matted hair away from his brows where it dripped stinging sweat into his eyes. "Okay. That's as much as we can do. Everyone take some salt and spread it. Be thorough."

The work they had done was impressive. The three of them had created a barren circle stretching almost seventy feet across. It was an expanse of desolation amid the plain, and Monty thanked the saints that it wasn't yet cold enough for the ground to be harder.

There was still plenty of light left, but there was more to be done before the sun descended. So they salted until the bag was empty, then they went back to the house so Monty could drudge up some papers. It didn't matter if they were the deed or a shopping list. He just wanted them in his hands.

"What about the bugs?" Terra pointed out as they walked back to the house. The circle they had made was not far from the house; it could be seen through the window. "Aren't there a lot of bugs in the ground? And worms, and other things?"

"I wouldn't worry about that," Iselle told her. "If chickens don't have souls, then it's fair to assume that all the crawlers in the dirt don't have them, either."

"But the trees do," Terra insisted, looking back at the Dromm forest, where the green leaves were starting to get thick enough to block out the sun. "And the grass. And the other plants in the Dromm. Nal'Gee was eating them all."

"There's still bugs in the Dromm," Monty told her. "You know that."

"I just don't understand." Terra flopped the empty salt bag, shaking out loose grains and rocks.

"I don't think that plants have souls," Iselle mused, looking down at the grass as they stepped out of their circle. "That's an awful lot of souls to account for in the beyond. And how do you determine where a bush or a tree deserves to spend the afterlife? No...I think it's a shared soul. The soul of the earth, maybe."

The storyteller smiled, her face alighting. "Now there's a thought. The tale of the earth spirit, under our feet at all times. *If you hold perfectly still, you can feel the ground breathing.*" Iselle chuckled. "Imagine being able to ask Nal'Gee about that. How she leached off the world to survive."

"We're not bringing her here to ask her questions," Monty said. "That circle is for her to die in. We can't go off the plan."

"I know, I know," Iselle said. "It's just a...fantasy."

Is she always this calm—this unfocused—*when her life is in danger? Or does she just not care because she lost her family?*

But that wasn't fair. He was being just as reckless, even more than Iselle, considering he was involving both her and Terra. If his mother were alive, would he be so headstrong?

Don't judge her, he told himself. *Just trust her.*

"The sun's coming down," Monty noted, eyeing the horizon. They were stopped outside the house. The fading light brought another task to mind. "I'm going to need a torch. He needs to see me and be drawn to the circle. And the Gartens...I thought we'd have more time."

"We already talked about that," Iselle said. "Their house is too far away. She couldn't possibly leap all the way there. You have to stay focused on yourself. She's going to have one place to go, Monty, and that's you."

"Yeah." He looked at the house, where Mullen's thick book of rites was waiting on the kitchen table. "Yeah, okay."

"I think I should do it," Terra said, not for the first time. "If she tries to get to me, I can stop her better than Monty."

"It's not happening," Monty said, and he looked right in Terra's eyes. "I'm not gonna say it again. It's enough that either of you are involved in this at all. It's going to be me and Mullen in that circle, and that's it."

Terra met his gaze, unflinching. Her head reached to just underneath Monty's chest. There was determination there, but she didn't retort. She turned away and went into the house.

"Iselle," Monty said, looking away from the front door as it closed behind Terra. "Thank you for helping us. The Gartens are far enough away, but like we talked about—"

"Yes, yes, I should go." Iselle sniffed, but Monty could see that she was mocking him a little. That was okay. He'd take a little mocking from her, and a little ire from his sister, if it would save both their lives in the end.

"I'll try not to be offended by the lack of potential you see in me," Iselle continued, and now she was really laying it on thick, enough to break his stern countenance into a smile.

"Keep Terra with you, however far away enough you feel is safe. You can come check on me after a good enough time has passed," Monty said. "One way or the other."

"Let's hope it's the good way," Iselle said. "If I just dug out a whole planting field for no reason, I'm apt to be very sore with you."

51

Elrich felt like he weighed an extra hundred pounds. He hadn't been this sick since...well, he couldn't remember *ever* being this sick. Even though his brain felt hot and addled, he knew that if he were in his best, most clarified state, he still wouldn't be able to pull up a memory of feeling worse.

But that didn't matter. He was hours away from having everything he wanted.

The timeline had to be moved, and what had spooked him (though he'd never use those words) was the fact that that the vagabond storytelling bitch had managed to slip between his fingers. If something so simple could go out of his control, there was no sense in leaving anything else up to chance and time. The fact that Monty had agreed so quickly was an added boon.

"About time something went right here," he muttered to himself, wiping his forehead. He was burning hot. If there were a frozen lake at his feet, he would have fallen forward into it without a second thought. But there was only polished wood.

He swallowed, his mouth as dry as his floor. There was water in the kitchen, and he went there, staying upright. He refused to lean against the wall for support as he made his way around his own home.

I'll do that when I'm old, I'll do that when I'm old and I own half this kingdom, I'll—

Elrich plunged a silver mug into the water basin, splashing cold wetness around his feet. He drained the mug, then filled it and drained it again. He couldn't get enough water to sate the thirst he felt. Let alone the hunger—though that was fading some. He'd have to eat something before he left the house.

He shuffled to the pantry, hot and exhausted and still thirsty, somehow, though his belly felt full enough to make him nauseous. There was a lock on the door, a simple latch he'd lifted a thousand, thousand times. His fingers struggled drunkenly against it.

Eventually, he managed to lift the latch and let it swing away from the door, and it was then that a wave of exhaustion crashed into him and he leaned his head against the wood. His hair, short and stiff, splayed against the painted door, his arms dropping down to his sides and hanging there. The world faded from white wood to dim nothing.

He awoke with a start, snapping back, then falling forward and catching himself against the pantry door with his palms.

"What..."

How long had he been nodding off in his kitchen? His shoulders ached, and his forehead felt raw. He rubbed a hand against it and winced, then turned to the window to see that the daylight was brushed with orange.

Hours. He'd been in here for hours. Unbelievable. Why had he been in here at all? He wasn't even hungry.

"Office," Elrich mumbled, clearing his throat. It was somehow both dry and blocked with phlegm. "Get to the office."

He turned and saw the water basin, and his thirst screamed at him again. He filled and drained the mug, then dropped it into the water. It sunk to the bottom. Water dripping from his lips, he pressed at his bleary eyes with the backs of his hands and tried to run an inventory in his mind. Anger clawed as he pressed at his temples, focusing as best he could. He ground his teeth together. Was there anything that he needed from here?

"No," he said, and he was sure of it. "No." All of the Bellamy documents were in the office at the Commons.

Elrich lowered his hands and swallowed a deep breath. He felt a little better than before, and as his thoughts came into sharper focus, that steady feeling improved. He was in control. He was the architect of his destiny, and he was about to break ground.

"Three signatures," he said to himself, looking down his robes to ensure he hadn't somehow made a mess there and finding them clean. "That's all I need."

He closed his eyes and imagined the brats solemnly signing over their farm, quiet and tractable. If this didn't go perfectly—if Monty or the little girl gave him any resistance, any last-minute begging or pleading—he'd have them killed anyway, signatures or no signatures.

In fact, it was best to get rid of them regardless. Why didn't he think of this sooner? No need to have rumors of the deal floating around. This was the first step to earldom, at the very least, and his rise to the top would be unmarred.

The thought made him feel better than he had all day.

Breathing easier, the Judge left his home and locked the door behind him.

52

Monty went to the barn to get the last thing he would need, which was a standing torch to plant in the dirt. Inside the barn, he rolled it in tar and then carried it out. He stopped at the bare circle and drove it into the ground, gripping it hard enough to hurt his hands, then lit it where it stood. It would burn tall, and it would bring Mullen right to him.

Terra came out of the house as he left the circle. She had the rites book in her hands.

"Thanks," he said, taking it from her.

"I marked where the rites start," she said, and Monty looked down to see a few papers nestled in the book, all sticking out slightly from the same spot in the pages. "And I just grabbed those from mom's desk. Are they okay?"

"That's fine," he said.

He knelt down so he could look at her better. She was quiet and subdued.

"I know you want to be there for this part," Monty told her. "I get it, really. You've already done a lot. Don't think you're not helping."

"I know," Terra said, not sounding convinced. "But we're doing this for mom. I should help you fight."

"We're doing this for everyone," he said. "Everyone in town, and everyone who's not there anymore, too." He patted the thick binding of the book. "This isn't a fight. It's more like a...magic spell. It's either going to work or it's not. There's no reason for you to be in danger in case it doesn't."

"You really want me to just run away with Iselle if Nal'Gee kills you?" Terra asked bluntly.

He blinked at that. They'd agreed it was the only recourse, but it didn't sound great out loud.

"It's better than staying here and dying," he said, and when he blinked again his eyes were hot and his vision was getting blurry. He lowered his head and rubbed at them, quickly. "And that's exactly what'll happen if this doesn't work. So, just promise me you will. If things don't—if I don't make it. Promise me you'll get the hell out of here. Okay?"

"I already promised."

"Yeah. I want you to do it again."

"Fine," she said, and Monty saw her eyes were shining too, but she wasn't trying to hide it. "I promise."

He smiled. It was a real smile, but a sad one. He let the book drop to the ground and pulled Terra into his arms, hugging her close.

"I'm sorry," he told her. "I'm sorry I wasn't there when I was supposed to be."

"It's okay," she said into his shoulder. He heard the words and he felt them. "Just don't let her get you."

"All right." Monty squeezed her, hard. She felt thin. He let her go and said, "I won't."

Terra just nodded and wiped at her face.

Monty gathered up the rites book and stood again. Iselle came out then, letting the door shut loudly behind her.

"Looks like it's about time," she called, idling on the front step. The sun lowered in the west, making the thin clouds look like smeared blood in the sky.

"Go on," he told Terra, offering her another small smile. "Get as far away from here as you can. Then I'll come and find you."

"I'll find _you_," Terra said, and she left it at that, turning to join Iselle as she came up to them.

"You're ready? Did we manage to take care of everything?"

"Yeah," Monty said, snapping his fingers twice, quickly. "Everything that I could think of, anyway. Thank you."

"It's done, then," Iselle said with a nod. "Good luck. I'd stay to help more if I could, but...well, we know why that's not the best idea." She gazed at the circle they had dug out.

The plan, rushed in formation and patched together as they worked, was to force Nal'Gee out of Mullen's body. Initially Monty had just planned to read the rites from memory as best he could, but when he saw the Judge's office open, it was like a sign to steal the book itself. He felt a bit more confident holding it in his hands, like the weight of the pages lent to the power of the words inside.

Once Nal'Gee was forced out of Mullen's body, she would have nowhere else to leap to, since they had dug out all the grass and salted the earth itself to make sure even the tiniest new sprouts wouldn't take hold. If she went back to Mullen, Monty would just read her out again. The circle was big, and as far as they knew, Nal'Gee had never made a leap farther than just a few feet.

It was the biggest *if* of the whole plan, and it was why Monty wanted Terra gone, and especially Iselle, who might be (but almost certainly was) more vulnerable to being taken by Nal'Gee.

If there was nothing to latch onto, and not even grass to cling to, then Nal'Gee would have to relinquish herself to the beyond and be gone from them forever. He hoped.

Of course, Monty himself would still be in the circle, and she would attack him, or try to harbor herself in his body. It would be her only option. He had to be prepared, and he had no idea how to do so. How could anyone prepare for something like that?

Just stay strong, he told himself. *If you stay strong, she can't take you.*

"You all right?"

Monty snapped to focus. Iselle was peering at him, looking over his face intently.

"I'm fine," he said. "You have to hurry away from here. Go wide of the path so you don't run into Mullen. Terra knows a good way."

"I'd argue with you if there wasn't a half-decent chance it would get me killed," Iselle said, and she stood up straight again and beckoned to Terra as she pulled away. "Come on. We'll be back after it's been dark for a little while, so try to have it done by then."

"I'll do my best," Monty said, Iselle's offhand affection warming him a little bit.

"We're coming back *soon,*" Terra insisted, pulling at her hair as it dangled.

Monty agreed to that just so she would get moving. He breathed a little easier once they finally got on their way, and easier still as they grew smaller and smaller on the horizon, winding far to the right so as to avoid the beaten path from the farm to town. Mullen wouldn't see them, but even if he did, Monty thought that he probably wouldn't care. He had much more pressing things on his mind.

Monty stuck his thumb in the book where the ritual began, pulling out the loose pages. He looked ahead, where the bare circle swept across the field and the lone torch burned ever brighter as the day's light faded. He knew there was a chance that, once he stepped inside, he would never leave that patch of earth again.

He got moving.

53

The day's light disappeared quickly. The stars were not plentiful tonight, and he was surrounded by a dense darkness that closed in on him more with each passing moment.

That's good, he reminded himself. He wanted Mullen to see him standing here and come right to him. The torch was a flaming beacon to summon him this way.

But Mullen wasn't coming, and the minutes wore on.

"What if she got him?" Monty asked himself, straining his eyes to scan a horizon he couldn't see. "She could have overtaken him today and drained him dry, and now she's in someone else and Terra's in town with Iselle. They could be right next to her."

Or she could be in them.

Maybe he could go to town. If Mullen was laid up at home, sick and dying, he could confront Nal'Gee before she got him entirely and moved on. Why hadn't he thought of this possibility?

The cracks in the plan were starting to show. Soon they'd be big enough to fall through.

He stood there, paralyzed by indecision, the seconds rolling by too fast and too slow at the same time. The torch burned beside him, licking fierce tongues of heat along the right side of his face and neck.

How much longer could he wait here without going crazy?

Footsteps rustled through the grass from somewhere ahead. Monty's breath froze in his throat, a solid slab. He forced himself to breathe normally, taking a small step back to make sure his face was in the light.

It was Mullen. Inside, Monty let out a sigh of relief which was lost immediately in the storm of trepidation. He held the book behind his back, his thumb still marking the rites. Its weight made his wrist twinge and the corner dug into his skin. With his other hand, he held forth the loose pages that Terra had brought him.

"Monty," Mullen said. He was barely visible, lingering on the edges of the light. "What...what is this? This is to be done inside. There's...there are signings."

"I can't hear you, Judge." The lie slipped through Monty's lips easily. "Come closer."

Mullen did, and Monty saw that the Judge looked about five times worse than when Monty had seen him earlier. Even in the flickering light, the sweat shone on his forehead. He looked thinner, both in his face and in how his robes hung from him. He was stooped over, and his mouth was partly open, drawing in struggling breaths, like the walk over here had brought him to the edge of death.

Except it wasn't the walk.

The Judge didn't look down, either not noticing the fact that he was now walking on bare dirt instead of grass, or just not caring. Under one arm, he had his own folio, stuffed sloppily with papers that threatened to catch the weak breeze and fly away.

"Inside," he said to Monty. "We'll go inside...we take care of this. Swear to the saints...I will have your head if you...try to cross me."

The threat wasn't as palpable with the Judge gasping for breath between the words. Still, Monty raised the hand that clutched the papers, putting it close to the torch.

"The deed is here," he said to Mullen, though he had checked to ensure that it was not. "We do this here, or I burn it all. I don't want you stepping foot in my house."

He felt confident dealing with Mullen; his voice rang strong. Right now, the Judge was a drained man with a singular focus, and all that mattered to him was the land.

"Don't do that!" Mullen snapped, and he took several steps forward, almost running but not quite. His foot caught in the dirt and he fell, dropping to his knees.

He was within ten feet of Monty now. It was time.

Monty pulled the book of rites from behind his back and let the papers fall. Mullen's eyes went first to the loose sheets, then to the book in Monty's hands, widening as surprised anger twisted his mouth into a scowl.

"You little thief, you—"

Monty opened the pages and began reading before Mullen could get to his feet. Whatever else the Judge said was lost in the flurry of pounding heartbeats in his chest and ears. He found the words on the page and let them out.

"I speak to the soul of our friend, Elrich Mullen," he said, quiet at first, then louder as he went on. "I brace thee in the comfort that the beyond awaits, and that the souls of those before you..."

Mullen began to stand slowly. His limbs shook with the effort; first his arms, as they pushed him from the ground, then his legs as he stood. He was muttering to himself, but Monty couldn't hear it. He watched Mullen's lips move for a moment before he focused on the page again.

"...the souls of those who have passed before you await your passage now. Your journey will be eased by the mortal efforts..."

Monty trailed off, briefly, to watch the Judge get fully to his feet. There didn't seem to be any effect on the man. Mullen struggled to stand and take a step forward, but the rites weren't holding him back. He was fighting with something else. Mullen's hands clutched at his stomach, and he bent over, groaning. Still, he moved forward.

Monty read.

"The mortal efforts to set you onward! I speak for the first saint, Allon, when I confirm that death is the end of all things here, but not else! I speak for the second saint, Thielle, when I tell your spirit that its work here will not be in vain! I speak for the third saint, Matilla, when I tell you..."

Mullen's moaning grew louder, and the sound warbled with pain. It was thick, like there was ichor in his throat that it had to bubble past. He took another step forward and fell down, this time not catching himself on his knees, collapsing facedown in the dirt. His teeth snapped together—*crack!*—as he hit the ground.

With his heart still threatening to beat through his chest, Monty read on through to the sixth saint before snapping the book shut and holding it in a death grip. Mullen hadn't moved in—what had it been, two minutes? Longer? Monty wasn't sure, but his whole body felt electrified.

He waited for something—some sign that Nal'Gee was swirling toward him, rushing to clamp onto his soul and drag his being into her own.

Nothing came.

Monty moved forward cautiously, not taking his eyes off the Judge, who lied before him in a puddle of robes. There was no movement. Was he dead? Or was Nal'Gee simply waiting to strike?

More, he thought, hefting the book up again. *I stopped too soon, I—*

He opened the book and flipped through the pages. He hadn't marked his spot, and he didn't remember any more. Where was it? A page tore as he yanked it aside; he let it fall to the ground, frantically searching.

He only noticed Mullen moving once the man was already on his feet. And when he looked up from the pages, he saw a completely different Judge. Mullen was no longer weak and doubled over in pain. He was alive with color, and the grin on his face was massive and mirthless. It was a grin of hunger.

"Stupid child," Mullen rasped in a voice that wasn't his. "That won't work on me."

54

Monty barely had time to think before Mullen darted forward and snatched the book out of his hands. He tore the thick binding to shreds like it was a loaf of bread, throwing the pieces to the dirt. Chunks of the black rites book lay scattered about like they'd been dropped from the sky.

"You thought you were trapping me, is that it?" Mullen looked around. "Thought you could just...*send me?*"

It sounded like Mullen, a little, but this wasn't him. Yesterday, Nal'Gee had turned the shriveled head of Dr. Tobias toward him and spoken faint, growling words. But now...

"You're using his body," Monty said in a tone of accusatory awe.

"Yessss," Nal'Gee hissed with Mullen's mouth, her eyes on Monty's for fleeting seconds, darting around as though she were seeing a million things that he could not. "For now."

Monty's heart dropped like a stone, torn like the shreds of the rites in the dirt. He hadn't ever suspected that she might be capable of something like this—another stupid, stupid error. She'd moved Tobias's head—he knew that, he'd seen it! Yet to think she could take over someone's entire body, to move of her own free will...it changed everything.

He understood immediately that he was going to die.

"I have a treat for you," Nal'Gee said, her eyes wide and watching, her mouth wet and grinning. "This man, you hate this man, don't you?"

"What?" Monty was poised on his feet, shaken but ready to run. Not that he would get far. He'd seen how fast she moved. "I don't know what you—"

"After your land, isn't he?" She twisted Mullen's hand, sweeping it broadly across his body with the fingers spread. "All of this! And there's murderous intent here, too. I feel it. He told you—" She cackled now, tilting Mullen's head back and wiggling his fingers. "He said he'd kill you and your sister! He means it, child. I can tell you that he means it."

Monty tried to think, ignoring whatever Nal'Gee was spitting at him. There had to be something else he could do; another way to fight her. He had no backup plan—everything had been so rushed. But he hadn't had a choice! There was no time.

Nal'Gee's wild motions stopped suddenly. She stood straight, staring in his eyes. Mullen's mouth drooped. "Answer me, or I tear out your throat."

"Yes," Monty said slowly, glancing at Mullen's arms where they hung limp. "He wants our farm, and he said that he would kill us to get it."

"So kill him," Nal'Gee said.

Mullen's body was absolutely still except for his mouth. His eyes were unblinking, locked onto Monty's. There was no wind, so even his robes stood still, like he was a puppet hanging from strings.

"You're not—this isn't Mullen," Monty said, desperately trying to understand Nal'Gee's intention.

"This isn't Mullen," she mocked, crinkling his eyes slightly with the tease, then dropping them back to dead stillness. "This is Mullen. This is his body, which is all that he is. His soul is mine. His body is what brought the harm to you, is it not? So kill him. Won't you feel better?"

A sudden move from Nal'Gee; she swept the robes away from Mullen's ankle and pulled out a blade that was strapped to his leg. Monty twitched, and she threw the dagger into the dirt at his feet. The pointed tip stuck into the ground, handle up.

She was still again.

"He brought it to kill you," Nal'Gee said, voice dripping with mirth. "Are you surprised? You don't look surprised. He was going to kill you and your sister. You know that."

But Terra's not here, he thought, and he thanked the gods and saints for that, then asked them to take her further away. Far away. Across the oceans.

"Pick up the dagger and put it through this bastard's heart," Nal'Gee commanded, stepping up close to Monty, within arm's reach. She slipped Mullen's hands behind his back and thrust his chest up. "You've thought about it, don't say you haven't. Kill this man."

She's crazy, Monty thought, but he quickly realized that was a dangerous straw to grasp. Nal'Gee was cunning, not insane. She was goading him into murdering Mullen, and there had to be a reason for it.

"You can't get free of him, can you?" Monty looked the body up and down. Possessed or not, Mullen looked far from death, far from succumbing to *the black.* He was strong, perhaps stronger than Nal'Gee had suspected. "You're trapped until he's dead. And...and you can't make him kill himself. You would have done it already."

Nal'Gee didn't react to Monty's words. She just looked at him, holding still, and said, "You will never have another chance like this, Monty Bellamy of the Dromm. Take your revenge."

Monty set his jaw. He stomped on the dagger's hilt, burying it in the dirt. "I'm not from the Dromm. You are."

"Most people are not as stupid as you," Nal'Gee whispered, and she drew Mullen's hands out from behind him, taking a step back. "I will tell you one thing, Monty Bellamy, and it is that you do not know anything."

An inane thought crossed his mind—*I should have kept the dagger.*

Nal'Gee let the arms drop, and Monty watched in horror as the very life was pulled from Mullen's body.

First was his hair, growing shorter and wispier, shrinking into his skull. His face lost its color, draining like a pierced tin mug, running from impassioned red to icy white, then dark and darker till it was black and shrunken. Mullen's legs gave out; he crumpled sideways to the ground, his arms flying over his head and landing in the dirt above him. Almost weightless, they made no sound.

It was all over in a few seconds.

Monty saw the air shimmer around Mullen's body, disturbed in the firelight. He slid one foot backward, but knew he had to stay in the circle. Had she been visible like this before, or was it just because she was so powerful now?

She could kill him after all, Monty thought, and then he was wrapped in superheated air and struggling to breathe. It was like a heavy blanket was wrapped around him in an instant, so strong and dense that he couldn't stay upright. He fell backward to the ground, narrowly missing the thick wooden pole of the torch as his head smacked the dirt.

Nal'Gee was taking him.

He couldn't move or scream. It felt like there was a huge python wrapped around his body, crushing him into one small piece. But more than that, he felt Nal'Gee inside his head, doing the same thing to his mind. She was wrapping around him, trying to pry her way into his soul through any angle she could find.

It gave him a strange hope. If she was struggling to grasp him, then he was resisting her. No one else had been physically attacked by her specter like this. But he was losing air. He couldn't breathe.

As soon as he thought that, the pressure on his throat cleared. He sucked in a choking, gasping breath, wiggling his fingers. That, he could do. But the powerful grip around him was too strong to push off. He felt the weight in his mind, like probing, wriggling fingers deep behind his ears. It touched something inside of him, sending a forking lightning bolt of deep-seated pain from his skull down to his ankles, but it wasn't his body that hurt; it was something else.

She's touching my soul, he thought, and Nal'Gee's intentions crystallized within him at that moment. The connection of their essences was violent and painful and unholy and intimate, and Monty read her aspirations like they were written in glowing ink on the backs of his eyelids. She didn't want to kill him.

Nal'Gee wanted his body forever.

Mullen was too old, and too short. Monty tasted her disdain for the man, and it ran through him like sour cranberries. She didn't want to spend eternity in his shell.

The golem in the woods was hers, but only if she couldn't get the power she needed to capture a real, living body. She found that power. Monty saw with some great pain that it had come mostly from Delila. Her resistance to Nal'Gee's invasion had only given her more to drink. It was with her death that Nal'Gee's new plan had come to life.

And his family, all of them—they were on her land. The Gartens, too, but Nal'Gee wasn't interested in them. They weren't even worth the souls they carried, not to her. This family Bellamy was ripe, and their youngest was young enough to be fooled. To be used. To be lured by a tragedy she was yet to overcome.

It was her way out, and it worked better than she could possibly have hoped.

Anger. Fury. Monty saw red, and the connection with Nal'Gee broke, recoiling like a hissing snake. He bent his arms, trying to grab at the invisible bonds that held him, but there was no purchase.

They were all just food to her. Everyone in the village was a different course, and Monty, well—he was the dessert, in a way. She had eaten all she needed, and now she was ready for a body so she could wield her magic again. Only this time, it wouldn't be to grow the plants and the flowers. She would strangle the world, one village at a time. After all, they'd done the same to her.

The connection pieced together again, and Monty snapped back flat on the ground, groaning. He couldn't speak; could just barely breathe. Black crept in around the edges of his vision as Nal'Gee wormed her way into his spirit, her tendrils virile and long.

She could have any other body. There were people younger and stronger. But she wanted this Dromm boy, the one who had dared to live on her land and make money from its yield. The one who had dared to walk through her woods and discard their dangers. The one who found her and thought he could stop her.

His mother's death was a piece of sweet revenge. Taking Monty would be far, far sweeter.

55

M onty was falling into a hole. It was a slow fall, like he was being forced down through the ground by powerful hands, but he couldn't slow the descent. There was nothing to grab onto. His vision was small circle of light being swallowed up by pure black.

This is where Mullen went, Monty gasped inside his own head as he sank. *This is where Mullen went when she took him.*

And where does a taken spirit go? Without death, could he be released to the beyond? Or would he stay in this blackness forever?

He breathed from somewhere far away, feeling his chest miles above him. Terra wouldn't know what happened, would she? She'd see his face and think it was him, and then Nal'Gee would...

Monty clawed at the pinprick of the world above him with ethereal hands, reaching up towards surface. There was something to hold onto, something that resisted the forces pushing him down. But it was like getting one hand on top of a ledge while a bear pulled on your leg.

Or grasping a fistful of sticks while someone three times your size yanked you from your mother's funeral pyre.

It hurt to hang on, hurt him somewhere so deep inside that he didn't know where it was, but he held on. He wasn't strong enough to pull himself up, not even a little, but he could resist. He could resist the darkness; the heavy weights on his mind; the incredibly vast, looming consciousness of Nal'Gee, smothering him into nothing. He could breathe for a little while, but for how long?

And what was the point?

It was when that thought crossed his mind that his flimsy grip weakened even more, and he started to slip. The tiny hole above grew smaller; the pressure above him grew stronger.

I'm giving up, he admitted to himself. *And it's letting her take me.*

Then he felt a new presence. It was warm, and where it touched him it didn't bring pain. It soothed him, like slathering the gel of an aloe leaf over a fiery sunburn. He leaned into the feeling, casting himself up toward it, and it granted him strength and brought peace to his flurrying mind. What was it?

Monty tried to call out to it, to ask, but he couldn't hear anything, not even his own voice. He didn't know if he was talking. He could see only darkness, but light was filtering in, dissipating the black to a deep, fuzzy gray. Still, he was miles away from the world that he knew.

Monty followed the warmth, ignoring the stinging pain of Nal'Gee's tendrils slapping back at him, pushing down at his consciousness. His muddled thoughts grew clearer, and he understood that his eyes were closed. He forced them open.

The world was dark and silent. He couldn't feel the heat from the fire nor the cold of the air, but he could see the few stars in the sky. Nothing reached his ears, not even the crackling of the torch fire or the chirping of nighttime crickets. It was like he was in a glass box.

I didn't open my eyes at all, he thought. *It was Nal'Gee. She's letting me see through them like windows, and that's all. I'm not even here.*

But her presence in his mind was muted now—still there, still digging into him and trying to suffocate him, yet different from before. And if she had him wholly now, would she still be trying to fight?

He felt a hand on his face, and it was like coming back from the dead. Even just these few dragging, endless moments where he could feel the touch of *nothing,* not even the air on his skin, made him feel alone and lost in ways he never could have imagined. That soothing warmth hit him hard now, and his cheek went from nothing, to warm, to flushed, and then he could breathe a bigger breath and he pulled it in like it was the last he'd ever take.

A face blocked his vision. No—it filled it.

"Terra."

Monty couldn't hear himself say it, but he felt the words rumble his skin, felt his mouth move. He was in control of that, not Nal'Gee. The rest of his body was still pinned, cold winter air brushing against his ankles where his pants had hitched up.

"Mon..."

Terra's voice, small and distant, brushed at him. He lunged toward it, his body not moving at all.

"...ty! Mon... Monty!"

Two hands on his face now, and Terra was inches from him. He could hear her voice louder, but it was still a whisper, and it looked like she was screaming. Her fingers clutched his head and dug into his cheeks and hair, surely painful, but he didn't know.

Pain wracked him as Nal'Gee's essence squeezed its coils, deadly. His eyes fluttered and his jaw tensed, teeth grinding against each other. He was pulled between the craving of the warmth and the sweet, black retreat from the pain.

Terra's voice was drowned out and overshadowed by Nal'Gee's screeching consciousness, a banshee storm cloud draped over Monty's soul.

"Mine you're mine you're mine give the body to me it's mine it's MINE IT'S MINE"

She cracked his insides like porcelain, running tracks through his brain and trying to break pieces off to swallow. Trying to break big enough pieces so that what was left would be fractured enough to gather up and swallow in one gulp.

Monty felt his soul being pulled apart. It was agony.

But he fought.

Terra's face was still there; her hands were still on him. He let the pain rip through him as he stretched forward past Nal'Gee's billowing weight, reaching out to clasp onto something else. It felt like he was jumping high in the air and waiting to fall back down, hand outstretched and grasping.

When he found the grip, he knew instantly that it was Terra, that his soul was reaching out to hers and she was anchoring him to herself. If he was pulled away, then she would be pulled too, and Nal'Gee would eat them both.

"Don't," he said, and Terra blinked, not knowing what he meant. Whatever she was doing, it was on a level beyond recognition, beyond decision—it was instinct; it was love. She couldn't stop it if she wanted to, and she didn't.

Monty waited for the scale to tip to Nal'Gee.

Waited.

And for the first time since falling to the ground, he felt whole. Balanced. He was being pulled on and clawed at, but he was...secure.

It's not me, Monty thought, looking at Terra in wonder as his younger sister held his face and called out his name, telling him to come back. *It's her.*

Terra was strong. More than that—Terra was steel. Monty held onto her and he felt all the unwavering power of her conviction and belief. Her assuredness that they would triumph over Nal'Gee; that good would beat evil. Her fear, yes, of losing her brother, but also the incredible lengths she would go through to stop that from happening. The potential there, and all that she could accomplish.

It was beautiful.

Panic pulsed from Nal'Gee now, a narrow wave that tickled prickly fingers through Monty's head and left him shivering. The spirit's desperation was showing itself, peeking through the torrent of latching arms she shoved at Monty. Each time she bounced off or lost a hold, that desperation grew. He could feel everything she felt, but that connection was slipping away, too.

Nal'Gee flew away from Monty and leapt for Terra.

56

A ll at once, Monty was free. He sat up immediately, gasping for air. Terra, meanwhile, had fallen back, sitting in the dirt. Her arms jutted out behind her, palms flat on the ground. Her head was tucked into her chest and her hair was wild, twisted over her face. She sat almost perfectly still, but clearly strained against the onslaught, her legs trembling and her hair shifting as her head twitched.

Monty reached forward and put a hand on her knee. He got something, but he wasn't able to feel Terra the way he had when she was reaching out for him. What he did feel was enough for him to know that the battle he had fought with Nal'Gee was nothing like the one happening inside of Terra. There was no pain there, no frantic struggle.

Nal'Gee could not hold on.

I was right about one thing, Monty thought wildly, as pride for Terra burned inside him. *She needs something. She needs someone. Nal'Gee is reaching out for a life and there's nothing she can steal.*

"She's panicked." Monty spoke his thoughts aloud, surprised to feel an awed grin coming across his face. "She knows. You know, Nal'Gee! *You know you've lost!*"

Invisible teeth snapped at Monty's fingertips, forcing him to withdraw them from Terra's leg. His sister curled in tighter on herself, drawing her legs up to her forehead. Monty's grin disappeared.

"Get her away, Terra," he said, not sure if she could hear him. "You're stronger than she is. Nal'Gee knows it, and she's scared."

He unconsciously snapped his fingers where they hung by the dirt. "Make sure it's the last thing she ever feels."

In that moment, if he could have grabbed Nal'Gee with both hands and torn her in half, he would have done it. It was infuriating, knowing that she was trying to steal his sister's life away in front of his eyes and he could do little more than watch.

The tightness in Terra's shoulders and legs started to relax, her feet sliding along the dirt, her fingers straightening and pulling out of the ground where they had curled in.

It happened slowly, then all at once. Terra fell backward, lying flat on the ground. In the intermittent light of the flickering torch, Monty saw sweat soaking her forehead. Stray hairs stuck to her skin.

"Terra! Hey." Monty knelt over her, grabbing her hand in his. Her eyes were closed, but he could see that they were moving. "Hey! Are you okay? Is she—"

Terra's eyes shot open, looking directly into the night sky. Monty followed them as she clutched his hand, and there he saw it. They were witnessing Nal'Gee's rejection; her spirit and essence being cast away from Terra.

She was massive. Vast. It was like a storm cloud had come down from the skies to drop upon them, except it was rising upward. She faded in and out of existence, slipping between the planes of life as she drifted, a swirling black cloud that grew gradually grayer and smaller.

The souls are leaving her, Monty thought. Black grains of weightless sand pulled free from the cloud, disappearing in the dark night sky. *All the souls she took.*

"Mom's up there," Terra said, and she pointed, but Monty couldn't tell where her finger was aimed or what she might be seeing. Whatever vision was in her eyes was for her, and that was okay. If their mother was seeing Terra, he hoped that she could see him, too, and feel what he felt.

There was no sound, no grand final scream or swear of revenge from the witch. Her spirit shrank until it was nothing but a wisp, just barely visible. Then she was gone in the time it took to blink.

Slowly, Monty lowered his head to Terra, who was straining to get back to a seated position. He helped her up and dropped down on the ground next to her.

"Are you hurt?" he asked.

"No," she said. "Just really tired."

"Okay." He was still holding her hand, and he let it go, watching her stretch the fingers out. "Why'd you come back?"

"Stop it," she said, looking at him. She looked sleepy and beaten, but her eyes were alive with light as the fire behind him danced, reflected. "I wasn't gonna leave you to fight her all by yourself."

"You promised," he pointed out.

"You made me," Terra said, adding, "and it was a stupid promise."

Monty laughed, something he didn't think he was remotely capable of doing right now.

Terra matched it with a grin. "I told Iselle that I was going back and that she shouldn't follow me. She tried to stop me, but she couldn't grab me. She got close, and chased me for a little bit, but she knew she couldn't come to the circle."

"Good thing," Monty said, looking in the direction of the town. If Iselle had been here, she would have been fodder.

"Did you see how big she was? Nal'Gee?" Terra craned her neck up again, although there was nothing to see. "I don't think we needed to pull up all that grass. No way she would have fit."

"Maybe," Monty said, then he laughed again. "Don't tell Iselle that. She'll be—what did she say? *Sore* at us."

"She's gonna want to know what happened, though."

"She deserves to." Monty finally got to his feet, the shakiness and nerves subsiding as he and Terra talked. He brushed the dirt off his clothes, then pulled a big clod from the ground and used it to snuff the torch. A burning smell drifted through the air. "We should go and find her."

"Yeah." Terra stood up, brushing herself off as well. She turned, looking at the lumpy robes on the ground. "Um, is Mullen...is he...?"

"Oh, hell," Monty said, eyeing the body. "I forgot, somehow...but yes. He's dead. Nal'Gee killed him, right in front of me. Drained him dry."

"Eugh." Terra shivered, stepping back from the corpse and closer to Monty.

"I guess both our problems are solved," Monty said, bitterly and without humor. He looked from the body to the scattered pieces of the rites book, barely visible in the muted moonlight.

"Do you think she's really gone?" Terra was looking at the sky again.

"I was going to ask you the same thing," Monty said. "We can't really know, not yet. We'll have to watch and wait...see if anyone else gets sick, or if the Dromm starts to die again. But...I do think so."

"How do you know?"

He shrugged. "I can...feel it. I *felt* it, when Nal'Gee was trying to take me, and then when she tried to take you. She was trying to hold on to save her own life, and she couldn't. She knew she had everything to lose."

"And she lost," Terra finished, pulling her eyes from the sky and looking to Monty.

"Yeah." Monty grinned. "She lost."

Terra seemed to accept this. She closed her eyes for a moment, breathing, then opened them and said, "Iselle's gonna be mad at me. She was yelling a lot of stuff when I ran away."

"By the time we're done telling her what happened," Monty said, "she won't even remember why she was mad."

57

When they found Iselle pacing the outskirts of town, the storyteller ran at them. At first, Monty feared she was indeed mad enough to lash out, though it didn't come to that. She did have some words for Terra, but the fire behind them dissolved almost as quickly as it had come.

"I'm glad you're okay," she finally said, her breath slowing down, and the look on her face showed she meant it.

They went back to their place in Irisa. Monty figured that it was safe now—no one saw them come and go in the dead of night, and it would already have been checked by Mullen's men, if they were even still operating without his orders.

"So the Judge is dead, then," Iselle said. They were all sitting as they had before, in an array of chairs pulled from around the house. Several candles were lit, placed around them on tables and ledges built into the walls. "Good riddance."

"They won't think Monty did it, will they?" Terra brought up.

Monty winced; he hadn't considered that.

"How could they?" Iselle shrugged. "You said Nal'Gee got him with the black, right? The body will show it."

"Yeah," Monty said. "I guess I'll just tell someone in the Commons I found him in the field like that. It's not very far from the truth." *And also nowhere close.*

"Sure," Iselle said, and leaned forward in her chair, her fingers arched and pressing into her knees. "Now, I want the meat. What happened in that circle?"

Terra, too, listened intently as Monty recalled the events of the past few hours, starting with his initial conviction that Mullen wasn't going to show up at all, and ending with what he and Terra had seen as Nal'Gee was ripped away from them and disappeared.

Iselle sat back in her chair with a mirthful smile on her face, giving her head a little shake.

"What?" Monty asked. "You don't believe me?"

She held up a hand. "Please. Save that for the people who don't make a living from this. I believe you, I'm just amazed at what Nal'Gee did."

"Impressed?" Monty asked.

"Hardly." Iselle tossed her hair to the side, her scarf nowhere to be seen. "She was cocky, and she was stupid. And it seems she must have truly hated you and your family, to want to take her revenge by taking your body."

"I had no idea she could do something like that!" Terra said.

"Nor I." Iselle shrugged. "Can all spirits? Or only ones as strong as she? We may never know. Which is probably for the best."

"She was so attached to the land," Monty said, "that she hated us just for living on it? Enough to kill us?"

"Nal'Gee didn't discriminate much in who she killed," Iselle said. "She went for whoever was closest, right? Somewhere along the way, she discovered the power to take bodies, like she took Mullen's—and others, for all we know. So her goals changed.

"But—and I mean this—she was stupid. She wasted Mullen's body in a show of power, killing him to scare you and get more strength for her attack. She assumed she'd be able to take you."

"She was right, though." Monty looked over at his sister. "If Terra hadn't shown up, she would have had me. I was almost gone."

"It's good that I couldn't catch her, then," Iselle said, and Terra let out a surprised laugh. "Nal'Gee was foolish to kill Mullen, arrogant to try to take you, Monty, and then outright dumb to think that she'd have a chance at taking Terra."

"She was desperate," Monty responded, remembering the spirit's thumping panic that had bled its way into his own feelings. "She had nowhere else to go."

"And now she's gone." Iselle clapped her hands.

Terra pulled her legs up into her chair, sitting on them. "Is it really over?"

"Time will tell," Iselle said. "But it does sound like the plan worked."

Monty said, "Well, the plan didn't really go through, but I do think she's gone. What we saw—she lost all her power, and there were no other lives that she could steal."

Terra turned away from Monty. "I wish...I wish I could've saved mom. If I knew what was going on, I could've. I just let her lay in bed because that's what she said I should do."

Monty, who had experience with exactly this type of thinking, was quick to leap on it. "Don't dwell on that," he told her. "It won't do you any good. We didn't know, and there was nothing either of us could have done."

"He's right," Iselle said, watching Terra until the girl turned her head to meet her eyes.

Terra gave a little nod. "I know...I know."

"Besides," Iselle said, "both of you should take a moment to be happy! Happy this is all over, and that Mullen went down in the bargain." She was smiling; it faded as she looked over the two of them.

"It's..." Monty began, unsure of what he wanted to say.

Iselle held up her hand, stopping Monty before he could try to piece together his thoughts. "Sorry. One good thing doesn't undo all the bad things that happened."

That's actually...pretty close to what I was thinking.

Monty leaned back. He was far from perfect, but he felt a good deal better. Some of the weights and worries on his shoulders had been lifted, leaving far fewer behind. He rubbed the back of his neck against the chair. "I'm exhausted. Feels like I've been awake for three days."

"Me too," Terra said.

"The fight took a lot out of both of you," Iselle said. She stood up, stretching her own arms behind her back. "And these chairs aren't very comfortable, truth be told. No offense."

"They're not really our chairs," Monty said with a tired smile, looking around the rented room.

Iselle chuckled. "I haven't seen a lot of this place. Is there another bed?"

"There's four," Terra said. "It's too big for us. I'm glad we're not gonna keep it anymore."

"Just for a couple more days," Monty said. "Till the Judge's money runs out."

"Then what?" Iselle asked, already peering around to find a bedroom.

Terra looked at Monty, asking the same question with her eyes.

Monty stood up from his own stiff chair, thinking of the farm. Where they had grown up and where they had lost their father. Where they'd learned almost everything they knew, and where they'd seen their mother die. Where they'd fought with their very souls in defense of their family, their land, and their village.

"We're going home," Monty answered, the words springing warmth in him. "This time, for good."

Epilogue

As was expected by Iselle (though it had still worried Monty), Elrich Mullen was ruled as a victim of the black, and his body was taken the same as all the others. The man's office and house remained locked up, and when people in Irisa spoke of him, they did it in whispers. Mullen had burned many bridges—savagely ripped them apart, in fact—and it was the general wish that he be forgotten.

Few were in attendance at his sending. Monty, Terra, and Iselle were among them, watching the pyre burn with stony faces, though there was some satisfaction in the storyteller. Her revenge drifted into the air, smoke and ash. While the final rites were read, she let herself mourn her caravan family. She had abided by the rule of moving onward for days, and felt it was finally time to let it bend, just for a few minutes.

Terra had reached over and taken her hand, and Iselle didn't refuse. When Terra asked her later if she was okay, Iselle just gave her a thin smile and said she might never feel better than when she'd watched Mullen burn.

It was a lie, but that was okay with Terra.

No one else in Irisa fell ill, at least not with the black. The wave of deaths was over, and the mood around town had brightened considerably. Monty wondered what Bradley would spread rumors about now.

They invited Iselle to stay with them, at least through the winter. They were not surprised when she refused, though they were a little disappointed, especially Terra. Iselle said she'd already been here far too long.

"Where are you gonna go?" Terra asked her, once her small arguments against Iselle's departure were over.

"I never know," Iselle said, "but I have this country back to front. Show me a painting of a road, and I'll tell you where it leads. The caravan and oxen are in fine shape—the stable that kept them did a better job than most have in the past. And that broken wheel is good as new."

"It's an entirely new wheel," Monty pointed out.

"That's what I said." Iselle held his gaze, straight-faced, until Monty's composure broke and he laughed.

"Make sure you travel through here again," he told her, and Terra reaffirmed the sentiment. "And come here for dinner."

"As long as you get more salt," she told him. "I'll be coming back to make sure the story makes a complete circle through everyone. So when you see me again, you better have heard some tale about all of this from someone else, or I'm the worst storyteller to ever ride."

After she left, Monty found her scarf in their house. It was in Terra's bedroom, folded and placed in the corner where it wasn't easily seen. She hadn't worn it since they'd reunited outside of town, and Monty just assumed she had finally shredded it to pieces between her fingers.

"She hid it because she knew if you found it, you'd try to give it back," Terra said, holding the blue cloth.

"Hm." Monty considered that. "Iselle is too smart for us."

"I think she let me go," Terra said. She tucked the scarf in her pocket. "That night, with Nal'Gee. I think she could have caught me, but she didn't. She knew I needed to be there."

"And she knew I couldn't let you," Monty said.

"We're really lucky she was here," Terra said.

"Yeah." Monty looked out of Terra's bedroom window, which faced the circle of earth in the field that would forever remain barren. "It cost her a lot, though. And I don't think being part of the story makes up for it."

The winter stretched on ahead. Monty got the farm animals back from the Gartens and brought them home, sincerely thanking his neighbors for all of their help. Life was almost back to normal, save the absence of their mother, which they felt every day.

But there was one last surprise waiting for them.

It came in the form of a missive, run out to their farm by yet another new courier who was even younger than than the last. He was the temporary Judge's son, a boy by the name of Nick. He was polite and kind, and it seemed he had learned that from his father. Monty had met the Judge once, when he arrived to town two days prior, just after Mullen's sending. It seemed that he had been on his way already to assist Mullen.

Judge Selton was not particularly esteemed, but was thrust up from the role of assistant Judge to interim Judge, and would likely be chosen to fill the role permanently. The people liked him, as did the king, who had appointed him personally. Monty thought he was fine. The bar for being better than Mullen was quite low, and Selton stepped over it comfortably.

Nick handed Monty a very small scroll and then quickly disappeared from his front door, as a good courier should. The seal was not from the Judge's desk, but from the town treasurer.

"A pickup?" Monty read, confused. His neck tingled, still on alert. Mullen was dead, but his sycophants might still linger. Could it be a trap?

"Let's go," Terra said immediately once she told him. "Iselle might still be in town, maybe we can see her and I can thank her for the scarf."

"All right."

He'd be damned if he was going to spend any more time being worried about betrayal and deceit in his own village. He'd seen the evil leave with his own eyes.

They walked through the thin sheet of snow that covered the ground on the path to Irisa. Flakes fell from the sky, but they could see the outlines of footprints still, both Iselle's and the courier's. Monty held the scroll curled in his hand, keeping it shielded from the snow.

The treasurer's office was a small, square building on the corner past the Commons, with inches of space between it and the buildings next to it. The officials called it the box. It was tight and short, and there was room for about four people as long as one of them wasn't Rodney Talhauer.

"Hi, Peter," Monty said to the treasurer when they arrived. He'd run messages for the man before, and had always liked him. The town treasurer was slightly pudgy and spoke fast, but usually with a smile. He was one of three people in town who wore spectacles, and he complained often about losing them, only to find them moments later.

"Monty, it's been a while," Peter said, his hands moving as fast as his lips while he arranged papers and scribbled down notes. His spectacles hung on the edge of his nose, and his short brown hair was thin and a little wild. "Pardon me for not chatting, but it's been a whirlwind here with the arrival of the new Judge. I should have gotten that message to you sooner."

"It's no worry." Monty set the scroll on the desk. "Peter, this is my sister, Terra."

"Charmed," Peter said, but he didn't look up from his desk. Monty looked down to Terra, and she shrugged.

"So, what's this pickup?" Monty asked, and before he had finished speaking, Peter hefted a lockbox onto the desk. He had to use two hands, and he groaned with relief when it slammed down onto the wood.

"Hope you brought a wagon," Peter said. "It's eighty-and-one-seven-tenths pounds of heavy coin. From the late Judge Mullen."

Monty blinked. "What?"

"Again, I apologize. It's been here for days. It was actually the last order he gave me before he passed." Peter was already working again, eyes on paper and pen and coin. "You should have had it sooner. I hope you didn't take out any loans in the last few days. Just kidding, I would know."

Eighty pounds of coin was what the farm would bring in with five years of extremely bountiful harvest. *Extremely* bountiful.

The money for the land, Monty remembered. *Mullen put it through before he came to me. And now he's dead.*

He hesitated for only a moment. "Peter, can you hang onto it for just another few minutes?"

"That's fine. I'll be here all day. And the next day. And the day after," Peter muttered, looking up only briefly. Monty gave him a short nod, and he whispered to Terra, who reacted with a gleeful smile and ran from the treasurer's office.

Monty took a sack of coin with him from the box before he left. Peter weighed it out to be exactly forty-one pounds. There wasn't a perfect amount for this, but that would be good enough. The gold bulged through the heavy burlap.

Terra was back shortly, breathless but happy.

"It's still here," she said, pointing deeper into Irisa. "It's behind Kettle's. I don't know where Iselle is, but she must be leaving soon. The oxes are hitched to it."

"Oxen," he said, and she smacked him in the side.

"Shut up," she panted. "I know. Is half fair?"

"We did all the work," Monty joked. "Except for tearing up the circle."

They hurried to Kettle's, going wide around the neighboring buildings to slip behind the general store where Iselle's caravan was sitting. A pair of beefy oxen stood before it, snorting puffs of white air from their nostrils.

"She must be inside getting supplies," Monty said. "Let's hurry."

"Shouldn't we tell her?" Terra asked, then answered her own question. "No, you're right. She left the scarf. So we leave the gold."

"She wouldn't take it if we gave it to her," Monty said, and he looked around to be sure no one was watching as he placed the tightly-tied bag containing a small fortune in the back of her covered wagon, shifting some rope and small crates so that it was hidden. "And I'm not gonna argue with her about how stories won't buy her food. So we just have to trick her a little bit."

"I don't think she'll be mad," Terra said, crackling with laughing energy. "Okay, let's go!"

They ran from Kettle's, clearing the area without being seen. On the sack, a small note was pinned.

It read, *For your field labor.*

With half the weight gone, Monty was fine carrying the lockbox back to the farm. He and Terra hauled it up to the second floor of the barn, to the safe hiding space their mother used to store the season's earnings. The twelve-and-some pounds from the last sell were still there, piled neatly in the iron box beneath the wood and straw. The rest of Mullen's gold filled it almost to the top.

It would be nice to have the money, but better to grow the crop and make their own.

That winter, the leaves of the Dromm faded from green to brown, and then to black. They fell off their branches and died in the dirt, dissolving into nothing. This went unnoticed, or at least was not marked as unusual. For once, the trees in the Dromm behaved like all the other trees around them.

When spring peeked its head through the snow, the other forests were in bloom and bud, welcoming the warmth. The breeze rustled their branches.

The black forest did not grow.

THE END

ABOUT SHANE LEE

Shane has been a horror fan for decades and has been writing almost as long. He lives in Western New York with his wife and their extremely handsome cat, Mordecai, and he likes to golf when the weather's nice and stay in to read when it's not.

A note from me: I love hearing from readers! Come say hi anytime on Facebook and Twitter, both @ShaneLeeBooks!

CPSIA information can be obtained
at www.ICGtesting.com
Printed in the USA
BVHW041012041222
653418BV00005B/224